THE SURFACING

TERRANCE COFFEY

Printed in the United States of America. All rights reserved. No part of this publication may be reproduced, distributed, or transmitted in any form or by any means, including photocopying, recording, or other electronic or mechanical methods, without the prior written permission of the publisher, except in the case of brief quotations embodied in critical reviews and certain other non-commercial uses permitted by copyright law. This is a work of fiction, all people, places, and the events surrounding them are products of the author's imagination. Any resemblance to actual persons, living or dead, or actual events are purely coincidental.

The Surfacing © 2024 Terry Coffey
Helm House Publishing
ISBN-13: 979-8-218-26672-1
ISBN-13: 979-8-218-26673-8
Library of Congress Control Number: 2023915685

Cover Art by Creativindie Covers
Editor: Allister Thompson
First Edition: January 2024

10 9 8 7 6 5 4 3 2 1

*This book is dedicated to Richard L. Evans (1932-2014)
whose insight and kindness went far beyond this world…*

CHAPTER 1

KADEN BOLTED OUT the door and down the porch steps, worried they were already dead.

The bucket he clutched swung wildly, soapy water sloshing out onto the cracked pavement as his foot hit the sidewalk. A repugnant odor, a noxious blend of foul and savory, assaulted his senses, akin to raw meat roasting at a barbeque. *Why would anyone want to kill an animal, and even worse, cook and consume it?* Kaden's nose wrinkled in revulsion at the nauseating smell. He marched around the perimeter of the weathered house, his eyes fixated on his cherished bicycle, painted in his favorite shade of blue, mirroring the ocean and the boundless open sky. The titanium-white seat bore intricate blue threading around the edges, and multicolored tassels hung from the handlebars. The bike rested against the hedges that separated his house from the massive, wooded lot next door. The bike had been a gift on his sixth birthday from his father, his only request fulfilled.

Amid the lush green expanse of Appalachia, Virginia, riding his bike had become his consummate joy. Undulating mounds and shallow dunes peppered the landscape, offering wide open spaces for testing his bike's durability. But on this day, there was no time for such things. He placed the bucket over the handlebars, mounted his bike, and veered onto the gravel road singing,

"Twinkle, twinkle, little star, how I wonder what you are.
Up above the world so high, like a diamond in the sky.
Twinkle, twinkle, little star, how I wonder what you are…"

Kaden, with his dark curly hair and ocean-blue eyes, exuded an angelic aura that matched his singing voice. He steered around the bend among red and white oak trees lining both sides of the road. Oblivious to everything else around him, he pedaled with unwavering purpose, his singular goal to reach the lake's edge before it was too late. Kaden glanced over his shoulder to ensure there were no approaching cars as he sang the second verse of the nursery rhyme.

"…When the blazing sun is gone, when he nothing shines upon,
then you show your little light, twinkle, twinkle, all the night…"

He arrived at a clearing and transferred the bucket from handlebars to hand. With deliberate steps, he descended the embankment on a mission, careful to watch his step the entire way so that no arthropod would meet an untimely end beneath his feet. It would be awful to unwittingly crush an innocent bug trying to make it home safely to its family.

Upon reaching the lake's edge, a flock of tundra swans flew overhead in the cloudless morning sky, emitting piercing high-pitched hoots. Kaden shielded his eyes from the radiant sun, granting him an unobstructed view of the swans adorned in alabaster plumage with long graceful necks landing majestically on the water. Nearby, a lone mallard fluttered her wings in the shallows, her ducklings following her in a frantic dance. Their tiny bodies bore the black stain of oil, hindering their feeble attempts at flight. Kaden feared the mother, unable to recognize her own offspring, might fly away and desert them.

He crept over to the beleaguered ducklings, his heart overflowing with empathy. "It's okay, don't worry. I'm gonna clean you all up. You'll be just like new, and Mama duck will love her baby ducks again."

With trembling hands, he gently submerged one of the four ducklings into his bucket of soapy water. Its tiny sneeze sprayed soap suds across his face, eliciting a delicate smile. Kaden worked tenderly, his nimble fingers navigating through the viscous oil. Some patches had

solidified, demanding a more aggressive effort to cleanse. The ducklings'
fate hinged on his determination to get them clean.

A rustling branch disrupted his solace, voices and sporadic laughter
followed in the distance. Kaden placed the duckling gently on the
ground and sprung to his feet. Just a stone's throw away, remnants
of an old and narrow fishing pier led into the lake, its wooden planks
groaned under constant treading. Kaden braced himself for the arrival
of strangers.

Two boys emerged and strolled onto the pier: Jeb and Travis, both
tall and lanky thirteen-year-olds, were followed by Jeb's younger brother,
Charlie, a stout preteen who had recently turned eleven. Kaden observed their arrival with a mixture of trepidation and anger. As the trio
converged on the fishing pier, they took turns bunting empty plastic
bottles over the lake with a wooden bat. Jeb reveled in the moment
when Charlie lofted a bottle his way. He sent it soaring far beyond the
shore into the lake.

"That's a homer!" Jeb declared.

"Nah, mine went out way past that," Charlie said.

"You're delusional. I left you in the dust."

Travis snatched the bat from Jeb's grasp. "It's my turn," he said. "Let
me show you losers how it's done."

Kaden watched from a distance. Anger simmered beneath his stoic
exterior, stifling him from speaking, and his expressive face was incapable of hiding it. Travis acknowledged him with a smirk and a nod before
tossing a plastic bottle in the air and bunting it. The bottle landed
ahead of the others in the lake. "What did I tell you bean-heads? I'm
the master at this," Travis boasted.

Kaden marched up onto the pier, still silent. He stared at the boys
as if they were from another world. Jeb returned his stare. "What? You
want a turn?"

Kaden shook his head.

"You got a problem or something?" said Travis.

Kaden didn't answer. Travis looked over at Charlie. "Who is this
kid?"

Charlie shrugged. "I don't know. I've never seen him before."

Kaden stepped onto the edge of the pier and yelled at the top of his lungs at them. "Stop it!"

The outburst startled Jeb and Charlie, while it only amused Travis. "Oh, look, the little brat is throwing a temper tantrum," he said.

"Stop what?" asked Jeb.

"The lake is sacred, and you people are poisoning it with all your garbage," said Kaden.

"Sacred?" Travis scoffed. "What's sacred about a stupid lake?"

Kaden shot Travis a contemptuous gaze. "And you," he said, pointing at Travis with conviction in his voice, "your behavior is especially putrid."

Charlie chimed in, squinting at Jeb. "What does putrid mean?" Jeb had no idea and left the question hanging in the air unanswered. "You should go home, little dude, before you get hurt," said Travis. "Yeah, we don't like little kids," added Charlie.

Kaden, resolute, refused to back down. "This is my home. You go."

Undeterred, Travis retrieved another plastic bottle from his backpack. "Well, this ain't your lake. It belongs to everybody. We'll do whatever we want to it."

Travis tossed the bottle up into the air, and as it descended, he whacked it as hard as he could. The bottle soared into the sky before it dropped into the lake. Kaden bolted off the fishing pier and dashed to the lake's edge. He rushed to remove his sneakers, and while fully dressed in his cargo shorts and plaid collared shirt, he waded into the water.

"What's he doing?" asked Charlie.

"Somethin's wrong with him," Travis quipped.

Kaden swam up to the plastic bottle, grabbed it in one hand, and headed back toward the shore.

"Let's give him some more," said Travis.

Before Kaden could make it back to dry land, Travis bunted another plastic bottle into the lake, followed by another and then another. "Hey, little dude, there's another one. And don't forget the one on your left," Travis mocked.

He laughed hysterically at Kaden scrambling for the other bottles while struggling to hold onto the one he had in his hand. He finally managed to guide three of them back to the shore, though the last one had floated out much farther than the others. Kaden gazed at it, looking unsure of what to do.

"You think he's gonna go after it? He's looking at it pretty hard," said Jeb.

"Who would be crazy enough to swim halfway across the lake after a bottle?" Travis replied.

"I bet he's gonna do it," said Charlie.

"No way," Jeb said.

Unable to hear their conversation, Kaden softly counted backward to himself, "Seven, six, five, four, three, two..." When he reached *one*, he swam out toward the bottle. The boys stood there in disbelief as Kaden slowly dog paddled. Each time he approached to grab it; the bottle drifted farther away from him. His arms and legs fatigued after several failed attempts, and the stress from it tugged creases across his forehead. Kaden took in a deep breath, closed his eyes, and without any forewarning, collapsed beneath the water's surface.

Seconds ticked by and he had not emerged. Jeb was first to express his uneasiness. "Hey, where did he go?"

The boys wandered several yards around the lake's edge, searching for him. There was no movement in the water, only silence—an eerie, dire silence.

"You think he drowned?" asked Charlie anxiously.

"I dunno," Jeb answered.

"We're gonna get blamed for this if we stay here," said Travis.

"What're you talking about? He needs our help, we can't just leave him," said Jeb.

"How can we help him, moron, if he's underwater?"

"We go in after him."

"We can't," said Charlie. "Rebecca says there're parasites in the lake that swim into boys' pee-holes and eat them alive from the inside."

"She's lying," Jeb sneered. "Why do you believe every crazy thing she says?"

"Rebecca doesn't lie."

"Everybody lies; she's no different."

"She's not like everybody. You don't know her like I do."

"Hey, will you two shut up and look?" said Travis. He pointed at Kaden in the middle of the lake. He had emerged from the water and was floating on his back, unconscious, his arms spreadeagle.

"Oh no, is he dead?" asked Charlie.

"He looks dead," said Travis.

Jeb sat on the ground and rushed to untie the shoelace on one of his sneakers.

"What are you doing?" Travis asked.

"What do you think? I'm going in after him," said Jeb. He tossed his sneaker and hurried to untie the other.

"Travis has a phone. He can call for help," said Charlie.

"Nope, it's at home charging," Travis said.

"It's not enough time anyway," said Jeb as he rolled off his sock.

"You can put your clothes back on, superboy. Look who's coming right at us," said Travis.

Jeb sprang to his feet, one sneaker donned, and the other held firmly in his grip. Their eyes were fixed on Kaden floating on his back spinning toward them, but how? There was no current. There had never been a current in the lake.

Charlie gnawed on his thumbnail. "What's going on?"

The boys shuffled backward as Kaden's lifeless form drifted ominously to the lake's edge. There he lay, suspended, floating above the water's surface like a discarded plastic bottle adrift on the tide. Jeb made a move to pull him ashore, but a sudden commotion stalled him. From the thicket, a towering stag covered in reddish-brown fur, with newly-formed antlers, burst forth. Panic surged and the boys ran in the opposite direction but stopped short when they glanced back at the stag stepping into the water toward Kaden.

With anomalous strength, it seized Kaden's shirt collar between its gnashing teeth and dragged him ashore. The animal dropped Kaden and raised its head toward the boys, challenging them with haunting amber eyes and a threatening stance. Fear engulfed Jeb and Charlie, causing them to flee. Travis wavered on the precipice of curiosity and self-preservation, lingering, as the stag, sensing an impending revelation, retreated a step.

As Kaden lay unconscious, blue-tinted dust particles escaped his mouth and nostrils, swirling above his head in a perpetual moving halo-like formation. Travis watched in awe, bewildered. Self-preservation finally trumped his curiosity and he fled into the woods in fear just as Jeb and Charlie had.

The stag, unrelenting in its vigil, nudged Kaden's cheek with its wet muzzle, triggering an abrupt cough that expelled lake water from the corners of Kaden's mouth—a sign of life. The ethereal blue dust particles suddenly reversed course and spiraled back into his body through his nostrils. After pausing to witness the reentry of every single particle, the stag sprinted away through the dense underbrush, vanishing as mysteriously as it had appeared.

CHAPTER 2

NO MORE BEING ignored and taken for granted, and no more keeping silent about it. Those days were over for Clay Krutcher. He had memorized exactly what he wanted to say, and with some help from his courage-in-a-bottle he was emboldened to demand what he deserved. On a mission to say his piece, Clay traveled the main road in Lynch, Kentucky, the KY 160, to his job at the Pineville Coal Mine, even though that route took him twenty minutes out of the way. The dirt roads were quicker, but by the time he made it to work, his red pickup would be completely covered in dust. To avoid mucking up his truck, he took the main road instead.

He arrived at the mine's security gate, typed the security code into the keypad, and prepared to wait an annoying amount of time for the gate to slowly open. Once it was clear, he floored it and sped down the path toward the office trailer. He drove so fast that he didn't see the pothole in the middle of the trail until it was too late. Clay hit the brakes hard but couldn't avoid slamming his left wheel into the hole. With a squeal and a bang his pickup came to a standstill.

"What the—?"

Clay jumped out and trotted to the front of his truck. Jagged cracks in the ground led away from the hole into the barren field. He followed alongside it, eyeing one of the cracks that had widened into a crevice near the border of the fence. Clay reached into his jacket pocket and pulled out a flask. He unscrewed the top and took a swig. After two more swallows, he knelt and peered into the crevice. It was too dark to see anything. The smell, however, was a rancid mixture of hot tar and camphor. He dipped his hand into the crevice to see how deep it was. His arm went in all the way to his shoulder. When he lifted his hand out of the crevice, a tar-like substance slicker than oil dripped from between his fingers.

"Ugh," Clay muttered. He wiped his hand on his jeans and headed toward the office trailer.

Jared Henson and Odin Lars were inside finishing up the mine's progress report for the month. In his early fifties, overweight, and gray around the edges, Lars had been the supervisor of the Pineville mine for eleven years. Henson had been a coal miner there for less than six. Despite Henson's imposing, muscular appearance, he embodied a friendly and amenable persona. Lars's method of grooming him to take over his supervisory position involved pushing the boundaries of Henson's amiable traits.

Seated at his desk, Lars thumbed through a stack of invoices until he found the one he was looking for and handed it to Henson. "Why didn't you bring this to my attention last week?"

"It wasn't that much," Henson said. "I didn't think it mattered."

"You don't make those decisions," said Lars. "I do."

Clay pushed the trailer door open and plopped down on an office chair next to Henson.

"What are you doing here? The shift doesn't start til' noon," said Lars.

"My truck hit some kind of hole out there. You didn't notice the cracks in the ground?" Clay said.

"We got potholes, so what?"

"I'm not talkin' about a pothole. I'm talkin' about cracks in the ground that I can stick my arm all the way down to my shoulder in, and what's that black, oily stuff that's seeping up out of it?" said Clay, slurring.

"You smell like a whiskey factory," said Lars.

"I had a beer, so what? What does that have to do with what happened out there to my truck?"

"I don't let anyone work here drunk," said Lars.

"I'm not drunk. If you don't believe me, go out there and look for yourself."

Lars and Henson didn't say anything.

"I'm serious. One of my tires is stuck in a hole out there," said Clay.

Lars grabbed his set of keys from his desk drawer. "You better not be wasting my time," he said and dashed out the door.

Things weren't going the way Clay had expected. The wheel of his truck slamming into a crevice had totally disrupted his plan. He stood there trying to remember what he had rehearsed to say to Lars.

"You gotta stop coming here after you been drinkin'," said Henson. "He's gonna fire you."

Clay scoffed. "What I do when I'm not workin' is my business. When I'm here, I do my job, and I do it as well as everybody else. You know how long I've been workin' at this place?"

"Yeah, you keep reminding me. A year more than me," said Henson.

"It's a year longer than anybody else. So why has everybody gotten a raise except for me?"

"You know why. How many times have you been written up for stupid stuff you could've avoided?"

"I've been loyal to Pineville. It's time they showed some loyalty to me," said Clay.

Lars returned and took a seat at his desk. He thumbed through more invoices without saying a word.

"Well? Did you see it?" said Clay.

"I warned you not to waste my time. Why don't you take today off?" Lars said as he continued marking off the invoices.

"What?" Clay said in disbelief.

"The next time you come here inebriated, you're fired," said Lars. "I'm giving you the day off so you can deal with your hangover. Now get outta my office."

That was the last straw for Clay. He had to say something now, or it would never happen. "I don't need a day off," he said. "I need to be paid what I'm owed, and being written up a couple of times is no excuse not to do it. Everybody's had a raise here except for me, and I've been here the longest. If I'm gonna be the chosen canary in the coal mine, I wanna get compensated for it. I'm not going down like Lankford did with black lung and having nothing left for his family to show for it."

"Clay!" Henson shouted.

Clay ignored him. "That crevice out there in your coal mine damaged my truck, and I'm gonna need the money you owe me to fix it, on top of everything else this company has screwed me out of."

Lars gave him the eye and returned to marking his invoices.

"Are you hearing me?" said Clay.

Lars put his pen down and stood. He looked Clay in the eye, stone-faced. "Yeah, I heard you. Now I want you to hear me. Get out, and you don't have a reason to come back because you don't have a job here anymore."

Clay had a what-just-happened look on his face. "Are you serious?"

"Does it look like I'm kiddin'? Let him out, Henson," said Lars.

Henson opened the trailer door. "Clay, you gotta go."

Clay stepped up to the trailer door and slammed his fist into the wall as he walked out. A framed picture of him with the other Pineville coal miners fell to the floor and shattered. His plan to get his fair share had not only failed—it had backfired. Coupled with everything else that had gone wrong that week, he would now have to contend with breaking the news to Tara before she got word of it from someone else.

Clay walked back to his pickup with no plan in mind. The cracks he had seen on the ground were not there anymore. When he reached his truck, he knelt in front of the left tire again and rubbed his hand across smooth and solid ground. There was no crevice.

"I'm not drunk," he said aloud in an attempt to convince himself. *This is crazy. Am I hallucinating?* He checked his jeans. The tar-like substance was still there, smudged across his pant leg.

○ ○ ○

Officer Brian Holt turned off his onboard computer screen and stepped out of his squad car. At twenty-three years old, he was the youngest officer in the district, a fresh graduate of the police academy. Physically fit, ambitious, and slightly cynical, he figured law enforcement was a good career match until in only his second week of duty he was bombarded with a truckload of paperwork. He assumed filling out forms and writing reports was all part of the job, but he never expected it to be the bulk of it. Serious crimes were rare in Appalachia, and even minor ones like parking and speeding tickets were issued maybe forty or fifty times a month at its peak, so when Officer Holt got the call to investigate a possible criminal assault, he jumped to the task. It wasn't a serious crime, but at least it was *real* police work.

He had his questions ready when he marched up to the front door of the Aaron residence. He looked for the doorbell and found it detached and hanging loose from exposed wiring. Officer Holt pressed the button anyway and heard it ring. The door cracked open, but the chain lock prevented it from opening any farther. A woman in her late thirties with a short pixie cut of dirty-blond hair peered back at him from the other side.

"Ma'am, I'm Officer Holt of the Appalachia Police Department. Is this 5447 Vanley?"

"Yeah, it is," she answered.

"Are you the one who called 911 dispatch this morning?"

Susan shut the door and removed the chain lock. She opened it again and invited Officer Holt inside. "Thanks for coming."

"I appreciate you calling the station, ma'am, and telling us what happened. Paramedics were able to get there in time."

"My boys, Charlie and Jeb, deserve the credit. They saw it happen. You guys find the stag?"

Officer Holt ignored her question. "With your permission, ma'am,

I would like to get a first-hand account of what happened from your boys, since they were there at the scene of the incident. Are they here?"

"Yeah, but they're gettin' ready to leave for school soon."

"It won't take long."

Susan shouted toward the top of the staircase. "Jeb, Charlie, get down here."

Jeb and Charlie came rushing down the stairs into the foyer with their backpacks over their shoulders and stood next to their mother. Charlie was biting his fingernails in a nervous twitch.

"Cut it out," said Susan. Charlie lowered his hand.

"Officer Holt needs to ask both of you a few questions about what happened today. Tell him everything you told me, okay?"

When their mother stepped out of the room, they gave Officer Holt their full attention. Though he didn't expect to hear anything out of the ordinary, he pulled a notepad and a pen from his pocket for note-taking.

"You know what this is about, right?" asked Officer Holt. They both nodded. "So what happened? Do you guys know how the kid ended up in the lake?"

Charlie looked at Jeb, expecting him to answer.

"We were bunting bottles," said Jeb, "and when we—"

Officer Holt interrupted him. "Bunting bottles? What's that?"

"It's hitting plastic bottles with a bat. We try to see who can bunt them out into the lake the farthest," said Jeb.

"We were gonna clean it up. I swear," said Charlie.

Officer Holt placed a reassuring hand on Charlie's shoulder. "You're fine. That's not why I'm here. Go on, what happened?"

"Then this kid came over to us," said Jeb, "and told us to stop, but we ignored him, so he got mad and dived into the lake, trying to gather up all the bottles we were buntin'. Then a minute after that we didn't see him in the water anymore."

Charlie added, "We were gonna go in after him, but we didn't want a parasite to swim up in our pee-hole and eat us alive."

Jeb elbowed Charlie in the arm to get him to shut up. "That wasn't the reason," he said. "Anyway, we waited a while, and all of a sudden this huge deer came bursting out of nowhere with its antlers and pulled him out of the water."

Officer Holt gave him a puzzled look. "Really? A deer?"

"Yeah, a big one. I thought he was gonna impale us with those things," Jeb said. "It was just standing there like it was guarding the kid or somethin,' so we ran."

"Yeah, we didn't wanna get impaled," Charlie said.

Officer Holt didn't buy it. They were either hiding something or outright lying, but soon enough, he would get the truth out of them. "Hey, if you guys were horsin' around and somehow ended up pushing the kid in the water, just tell me that. Don't make up stories."

"We're not makin' it up. All three of us saw it," said Jeb.

"Who was the third?"

"Travis Morley. He was there too."

Officer Holt jotted the name down on his notebook. "You're sure all three of you saw this deer?"

"Yeah, we did," said Jeb. Charlie nodded. He gazed back at his mother, who was seated in the kitchen, listening to their conversation. "We swear," he said, looking her in the eye.

Officer Holt placed his pen and notepad back in his pocket. "Does Travis live around here?"

"Yeah, but he's probably on his way to class now. He has first period like we do," said Jeb.

Susan stepped back into the room. "Officer, they need to go now so they won't miss their bus." She opened the front door. "Go ahead on. And I want you to come straight home after class. Both of you." Jeb and Charlie hurried out the front door.

"And no stoppin' off at the lake either," Susan warned. She closed the door and faced Officer Holt.

"They're good kids. They don't get into trouble, and they certainly wouldn't push another kid in the lake, if that's what you're thinkin'," said Susan.

"It's part of the job, ma'am. I have to ask."

"How's the boy doing? Is he okay?"

"He had a mild case of hypothermia and took some water in his lungs, but he'll be all right."

"What's his name?"

"Kaden. His parents are Doug and Pamela Lofton. You know 'em?"

"Nope, never met 'em. Must be new to the neighborhood, but then again, I don't do a lot of socializin'."

"Let me ask you, Miss...?"

"It's Miss Aaron," she said, stone-faced.

"Miss Aaron, I'm sort of confused.

"About what?"

"I don't know why your boys are making up a story about a deer unless they're not being completely honest with me."

"Listen, I didn't raise my boys to be liars. They told me the same story they told you. I believe my kids."

"You're welcome to believe whatever you like, but there are no deer in this area of Virginia, especially the stag that they described and even if by chance one strayed into this area, it would be impossible for it to behave like what your boys described."

Susan folded her arms in a defensive stance. "Oh yeah, and why not?"

"Stags view humans as their predator. They would never get close to one, let alone rescue someone by dragging them out of the lake. That's a pretty wild story, Miss Aaron. Deer are not dolphins."

○   ○   ○

It didn't bother Travis that he had missed his school bus and would be late for first-period class. If he jogged all the way, he could make it there in twenty minutes. But why make an effort for a class he hated? Resolved to be at least thirty minutes late, he trudged the last block of the residential street into a dense field, following a pathway through the dead trees and bushes made by other students who had taken the same shortcut hundreds of times.

Travis's thoughts drifted to what he witnessed at the lake—the stag dragging the boy from the lake, and the strange blue dust floating out of his mouth. *What could that have been? It couldn't be real.* Maybe he was imagining things, but the stag had to be real, or was it? He planned to meet up with Jeb and Charlie after class and compare what they saw and then he'll know for sure.

He tightened the strap on his backpack to prevent it from sliding down his shoulder and continued another hundred yards. Dried leaves crackled from something heavy trotting across them. Travis froze, and the sound stopped. He started walking, and the crackling sound returned. He stopped again, and the sound stopped for the second time. Something or someone was following him. He pulled out his pocketknife and turned around. The deepest black eyes he had ever seen stared back at him: the eyes of a stag. Unlike the one he had seen at the lake, this one had antlers fully formed, jagged and razor-sharp. It stood fifty feet away in a menacing stance. *This is crazy. There's more than one of these things? Where are they coming from?*

Travis made a half turn, and another stag appeared from behind the bushes, leering at him from the same distance as the other. It wasn't unusual to see deer roaming the rural areas of Virginia, but a sighting of three male deer near a residential neighborhood wasn't normal. One of them lurched toward Travis, and seconds later the other one did the same. Travis slowly took his backpack off his shoulder and set it on the ground in case it became necessary for him to sprint away.

If I run, they'll chase after me. They could easily outrun me. What if they try to stab me with their antlers?

Unsure of his next move, Travis took small steps backward with the pocketknife clenched in his hand. His eyes darted back and forth in both directions. The time to be afraid had passed, he needed a way out of it. Crunching noises of hooves bearing down on crisp leaves echoed from the brush, and to his dismay two more stags crept out from the overgrown bushes. All four creatures approached him in sync from every direction. Travis jumped up and down, flailing his arms. "Ha! Go! Get outta here!" It had no effect. The animals marched closer until they had him cornered.

CHAPTER 3

IN ITS HEYDAY, the border town of Lynch, Kentucky had thousands of employees working in hundreds of coal mines, but when the demand for coal left, so did most of the residents. Only four thousand people now lived in Lynch, and out of hundreds of mines only one underground coal mine was still open and operating, the Pineville mine.

Camilla Bailey was the only woman ever hired as a coal miner at the Pineville mine and always the first in her shift to arrive at the underground shaft for work. Covered head to toe in her miner's uniform, she hurried into the shaft hefting her equipment in a satchel across her back. Underneath the hard hat, the goggles and the mask was an attractive woman in her early thirties.

Bailey emptied the sack and dropped the bag on the moving conveyor belt as it carried pieces of coal up through the underground tunnel and onto a shuttle car. After preparing the coal face for extraction and securing the area on the opposite side of the shaft, George Stanley carefully opened boxes of blast caps and unpacked them next to the rock wall. Lars climbed inside the drill jumbo's cabin, extended the boom, and drilled strategic angled holes through the coal seam while Bailey shoveled remnants of coal onto the mining car. Dressed in their uniforms, hard hats and PPE safety equipment, all three were meticulously performing their assigned jobs in silence. Lars drilled the last blast hole in the wall and retracted the boom. Stanley inserted a blast cap into the bottom of each hole. The next step was to fill the holes with the explosive material, but Lars didn't see the ammonium nitrate pellets anywhere in the vicinity.

"Where's the nitrate?" asked Lars.

"That's on Henson," Stanley said.

"Well, where the heck is he? Bailey, check on Henson with my nitrate."

Bailey dropped the shovel and trudged to the elevator cage.

Henson was outside the mine on his way back to the mineshaft when he spotted cracks in the ground. He traced them toward an even wider jagged crevice and knelt beside it. The crevice appeared to go deep underground. *This has to be what Clay was talking about.* But why hadn't he and Lars seen it there before?

A tar-like substance seeped out of the crevice onto the ground. Startled, Henson jumped to his feet and walked away. He reached the elevator cage, picked up two boxes stacked next to it, and loaded them inside. Henson stepped in, closed the half-door, and pushed the square green button. The elevator slowly descended and stopped seconds later. When he stepped out with the boxes, Bailey was standing there waiting for him.

"What took you so long?" she said.

"Bailey, he's right. I saw it. It's out there in the ground."

"What're you talkin' about?"

"The cracks in the ground and the black oily stuff that Clay said he saw. It's there. I can show it to you."

"Henson, they need the nitrate, now," she said, brushing it off.

Henson stepped past her into the mineshaft and set the boxes of nitrate pellets on the ground next to Lars. "There's somethin' seeping out of the ground out there," he said.

"Oh yeah? What do you want me to do about it?" said Lars. He opened the boxes of nitrate pellets and layered them with diesel fuel inside a container. He carefully used a shovel to mix it together.

"Maybe Clay was right," said Henson. "Somethin' we're doing here could be causing it."

"You don't know that," Lars said.

Stanley pumped the explosive ANFO mixture into the blast holes on top of the caps, looking concerned by what Henson said.

"I'm just saying, it wouldn't hurt to get somebody out here to check it out to make sure we're safe," said Henson.

Lars didn't react. He and Stanley connected the detonator wires from the blast caps to the blast machine.

"If it concerns you that much, you're welcome to leave. I ain't holdin' nobody hostage here," said Lars. He hopped back into the drill jumbo and drove it away. They all followed behind to a safe distance from the explosion area.

Lars exited the jumbo's cabin and grabbed an easel and a pen from a steel tray and checked safety protocol procedures off a list.

"Henson!" shouted Lars.

"Clear," Henson said.

"Bailey!"

"Clear."

"Stanley!"

"Clear."

Lars reached for the handle of the blasting machine. "Fire in the hole," he yelled.

He waited a few seconds and activated the detonation button. It sent an electric signal to each blast cap, initiating sequenced explosions from one end of the wall to the other. The coal seam fractured, and the rock wall imploded leaving a cloud of dust that enveloped the area. After waiting for it to clear, Lars headed toward it.

"All right, let's go," he said.

They all searched the blast area for misfires and unexploded charges and found none. Everyone returned to their posts around the shaft, except for Stanley. He was staring peculiarly at something through the dust cloud. "Did you guys see that?"

"What?" asked Bailey.

"Somethin' moved."

"What do you mean *somethin*?" said Lars.

"Somebody just walked past the blast area to the other side of the shaft," Stanley said.

"Who was scheduled to do the check?"

"I was. I did it, we're clear. There's no one else down here but us," said Bailey.

"You think Clay came back?" said Henson.

"It didn't look like a man," said Stanley.

Lars scoffed. "You're imagining things. No one is down here."

The dust cloud evaporated. A silhouette trudged toward them through the dark, winding shaft. Stanley pointed his flashlight toward it. "Then who is that?"

The image took several steps toward them and stopped. The lights on their helmets partly revealed a woman wearing only an undergarment standing motionless in the distance just forty feet away. Her face was soiled with coal dust. Long locks of jet-black hair concealed her chest and were littered with specks of leaves and debris. She stood quietly amid the dust cloud, undeniably alluring but with no discernible expression on her face. She glanced at each of the miners until her eyes found Lars, and laser focused on him. Lars looked as though he'd seen a ghost.

"What in the world?" he said, gaping.

The woman lifted her hands in front of her eyes to block the light from Stanley's flashlight. It illuminated a spiral-shaped tattoo on the palm of her left hand.

"For your own safety, lady, you need to come out now," said Henson. He couldn't conceive how she got past the security gate and over the electrified fence. The biggest mystery was how she was still alive.

"How did she survive that blast?" Henson asked.

The woman took a step toward them and stopped again. "I've come for Clayton," she said in a demure, raspy voice that sounded quasi-feminine.

Henson gazed at the other miners looking for their reaction. Had they heard the same thing? He couldn't tell.

"Did she ask for Clay?" said Henson. No one answered him. Bailey caught the woman's attention and asked her again. «Are you looking for Clay Krutcher?"

The woman put her left hand behind her back. The miners couldn't see the spiral tattoo glowing and pulsating on her palm. A rumbling sound followed.

"Where is the one you call Clay?" the woman asked again.

There was no ambiguity. She repeated Clay's name. Her eyes darted back and forth at all four of them. The rumbling intensified and the rock ceiling vibrated, but she appeared unaffected by it. Lars glanced up at the roof and then at Henson. "We don't have the roof support. We gotta get outta here. It's comin' down," Lars warned.

A high-pitched alarm squelched intermittently as crumbling rocks fell from the ceiling around the woman. She didn't move, nor did her deadpan facial expression change.

"Come on, lady, you're gonna get crushed," Lars said.

The woman still had no reaction to their warnings. Lars glanced over at the other miners. "We have to abort. Let's go."

Lars hurried toward the elevator with Stanley and Bailey following. Henson was left standing alone. "So that's what we're doing? We're leavin' her behind?"

"We don't have a choice," Lars said.

The rumbling and shaking escalated as more debris from the shaft's ceiling fell around the woman, but oddly not *on* her. She remained motionless.

"If we don't grab her and pull her out, she'll be killed. We can't just let her die," said Henson.

"I'm not riskin' the safety of my team for some crazy-in-the-head naked woman. Let's go, Henson," Lars said.

Henson reluctantly fell in line behind the other miners, and they all rushed to the elevator and piled inside. As the alarm squelched to an excruciating volume, Lars pushed the elevator button, and it quickly ascended, shaking and tossing them around. It reached the top in a matter of seconds, and Lars, Henson, Stanley, and Bailey all exited and stepped foot on solid ground at the entrance of the mine. The rumbling and shaking subsided, and an eerie quietness hung in the air.

Lars removed his helmet and mask. "I'll call MSHA and an ambulance."

He scrambled into the communication system trailer. Stanley and Bailey were left standing in front of the mine, silent, not sure what to do next.

"We have to go back and get her," said Henson, breaking the silence.

"You know we can't do that. Not until we get clearance," Stanley replied.

"If she dies in there, they'll shut this place down."

"MSHA has to determine whether there's a black damp hazard. We can't go back. You know the regulations."

"This is crazy," said Henson as he defiantly headed to the entrance of the mine. Before he could walk back inside, Lars stuck his head out the door of the communication trailer. "Henson, if you step one foot in that mine, don't expect to have a job when you come out," he warned, before disappearing back into the communications trailer.

Frustrated, Henson made an about-face. "Unbelievable," he said and took off his helmet. He strode past Bailey in the opposite direction.

"Where you goin'?" she asked.

"If you wanna stand around and watch an obviously mentally ill woman lose her life and not do anything about it, go for it," said Henson. "I'm outta here."

○　○　○

Neither Clay's inviting smile nor his outgoing personality were what caught Tara's attention; it was his slightly pigeon-toed walk that exuded his confident swagger and fearlessness. Coupled with an intense resting face, Clay appeared threatening and empathetic at the same time. His kindness was what eventually sealed the deal for her. At six-one, Clay was considered exceptionally tall in comparison to the average guy in Lynch. He had a solid, athletic frame with blond, cropped-cut hair and deep-set hazel eyes. He wasn't what she would normally consider handsome, but he was attractive.

Tara and Clay were an unlikely couple, especially for Lynch. African Americans accounted for only two percent of the town's population, making the probability of interracial marriage rare. Because they were young, in their mid-twenties, most of the townspeople assumed they were being rebellious or were in it for the novelty. No one believed their relationship would last. Married couples had enough problems to deal with; bringing race into the equation would only make it many times worse. Because Clay could care less about what people thought about them, it encouraged Tara that they would be the exception. No matter the circumstances, they'd listen to each other and not keep secrets. It was a promise they made from the beginning; a promise Clay had trouble keeping.

He parked his truck in the drugstore lot. Tara stepped out and entered the store. An elderly clerk side-eyed her as she picked up a basket and walked past the front counter. Tara ignored his stare and turned down the middle aisle, browsing oral care products.

A middle-aged man with an overextended beard and layers of mismatched clothing entered the store. He had the appearance of a mentally challenged homeless person moving aimlessly through the aisles. The man turned into the same aisle as Tara, lugging a burlap sack over his shoulders. She caught his stare as she placed a tube of toothpaste in her shopping basket.

Tara forced a smile and stepped over to the next aisle. She browsed the shelf until she found what she was searching for, an early pregnancy test kit. She placed one in her basket, and when she turned, the man was standing only a few feet away, staring at her. Tara ignored him and walked over to the counter to purchase her items. The man followed. Tara pretended it didn't bother her as she took her items from the basket and placed them on the counter.

After the clerk rang them up on the register, she handed him her credit card. He examined it thoroughly, back and front, as if he didn't trust its validity. She scoffed that he paid no attention to the homeless man who had followed her down the aisle. Tara wondered if the gratuitous effort he put into scrutinizing her was because her skin color. Miffed, she flashed him her driver's license before he had a chance to ask for it.

The clerk didn't say a word to her as he bagged her items and gave her the receipt.

Tara exited the store, reached into her pocket, and clenched the vial of pepper spray she always carried with her. She sensed the homeless man still trailed behind her, and a quick glimpse over her shoulder confirmed it. Tara cringed and took her hand out of her pocket, still clenching the pepper spray. When she reached the parking lot, he called out, "Tara?"

She panicked. *How does he know my name?* She turned around. The homeless man held her driver's license up. "I think this belongs to you," he said.

Tara put on a smile and walked over to him. He smelled soapy-fresh, like he just got out of the shower, not foul-smelling, as she had assumed.

"Oh, thank you. I thought I put it back in my wallet," she said.

He handed her the license. "Congratulations," he said facetiously.

"Excuse me?" said Tara.

"I saw you buy an early pregnancy test."

"Oh, that's not for me," she said in a knee-jerk response.

He smirked. "You're not deceiving anyone but yourself."

Tara stepped back from him, speechless. She masked her embarrassment and hurried into the passenger's side of Clay's truck.

CHAPTER 4

THE MUD STAINS on Travis's khakis appeared suspicious to Officer Holt. Travis had a bandage wrapped around his left hand, and his shirt had deep wrinkles throughout. He wandered down the school hallway over to his locker and examined it as if he wasn't sure it belonged to him. He dropped his backpack off his shoulder, removed his chemistry book, and placed the backpack in his locker. Officer Holt approached Travis, curious about what he had been up to, and if it had anything to do with why his shoulder-length hair was wet and his face dripped with sweat.

Officer Holt handed his cell phone to Travis. "Is this you?"

Travis gazed at the picture on the phone. "Yeah, it's me. Why do you have that?"

"The principal forwarded it to me. I wanted to be sure who I'm talking to. So, you're Travis Morley?"

Travis nodded and handed him back his phone.

"I've been waiting for–" Officer Holt glanced at his wristwatch. "–thirty-two minutes. That makes you about forty minutes late for your class."

"I had an emergency. What do you want?" said Travis.

"You witnessed an incident and I have questions about it."

"I didn't witness any incident."

"Are you telling me you weren't with Jeb and Charlie Aaron yesterday at the lake?"

Travis bowed his head and nodded. "Yeah, I was there."

"I'm not trying to blame anybody for anything, Travis. I just wanna hear in your own words what happened with the boy. How did he end up in the water?"

Travis shrank. "I didn't do anything to him."

"I said I'm not accusing you. I wanna know what happened," said Officer Holt.

"We were playing bottles and he jumped in the water after them."

"Why do you think he would do that? It doesn't make any sense."

"We were polluting the lake, and he was trying to clean up behind us. We shouldn't have done that, and I'm sorry."

"I don't care about the polluting. Explain to me how he almost drowned."

"All I remember was that he was swimming in the lake, and all of a sudden we didn't see him anymore. We thought he might've drowned, so we ran to get help."

"Is that the whole story? You didn't dare him or push him in the lake?"

"No."

"What about this so-called stag?"

"What stag?"

"Jeb and Charlie said you guys saw a stag pull the boy from the water."

Travis looked confused. "I've never seen a stag in my life. Maybe on TV, but not in person. I've seen a baby deer once with its mother."

"Why do you think they're making that up?"

Travis shrugged. "I dunno. Maybe to get attention from their dad? He never comes around to see 'em."

"That's a really odd thing to say."

"I don't know what else to tell you. It's true."

Blood droplets on the white bandage wrapped around Travis's hand caught Officer Holt's attention. Why was he bleeding? And why did

Jeb and Charlie show more conviction with their crazy stag story than Travis did with his denial?

"What happened to your hand?" asked Officer Holt.

Travis glanced at it. "Oh, this? I fell on a piece of glass. I deserved it."

"Really? Why would you deserve to get cut like that?"

"I'm the one who dumped the motor oil in the lake. It's my fault the birds that swam there died. So if you wanna arrest me, go ahead," he said.

"I'm not here to arrest anybody. I actually think it's a very mature thing to take responsibility for what you did wrong, but what I don't understand is why."

"Why I did it?"

"No, why you would admit it."

Travis shoved his chemistry book under his arm. "If I don't get to my chemistry class, I'll be marked down as absent. That's worse than late."

"All right, you can go. By the way, what was the emergency?" asked Officer Holt.

"What?"

"You said you had an emergency. What was it?"

"It was nothing to worry about, I took care of it," said Travis as he hurried down the hall and into his chemistry class.

o   o   o

Clay considered telling Tara he lost his job but later decided against it, thinking she would needlessly worry. Waiting until he found a new one seemed like a better idea. *How hard can it be to find a decent job anyway?* He drove out of the parking lot more concerned about confronting his father than anything else. Tara had spurred him on a peacemaking mission, and he found himself back on KY 160, headed to his father's auto shop.

"I don't know why I'm doing this. It's not gonna change anything," he said as he traveled down the road.

"It doesn't matter if it changes anything. Your father should hear the truth from you," Tara said.

"He's not gonna listen. He doesn't give a crap about me, he never has, and I'm not gonna let him disrespect you again."

"I'll stay in the car. He won't have to see me."

"It's still a bad idea."

Tara put her cell phone away. "There's some good even in the worst person, Clay, if you're open to receiving it. You need to settle this with him."

Though she had no idea how wrong she was about him and his father's predicament, he admired her peacemaking effort and her optimistic attitude about life in general. It was more than the little things she would say that had made him fall in love with her, there was an obvious physical attraction from the moment they met. He adored her sun-kissed curly dark hair that reached just below her shoulders in soft waves against her caramel skin. When she smiled, her dimples would deepen, accenting her delicate jawline and her gentle almond-shaped eyes. How lucky for him she didn't realize how attractive she was. Tara made him feel good about himself—she made him a better person. Whatever amenable trait she saw in him, he could only hope he would always have it.

He drove his truck up to the side of an auto repair shop. The rusted sign on the marquee read *Gee's Auto*, and inside was just enough space for two side-by-side repair stations.

Clad in his oil-stained mechanic overalls, Gerald glanced at Clay's truck parking on the side of his shop and turned a blind eye to it. Gerald laid back across a rolling platform exasperated and slid under a vintage Camaro that he had jacked up on one of the repair stations. He ignored Clay's entrance and kept tinkering under the vintage car. Clay assumed no one was there until he heard a muffled voice. "You got some nerve comin' here after what you did," said Gerald, his face obscured beneath the car.

Clay caught sight of Gerald's legs extending out from under the Camaro. "I knew you were gonna blame me. I had nothing to do with it," Clay said.

"If you didn't come here with my car or the money I paid for it, you should leave. I got things to do."

"Pops, will you please come from under the car so I can talk to you face-to-face?"

Physically fit for a man in his late sixties, Gerald slid out easily from under the car. Clay gave him a hand and pulled him up to his feet. "All right, we're face-to-face. Now what do you wanna say?"

Before Clay said a word, Tara strolled into the shop and stood next to him. It bothered Clay that she had completely ignored what they discussed and agreed to moments ago– that he would handle it alone with his father. Now he had to change his plan.

Gerald had a disgusted look. "I should've known," he said. He grabbed a towel from the counter and wiped the oil from his hands and arms. "I see you brought your backbone with you."

"She's my wife, Pops, and she knows I didn't steal your car. Anybody could've taken it. You're always leavin' the keys inside."

"And you're the only one who knows that."

"Gerald, why would he steal your car when he has a truck that works perfectly fine?" said Tara.

Gerald scoffed. "A woman is best seen and not heard. Stay in your place or leave my property. It's your choice." He opened his toolbox and rambled through it.

"Pops, you're gonna respect my wife. She's stayin' here next to me," said Clay.

"Great, then both of you can get the hell out. I told you I'm busy," Gerald said.

"I'm not leavin' until we settle this," said Clay.

"Settle? Is that what you want? You want me to settle with you?"

"I want you to believe me."

Gerald chuckled, though it quickly turned serious. "Just because you're my son doesn't mean I'll play stupid for you. You've lied to me before, so I know what to expect. Don't ask me to do somethin' you know I can't do."

Gerald lifted the hood of the Camaro and used the wrench to

unscrew an engine bolt. Clay and Tara stood there awkwardly watching him in silence. Finally, Clay couldn't hold it in any longer.

"Okay, Pops, I admit it. I parted out the car, but I'm gonna pay you back. Whatever the car was worth, I'm gonna pay you back every penny. Just give me some time."

Tara's mouth fell open in shock. "Clay are you serious?"

Clay took her hand. She snatched it away. "We needed the money. I'm sorry," he said.

Gerald winked at her. "What did I tell ya? I know him."

"Pops, I mean it. I'm gonna pay you back."

"I'm givin' you one week to give me my money, or I'm callin' the cops and pressin' charges."

Tara stormed out of the auto shop. Clay wanted to run after her, but first he needed to make good with his father.

"I'm gonna need more than a week," said Clay.

"One week, Clay. That's it."

Clay left the auto shop, hopped in his truck, and started the engine. He paused to look over at Tara in the passenger seat. She stared aimlessly out the window, refusing to look at him. "I vouched for you," she said, still staring out the window. "I told everybody you had nothing to do with stealing that car, Clay, and you couldn't trust me enough to tell me the truth?" She turned and faced him. "The whole time you were lying to me, and I believed you. You let me humiliate myself in front of your father. How could you do that to me?"

"I don't know what I was thinking," said Clay. "I guess at the time I didn't feel I had a choice."

"Everyone has a choice, Clay. You could've just told me. What am I doing that makes you choose to be dishonest with me?"

o   o   o

The day after the coal mine accident, uniformed MSHA inspectors had taken over the Pineville mine, placing it on lockdown and shutting off the power grid. The inspectors had respirators that covered their faces as they trudged in and out of the mineshaft, removing tanks of diesel fuel and nitrate pellets and loading them onto the waiting trucks. Bailey and Henson had returned and were standing together on the sideline watching them, waiting for any sign of the woman.

"You think they'll find her alive?" asked Bailey

"I doubt it. The explosions probably caused the roof to collapse over her," said Henson.

"The whole thing is just…crazy. What was she doin' in there? And was that a tattoo on the palm of her hand? Did you see it?"

"Her hand was not the body part holdin' my attention."

Bailey rolled her eyes at him. His blunt candor didn't work. "You're such a cad," she said.

She took off her hard hat and unpinned her hair. Her long auburn locks fell over her shoulders and softly framed her face. Henson caught himself gazing at her. Maybe humor would be his way of finding out if she had the slightest attraction to him.

"You ever wonder how things would be if we were single?" asked Henson.

"No, never," she answered.

"I don't believe you."

"It doesn't matter to me what you believe."

"You're only foolin' yourself, Bailey. People can see it."

"Really?" she said, grinning. "What is it they see?"

"The sexual tension between us."

Henson couldn't keep a straight face after he said it. Bailey laughed along with him. "You're such a narcissist."

"We're two consenting adults," said Henson. "We should be honest with each other. I'm just sayin'."

"Does your wife know how horny you are, Henson?"

"I don't think she cares."

"Well, your wife and I have something in common. Neither do I," said Bailey.

The lead MSHA inspector and two safety workers dressed in hazard uniforms walked out of the mine carrying a stretcher. Bailey and Henson went over to get a closer look and discovered an empty stretcher. The inspector walked past them and over to where Lars stood, pensive. He had an easel in his hand, as he watched the safety workers load the empty stretcher into a waiting ambulance. Curious about what the inspector was telling Lars, Henson trotted over to them with Bailey close on his heels.

"You didn't find her?" asked Henson.

"Nobody's in there. We searched the entire mine," the inspector answered.

"That doesn't make sense. Could she have slipped out another way?" asked Bailey.

"There is no other way," said the inspector. He hurried away into the MSHA van, leaving Lars, Henson, and Bailey standing together.

"Okay, you heard him. There are no dead bodies here, at least none that were found," said Lars sarcastically. "Let's close it down. They'll be back Friday to retrieve any remains and do the final inspection."

"What if she's still alive?" said Bailey. "Friday will be too late."

"I said we're shuttin' it down," said Lars.

"We can't pretend that we didn't hear her ask for Clay. Maybe we should call him and see if he knows who she is."

"Actually, she asked for Clayton," said Henson.

"Clay, Clayton, it's the same name," Bailey replied.

"Either way, there must be at least a thousand guys with that name here in Kentucky. If we contact anybody, it should be the FBI."

Lars gave them both a warning glance. "Did you hear what I just said? We're not calling the FBI, and we're not calling Clay. We're closing it down now. Whatever is left in that mine will be taken out in a body bag tomorrow. Rain or shine, we're back to business as soon as we get clearance."

CHAPTER 5

DOUG AND PAMELA Lofton were the only people seated in Dalton Children's Hospital triage. Waiting on answers frustrated them, and they had been waiting for an update on Kaden's condition for over an hour. Doug sensed his wife's concern, though he didn't share it. He reached over, took Pamela's hand, and squeezed it gently. She looked him in the eye with a worried smile. The nurse approached, and they both stood.

"Are you Kaden's parents?"

"Yes, we're the Loftons. How's he doing?" said Doug.

"He's doing fine. He's a trooper. If you follow me, I'll take you to his room."

They followed the nurse down the narrow corridor. "I know the doctor told you yesterday that Kaden may have a bacterial infection from ingesting the lake water, but we ran some tests this morning, and he's negative for that infection. We were able to expunge all the bad bacteria and stabilize the hypothermia as well. The doctor will give you a prescription for an antibiotic."

Relieved, Pamela exhaled. "So everything is okay?"

"Everything checked out normal. He's one of the healthiest six-year-olds I've ever seen. But I must tell you, he still doesn't remember what happened to him or even how he ended up in the lake. Probably best not to bring it up unless he wants to talk about it."

The nurse stopped at room 103 and stood in front of the door. "I know he doesn't want to, but the doctor suggests Kaden stay with us another twenty-four hours, just so we can monitor any adverse reaction he might have to the antibiotic."

"Thank you," said Doug.

After the nurse walked away, Pamela and Doug entered Kaden's room. He was sitting up in bed with a Petaminx Rubik's cube in his hands, turning it rapidly in an effort to solve the puzzle.

"Can I go home now?" he asked without taking his eyes off the cube. Pamela went up to Kaden's bedside and caressed his forehead. His eyes didn't stray from his puzzle as he continued rotating the sections to solve it. "Is it necessary that you touch me?" He said with a deep frown.

Pamela froze from embarrassment. She took her hand away and regained her composure. "How are you feeling?"

"I'm fine," said Kaden.

"I was worried. I can't help it."

Kaden smirked without turning his attention away from his Rubik's cube.

"The doctor recommends you stay another day," said Doug.

"I don't care what he recommends. I wanna go home."

"You almost drowned," Pamela said.

"No, I didn't."

"Yes, you did," Pamela said. "The doctor needs to make sure your body doesn't have a bad reaction to the antibiotic. You have to stay until tomorrow."

"I think it's best you leave now so I can talk to *Dad* alone," said Kaden.

Pamela stood her ground and didn't budge. Doug nodded at her, a signal that she would be better off doing what she was told. Pamela stormed out. Doug was left watching Kaden try different combinations of turns on his cube, not sure when to interrupt him or even if it was safe for him to do so. After minutes of dead silence, Kaden spoke. "Have you found him?"

"We're close, but we—"

Kaden cut him off. "Have you found him, Doug?"

"Not yet, but I tracked the town where he lives."

Kaden scoffed. "I know where he lives. He's in Lynch, Kentucky. Why isn't he here in Appalachia?"

Doug didn't have an answer that Kaden would accept, so he didn't answer him at all.

"Let me guess," said Kaden. "You're workin' on it."

Doug nodded. "I am."

"Of course you are. You're always *workin' on it* but hardly getting anything accomplished."

Kaden made one last turn on the Rubik's cube. It made a hollow clicking sound, confirming it was solved. He tossed the cube onto the bed and finally focused his attention on Doug for the first time since he had entered the room. "Clay Krutcher poses a threat to all of us," said Kaden. "It's imperative you get him here before Zarian finds him. Can you do that, Doug? Or do I need to enlist someone more competent?"

"That's unnecessary. I'll complete the task, but it's best for you to follow the advice of the medical professional and remain here for another day," said Doug.

Kaden sneered. "No! I wanna go home. Now!" he screamed.

o   o   o

Lily and Frank Astin couldn't hold their marriage together after the disappearance of their son Jeremy. The glue that had once kept them bonded had vanished without a trace. With that connection broken, the couple's marriage was destined to fail, and within five months of Jeremy's disappearance they were divorced. Lily moved in with her mother in the neighboring city of Benham and left the house to Frank.

It had been a total of six months since Jeremy vanished outside his home in Lynch, Kentucky. He was five years old at the time, and the local police department had no leads or answers to the mystery. How could a young boy vanish from a town of fewer than four thousand people? Frank never accepted it. He conducted his own search, scouring the city and the entire peripheral area of Harlan County in Kentucky, and had found nothing, not a single clue to Jeremy's disappearance. His son, a dyslexic with a severe case of autism, required special attention. He had trouble communicating and adjusting to social situations. He needed his parents, but they needed him more.

Frank's depression consumed him, and by isolating himself from the world he was able to conceal it from everyone except Lily. She knew him better than anyone. When Frank stopped answering her calls, her gut instincts told her something was wrong, and she drove over to his house to check up on him. She took a stack of Jeremy's flyers with her in hopes of getting Frank to leave the house and join her in her own search.

Before Lily could knock on the front door, Frank opened it. His passive glance suggested he had anticipated her visit. It jolted her to see him with a full beard, something she had only seen once in their entire ten-year relationship. He appeared gaunt and pale and exuded an unkempt odor. His hair was plastered to one side, like he had just rolled out of bed. Without a word, he sat on the couch, silent, in front of his laptop and scrolled through a search engine.

Lily stepped into a house in complete disarray: papers strewn everywhere, and dirty dishes scattered throughout the living room with spoiled food still in some of them. It disgusted her, and she tried her best to ignore it. "Why haven't you returned my calls?"

Frank typed something and pushed *enter*. He scrolled through it as he read to himself.

"I've been busy," he said. "What do you want, Lily?"

She accepted she wouldn't get a real answer from him and continued with her intended mission, placing the stack of flyers on the table in front of Frank. The flyers had a picture of Jeremy and contact information in case he was sighted.

"We printed up a hundred. I brought you half," she said. Frank glanced at it but went back to his laptop.

"They got a lead on a red Honda Civic," said Lily. "The police said there's only about thirteen of 'em registered in Harlan County, so it shouldn't take long to—"

Lily stopped to study Frank. His eyes were bloodshot. "You haven't slept at all, have you?"

Frank gave her an *I-don't-want-to-talk-about-it* glimpse.

"You're making yourself sick, Frank."

"How is sleep gonna help?"

"I'm worried about you. That's all," said Lily.

"Don't worry about me. You should be worrying about Jeremy."

Frank's vicious comment crushed her heart and pushed her off balance. "Don't you dare speak to me like that. You think I enjoyed waking up this morning knowing my Jeremy is not with us? That he could be somewhere dead in a field?"

Frank still hadn't taken his eyes off his laptop. Infuriated, Lily slammed it shut in his face.

"Frank, look at me," she demanded. He finally made eye contact with her. "You don't think I suffer as much as you? You don't think I'm doing everything I can to keep from losing my mind over this?"

Tears flooded Lily's eyes, and it only made her angry that she wasn't strong enough to hold them back. Why did she allow him to drive her to the point of losing control? She had been the strong one, the one who kept them united or at least cordial, for Jeremy's sake. Frank didn't say callous things to her to be mean; it was because he blamed himself for Jeremy's disappearance and was incapable of dealing with it. She was intuitive enough to know that, yet she still let him get to her.

"This is not on you, Lily," Frank said, pushing his hair back from his forehead. "It didn't happen on your watch. It happened on mine."

He got up and went into the bathroom. Lily followed him up to the closed door empathetic to the guilt he harbored.

"I can make you some coffee. It'll only take a minute," she said.

"I don't want any," he replied from the other side of the door.

"Then I'll just clean up the dishes real fast."

She had gathered most of the dirty dishes to the sink when Frank walked out of the bathroom. "I wanna be alone, Lily. Just leave it."

She set the plates down. It was an awkward time to mention what she really needed from him, but it was now or never. "We're having a candlelight vigil tomorrow night at my parents' house for Jeremy," she said. "Before that, we'll be searching Bolton Creek with a few volunteers around four in the evening. I would appreciate it if you came out and supported us."

Frank sat down and stared at Jeremy's flyer. "A vigil means we're giving up hope that he's still alive," he said. "I'm sorry, I'm not there yet. Lock the door on your way out." He hurried back into the bathroom and vomited.

CHAPTER 6

I HAVE TO get there.

Kaden bulldozed his way down the dirt road on his bike. The lake had never seemed so far away as it did at that moment. His legs grew fatigued, and the constant pedaling caused his feet to sting, but he refused to stop. There was no time to consider the pain. His way was to block all of it out of his mind, to completely ignore it until he couldn't feel it anymore.

And what if it's too late? It's been a couple of days. Are they even still alive?

An SUV drove up behind him with a golden retriever seated on the passenger side. Kaden steered over into the grassy area to put some distance between himself and the oversized vehicle. As it slowly passed, the dog stuck its head out the half-opened window and barked ferociously at him. Kaden looked the dog in the eye and the barking stopped, its ears perked, and the dog tilted its head to the side and whimpered, seemingly mesmerized by Kaden. The car revved up and sped off ahead of him.

Kaden kept pedaling until he reached the clearing between the oaks. He dismounted, dropped his bike on the ground, and ran down the embankment to the shoreline. He stopped at the sight of his bucket buried halfway in the dirt. His head dropped, and he stood there frozen, afraid of what he might see next. He nervously rubbed his arm as he took slow steps toward his bucket, cringing as he got closer to where the flies were circling and buzzing around in one specific area. And there, scattered across the grass, were the four ducklings, still covered in motor oil, dead.

"No, no, no, no, no, no," Kaden shouted. Tears flooded his eyes and poured down his cheeks. He swiped the flies away and picked up one of the ducklings. He gently caressed its lifeless body with his fingers.

"Why are you crying?" he muttered to himself in a harsh voice. "It's not gonna change anything, now is it?"

He shook his head as if he was someone else answering the question.

Kaden wiped his eyes, placed the duckling on the ground, and used the bucket and a stick to dig a hole next to a tree. When the hole was big enough, he placed all four ducklings in it and covered them over with dirt. Kaden walked back to his bike with his bucket in hand. He tossed it over the handlebars and pushed his way up the embankment. Nothing else could be done. He had returned the ducklings to the ground from where all sources of life began. They would become dust, and he had assured himself that one day soon the dust would be swept away in the wind to a new life.

Kaden rode away on his bicycle, homeward bound. A dido butterfly abandoned the safety of an empty bird's nest and flew out into the open air onto his path. When Kaden caught sight of it, the butterfly fluttered away, rolling up and down, side to side, but still on the main road's path. Kaden continued to follow it even after it made a sharp turn into an open meadow. The butterfly landed on a mulberry bush, perched atop one of its lower branches.

He dismounted and walked up next to the bush. The butterfly's luminous yellow and turquoise wings fluttered in the wind. Kaden smiled, in awe of how beautiful it was, and extended his open hand. The butterfly ascended briefly before descending onto his palm. He studied it as he caressed its delicate wings with his index finger.

Two monarch butterflies flew out from the other side of the bush and landed in Kaden's palm alongside the dido. Admiring the contrasting deep orange and black wings, he raised the palm of his hand above his head, and all three butterflies flew away into the sky toward the sun. When he raised both hands, the wind billowed. He waved them back and forth, and the oak branches seemed to sway from the surging wind in sync with his hand movements.

Someone reached out from behind him and grabbed his shoulder. He jolted around and was face-to-face with a young girl. She had strawberry-blond hair and cheeks sprinkled with freckles. She looked older than him, maybe seven or eight. He wasn't sure.

"Who were you waving at?" she asked.

More than her question, it irritated Kaden that she smacked her gum as she chewed it. How long had she been spying on him? "I wasn't waving," he finally said.

"Yes, you were. I saw you. Why were you doing that?"

"Why do you care?"

"Because I wanna know."

"I was pushing the wind at the tree branches," said Kaden.

She giggled. "You think waving your arms in the air will make the wind blow?"

"I just did it."

"No, you didn't," she said. "It's windy here. It's been windy all day. C'mon, you can tell me. What were you *really* doing?"

"I told you. I was pushing the wind forward."

The girl placed her hands on her hips in an I-dare-you stance. "Okay, then. Do it now."

"Do what?" said Kaden

"Make the wind blow, smarty pants."

Something about her jarred Kaden's memory. Something he didn't particularly like. Where had he seen her before? Had he forgotten he already met her? And why did she think she could dare him to do something? Nobody dares a stranger to do anything, but maybe if he proved what he said she would go away.

Kaden gazed upward at the treetops, raised his arms, and waved them back and forth. The branches shimmered in the wind. He turned to her. "See, I told you."

She giggled at him again. "You didn't do that."

"Yes, I did."

"Okay, watch me." The girl raised her arms in the air and waved them back and forth, mimicking Kaden. Again, the branches shimmered in the wind. "I did the same thing you did," she said. "But I would never say I was pushing the wind. The wind is blowing because it's always windy in September, you silly goose."

Kaden had enough of her. He picked up his bike and led it away. To his annoyance, she followed.

"Hey, I'm only teasin'. You don't have to leave," she said.

"You speak to me like I'm a child, and I don't like it."

"But you appear as a child."

"And so do you."

"I'm not the one that's angry about it, you are."

"I'm not angry," said Kaden. "You're incapable of understanding, so how could I be angry by your inadequacies when you have no control over it?"

"Oh yeah? Tell me exactly what I'm incapable of understanding?"

"*I know who I am.* You can't dominate me. No one can."

"I don't wanna dominate anyone."

He stopped and turned around. She feigned a smile and held out her hand for a shake. "I'm Rebecca, and I'm guessing you must be… Kaden?"

He ignored her outstretched hand and stared at her curiously. What had made her appear so familiar to him came to light. "Did someone tell you how to find me?" asked Kaden.

"What is there to tell? It wasn't that difficult."

With that admission, Rebecca had all but revealed her true identity. He would speak to her in one of the old languages to be certain.

"*Man anta?*" he asked her in a distinct Middle Eastern accent.

Rebecca took a moment to answer. "I told you already. My name is Rebecca."

It was enough to confirm his suspicion. Kaden mounted his bike. "Interesting that you speak Arabic, Rebecca," said Kaden.

She responded by stepping even closer to him. "So where you goin'?"

"I have to find my puppy. He ran away yesterday while I was gone."

"Oh no, that's terrible. I can help you look for him. I'm good with dogs, especially puppies."

"I don't want your help," said Kaden as he rode off onto the main road leaving her behind.

"You're very rude, Kaden," she said in an undertone to herself.

A sudden gush of wind snapped a branch off a tree. It crashed on the ground behind her. She didn't flinch, nor did she turn around to look.

○ ○ ○

Clay didn't frequent the Black Mountain Bar for the sports talk or the social scene; it just happened to be the nearest place that would serve him drinks in the afternoon. A tall, frosty mug of Avery Ellie's Brown Ale started his binge, and he would have plenty of time to chug down a few more and disappear before the evening crowd invaded his space. The mug in front of him had his full attention until Jimmy walked in and sat next to him, dampening the mood. He expected a lecture next.

"Now, how did I know my little brother would be held up at a bar drinking at three in the afternoon? How would I know that?" asked Jimmy.

Clay downed another swallow of his beer and didn't say anything. "You wanna know how I knew?" said Jimmy.

"It doesn't take a genius. I'm guessing because there are only two bars in Lynch, and this was the only one open."

"No, because it's a habit, Clay. You're predictable."

"Tara send you here?"

"I haven't talked to Tara."

"It was Abby, wasn't it? She's always stickin' her nose where it don't belong," Clay said.

"She's trying to help."

"I don't need her help."

"You need somebody's help. If you keep goin' like this, you're gonna lose everything, including Tara."

The bartender walked over to their side of the bar and placed a napkin down in front of Jimmy. "Can I get you somethin'?"

"I don't drink," said Jimmy.

Clay rolled his eyes. "Since when did you stop drinking? Was it the day Abby told you not to do it anymore?"

"I've never been a drinker like you," said Jimmy. "And you, buddy, better pay Pops back for his car before he calls the cops on you. Why would you steal a car from him when you have your own truck?"

"You mean I finally did something that got his attention?"

"Don't avoid the question. Why did you steal his car?"

"Honestly? To sell it. I needed the money."

Jimmy sighed. "You can be an incredibly selfish guy sometimes. Why is everything about what you want or what you need, Clay?"

Jimmy wasn't just Clay's only sibling; he was his only friend in the world. What his brother thought of him meant something, even if it was for the wrong reasons. "Look, I'm gonna make it right with Pops," said Clay, "but I need more than a week. Can you talk to him?"

"How ironic. He asked me to talk to you."

"C'mon, it's not a big deal, the man has four cars. How is one less gonna make a difference in his life?"

Jimmy scoffed. "You still don't get it, do you? That's not the issue. You took something that belonged to him, something he worked hard for. It doesn't matter whether he had five or fifty cars. They're his. Why can't you understand that?"

"Like I said, I'm gonna take care of it. Heck, I'll pawn my truck if I have to. Can he get off my back and let me—"

Jimmy interrupted. "–Let you do what? Why should he wait, Clay? If he didn't stay on your case, you wouldn't do anything."

"Jimmy, he needs to trust me. He's never trusted me."

"You never give him a reason to. You're always screwing things up."

Clay took another chug at his beer and nodded. "Yeah, I know. He's been telling me that all my life. *If you could only be like your brother*

Jimmy, he would say. You know what? I tried that, but it still wasn't enough for him, so I gave up."

"Okay, he wasn't the perfect father but at least he was there," said Jimmy.

Clay snickered. "He was there for you; he worshipped the ground you walked on."

"That's not true, Clay. He tried to be there for you."

"Why did he have to try when he could've just done it?"

Jimmy sighed. "Holding a grudge ain't gonna help anything and stealing from him doesn't make it any better. The gamblin', the drinkin' thing... You're my little brother and I'm worried about you. Let me help you, Clay. Let me get you to a rehab."

"You know how you can help me?" said Clay. "Loan me five hundred dollars."

"What?"

"Just until the weekend. I swear I can pay you back. I'll even give you interest on your money."

"No, I'm not doing it," said Jimmy. "I'm not bailing you outta this one. Why would you even ask me that? You know I can't loan you another dime or Abby would kill me. I'm not tryin' to break up my marriage because of you."

"Why do you even have to mention it to her?"

"Because she's my wife, Clay."

"Or because she has complete control over your mind," Clay said.

"You know what? This is a wasted conversation. I gotta go. Pops wanted me to talk some sense into you, but obviously that's not going to happen."

Jimmy stood to leave. Clay grabbed his arm. "You know I wanna do right by him. I just need more time. Look, none of this would even be an issue if I had my own eighteen-wheeler. Do you know how much truckers who have their own trucks make in a week? Thousands. I could be working for myself instead of Pineville."

"Even a used eighteen-wheeler is at least sixty grand. How are you going to get that kind of money?"

Clay took another swallow of his beer. "I want my own truck. I'll find a way."

"Pineville is a decent job. You're lucky to have it. I gotta go," Jimmy said.

Clay wanted to tell him he had been fired, but now that was out of the question. "We're goin' on our hunting trip this time, right? No cancellin' on me."

"Yeah, but take care of your situation with Pops. Please."

As Jimmy exited the bar, Clay gulped down what was left of his beer. "I'll take the check," he said to the bartender.

"It's already taken care of," the bartender said.

Clay assumed Jimmy must have slipped the bartender his credit card before he left, but why didn't he remember seeing him do it?

"Who took care of it?" Clay asked.

"The gray-haired guy at the table over there.

"What gray-haired guy?"

The bartender pointed to an empty table in the corner of the bar. "Guess he left."

Clay went over to the table. There was a note written on a paper napkin. He picked it up and read it. The note said, "They are watching you."

CHAPTER 7

BOLTON CREEK WAS the farthest forest preserve from Lily's home, which was why it had never been formally searched. With the help of her friend Rosalind, a recently promoted deputy sergeant, they assembled a team of volunteers, including off-duty police officers and ordinary civilians, to help search for any trace of Jeremy.

Rosalind and Lily had become fast friends after her assignment to Jeremy's missing persons case, and Rosalind had taken on the responsibility of dividing the groups into teams that were evenly spread out over Bolton Creek. They combed the ground with long metal rods, while others used long sticks to navigate the dense shrubs and overgrown weeds.

Rosalind tapped Lilly's shoulder to get her attention. A man she didn't recognize marched toward them with a scowl on his face.

"Is that your husband?" asked Rosalind.

Lily turned around and recognized Frank looking like he hadn't slept in days. "We're divorced," she said.

Frank marched right up to them, ready for a confrontation. "You won't find him here," he said. "Why do you have all these people wasting their time?"

Rosalind stepped in front of Frank to shift his attention away from Lily. "We don't know that yet."

"What I do know is that we searched this area months ago," said Frank.

"There was never a formal search of this area," Rosalind retorted.

"I know for a fact there was no trace of Jeremy ever found here. Some sick maniac has my little boy, so stop looking for a gravesite and look for him."

Lily got face-to-face with Frank. "Why are you making this harder than it already is?"

"Lily, this is crazy. They're wasting time."

"I have to know, Frank. If he's dead, I want to bring him home. I don't want my little boy lying out in some godforsaken field alone, thrown away like a piece of trash."

Frank grabbed her firmly by her shoulders and looked her in the eye. "Listen to me. I'm telling you that he's not here, Lily. He's alive."

"How can you know that for sure?"

"I can feel it. You gotta trust me."

"You have some information you want to share with the police?" said Rosalind.

One of the volunteers waved his hand above his head and shouted, "Over here, over here!"

Everyone hurried over to where he had discovered a rusted frame from a child's bike. They determined the color was candy-apple red, though most of the paint had rusted to an orange-brownish shade. The chain was broken, and the front wheel was missing.

Lily buried her face in her hands at the sight of it, crying.

Frank walked up next to the bike. "Just because it looks similar doesn't mean it's Jeremy's, Lily," said Frank as he eyed her sobbing. He picked up the bike frame and closely examined it.

"What do you think you're doing?" said Rosalind, appalled.

"I'm looking for the serial number," said Frank.

"Put it down. It could be evidence."

"Evidence to what?"

"A possible homicide."

"It's not a homicide. We don't know who this belongs to."

"It's Jeremy's. I know it is," said Lily.

"Put down the bike, Mr. Astin," Rosalind demanded.

"Not until I find out the serial number," he said.

"I'm serious. Put it down or I'll call for backup over here."

"Call whoever you want."

Frank grabbed the bike frame and strode away with it under his arm.

"Frank, stop it!" Lily shouted.

He ignored her and kept treading through the field.

"Mr. Astin, I wouldn't do that if I were you," said Sheriff Jenkins. His voice sounded more intimidating than threatening, and the gravelly timbre of it was familiar to Frank. His first inclination was to ignore it, but when he considered the possible consequences, he stopped walking and turned around. Sheriff Arthur Jenkins stood there behind him, a short and stoutly built man in his mid-sixties. He wore a Stetson that hid most of the gray, and his stern countenance implied he meant business. "I thought you and I had an understanding, Mr. Astin," Sheriff Jenkins said. "We have a job to do here, and you're making it unnecessarily difficult for us to do it. I get this process may not be moving fast enough for you, but this is a crime scene investigation now, and we're gonna do this my way. Put the bike frame down."

Frank hesitated.

"Now, Mr. Astin," said Sheriff Jenkins, lifting his brow. He unhooked the strap on his gun holster and rested his hand on the gun's handle.

Frank finally got the message. He laid the bike frame on the ground and took a step back. "I don't believe it's Jeremy's," he said.

"It's a free world. You're welcome to believe whatever you like, but we deal in facts and proof here. Why don't you go on home and settle down. I have your number. You can expect a call from me when and if we learn something."

○　○　○

If Kaden Lofton's parents were guilty of neglecting their child, Officer Holt would find proof of it in their interaction. The most likely scenario was the kid had decent parents and the accident was just that, an accident stemming from older kids bullying a younger kid.

Holt knocked on the Loftons' door. When Pamela opened it, she put on a worried face.

"Hi. I think we spoke over the phone yesterday regarding your son Kaden's accident. I'm Officer Holt."

"Oh, yes, I remember," she said.

Pamela Lofton looked much older than he expected. Kaden was six, yet she appeared to be in her late fifties or early sixties. It didn't seem probable she would have a son so young from natural childbirth. Odd but not impossible.

"I came to update you on his case," he continued. "Do you have a moment?"

"Sure, please come in." Pamela held the door open as Officer Holt stepped inside.

The living room was minimally furnished with a couch, a chair, and a cocktail table placed in the center. Custom-framed photographs of lions, cheetahs, alligators, hippos, moose, and peculiarly stag in their natural habitat covered the walls on all sides.

"Please, have a seat," said Pamela.

Officer Holt took a seat on the couch, still taking in the unusual amount of animal pictures on the wall.

"Can I get you a cup of coffee, Officer?"

"No, thank you, ma'am."

"What about doughnuts? I hear you guys like those."

Officer Holt chuckled. "That's a myth. We're not all doughnut lovers."

"Of course not."

"So, tell me. How's your son doing?" said Officer Holt.

Pamela took a seat on the opposite side of the room. "He's fine. Back to being our rambunctious little Kaden again."

She smiled to herself after she said it, but it didn't appear genuine.

Something still bothered her. Doug Lofton's sudden appearance in the living room put her at ease, and she was more than willing to let him take over the conversation. He had reading glasses that were too small on his nose. Even with that, he had to be at least twenty years younger than his wife. Odd again but not unheard of.

"Douglas, this is the officer who helped save our boy's life, Officer Holt."

Officer Holt shook Doug's hand and noted how freezing cold and excessively firm it was. *Does this guy bench-press icebergs?* Holt took his hand away.

"Call me Doug," he said before taking a seat next to his wife.

"So, where are you from originally?" asked Officer Holt.

"What do you mean? We're from here," said Pamela.

"You're from Virginia?"

"Actually, we're new to this area," said Doug, looking Pamela in the eye. "My wife misunderstood your question. We're both from Kentucky."

"Really? My family is from Kentucky. What city?"

His question silenced them. It was strange they had to think about what city they were from. Doug finally answered, "Fenton Bay."

"Fenton Bay? Can't say I heard of it," said Officer Holt.

"It's a small town. Not much goes on there," Doug replied.

"Hey, do you mind if I get a closer look at your photos?" said Officer Holt.

"Sure, go ahead."

Officer Holt walked over to the framed wild animal photos on the wall for a closer look. "These are amazing photographs," he said as he stooped lower to see the others at the bottom of the wall.

Doug walked up next to him, admiring his own work. "Most people assume I used a high-powered zoom lens because of the rich detail," he said. "But it was a basic 35-millimeter lens. Animals trust me. They can sense if you're an animal lover, you know."

"How long have you been photographing animals?"

"For a while. It's a hobby of mine. Are you an animal lover, Officer Holt?"

"I don't have anything against 'em. They're okay."

"Kaden loves animals," said Pamela. "I think he loves them more than people."

"I wanted to ask you about that. Has he ever ventured out into the water chasing after a duck or anything?"

"Kaden doesn't chase after animals; they come to him," said Doug.

Officer Holt's brow lifted. "They come to him? What do you mean?"

"Kaden's our little animal-whisperer. Animals are drawn to him," Pamela interjected.

"Well, we have to consider every possibility of what could have caused your son's accident."

"Chasing after an animal is not a possibility. Someone must've lured him into the water," Doug said. "We were told a group of teenage boys were there at the time. If we had known that it was a hangout for delinquents, we wouldn't have allowed him go there."

"How old is Kaden again?" asked the officer.

"He's six," said Doug.

"Isn't that kind of young to let him go somewhere unsupervised?"

"Kaden has a curfew like every other child. Sometimes he forgets and comes in a little late, but the lake has always been a safe place for him."

Officer Holt returned to his seat with the impression the Loftons might be more than a little eccentric. "I spoke to the boys who reported seeing Kaden in the water. They made up some wild story, which I think was used to cover up the fact they may have egged him on to swim farther away from the shore or maybe even pushed him in, but if we don't have proof, the judge can't prosecute them. I would have to hear from your son what happened in order to do that."

"Wait a minute. We never said we wanted to prosecute anybody," said Pamela.

"Not necessarily prosecute, but hold them accountable."

Doug pinched the tip of his nose. "What my wife is trying to say is that we don't wanna make this more than what it is." Pamela nodded in agreement.

"I must've gotten the wrong impression," said Holt. "Fine, then I would suggest you keep Kaden away from the lake, unless he's supervised. Kids can be pretty cruel to younger kids, and most of the time they don't think about the consequences of their actions. Just curious, did Kaden tell you anything at all about how he ended up in the water?"

"He doesn't remember," said Pamela.

"That's understandable. Well, unless you have any other questions, I'll file the report today, and his case should be all wrapped up by tomorrow."

Doug scratched his chin thinking about it. "You said the older boys told you a wild story about what happened to my son. What kind of wild story?"

"Something about a stag…" said Officer Holt.

Doug eyes widened at his answer.

"It's nonsense," Officer Holt said. "There are no stag roaming the lake in these parts, and the wild story they made up is just an excuse for kids who were most likely doing the wrong thing. But anyway, I'm not gonna take up any more of your time." He went over to the door. Pamela and Doug followed behind him.

"Thank you, Officer, for coming by," said Pamela. "Kaden lost his puppy on top of all of this, so he's taking it pretty hard, sleeping a lot. Otherwise, I would have him say hello."

"I'm sorry to hear that," said Officer Holt.

Kaden strolled into the living room and slipped on one of his sneakers, surprising all of them.

"Oh, he's awake," said Pamela.

Once Kaden had the other sneaker on, he stepped in front of the officer and turned the doorknob to leave.

"Kaden, where are you going?" asked Doug.

"Out to ride my bike."

"Don't be rude. Say hello to Officer Holt," said Pamela.

Kaden gave him a quick glance and turned back to her. "I don't wanna say hello. He irritates me."

Kaden walked out the front door. Pamela giggled out of embarrassment. "Kids say the darnedest things, don't they?"

Doug joined his wife's reaction by feigning a smile. Officer Holt chalked it up to another bratty kid who craved more discipline from his parents. "Have a good evening," he said as he opened the door and stepped out.

In a quick reflex, Pamela blurted, "Help me!" She immediately covered her mouth with her hand, looking shocked and frightened by her host's cry of desperation that had somehow slipped out.

Officer Holt turned back. "What was that?"

Doug stepped in front of her. "She asked for my help, Officer, goodbye," he said and closed the door in Holt's face. Pamela stood with her hand still over her mouth, confounded by what she had unwittingly said.

Doug turned sharply to Pamela. "You've lost control of your host," said Doug. "Silence it permanently or you will leave me no choice but to report your deficiency to Kaden. He will extract you and scatter your particles over the lake and you will be eliminated."

The iris in his eyes morphed from brown to ocean blue. He leered menacingly at her and questioned her in Arabic, "Hal tafham?" *–Do you understand?*

Pamela nodded. He wasn't convinced. Doug grabbed her by the throat with both hands and slammed her against the wall. She shrieked, unable to swallow. The iris of her left eye changed to blue, though the color was not as intense as Doug's mutation.

He repeated it in Hebrew inches away from her face. "At mevina?" *–Do you understand?*

"Yes," she mustered from trembling lips, strangled by his relentless vice-like clasp on her throat.

CHAPTER 8

THE LAST PLACE Tara imagined she would end up living was in a trailer. Trailer parks were for rednecks or the poor or those who desired a reclusive lifestyle. It was certainly not for her, yet it was where she had ended up—in the East End Mobile Home Park. Clay's Grandpa Ellis owned it. As a child, his grandpa would preach to him how acquiring money and owning property was a means to an end, a sure way out of any sort of problem. As far as Clay was concerned, Grandpa Ellis knew everything, and he would boast to Tara that his grandpa's long gray beard was proof of his unchallenged wisdom. When he died unexpectedly, Gerald discovered in his father's will that he wanted Clayton, his favorite grandson, to have it.

Now that Tara had been living there with Clay for over a year, her feelings about it had changed. The park itself was well maintained. The residents took pride in their mobile homes, and as far as she could tell there were no rednecks in the area, and even if there were, she wasn't sure what one would look like outside of being Caucasian. Everyone in the park socialized with each other, had a decent car, and had shoes on their feet—not ragged sandals as she had imagined. The best part of living in their trailer was that she and Clay didn't have a mortgage or rent to pay, only a lot fee of two hundred dollars a month. They were secure there, but Clay's inability to be honest with her was eroding that sense of security and mulling over it kept her up all night.

She lied in bed on her side in the dimly lit room, her eyes wide open. Clay entered the trailer and grabbed a beer out of the refrigerator. He must have gulped it all down before he entered the bedroom.

Clay sat on the bed opposite Tara, sodden. She didn't budge or acknowledge his presence, nor did she pretend she was asleep.

He took off his shoes and placed them under the bed. It didn't matter what he wanted to say to her next. She didn't want to hear it, especially with the pungent odor of alcohol on his breath.

"Is it too late to say I'm sorry?" asked Clay.

What a stupid question, she thought.

Clay waited a moment before he tried again. "I know I should have told you the truth. I just wanted to fix everything before it got outta hand."

Clay took off his shirt and tossed it on the chair. He glanced over at Tara. She was determined not to respond to anything he had to say.

"We needed the money for the note on the truck and the other bills," said Clay. "I was too ashamed to tell you I lost it.

He chose not to admit the real reason he needed the money, and it made her angrier. "You didn't lose it. You gambled it away," she said.

Clay reached out and laid a hand on her shoulder. Tara tensed. He took his hand away.

"It won't happen again. I'm gonna pay back Pops, and I'm gonna put all this behind us and make it right."

"You need help, Clay."

Clay took off his jeans and got into bed. "Baby, listen to me. I don't need anybody else to tell me how much of an idiot I've been. I know what I have to do. I'm gonna show you I'm serious this time. I won't let you down. I promise."

Tara wanted to believe him and be the supportive wife, but he hadn't convinced her he was being genuine. She handed him the EPT wand anyway, hoping the man she married—the man she had fallen in love with, was still in there somewhere and would be mindful of her insecurities, as he always had been in the past.

"What is this?" he asked. He took a closer look. "You think you're pregnant?"

"It says I am," said Tara.

Clay gazed at the wand again. His eyes lit up. "We're gonna be a real mom and pop? Is this for real?"

Tara didn't share his excitement. This had been weighing on her since the moment she read the results. Coupled with the problems they were already having, it was far from good news, and her face conveyed her anxiety.

"Baby, what's wrong? This is what we wanted, right?"

She got out of bed and stepped over to the window.

"You don't want our baby?" he asked.

"Of course I want our baby, but it's too soon, Clay."

"Why is it too soon?"

"We're barely makin' it with just the two of us. It's not the right time."

Clay walked over to her, placed his hands on her shoulders, and looked her in the eye. "Honey, I'll get two jobs. I'll do whatever it takes. We'll make it work. We can do this."

Tara sat back down on the bed. Clay sat beside her and sighed. "When is the right time, Tara?"

When she didn't respond, Clay took her hand. "Was it the right time when we got married? Or didn't we do it because we loved each other and didn't care what people thought about it?"

Tara stared at the ground, silent and aloof.

"Tell me. What is it then?" said Clay.

She finally gave in. "I'm scared."

Clay caressed her hand. "Honey, you're not alone. It's both of us. We're a team, right?"

"Are we?" she said. "You don't make me feel like we are."

"I know… I'm sorry. I'm gonna change that, and I'm gonna give this baby everything it needs," said Clay. "I promise you. I'm gonna take care of us."

Clay's excitement over her pregnancy complicated everything. Tara pondered what to say.

"Tara, look at me."

She snapped out of it and faced him with her ultimatum. "No more hiding things from me, Clay. No matter how bad it is, I wanna know the truth. I have to feel that I can trust you. If we can't trust each other, what do we have?"

"Just don't give up on me," he said and kissed her forehead. "Look, I wanna show you something."

Clay hopped up from the bed, excited. He rushed out into the living room and returned with a magazine. "Take a look at this," he said and handed it to her.

Tara scanned the cued page. "What is this?"

"Go ahead," he said.

Tara turned the pages. The magazine featured stunning photos of a city with oceanside bluffs, flower-studded fields, scenic oceanfront trails, mansions, and people strolling carefree on white-sand beaches. It was gorgeous, picturesque, and…confusing.

"It's a beautiful place," said Tara, "but I don't understand what it has to do with us."

"It's Carmel, baby. Carmel-by-the-Sea, it's the best place to be," Clay said with a big grin, as if he was reciting a popular slogan. "This would be a great place to raise our kid."

"Carmel? Are you serious?"

"I'm very serious. There are people here who go through their entire lives without ever leaving this depressing town, and most of them are miserable for it. I don't want that for us and especially not for our kid. I want him to have a better life than I had."

"It's not so bad here," said Tara. "I mean, we do have our own place. We can afford it here, Clay. Where else can we expect to live for two hundred dollars a month?"

The Carmel thing was all out of nowhere, and she wasn't easily swayed by his passion for it.

"Honey, it's seventy degrees there in the winter," said Clay. "They don't even have sidewalks or streetlights because they don't need 'em. And you see the pictures? It looks great like that all year round."

"We can't just run away from our problems, Clay. They're gonna follow us."

"That's not what I'm tryin' to do. I wanna make a better life for us." Tara sighed.

"Be honest with me. You wouldn't want to live there?" asked Clay.

"Of course I would love to live there. It's beautiful, but we could never afford to live in California, Clay. The home prices there alone are ridiculous, and the price of living in a place like Carmel is way out of our league."

"Not with the kind of money I can make haulin.' When I get my own truck, I can call the shots and work as long and as hard as I have to. I wanna help you get your own salon like you dreamed honey, but in a nice place like Carmel. You're so talented, nobody deserves it more than you."

Tara blushed. "You're just saying that."

"No, I'm serious. You're really good at it and everybody says so. I wanna support my wife in whatever way that I can."

Clay spoke with such enthusiasm that Tara was inclined (though not convinced) to believe in herself as much as he did.

He caressed her stomach. "How long before you can hear the heart-beat?" he asked.

"I don't know."

He pressed his ear against her stomach and listened. When seconds went by and he hadn't said a word, Tara was curious. "You hear anything?"

"Shhhh…Wait. I think I hear it."

Tara perked up. "You do?"

"Yeah, there are two different heartbeats."

Tara gasped. "Oh my God, are you serious?"

Clay couldn't keep a straight face. "No," he replied and burst out laughing. She punched him on the shoulder. "Clay, that wasn't funny. You scared me."

"Why? Two is better than one."

"One is more than enough," she said.

Clay smiled at her. "If our kid looks like you, it'll be beautiful."

He kissed her passionately as they lay back across the bed.

○ ○ ○

Susan stepped out onto her front porch to get some air. It had been a rough day juggling the kids, her ex, and trying to make things right. For the third time that month, her ex had promised to spend time with their kids, and for the third time he hadn't shown up. He made sure to leave a lame excuse why he had to cancel on her voicemail. Jeb and Charlie both claimed it didn't bother them, yet neither concealed how disappointed they were.

She wished there was something she could say or do that would make it okay, but for the time being the soothing night breeze against her face was helping her not to stress too much. It wouldn't be long before Sherlock, her cat, would come trotting by and climb onto the window ledge so she could carry him back into the house. She waited longer than the usual time for him, but Sherlock never appeared. Susan stepped off the porch onto the sidewalk. A radiant moon illuminated her tranquil neighborhood of single-family homes.

"Sherlock…Sherrrrlockkkkk," she called out. "Sherlock, c'mon honey. It's time to come in."

In response were voices—several voices chatting at the same time, emanating from her backyard. Susan walked around to the back of her home to investigate. The closer she got to the backyard the louder the voices became, and the clearer the exact number of people who had chosen for some unknown reason to have a meeting in her backyard. A total of seven adult men and women in their thirties and forties, were huddled together chatting with each other. One of them caught Susan's stare, and all of them turned their heads in sync and gazed at her.

"Hey! What are you people doing on my property?" said Susan.

The moment she spoke, they all scattered about in different directions like a disturbed ant colony. A young boy was left standing alone with his bike lying on the ground next to him. He had a tabby cat in his arms, petting it.

"What's going on? Who were those people?" asked Susan.

Kaden ignored her question and gently stroked the cat's head, gazing into its piercing emerald eyes.

"Do I need to call the police?" said Susan.

Kaden shot her a glance. "I was having a conversation with my friends. It would be foolish to call the police for that," he said.

"Those were adults. Are you related to them?"

"No. I told you they're my friends."

"Adults are not friends with children."

"I don't follow your rules. I can be friends with whomever I choose," said Kaden as he stroked the cat from its head down to its tail.

"Where did they go?"

"Who are you referring to?"

"Those people that were standing around you. Where did they go?"

"I suppose they went home. As you said, they're adults. They can do what they please."

Who is this child? And why hadn't she seen him on their street before?

"What's your name?"

"Kaden," he replied.

"Oh, you're that Lofter kid, aren't you? The one who was in the accident."

Kaden shook his head.

"It wasn't you?"

"It's not Lofter. It's Lofton." He spelled it out, "L-O-F-T-O-N, Lofton."

How bizarre he's allowed to ride around the neighborhood at midnight. And what does a group of adults have to discuss with a child at night in a stranger's backyard? Besides the peculiarity of it all, it was clear he was being neglected.

"Why on God's earth are you out at this time of night? Where are your parents, Kaden?"

"They're at home, as they should be, and I can do whatever I want," he said.

Susan took a good look at the cat Kaden had in his arms. It wasn't just any tabby cat—it was her Sherlock. "Is that my cat?"

"He came to me. I gave him some water 'cause he was really thirsty. Here, you can take him." Kaden placed Sherlock in Susan's arms and stepped back. "He hates the name Sherlock," said Kaden. "He prefers Sebastian. It fits his personality better."

He mounted his bike and readied himself to ride away. "Can you ask Jeb and Charlie for me where Travis lives? I need to speak to him."

He can't be serious? "It's past midnight," said Susan. "Jeb and Charlie are asleep. You're a child. You should be at home in bed as well. What's your phone number so I can call your parents and let them know where you are?"

Kaden creased his nose at her. "I was wrong about you, Susan," he said. "You're a very bitter woman. Goodbye." He rode away into the night, leaving Susan wondering (among other things) how a child she never met before knew her name.

○ ○ ○

Over seventy people had gathered on the front lawn of Lily's mother's home in the middle of the night. Each one was holding a lit candle in a scene that resembled an opaque night sky lit up by a million flickering stars. Tears welled in Lily's eyes as she scanned the crowd. They were working-class people from all parts of Harlan County, some of whom she had never met. They had not only taken the time to help her search for Jeremy in Bolton Creek but were now there again to support her at his vigil. Witnessing everyone huddled together touched her heart, and at the same time it deepened the blow that Frank (for his own selfish reasons) wasn't there. Despite his absence, she wanted to thank each one of their supporters on her and Frank's behalf for their unconditional kindness.

Lily wiped her eyes dry with her hand, lifted her shoulders, and composed herself before she stepped into the center of the crowd. Rosalind flashed her a smile of encouragement and stood behind her. Everyone quieted at Lily's cue.

"I want to thank you all," she said. "Thank you so much for supporting me, my family, and most of all for supporting Jeremy. For those of you who don't know anything about him, Jeremy is a special needs child. He is sweet and kind, and he loved everyone. He would be so happy to see how many of you care about him…"

To Lily's astonishment, Frank stepped out from behind the crowd and into the forefront. She glimpsed his bloodshot eyes, sensing the pain they bore—an agonizing pain that had torn them apart yet was still holding them together by a single thread. His presence made her feel secure.

"It's been exactly six months to this day," Lily continued, "that Jeremy was taken from us, and not one minute goes by that I don't think about him and wonder if he's okay. Is he getting enough to eat? Is he cold? Does he need a sweater or a coat?"

Lily paused to catch her breath. Voicing her concerns about Jeremy to the crowd had affected her composure. Rosalind put an arm around her and hugged her. The reassurance was enough to help her finish her speech.

"If it wasn't for you guys," Lily said as she gazed at Frank, "your love, your prayers, your time you so graciously donate to the searches, I don't know what I would… I don't know what I would do. Thank you so much, and please keep praying for Jeremy that whoever has him will take care of him and let him come home to his family that loves and misses him. Thank you."

Lilly walked over to Frank, and he fully embraced her. He held her so close that she could feel his heart beating as he rested his head on her shoulder. She had never seen him cry or even tear up over Jeremy's disappearance. It was the first time he had shared his heartache with her instead of using it as a weapon against her.

The next morning they drove around in Frank's SUV, posting the last of Jeremy's missing persons flyers around the outskirts of Lynch.

Frank spotted a light fixture at a busy intersection free of advertisements, a perfect place to post the last flyer. Lily held it against the light post as Frank attached it with tape. They got back into the car and drove away, leaving the unattached corners of the flyer flailing in the wind. In bold black letters at the top, it read *Missing*, and at the bottom of the flyer was *Jeremy Astin, six years old, from Lynch, Kentucky.* There was a black-and-white photo in the center of the flyer—an unmistakable photo of Kaden.

CHAPTER 9

WHEN TRAVIS OPENED his eyes, he was lying on his back looking up at a golden sky. A reddish hue scattered across the horizon, and it softened the sunlight away from his eyes. The golden hour before sunset was almost over, and all he could think about was getting back home before dark. Exhausted, Travis forced himself to sit up among the brush and tall weeds that surrounded him. The last thing he remembered was being cornered by four threatening stags, and beyond that he couldn't remember anything else.

Travis stood and grabbed his backpack. The moment he put it over his shoulder, he flinched. Standing in the tall grass a short distance away was Kaden, staring at him, watching his every move while he gently petted a stag. This one had muscular hind legs and oversized antlers that towered over him. The animal kept fidgeting, taking small steps back and forth.

"Calm down, it's only Travis. He means you no harm," said Kaden as he massaged the stag's cold, wet muzzle. It gently brushed its face against Kaden's cheek in requital to his soothing touch. Kaden smiled and waved at Travis. "Come say hello to him, Travis. Don't worry, he's a nice one. He won't hurt you. He's my friend, and now you'll be our friend."

Travis froze, perplexed. *It has to be a dream.* The thought settled him. All he had to do now was to wait for the nightmare to end.

"You think it's a dream, don't you?" said Kaden as if he had read Travis's mind. "If you truly believe you're dreaming, then you must be aware that a dream can't really harm you, can it? Come over and pet him."

Travis didn't want to go anywhere near it. The animal's obsidian eyes bore into his soul, but for reasons he didn't understand he was drawn to it. He took a step forward, and a crack formed on the ground under his foot.

"I think you should hurry," said Kaden.

The crack formed into a deep crevice and the ground vibrated underneath Travis. As the opening widened, the crevice spread ahead in a zigzag pattern as it speedily traveled across the ground. Clumps of grass and dirt fell into the opening. Travis was afraid to take another step.

"You're gonna fall into the ground, Travis if you don't hurry."

Kaden's warning seemed like a real possibility if he didn't make a move. Travis sprinted toward Kaden. The crevice followed him, opening the ground along its path as it trailed inches from his heel. The moment he reached Kaden, the crevice formed into a fissure deep enough to encase a whole human being. Dirt and debris thrust upward and out of the hole, and in a flash, it filled in all the cracks, sealing itself shut.

Travis checked the ground behind him, out of breath. The fissure was gone, and so were the cracks. The terror of what had just happened to him had no effect on Kaden. His attention remained on the stag as he continued to calmly stroke the animal's back.

"It's okay. Pet him, he's nice," said Kaden.

Travis was reticent at first, but Kaden's reassuring demeanor kept drawing him in. He reached out to touch it. The animal lurched back and ran off into the clearing.

"He'll come back," said Kaden. "He just needs to get to know you a little better."

He pointed at a bleeding cut on Travis's forehead. "Oh no, you cut yourself. You have to be careful. The bushes here have very sharp thorns."

He reached into his pocket, pulled out a tissue, and held it out to

Travis. "Go ahead." Travis took the tissue and wiped his forehead. There was a spot of blood left on it.

Kaden knelt. "There's something I want to show you, Travis."

With his back turned, Kaden scooped something up off the ground with both hands. He stood, turned, and faced Travis, holding a handful of blue-tinted dust.

"What is that?" asked Travis.

Kaden took a deep breath until his lungs were filled with air and blew the dust upward into Travis's eyes.

Travis sprang up from his bed with a guttural scream. His heart was beating so fast against his chest it stifled his breathing. He frantically wiped at his face. There was nothing there. He took a moment to curb his erratic breathing and glanced around the room. The light from the computer monitor on his desk dimly illuminated his bed, and his pillow was soaked in sweat. He was in his own bedroom, at home with his family, and had awakened from the strangest nightmare.

Relieved to know it was all a dream, he got up and trudged into the bathroom. He flicked on the light switch and turned on the faucet, cupped water in his hands, and splashed it on his face. Travis peered into the mirror. A drop of blood seeped from the cut on his forehead. He shuddered as he touched it with his finger. The blood was real.

○　○　○

Officer Holt made the decision to close the Lofton case. He didn't believe he would get any additional information from Jeb or Charlie, and Kaden seemed unaffected by the whole incident. Eccentric parents who allowed their young child to ride around places unsupervised may not necessarily be criminally negligent, but it certainly wasn't smart or normal. One last search of the area where the incident occurred would be the proper way to end the investigation and put a period on it. Holt figured he'd get an early start and take advantage of the bright morning sun.

He searched the grounds near the lake's edge, moving debris away with his hands as he trudged from one end of the bank to the other. He wasn't sure what exactly he was looking for when he came across the prints. They were from an animal but not one he could immediately identify. The prints led directly into the water. He reached for his cell phone in his shirt pocket and snapped a picture of it.

"All sorts of people show up here," said a young girl's voice from over his shoulder, "but I never see police officers. Is it serious?"

Officer Holt turned around. A preteenager stood there confidently, chewing a wad of gum. He smiled at her. "Naw, it's not serious."

She examined him from top to bottom. "I'm Rebecca," she said.

"Nice to meet you, Rebecca. I'm Officer Holt." He reached out.

Rebecca shook it. "I know. It says so on your shirt."

He glanced down at the name tag on his shirt pocket. "Yep, it sure does, doesn't it? You come here a lot?"

"I love the lake, so I come to visit as much as I can. Why does a police officer come here?"

"I'm just lookin' around."

"What're you looking for?"

"Nothing in particular, just looking."

"And taking pictures too," she added.

"Yep, maybe a couple of pictures."

"Is that part of your job? Taking pictures?"

"Sometimes my job requires me to. Hey, you wouldn't have happened to see any unusual things here at the lake. Maybe some kind of animal that doesn't belong here?"

"What do you mean? All animals belong here. This is their home."

Officer Holt smiled. She obviously didn't understand what he meant. "Well, what about unusual things?" he replied.

"Nope, haven't seen any unusual things, but I have seen some unusual people."

Officer Holt assumed she was kidding. "There was an accident here the other day. A kid named Kaden Lofton nearly drowned. Do you know him?"

Rebecca's cheerful demeanor faded. "Be careful. He's not a good person."

"Well, he's only a child. How do you know him?"

She picked a pebble off the ground and made it skip across the surface of the lake. "I don't know him that well. Just be careful." Rebecca turned away from the lake and walked away.

"If you see anything, anything unusual at the lake, call the police department and let us know, okay?"

"You don't believe them, do you?"

"Pardon?"

"They're telling you the truth. The pictures will prove it," said Rebecca. She skipped away toward the top of the embankment.

Officer Holt left the lake intrigued by their encounter and even more by what she said about the pictures he had just taken. He assumed she was friends with Jeb and Charlie, and that was how she knew what they had told him. He stopped to pick up his case files from the reception area of the Appalachia police department and dropped them on his desk. The Lofton case needed to be put to bed before he could even begin to shuffle through them. He turned on his desktop computer, clicked on Google, and typed "stag footprints" in the search box. Various pictures of animal impressions popped up on the screen. He scrolled through the pictures he had just taken at the lake on his cell phone. When he compared them with the known stag prints on his computer, they appeared identical.

○　○　○

Rebecca turned the corner in time to see Kaden laying his bike down on the sidewalk in front of her house. She gaped, and the wad of gum almost fell out of her mouth. The audacity he had to come to her house knowing she wasn't there.

Enraged, Rebecca ran toward him as he was stomping up the porch stairs to her front door. Kaden put his finger on the doorbell, but before he could press it, she reached the bottom of the stairs.

"What're you doing?"

Kaden gave her a dismissive look. "Oh, it's you. Hi, Rebecca. I thought you'd be at the lake now with the ones you seem to care so much about."

"I don't want you at my house. Ever," she said, grimacing.

"Why do you care? I'm not here for you. I wanna meet the people you call your parents. I have a message for them."

"They're not interested in your messages. Stay away from my parents, Kaden or else…"

"Or else what?"

"I mean it. Stay away from my house," said Rebecca. She turned her head and spat her wad of gum on the ground, eliciting a disgusted scowl from Kaden.

"You display all the vile traits of your human host—your opinions, the way you speak, the gum chewing. It's obnoxious," said Kaden.

"I am as a part of my host as you are. Neither of us can avoid merging with the human traits of our host's consciousness."

"There is no merging between me and the Jeremy boy. He does not exist within me any longer." Kaden spoke in Hebrew. "Hasarti oto."– *I've eliminated him.*

"You wouldn't do that. You're just as curious about them as I am," said Rebecca.

Kaden paused for a moment before he walked down the stairs and stood face-to-face with Rebecca on the sidewalk. "I will talk to your parents," he said. "Maybe not today, since you're in such a rotten mood, but it'll happen sooner or later."

"Whatever you need to say, you can say to me. This doesn't concern them."

A wry smile formed on Kaden's face. "They're not changed, are they?"

Rebecca offered no immediate reply. Her silence was enough.

"How long do you think you can keep hiding what you really are?" asked Kaden. "They'll find out, and they'll try to destroy you because that's human nature."

"Don't ever come here again," said Rebecca.

Kaden menacingly eyed her, but she refused to cower. He picked up his bike from the ground and mounted it.

"Your back tire is almost out of air," said Rebecca. "You must've run over a nail or something."

She reached down and yanked a rusted nail from his tire. It popped, and then a hissing sound emanated from it. Kaden dismounted and she handed him the nail. He frowned. "You're a mean friend."

"We're not friends," said Rebecca.

Kaden tossed the nail on the grass. "A cold, wet towel is good for nosebleeds," he said to her and strolled away. Rebecca watched him lead his bike down the sidewalk. *A cold, wet towel is good for nosebleeds? What does that mean?* Confused, Rebecca trod up the stairs to where her mother, Miriam, had been standing, waiting for her to come inside.

"Who was that you were talking to?" asked Miriam.

"Just a kid," said Rebecca flatly. She stepped past her mother into the house.

CHAPTER 10

JEB HAD JUST swapped textbooks in his locker when Travis side-swiped him and kept walking without saying a word. "That was freaking weird," said Jeb in an undertone to himself. He shut his locker and followed Travis down the hallway. He had never seen him walk so fast, and what was going on with the bandaged hand? He cradled it as if he was in pain.

Jeb ran up behind Travis just as he spun around the corner of the hallway. "Hey, wait up. Why didn't you answer my texts?"

Travis glanced back at him. "Who are you?"

Jeb chuckled. "Ha-ha, very funny," he said sarcastically.

"Oh, yeah, you're Jeb," said Travis.

"Are you serious? I'm always Jeb, you weirdo. So what's wrong with your hand?" Jeb asked as he trailed Travis down the hallway.

"Nothing," said Travis.

"So you wrapped a bandage around it for no reason?"

"I can't talk to you right now," Travis said and pivoted into the boys' washroom. The door closed in Jeb's face.

Travis checked all the stalls to make sure they were empty before he entered one himself. He locked the door behind him and unwrapped the bandage from around his hand, one layer after another, peeling it off until the bandage fell to the floor. A spiral appeared engraved into his palm. His heart raced.

Travis hurried out of the stall and over to the basin. He squirted soap onto his hands and erratically scrubbed them together, hoping it would wash it away. Soap and water had no effect, the tattoo was still there.

"What is that?" said a voice from over his shoulder.

Travis turned around and discovered Jeb had followed him inside. He ignored his question and went back to rinsing his hands in the basin.

"Was that a drawing on your palm? Did you get a tattoo?" Jeb asked again.

Travis turned the water faucet off and put both his hands–palms up, in Jeb's face. The spiral tattoo was gone. "I didn't get a tattoo, and it's none of your business anyway," said Travis. "Stop following me and leave me alone!" Travis yanked a paper towel from the dispenser and stormed out of the bathroom.

○ ○ ○

Miriam hadn't heard a word from Rebecca since she went into her room hours earlier. Concerned about her daughter's need for isolation, Miriam went upstairs to her bedroom. She opened the door expecting to see Rebecca on her bed scrolling through her tablet. She was at her desk instead, engrossed in a picture she was drawing. Watching her daughter so absorbed in her activity made her hesitate to interrupt the moment, but she needed her daughter to interact with her, to show her that she was getting better, that she could be *normal* again.

Miriam knocked twice on the opened door. "Hey, honey, your dad called. His flight comes in at seven tonight, so I'm thinking about making lasagna for dinner. You wanna help?"

Rebecca used to jump at the chance to cook with her mother, but she shook her head no and kept drawing.

"It would be nice to make him something special. What do you think I should make?" asked Miriam. Rebecca shrugged, swapped colored pencils, and continued coloring her drawing.

Unwilling to give up, Miriam tried again. "How about I make the lasagna and you make the dessert?"

"Can I make chocolate chip coconut cookies?"

"Homemade chocolate chip coconut cookies sound great to me," said Miriam.

Rebecca managed to smile. Miriam had hoped for a more excited reaction from Rebecca but she never looked away from her picture, not once.

"So what are you drawing, honey?" asked Miriam.

"Beautiful things…like flowers and animals."

"Really? Can I see it?"

Rebecca held the picture up at Miriam. She had drawn a doe and her fawn standing in a field of yellow dandelions. The artistry astounded Miriam. It seemed far beyond her daughter's years. How could she have been unaware of her daughter's artistic talent?

"Wow, it's beautiful, Becca."

Miriam's smile faded to a look of concern at the line of blood dripping from Rebecca's nostril.

"Oh my gosh, what happened?" said Miriam.

"What?"

"Your nose is bleeding, honey."

Rebecca touched the space below her nose. There was blood on her finger. Miriam rushed over and tilted Rebecca's head back.

"It's okay. Hold your head like this. I'll be right back."

Miriam went out of the room, and Rebecca, with her head tilted back, covered her nose with her palm. When Miriam returned, she sat Rebecca down on her bed. "Here, keep your head back and hold this on your nose."

She handed Rebecca a cold, wet towel and helped her place it over her nose.

"Hold it there tight. It'll stop the bleeding," said Miriam.

Rebecca whispered to herself, pensive on the last comment Kaden made to her. "A cold, wet towel is good for nosebleeds."

"What did you say, honey?" asked Miriam.

"It's nothing," Rebecca said.

After the bleeding stopped, Rebecca was in the kitchen with her mother, baking chocolate chip coconut cookies while Miriam made lasagna. They waited up as long as they could for Rebecca's father to arrive, but when he hadn't shown up by ten, she sent Rebecca to bed.

Miriam fell asleep an hour later on the couch in front of the television.

Movie credits scrolled on the television screen as Thomas, her husband, entered the house. The sound awakened her, and she got up and followed behind him as he pulled his suitcases into their bedroom. "Hey you," said Miriam.

"I didn't want to wake you," he said and gave her a quick kiss.

"How was your trip?"

"It was great until they lost my luggage and I had to wait two hours for them to find it."

"You should have called me. Rebecca and I could've picked you up from the airport."

"I didn't want her out so late. The Uber was fine," Thomas said.

Miriam followed him into the kitchen. He took a seat at the table in front of a stack of mail and loosened his tie before rummaging through it.

"You want me to warm up your dinner?" asked Miriam.

"I'm not that hungry. I can have it tomorrow, but I will have one of these cookies."

Thomas grabbed one off the plate of cookies on the table and took a bite.

"Becca made those for you," said Miriam.

"They're so good. She's great at baking."

"She loves doing it, and she really has a gift for it. It's the only time I can tell that she's happy."

"How has she been? Did she have any more episodes?" asked Thomas.

"No, nothing like that, but I'm still sort of worried about her."

"Why?"

"She had a bad nosebleed today," said Miriam.

"Is she sick? Let's take her to the doctor in the morning."

"No, she's not sick…she just a lot different than before."

Miriam couldn't find the right words to describe it. Rebecca wasn't herself. Something had changed.

"Different? What does that mean?" said Thomas.

"Her mannerisms aren't the same. They seem odd. Certain things she used to do; she doesn't do them the same way anymore. It's like I don't even know my own daughter."

"Honey, of course she's not the same. Think about the trauma she endured. That would change any child. She survived an abduction. Who knows what kind of brainwashing was done to her? We're lucky to have gotten her back alive."

"I know," said Miriam. "I just wish there was more I could do to help her. I asked Becca if she knew the person that had taken her and if he had harmed her in any way."

"And what did she say?"

"She said no, that she wasn't taken or harmed by anyone. I don't have a reason not to believe her, she's never lied to me. I don't even think she's capable of lying. I just don't want her to feel that I'm forcing her to do something she's not ready to do, but each day she seems more and more withdrawn."

"What did the therapist tell us? It's going to take some time. We're gonna have to be patient and let her find herself again. She's a strong girl. She'll pull through."

Thomas rubbed Miriam's back and stood up from the table. "I'm gonna go check in on her before I call it a night," he said.

Thomas went upstairs and opened Rebecca's door to a darkened room. A nightlight softly illuminated Rebecca in her bed sound asleep under the bedcovers. Thomas walked in and kissed her on the forehead. He gazed at her lovingly before he delicately closed the door and left the room. Rebecca opened her eyes.

"Can I go hug my dad?" she said in a soft voice.

"I'm sorry. I can't let you do that," she answered herself sternly.

"Why?"

"It's against the rules."

"Please, I won't say anything I promise. It's just one hug," the softer voice said.

"If the Council discovers that I even allowed you to speak, it will demand that I disable your voice completely and I would be severely punished. You have to remain silent for now. Do you understand?

Rebecca nodded.

"I promise I'll let you embrace your parents one day soon, but now is our time to sleep."

Rebecca closed her eyes, and the conversation with the entity inhabiting her ceased.

○   ○   ○

Clay reached over Tara and shut off the alarm on his cellphone. His kiss on her cheek stirred her awake, and she sat up in bed. He got up and retrieved a backpack from the closet. "You going hunting with Jimmy?" she asked.

"Yeah, what're you gonna do?"

"I'm gonna hang around here in case they call me into the salon early. We could use the overtime." Tara yawned, hopped out of bed, and put on her robe. "You want some breakfast before you leave?"

"I'll grab somethin' when I get to Jimmy's place," said Clay. He headed toward the bathroom.

"Clay, promise me you won't drink and drive."

He stopped in his tracks, smirked, and huffed because she knew him so well. "I'm not an alcoholic," he fired back.

"I didn't say that."

"It's seven in the morning. Why would I be drinking?" asked Clay, hoping it was enough to quell her suspicion.

After he showered, he put on his boots and hunting gear and walked out without saying goodbye—something he had never done before. Clay drove less than five miles before turning down the gravel road that led to Jimmy's house. He parked in the makeshift carport, pulled out a flask from his glove compartment, and took a swig of whisky. One swallow wasn't enough. He took two more and returned the flask to the glove compartment.

Clay exited his truck wearing his orange hunter's safety vest, camouflage pants, and a baseball cap. He trotted around to the front of the house and banged on the front door.

Abby opened it, still in her morning robe and slippers. She had huge pink curlers in her hair and was clutching a broom. *What could he possibly see in this woman?*

She opened a second screened door. "He can't go. You're gonna have to go alone," she said.

"Why? Because you won't give him permission?"

"It's not me."

Clay sneered. "It's always you." He pushed his way past her into the house. "Jimmy, let's go!"

He didn't get a response, so he hurried through the kitchen and hammered a fist on Jimmy's closed bedroom door. "Hey, c'mon," said Clay.

Jimmy answered from the other side. "I can't. A recruiter just called me for an interview."

"Are you kidding? We planned this months ago," said Clay.

"I've been trying to get this interview for months. I can't turn it down."

"Unbelievable. You're gonna stand me up again?"

"Hey, I didn't plan it this way."

"Why did you have me come here if you knew you weren't going?" asked Clay.

"Abby didn't think it made sense to cancel it just because of me. Plus, it's already paid for."

"Of course, it's what Abby thinks," he said facetiously. "I'm not goin' huntin' without you."

Jimmy shouted from behind the door. "Yes you are, you're gonna go and you're gonna bring back the biggest set of antlers ever, and we're gonna hang that trophy right over the fireplace downstairs. The trip's paid for, Clay. Go."

Clay relented. He grabbed the carton of orange juice from the refrigerator and poured some into a glass. The bottle of vodka on the counter got his attention and he filled the rest of his glass with it.

After he gulped down half his drink in one swallow, Abby snatched the bottle of vodka away from him and placed it inside the kitchen cabinet. "You've had enough," she said.

Jimmy burst into the kitchen in a sports coat, dress shirt, and slacks. He was of average height, stocky and dark-haired, a complete contrast to his brother Clay's tall, blond, and thin build—except for the eyes. They shared the same deep-set hazel eyes inherited from their mother.

A paisley tie hung loosely around Jimmy's neck, and he kept twisting both ends together in feeble attempts to make the knot.

"Honey, can you fix this?" he asked.

Clay studied Jimmy as he went to Abby like a lapdog to get her to tie the knot for him. His older brother who had thrived on independence and never needed anyone to do anything for him was long gone. Jimmy had become a wuss right before his eyes, and because it was his wife who he worshipped that influenced him, there was nothing Clay could say or do that would ever change it.

Abby effortlessly tied the knot for Jimmy and left the room.

"Does she need to hold your hand for you while you pee?" said Clay.

Jimmy rolled his eyes at Clay and tucked his shirt into his pants. "Honey, where's my sport coat?" Abby returned to the kitchen with it and helped him put it on.

"You'll like Silver Springs. It's a prime hunting spot," said Jimmy as he rushed back into his bedroom. Abby followed behind him, leaving Clay alone in the kitchen.

"So where exactly is this place anyway?" asked Clay.

Jimmy shouted back from his bedroom. "There's a map on the table."

Clay scanned the table. Nothing was there. Abby returned to the kitchen and handed Clay a folded map. "Here it is. It's about twenty miles away near Appalachia. Jimmy marked it in red."

Clay tucked it in his front jacket pocket and stepped up to Jimmy's closed bedroom door. "I'm outta here. Good luck on your interview."

"Take care of Pops, Clay. You've only got a few days left," said Jimmy.

Abby eyed Clay. "What is he talkin' about? A few days left for what?"

"It's none of your business," Clay said. Abby followed him to the front door. He turned and looked her in the eye. "Somethin's not right about you."

"What a coincidence. I was thinking the same thing about you. Happy hunting," Abby said with a half-smile.

She opened the door and Clay walked out. Abby waited for Clay to get into his truck, and as soon as he pulled away, she reached into the pocket of her robe, took out her cell phone, and dialed a number.

She put the phone to her ear and listened. Three staccato beeps were followed by a low-pitched fluttering tone that lasted for two seconds. Abby whispered into the phone in Greek. "Eínai sto drómo tou." –*He's on his way.*

As she slipped the phone back into her pocket, Jimmy walked up from behind and startled her. He had the folded map in his hand—the same one she had secretly thrown away and replaced with her own.

"Why was this in the trash?" said Jimmy. "Why didn't Clay take it?"

Abby never considered Jimmy would look in the trashcan. It worried her how quickly he was becoming a risk and that soon her lies would not be enough. She would have to deal with him, one way or another. She answered with the first manufactured excuse that came to mind. "He said he didn't need it, so I tossed it."

CHAPTER 11

CLAY HEADED EAST toward Appalachia, tracking the diagram Abby gave him. He scanned it again as he crossed the Kentucky line into Virginia.

Amid wide-open spaces, he drove past the Appalachia city limits sign and finally onto a rural road. Not a second had gone by after he had taken the turn than a child on a bike raced across the intersection, right in front of his truck. Clay slammed on his brakes. His pickup slid to a halt just inches from hitting the boy's delicate frame. Through the windshield, the boy looked him in the eye with an unusually calm expression, as if he hadn't a care in the world. He dropped to the ground with his bike out of Clay's view.

Nervous and worried, Clay jumped out and rushed over to the front of his pickup. He expected to see a shaken-up and injured child. Instead, there was Kaden, unharmed and kneeling beside a mound of blue-tinted dust. He scooped up a handful of it and put it in his pants pocket.

"Hey, you okay?" Clay asked.

Kaden nodded.

"What are you doing? What is that?"

Kaden put another handful in his pocket and said nothing.

"Hey, you almost got yourself killed. This ain't the place to be playing with dirt."

"It's not dirt," Kaden said. "It's the dust things are made of."

Clay grabbed Kaden's arm and gently helped him to his feet.

"You okay?" asked Clay.

"My puppy is gone," he said.

"What happened?"

"He was behaving badly, and now he's lost," said Kaden.

"What kind of dog is it?"

"He's a German shepherd, but I don't know what breed he'll be when he comes back."

What is this kid talking about? Maybe he's in shock or something.

A car drove slowly by. The male driver gazed at Clay before he picked up speed and drove away. "C'mon. Let's get off the road," said Clay. "There's too many weirdos around here." He picked up Kaden's bike, and they walked it over to the sidewalk. Clay examined it thoroughly and didn't see any damage.

"So what's your name?"

"Kaden."

"Nice to meet you, Kaden, and what's your puppy's name?"

"Puppy."

He must have misunderstood him. "No, what's your puppy's name?"

"I told you," said Kaden. "His name is Puppy."

"Well, I'm sorry Puppy ran away, but you need to stay off the road. It's dangerous," said Clay.

"Puppy didn't run away. He's out there," said Kaden, pointing at the spot in the road where he had knelt.

"No, he's not in the middle of the road," said Clay.

"Yes, he is."

"No, he's not."

"Yeah, he is," said Kaden defiantly. "I have to collect him."

Clay ignored his strange reply and stooped down to Kaden's eye level, inches from his face. "Listen, if you promise me you'll go home to your parents and stay outta the road, I won't take you to the police station. You know what they do to kids like you at the police station?"

Kaden shook his head.

"They lock them up for a very long time, and they never let 'em come out to play. You don't want that, do you?"

"Nope."

"So we got a deal?" asked Clay.

After waiting too long for an answer and not getting one, Clay was ready to leave.

"Go on home before you get yourself hurt."

"It's your turn," Kaden said.

"What was that?"

"You heard me," said Kaden. "I said it's your turn." He mounted his bike. "I'll see you around," he said and rode away.

Clay stood on the sidewalk, confused. "It's my turn? Crazy kid," he mumbled to himself while scanning his surroundings. A rustic building stood tall across the road with a marquee above that said *B&B Pawners*. It was an odd place for a pawnshop, but then again so was the whole area—an odd place with odd people.

He hopped back into his truck, searched the map again, and was back on the four-lane highway. The car behind him on his left sped up until they were driving side-by-side. Clay glanced over at the driver–a teenager wearing thick, black-rimmed glasses. He tilted his head to get a better look into Clay's pickup. Clay sped up, and the teen matched his speed like it was some sort of racing game. When Clay pressed hard on the brakes and slowed, the car raced past him.

"A bunch of freaks in this town," he said out loud to himself as he took the exit off the highway and pulled into a gas station convenience store.

A dark-skinned African American in his forties was the on-duty attendant. He wore dark sunglasses while he swept the floor with a push broom. Clay walked past him to the back coolers. He grabbed a six-pack of beer and set it on the counter. The attendant put the broom away and stepped behind the cash register.

"Give me ten Quick-Picks and five of those Instant Jackpots," said Clay.

The attendant ran slips through the lottery wheel and rang up Clay's beer.

"That'll be $21.59."

Clay gave him the money, and the attendant handed Clay the Quick-Picks, the lottery cards, and his change simultaneously.

"So you're determined to win this," said the attendant.

"Seventy-five million? Who wouldn't? It would make my life a whole lot easier."

"C'mon, you don't really believe that."

"Of course I believe it." He stuffed the change into his pocket. "Hey, I'm in Appalachia, right?"

"Yep, you're in the best town in Virginia," said the attendant with a wide grin.

"That's an interesting accent you got there. Where you from?"

The attendant paused and thought about it. "New Orleans. That's where I from," he said.

Clay pulled out the map and showed it to him.

"I'm trying to find a deer-hunting range called 'Silver Springs.' This map shows that it should be here, or at least somewhere in the Appalachia, Virginia area," he said, pointing to an area highlighted in red on the map. "Did I miss the exit?"

The attendant took off his sunglasses and gazed at the map before handing it back to him. His eyes were crystal blue, a striking contrast against his dark skin color.

"No, you're in the right area," said the attendant. "What you're really looking for is Oceola. They don't call it Silver Springs no more."

"Never heard of it either way," Clay said.

"Most haven't, and that's the idea. Nobody here wants to advertise our best place to hunt stag. The last thing we need is a bunch of big city folks over runnin' it, killin' ev'ry thing in sight. We're one big happy family here in this town, and we like to keep it that way."

"Best place to hunt stag, huh?" said Clay.

"Yep. They run in herds in Oceola, and I'll tell you a little secret." The attendant leaned in closer to Clay and whispered, "Some even say diamond deposits are in the creek beds."

"Is that true?"

"That's what they say. I say you'll find everything you want in Oceola."

"Your secret is safe with me. You know how to get there?"

The attendant put his sunglasses back on. "Just take a left out of here, stay on that road about a quarter-mile, and you'll see a horse stable on the left. Make a right and you'll be in Oceola. It's that simple. There are no signs around, so you just gotta follow the turns that I told you."

"Thanks for the info, bro."

The attendant narrowed his eyes at him. "We're not related, are we?"

Clay looked confused. "That's not what I–...No, we're not."

"I didn't think so. Bro wouldn't be a word you would use for someone who's not related to you unless you're some kind of big city folk. You're not one of those are you?"

"One of what?"

"A big city guy–a college educated jerk who thinks they're smarter than everybody else."

"That's not me," said Clay.

He stepped out of the convenience store puzzled at why the attendant had made such a big deal out of nothing. Clay tossed the six-pack onto the passenger seat before hopping into his truck and using his ignition key to scratch off all five lottery cards. All were losers. He crushed them in his hand. "Rip-off," he grunted.

He grabbed a beer from the six-pack, opened it, took a big gulp, then backed up and drove out of the gas station. He reached the horse stable and followed the attendant's directions. Clay had downed two tall cans of beer by the time he reached the lush forest area he assumed was Oceola. There were oaks on every side that seemed to go on for miles. Clay found a clearing and parked.

"This has to be the place," he said. He grasped his backpack and strapped his hunting shotgun across his shoulder. He trudged through the dense foliage and trees, spying for any sign of deer. It wasn't long before a familiar sound emanated from up ahead. Clay carefully opened his backpack, took out his binoculars, and scanned the area. He focused the lens until the blurry image became clear, and there it was: a stag. The animal gazed back at him through the lens.

Clay lowered the binoculars and adjusted the focus to get a clearer image. When he looked through it again, the stag had vanished.

Something splashed into the water, alerting him to the stream nearby. He trampled toward the sound but abruptly stopped at seeing someone in the distance standing on the edge of the creek. He peered through his binoculars at an elderly man with shoulder-length gray hair and a long gray beard. He was shirtless and sweating profusely as he dumped something out of two buckets into the creek.

Clay kept watching through his binoculars as the man carried the empty buckets up an embankment and into a dilapidated barn. Seconds later, he walked out lugging four buckets. He returned to the creek and emptied all four of them into it one by one. The man climbed back up the embankment with the empty buckets and entered the barn again, but this time he shut the door behind him and didn't come out.

Clay put away his binoculars and rushed curiously down to the creek. Sand was strewn over a bed of rocks, and the current was slowly carrying it away. Clay scooped up some of it in his hand and strained it through his palm and fingers. He was left with six small crystals that reflected sunlight. Could they be real diamonds? Clay wrapped them in a napkin and placed them in his pocket, recollecting what the attendant had said about rumors of diamond deposits in the creek beds. He reached into the stream to scoop up more of the sand, but the current had swept what was left of it away.

○　○　○

Raphael stood next to a grandfather clock, beaming like the proud father. He opened the clock's glass door to showcase its hidden features to two elderly women who were shopping for antiques. Raphael had been a co-owner of B&B Pawners for only a year and at twenty-five years old was one of the youngest Hispanic business owners in Appalachia. He dressed in sport coats and bowties, always ready to make the sale.

The bell signaled that someone had entered the shop. Clay stumbled in tipsy with a can of beer in one hand, and the bottom of both pant legs wet from standing in the creek bed. Raphael asked the women to excuse him for a moment and walked over to where Clay was staring at the jewelry behind the glass counter. "Is there anything I can help you with?"

"Yep, there is," Clay said as he read his name tag. "So you're Raphael."

"Yes, what can I help you with?"

Clay unwrapped the napkin and held it out to him. "Look at these and tell me if they're worth anything."

Raphael glanced at it and stepped back, startled.

"What's wrong?" asked Clay.

"Where'd you get 'em?" said Raphael.

"I'd rather not say."

"You're not from around here, are you?"

"Does it matter where I'm from? I'm just askin' you what they're worth."

"Sir, I have no idea what they're worth. I have other customers. If you don't want to tell me where they originated, I can't help you," said Raphael.

"I don't know where they originated. Don't you have one of those diamond tester things?"

Raphael didn't answer.

"C'mon, every pawnshop has one. It'll only take you a second, and I'll be outta here. I just need to know if they're real," said Clay.

Raphael gave in and disappeared behind a curtain into a backroom. Both women eyed Clay with disdain and he returned their stare, intimidating them into sauntering away to the rear of the shop.

Raphael returned from behind the curtain wearing rubber gloves, a clear visor over his face, and holding a moissanite diamond tester. He looked more like a uniformed inspector than a pawnshop clerk. He touched the crystals with the diamond tester. It made a buzzing sound. "As I suspected," he said, "cubic zirconi—"

Interrupted by a beeping sound, Raphael had an astonished look on his face. "That's odd," he said.

He turned the diamond tester off and then on again.

"What does it say?" asked Clay.

Raphael touched the crystals again with the diamond tester. It beeped several times.

"Are you going to tell me what that beeping sound means or what?" said Clay.

Raphael brought out a magnifying glass from under the counter and studied the crystals closer. He put down the magnifying glass. "These are showing up as three-and-a-half-carat diamonds," he said.

"Three and a half carats? What is that worth?"

"With this color and clarity, I would guess around twenty-five thousand."

"Total?"

"No, each."

"Are you kidding me? That's a hundred and fifty grand."

"They're stolen, aren't they?" said Raphael.

"Do I look like a thief to you?" Clay answered.

Suspicious of Raphael's questioning, Clay grabbed the diamonds from the counter and placed them back in his pocket.

"Did they come from the creek in Oceola?" asked Raphael.

"Thanks for all your help," said Clay, deliberately ignoring his question. He took a swig of his beer and walked toward the door.

"If I were you, I wouldn't drink and drive in this town," said Raphael.

"If I were you, I wouldn't either," Clay said. He stepped out of the pawnshop, grinning from ear to ear. "A hundred and fifty grand. I love this town!"

CHAPTER 12

TARA PLOPPED DOWN on the couch, clutching the second EPT wand that had affirmed her pregnancy. Though Clay had assured her it all would work out, that a baby was the best thing that could have ever happened to them, she still couldn't help but be nervous at the prospect of bringing a life into the world. Would it be normal? Would the baby be healthy? Would they make good parents? Could they even afford a baby? None of it mattered if the test turned out to be a false positive. She had only taken two. Maybe she needed to take a third just to be sure? It's possible both tests were false positives.

Wishful thinking wasn't going to change anything. She needed to accept they were going to have it and make the best of it. It might be rough at first with the added financial burden, but Clay loved the idea of being a father, and she had the potential to be a great mom. She would be loving, kind, and nurturing to her child, unlike what she remembered her mother had been to her.

Tara raised her blouse and stared at her stomach in the mirror. She imagined being nine months pregnant with a huge belly hanging over her jeans. She smiled and caressed her stomach with both hands. *I can't believe there's another human being growing in there.* A queasy feeling churned in her throat. It turned nauseous, and she ran into the bathroom, fell to her knees, and vomited into the toilet bowl. She never expected morning sickness to come so early in the pregnancy.

"What's next?" she said sarcastically to herself, and right on cue something crashed outside her trailer. Tara opened the blinds. The homeless man she had encountered at the drugstore was standing outside her trailer, staring back at her through her window. Tara closed the blinds and stepped back. Her fear turned to rage, and without thinking rationally she rushed out the front door to confront him. He was gone. She searched the perimeter of her trailer, but there was no trace of him.

On her way back inside, a deep, jagged crack in the ground leading from the adjacent road to her trailer concerned her. It was strange that it hadn't branched out to any of the others; it led only to her trailer.

Her cell phone rang, and she rushed inside and locked the door. Blue dust particles floated up out of the jagged crack in front of her trailer. The dust hovered three feet above the ground in a continuous circular formation, searching for its intended host.

Tara grabbed her phone, relieved to see Clay's name on the screen and anxious to tell him everything. She answered it with a question. "When are you coming—"

Clay cut her off as he sped down the road in his truck. "I'm on my way, but, baby, listen to me. You're not gonna believe this," he said. "Remember what I promised you yesterday?"

Tara ignored his question. "I think someone is following me."

It silenced him. "Following you? Who?"

"Clay, I need you here."

"Who is following you, Tara?"

"The homeless man I saw at the drugstore. He must've followed us home."

"What homeless man? What're you talking about?"

"I left my driver's license in the drugstore the other day, and this strange man, I dunno, he looked homeless, gave it back to me. I just saw him standing outside our trailer a moment ago. How could he know where we live unless he followed us?"

"Are you sure it was him?"

"Yeah, it was him," said Tara. "I'm sure of it."

"Honey, maybe he lives there in the trailer park."

"No, he doesn't. I've never seen him around here before."

"He must've got our address from your driver's license. You should call the police. You remember where I keep the Glock?"

"I'm not touching that thing."

Tara opened the blinds again and peered out. No one was there. "I dunno," she said. "Maybe I imagined it, but it seemed so real."

"We'll talk about it, okay?" said Clay. "But I need to tell you this before you hear it from someone else."

From his tone, Tara braced herself for the worse. "What is it?"

"Somethin' we were doing in the mine was creating crevices in the ground. I mentioned it to Lars and about not getting paid what I deserved. He didn't like me standing up for myself, so he fired me."

Tara had stopped listening before Clay admitted he was fired. She was more concerned about the crevice part and how she had seen the same anomaly outside their trailer. Maybe there was a connection.

"Baby, it's nuthin' to get worked up over," he said. "We don't need the mine. I found somethin' here that's gonna take care of all our money problems—a down payment on a house in Carmel and my eighteen-wheeler. Carmel-by-the-sea—here we come!"

"Clay, you're not making sense. Where are you?"

Static noises from a weak cell phone connection drowned out his response.

"Is Jimmy there with you?" Three beeps sounded before the line went dead. "Hello? Clay? Hello?"

On the other side of the line, Clay had lost the signal on his phone with Tara and hung up. He put the phone in his pocket and parked his pickup in the same place he had before, the Oceola hunting area. If he had been lucky enough to find six diamonds worth a hundred and fifty grand in a matter of minutes, it made sense that he could find five times that amount in an hour or two. The diamonds would mean a fresh start for him and his family and a better life in Carmel.

With his shotgun and binoculars strapped around his neck, Clay returned to the creek where he had found the diamonds. He searched it for remnants of sand for nearly an hour, but there was none, nor were there any diamonds left in the water to be found.

Clay turned his attention back to the dilapidated barn. He climbed to the top of the embankment and cautiously approached it. Rumbling sounds emanated from inside. He cracked open the door and peeked in. The interior of the barn was as rundown as the outside of the rotted and chafed wood-framed building. Clay gazed up at a perfectly shaped ten-foot-diameter hole in the middle of the barn's roof that framed a clear blue sky.

The old man he'd seen carrying buckets and emptying them into the stream was seated on a wooden stool directly under the hole in the roof, turning a hand crank on what appeared to be a medieval spinning wheel. The frame was ten feet long and five feet high, made of wood. A wooden wheel was attached to the end of the frame, and the spokes in the center were clear blue sapphire. A four-lobe pinion-pulley system shaped from burnished brass held leather straps over the wooden wheel, and a brass pipe extended out from the wheel into the ground, the other extended inward.

The wheel and frame were covered with strange symbols and weird writing that reminded him of a foreign language.

As the old man continued to crank the wheel, it spun a rainbow-like aura from within the blue sapphire spokes. Sand shot out from the pipe and into a bucket underneath it. Clay opened the barn door all the way and stepped inside. The old man leaped up from the stool, shocked by Clay's intrusion.

"Man, that's incredible. Is that how you dig up the diamond dust? With this contraption?" asked Clay.

Clay circled the wheel, examining it in detail. How could something so primitive-looking unearth something so valuable?

"You know how much dinero we could make from this thing?" said Clay. "What I could bring to the table is a lot more than you could ever do here by yourself. This could be our secret. You and me, partners."

The old man remained frozen in place, frightened into silence. His eyes followed Clay as he circled the wheel again, trying to decipher how it worked.

"This is freakin' incredible," said Clay. "Don't worry, you can trust me. All I want is a fifty-fifty split of this thing. You give me that, and I promise I won't tell anybody about this place. You don't want a bunch of greedy idiots down here looting your treasure trove. Especially an older guy like you. People would try to take advantage of that."

When Clay extended his hand for a shake, his shotgun slid out from behind his back. The old man raised his hands in the air.

"What're you doing?" said Clay. "I don't rob people. Put your hands down."

The old man dropped his hands and picked up the bucket of sand. He slowly backed out of the barn. Clay followed him out.

"Where you goin'? Are there more diamonds in the bucket?" asked Clay. "Look, I'm taking this off, and I'm gonna put it on the ground. See?" He carefully removed his hunting shotgun from around his shoulder and placed it on the ground. "Now we can do our handshake agreement, okay?"

Clay extended his hand again. The man dropped the bucket and bolted.

"Wait!" Clay shouted.

He chased the old man all the way down to the bottom of the embankment until he inexplicably disappeared in the distance. Clay gave up the chase and headed back up to the barn dumbfounded at how unusually fast the old man was for his age. He sifted through the bucket and cupped something small, round, and hard. Excited, he yanked his hand from the bucket holding a crystal diamond a half-inch in diameter.

"This is unreal," he whispered. "He really extracted diamonds with that thing."

Clay held the diamond between his thumb and index finger up toward the sun, admiring the refractions of colorful light and sizing up the potential wealth it would bring him. "This has to be the prettiest thing I ever—"

Something sizzled. The sound emanated from his hand—the sound of skin burning.

"Ahhh!" he screamed and dropped the diamond. A whiff of smoke dissipated, and when he glanced at his hand, the skin on his palm was charred, and his index finger and thumb were split and separated, revealing blood and bone. Clay rushed to remove his safety vest, his collared shirt, and finally his undershirt and wrapped it around his badly injured hand to stop the bleeding.

○　○　○

Rebecca's bright-yellow dress struck a stark contrast to the dark-green foliage that surrounded her. She strolled across the grassy field, picking dandelions that were the same shade of yellow as her dress. She kept gathering them until she had enough to form a dandelion bouquet. When she brought the bouquet up to her nose, she smiled, captivated by the muted fragrant scent. Rebecca spotted the only gray-seeded dandelion in the patch and plucked it off. She blew the dried seeds into the air and watched them float away like tiny helicopters.

Across from the field, a young boy was on his knees in his backyard, digging a hole in the ground with the opened end of a can. Rebecca dropped her bouquet of dandelions and ran over to him. "What are you doing?"

Startled, he stopped. "I'm digging a hole."

"Why are you doing that?" said Rebecca.

"Because I want my three wishes."

"No, you can't dig holes. It's dangerous."

Rebecca kneeled on the ground next to him. The hole looked almost a foot deep. She pushed the dirt back into the hole with her hands. "Kaden told you to do this, didn't he?"

"He said leprechauns are in the ground," said the boy. "And if I dig a really deep hole, I can reach down and pull one out, and it has to give me three wishes. Anything I want."

Hearing the boy repeat Kaden's lies as if they were the truth disturbed her. There were no boundaries to his deception. Children as well as adults were fair game to Kaden. Still, the best course for protecting the humans around her was to keep the human emotions of her host constrained. She didn't want to alarm the boy, but he needed to know at least part of the truth. "Don't believe him," she said. "He wants to hurt you and your family."

Rebecca pushed down harder on the dirt, compacting it tightly back into the hole. It was only a matter of time before one of her kind would use it to surface and change him.

The boy frowned. "So there are no leprechauns?"

"Leprechauns do not exist. It's only a story. It's not true," said Rebecca.

"What about the three wishes?"

Rebecca stood up. "You can't just wish for something and expect it to happen. It's not the way things work in this world."

The bottom half of her yellow dress had dirt stains below the hemline. She used her hands to brush off as much as she could, but a part of the stain remained. "There's nothing good for you down there," she said, pointing at the ground. "Bad things are below, and they will harm you if they surface—they will harm a lot of people. You mustn't do that again, okay?"

He nodded, but because he was so young, she didn't believe he truly understood the seriousness of her warning. She needed to teach him how to protect himself without revealing who and what she was.

"Is that the only hole you dug?" asked Rebecca.

"Not really," he said.

Rebecca turned and scanned his backyard. Half-dug holes were scattered everywhere.

o   o   o

Lars rushed out of the Pineville office trailer to his car in the parking lot. He opened the trunk and tossed a jacket and some work files inside. They landed on top of a ripped and soiled bra. He gazed at it for a moment, wondering why he hadn't gotten rid of it a long time ago. He slammed the trunk door shut, got in his car, and sped away.

Leaves from a hibiscus plant had fallen near the mine's entrance, and a tree squirrel darted out and grabbed one. With its tiny fingers, it gnawed and chewed on it as a crack formed on the ground inside the mine. The crack widened, generating crunching noises the squirrel ignored. When it finally had the urge to flee, it was too late. The crack had swept under the animal and formed a fissure. The squirrel dropped into the crevice deep below.

The noises stopped when the woman stepped out of the mine. She broke through the yellow caution tape, still semi-nude. Her face, arms, and legs were stained with blotches of coal dust, and as she walked toward the office trailer the cracks and crevices in the ground sealed up behind every step she took.

The company van was parked in front with the words *Pineville Enterprises* written across both doors. She tugged on the driver's side door handle, but the van was locked. Turning her attention to the office trailer, she pulled on the doorknob. It didn't budge. With a burst of inhuman strength, the woman ripped the knob clean off the door and tossed it on the ground. She smashed her fist through the glass door window and with a bloody hand reached inside and turned the deadbolt.

The woman stepped inside the office trailer. A desk, a file cabinet, and a couple of chairs were the only furnishings. A coal miner's uniform hung from a rack near the bathroom door. Drawn to her reflection in the mirror, she entered, staring at herself, and touching the skin on her face with both hands, as if she didn't recognize her own facial features. The woman retrieved a hand towel from across the basin and with soap and water used it to wipe the soil and coal stains from her face, legs, and arms and the blood from her hand.

Piece by piece, she plucked specks of leaves from her hair, and when she had removed all the debris, she put on the coal miner's uniform. The file cabinet seemed to interest her the most. She snatched open the drawer in anticipation of the contents. Inside were supply receipts and hanging folders labeled with the name of every Pineville coal miner:

Camilla Bailey, George Stanley, Jared Henson, and Lars Odin, but Clayton Krutcher's file, the one she wanted, was missing. She browsed through the others before taking them all. She opened the second drawer and discovered a set of keys for the Pineville company van and grabbed them.

CHAPTER 13

AFTER CALLING JIMMY and Abby repeatedly and only getting a voicemail, Tara drove over to their house for answers. Clay wasn't answering his phone, and she had expected him back home hours ago. Without a clue as to where he went hunting, asking Abby for information was her only option to find out where he had gone. She knocked on their door and didn't get an answer. Seconds later, Abby opened it. Her eyebrows raised at seeing Tara on the other side.

"Tara? What's wrong?"

"Have you heard anything from Jimmy and Clay?"

"Jimmy didn't go. Clay went alone," said Abby.

"Why? They were supposed to go together."

"Jimmy got a call for an interview with a recruiter. Come in."

Tara stepped inside. "I made a pot of that new coffee, Mountain Creek… Heard of it?" asked Abby.

Without giving it a thought, Tara said "No, I haven't."

"Miner's Market, on sale. It's supposed to be really good with rhubarb apple pie," said Abby.

Tara followed her through the house into the kitchen and took a seat at the table. "I'll get us some," said Abby. She grabbed two mugs from the cupboard and the coffee pot off the stove and filled both their mugs. "Got some sugar and cream if you want it."

"No, I like it black."

"Really? I wouldn't have guessed."

Abby's comment sounded like a jab at her relationship with Clay, but had she read too much into it? She weighed on the side of giving Abby the benefit of the doubt.

"So what's really goin' on? You look stressed," said Abby.

"Where's this hunting area that Clay went to?" Tara asked.

"Silver Springs, right on the Kentucky-Virginia border. I don't understand why you're worried."

"Clay called me. Something's wrong. What he said didn't make sense."

Abby put a couple of teaspoons of sugar in her mug, followed by an endless stream of creamer.

"And what was that?" asked Abby.

"He said he found somethin,' that it was gonna change things for us."

"Really? Did he tell you what it was?"

Abby took a sip of her coffee and removed four apples out of a paper bag onto the counter.

"The connection went bad," said Tara. "I kept trying to call him back, but it wouldn't go through."

"Is that it?"

Tara nodded. "Yeah."

"Then, honey, you're overreactin'. Sounds like he's drinkin' again. He was doin' it long before you met him."

With that remark, Tara remembered how Clay used to say how he never trusted Abby and how rude she was, though every encounter Tara had with Abby was just the opposite. She found her amenable, friendly, and easy to talk to. She never understood why Clay talked so negatively about her, but now she agreed with him.

"You weren't on the phone with him," said Tara. "It had nothing to do with drinking."

"Then you don't have a reason to be anxious." Abby took a knife from the rack and began peeling an apple on a cutting board. "I ran into

Gerald down at the hardware store today. He seems to have lost that gut of his. He's lookin' a lot better."

"Good for him," said Tara disingenuously.

"You two haven't patched up your differences yet, have you?"

"I don't have any differences with him. He has a problem with his son marrying outside his race because he's a racist. That's somethin' he needs to talk over with a therapist."

"He's not a racist. He's just pissed off at Clay for stealing his car. It has nothin' to do with you," said Abby.

"Clay is my husband. It has everything to do with me."

"We'll just have to agree to disagree on that one."

Abby forced an apple slicer down on an apple and tossed the core in the trashcan. She quartered the remaining apples with a knife and started cutting the last three.

"Clay wants to make it right with Gerald. I know he does. He's always wanted a real relationship with his father, but he doesn't know how to get through to him," said Tara.

"You don't do it by stealing his car from right under his nose and selling it for parts," Abby said.

"He promises to give him the money for it in a few days, Abby. Look, nobody's sayin' that Clay is a saint. He's not, though I wouldn't call Gerald father-of-the-year material either."

Abby dropped the knife on the table and took a seat across from Tara. She looked her straight in the eye. "If I were you, I wouldn't tread into their private matters. That's best left between father and son. You are aware Clay stole Jimmy's identity and ruined his credit?"

"He told me that was over ten years ago, Abby. He was a teenager. Kids do stupid things."

"And over ten years later we're still tryna fix it. You can't keep makin' excuses for him, Tara. He's a grown man, not your child."

"I'm not makin' excuses. He knows he's made mistakes, and he's workin' on himself to do better."

Abby smirked, amused by Tara's declaration of devotion. "You really think you can change him, don't you?"

Tara didn't answer. She didn't want to admit Abby was right. She wholeheartedly believed she could change Clay for the better. The qualities were there. He just needed a kick-start, and only someone who truly loved him could do that. Abby was welcome to think whatever she liked. Clay had potential and a good heart, and that was all that mattered. She listened to Abby, but she wasn't *hearing* her.

"We wanna believe we can change men, mold them into somethin' that we can at least tolerate," said Abby. "It's a waste of time, ' cause truth is, it's never gonna happen. They are what they are. Take it or leave it. What I don't understand is what you're getting out of all of this. You're smart, you're pretty. You don't come across as somebody who's hard-up for anything, so I don't get it."

"You don't get what?"

"Be honest. You had to know Clay was a loser, yet you married him anyway. Instead of being desperate, you could've done a lot better with someone of your own kind."

Tara recoiled in a conscious effort to control her anger. "*My own kind?* I expect to hear something like that from Gerald, but I never would have thought I'd hear it from you, Abby. Let's be clear, I'm not desperate for anybody. Clay is a good man who I happen to love very much. It wouldn't matter to me if he was green."

Abby took off her robe and draped it over her chair, leaving her in nothing but a delicate teddy. "You could do better, that's just my opinion. And for the record, I wasn't referring to his skin color."

"I didn't ask for your opinion. I have what I want," Tara said.

"Really? Now, why do I get the feelin' that's not the truth?"

Tara had enough. She stood up from the table and collected her things. "What happened to you, Abby? You used to be a nice person."

Abby took a sip of her coffee. "I was never nice," she said, "just practical."

Tara rolled her eyes and walked out of the kitchen to the front door.

"You haven't touched your coffee," said Abby. "Might be surprised how much you like it."

Tara continued out the front door. "If you or Jimmy hear from

Clay, let me know," she said. Abby followed her outside and stopped short of the front yard.

"If I didn't know any better," said Abby, "I would guess you're pregnant."

Abby's comment sent a chill through Tara and angered her at the same time. Clay promised he would keep her pregnancy a secret until they were both ready, but how else would Abby have known unless Clay told her?

She strolled to her car, pretending not to be affected. As her back was turned, Abby clenched her fist, and when she opened it, the spiral tattoo appeared on her palm. Cracks formed instantly on the ground beneath her feet. She squeezed her fist tight, and the tattoo pulsated a burnt-umber glow, sending crevices surging across the ground toward Tara. It came to a stop at her heel, reversed, and surged backward toward Abby, sealing and filling in the cracks completely. Unaware of what had happened on the ground behind her, Tara got in her car and drove away.

Abby glanced at her palm. The tattoo had stopped glowing. *Why?* Beads of sweat gathered on her forehead and her heartbeat quickened. She scanned her surroundings, expecting to see someone. There could only be one explanation: someone with stronger abilities over the elements had halted her assault on Tara, and that someone most likely remained there with her.

"I know it's you, Octavius," she said out loud, and when she turned around, he stepped out from behind her house. He was tall and slender, of Indian descent and in his thirties, but with premature salt-and-pepper hair. The spiral tattoo glowed and pulsated in Octavius's palm. She kept her eyes locked on it as she walked back to her front door.

"I'm warning you to leave her alone," said Octavius.

Abby spoke to him in Arabic. "Indama yamootoon, sanhya. Sanhod." —*When they are dead, we will live. We will rise.*

The tattoo faded from Octavius's palm, and he answered her in Greek. "An pethánoun aftoí, petháinoyme óloi." —*If they die, we all die.*

Abby backed away inside her house and slammed the door. She locked both deadbolts in a hurry and connected the security chain.

Henson stepped down from the kitchen door and into his attached garage with a wrench and a pulley belt, ready to go to work. He raised the hood of his vintage '77 Buick and tinkered with the engine. The restoration had begun over a year ago, and having time off from working the mine was incentive enough to get it completed and ready for resale.

He lifted his head from beneath the hood as a car wound its way down the driveway and into his garage. His wife, Edie, parked in the empty space next to him, and when she stepped out, he lowered his head back under the hood and returned to modifying the engine without acknowledging his wife's presence. A business professional, Edie was in a conservative gray pantsuit, toting a briefcase instead of a purse. The natural blonde walked past a preoccupied Henson, who still had his head buried under the hood.

"Thought you were sellin' that piece of junk?" said Edie.

Henson raised his head from the engine block and glared at her. His shirt, arms, and hands were soiled from engine oil. "If it don't run, I can't sell it, now can I?" he snapped back.

"Make sure you don't track that oil in the house. I just had the carpet cleaned," she said as she walked through the door into the kitchen.

Henson went back to work under the hood. The moment he removed the damaged engine pulley, another vehicle approached. The Pineville company van was driving up to the front of his house. It didn't add up. Why would someone use the van outside of company hours? And who at the mine would be making a surprise visit to his home? The van parked and idled. Henson couldn't identify the driver through the van's tinted windows, so he walked out of his garage to get a closer look. The driver's door swung open.

Inside the house, Edie was in the bedroom, sitting on the bed and massaging her feet through her stockings. The sound of something crashing to the floor interrupted her peaceful massage. She assumed Henson had dropped something metal on the concrete garage floor.

"Jared?" she shouted.

He didn't respond, so she left the bedroom, walked into the kitchen, and took careful steps toward the door that led to the garage. "Jared? Everything okay out there?"

She placed her hand on the doorknob, turned it, and slowly pushed it open. A woman dressed in a coal miner's uniform was standing in her garage with her back turned. Her husband lay flat on his back, unconscious, suspended in midair just inches above the woman's head. A pulsating glow emanated from the palm of her raised hand, illuminating his levitating body. Edie gasped and the woman clenched her hand shut and faced her. Henson's limp body dropped to the floor behind her with a loud thud.

"Tell me where Clayton is," the woman said to her.

Not waiting for Edie's answer, she rushed toward her. Edie slammed the door shut in her face and locked it.

○　○　○

A storm approached.

Dark, brooding clouds hovered in the sky above Clay as he trampled through the dense foliage. He nestled his injured hand under his shirt and checked his cell phone—still no signal. Fifty yards away he spotted the old man again, sitting rigid against a tree with his knees pulled up into his chest and his arms tightly around them.

"Hey!" Clay shouted at him.

The man's body shivered in the warm air, and his eyes bulged in fear when Clay caught up to him.

"What the heck is in that sand?" asked Clay.

The old man formed words with his lips, but no sound came from his mouth.

"Stop whispering and speak up," Clay demanded.

"He can't, Clayton," said a familiar voice from behind him.

Clay turned around. His eyes widened at the sight of Kaden, standing a footstep away watching him.

"His time has come to an end," Kaden continued. "That's why he's not allowed to move or speak right now."

Clay had just encountered the boy on the road, and now the kid was there again in the middle of nowhere. "You...you were the boy in the road. How do you know my name?"

Kaden shrugged.

"What do you mean you don't know?" asked Clay. "What are you and that old man doing here?"

"I can be wherever I want. I choose to be here."

Kaden walked away, singing, *"Twinkle, twinkle, little star, how I wonder what you are. Up above the world so high, like a diamond in the sky. Twinkle, twinkle, little star, how I wonder what you are..."*

"Hey, kid," Clay shouted.

Kaden ignored him and kept singing as he walked away. Clay followed. "Look, I don't care what you and the old guy are up to. I wanna know what happened to my hand. Is that sand some kind of acid?"

Kaden stopped singing and laughed at him. "Have you been drinking, Clayton? Do you really think someone would carry buckets of acid around? There's nothing wrong with your hand. It's fine."

"It's not fine. It's burned."

"But I'm telling you it's not. Go ahead, take a look."

Clay unwrapped the shirt from his hand, and when he examined it, there was no burn wound, no separated skin or bone, and the pain had dissipated.

"I don't understand. I know it was burned. This must be some kinda hallucination," said Clay as he walked ahead of Kaden.

"You're not hallucinating, Clayton. We're both here together, and it's real."

Clay pulled out his cell phone again from his pocket to check for a signal.

"Your phone won't work," said Kaden.

Clay checked his phone. The screen was blank. He held it up and swayed it around. He still couldn't get a signal.

"You're wasting time, Clayton. It's your turn," said Kaden.

Clay faced him. "Why do you keep sayin' that? It's my turn to do what?"

"Though you have inherited detestable traits from your kind, I have demonstrated to the Council that you are nonetheless redeemable. That's why it has chosen you to be the next."

"The next what? Who is the Council?"

Kaden gazed at him peculiarly. "You really don't know, do you? I assumed it would've been revealed to you by now. Oh well." He kneeled on the ground, took out a handful of blue-tinted dust particles from his pants pocket, and placed it in a pile in front of him.

"You're a real nut job, aren't you?" said Clay.

Kaden jumped to his feet, his nostrils flared in a silent, seething rage. "If you want Tara and your unborn child to survive, you will take your turn at the Wheel, Clayton!"

Clay froze. This kid couldn't have said what he heard. He marched up to Kaden and grabbed him by his shoulders.

"I never told you about my wife. I never told you anything about a baby. So how do you know all this?"

"I just know things, and I know what you are, Clayton. The Council knows too."

"I don't care that you're a kid," said Clay. "I swear I'll strangle your scrawny little neck if you don't tell me right now how in the world do you know about me and my fam—"

The blare of a foghorn cut him off. The deep, guttural sound pierced Kaden and Clay's ears, and they covered them with their hands.

Kaden shouted over the intense sound. "You hear what I hear, Clayton!"

"What is that?"

"The Council is angry. I can't control it anymore," Kaden said. "Turn the wheel before we all die, Clayton. It's in the barn. Go back to the barn!"

Kaden ran from the scene with his hands still covering his ears. Clay was left standing alone as the foghorn sound intensified. He glanced around. There was no way to tell where the sound was coming from.

Clay peered up at the treetops as they began to bend and sway from a surge of gusty wind. His body trembled, and when he examined his hand, it had returned to the same state of charred skin and exposed bone as before. Clay let out a primal scream from the extreme pain. His first reaction was to clench his fist, and when he opened it, the burns and the pain were gone and his hand was back to normal again, except now in the center of his palm was the spiral tattoo.

○ ○ ○

Henson awakened on the garage floor feeling like someone had beaten the crap out of him and for the *coup de grâce* hit him over the head with a brick. Henson stretched his neck from side to side and grudgingly lifted his upper body off the floor. When he stood his knees buckled, and he fell back to the floor again.

"Edie!" he shouted.

Not getting a response worried him more than the injuries he had sustained himself. Henson tried again to lift himself up off the floor. His legs managed to support his weight, and he forced himself up and braced himself on the car. The Pineville company van was gone, or maybe it had never been there at all. Somehow, he must've fallen unconscious and hallucinated this crazy dream of the woman coming to him and asking about Clay. The dream notion was quickly shattered when he discovered the garage door that led to the kitchen was torn off its hinges and lying on the floor. Henson limped over it and into the kitchen.

This cannot be happening. Where is Edie?

An unnatural calmness enveloped him, and he couldn't help but notice the intense metallic scent in the air. Blood droplets on the floor formed a trail that led from the kitchen down the hallway. Limping on one foot, he followed it.

"Edie?" he called out again.

When he reached their bedroom, he paused at the door. A morbid feeling enveloped him of what awaited on the other side. He pushed it open and stepped into what he had feared the most. Edie was lying face-up on the floor in just her bra and underwear, her eyes fixed on the ceiling in a look of shock. Henson dropped to the ground and cradled her in his arms. There was nothing he could do. She was already dead.

CHAPTER 14

THE OLD MAN pulled his knees in even tighter to his chest. Hurricane-force winds blew debris and dust all around him as he sat with his back still pressed against the tree. He covered his face with his hands to prevent it from getting into his eyes. A vein bulged through the skin on his wrist. He expected it to happen, though it didn't make the sight of it any less frightening. A bright-blue vein protruded from the skin and slowly traveled up his arm to his shoulder. The protrusion spread up to his neck, and when it reached his cheek, the vein constricted, swelled to three times its size, and pulsated through his skin in sync with his quickened heartbeat.

The old man's pupils dilated. He trembled and clenched his teeth in agony but never made a sound. The winds swirled around him, emitting howling that forewarned his fate. When the protruded vein reached his forehead, the man instantly transformed into a solid alabaster statue. A jagged crack formed in his plaster-like face and spread rapidly down to the bottom of the structure. Smaller cracks formed from the larger ones until they covered the entire statue. In a fierce eruption of energy, the statue imploded into specks, and what was left of the man crumbled to the ground in tiny particles.

On the north end of Oceola under the blare of the foghorn, Clay struggled against the wind's force pushing him backward. He resisted with all his strength until finally he had forged his way to the top of the embankment. He rushed up to the barn door and cracked it open. The foghorn sound stopped, and the windstorm fizzled out. Clay pushed the door all the way open.

The barn was lit by twelve oil lamps evenly spaced along the barn's walls and standing next to the Wheel amid the dim lamplight was Kaden. He gazed at Clay with a welcoming smile. "Come in."

Baffled by his presence, Clay didn't budge.

"It's okay, Clayton. Come in," said Kaden. He beckoned with his hand.

Clay stepped inside, and when he turned around, Raphael appeared out from the dark corner of the barn and stood next to Kaden. Clay pointed at him. "Raphael? You're the guy from the pawnshop. How did you get… Hey, I don't care what you people are doing up here. It's none of my business, but if this is about the diamonds, I'm not giving 'em back. I found them on my own on public property," said Clay.

"The diamonds are yours, Clayton," said Kaden. "It's what you crave, so the Wheel has given them to you in exchange."

"In exchange for what? This contraption can't be real," Clay said as he stared at the Wheel.

"You're wrong, Clayton. It's as real as you and I. The Wheel is alive, and it will remain that way if we keep the cycle."

Kaden traced the perimeter of the Wheel with his finger as he paced around it. "When the wheel shakes, you will turn the crank, as you saw the old man do. When the Wheel is calm, you will fill the buckets with the sand and empty them into the lake. The lake is our blood. It must be cleansed before it can return as energy for the Wheel. The cycle must continue."

"What're you talking about? I'm not turning anything. I'm leavin'," Clay snarled.

"You need to turn the wheel now before it gets angry again," said Kaden.

Clay ignored him and stepped toward the door. The wheel vibrated, and a creak erupted from it.

"Without the energy of the Wheel, there is no illusion," Kaden said. "And if there is no illusion, Clayton, the pain will return."

As soon as Kaden said the word "return," Clay made a piercing shriek and buckled over cradling his hand. His grievous injury had returned and so had the intense pain.

"Turn the Wheel and the pain will go away and your hand will be healed again," said Kaden.

Though the pain was excruciating, something deep within compelled him to resist.

Raphael stepped forward. "Clay, the Wheel is what regenerates us. If you take your turn, the life cycle of every living thing will continue. It's the noblest of all sacrifices you could ever make."

Annoyed by Raphael's pathetic plea, Kaden moved in front of him and pointed his finger at Clay's face. "If you won't turn the Wheel, then you must return the diamonds to where you found them in their place of origin."

Clay grabbed his shotgun and strapped it around his neck with one hand. The sudden movement caused him to flinch and moan from the pain.

"I said I'm leavin', and I'm taking what now rightfully belongs to me. If anybody gets in my way, I'll use this," he said as he stumbled out the barn.

○ ○ ○

Sally tucked the five-dollar tip in her apron and stepped behind the counter to ring up an order at the register.

A familiar face she hadn't seen at the Derby Diner in a long time walked through the door and sat down at a booth. Sally grabbed a pitcher of water and a menu and walked over to where Tara had just seated herself.

"Well, I'll be. Look at you, pretty lady," said Sally.

"Hey, Sally," Tara said. She stood up and gave Sally a hug.

"I don't think I've seen you since the wedding. How are things goin' with you newlyweds?" asked Sally.

"We're okay."

The man seated at the adjacent table had his eyes locked on Tara. His head was clean-shaven, and he had a bushy mustache that curled up on both ends.

"Can I get you somethin' to drink? Coffee, tea, juice?" asked Sally.

"Water is fine."

Sally placed a menu down in front of Tara and filled her glass with water.

"That had to be the most beautiful wedding dress I've ever seen," said Sally. "You were such a gorgeous bride."

"Thanks, you're sweet, and thank you so much for the blender. Clay and I use it all the time."

"You're welcome." Sally's face crinkled.

"What's wrong?" asked Tara.

"Hon, I don't mean to pry, but it really hurt her that you didn't invite her to your wedding."

Tara rolled her eyes. "I was not gonna let her make a scene, Sally. She ruined a lot of things for me. My wedding was not gonna be another checkmark on her list."

"Gloria can be a handful, I know, but in her heart she means well," said Sally. "You only get one mother in a lifetime, honey, and that woman cherishes the ground you walk on."

Tara didn't agree and chose not to respond. She fumbled through the menu until Sally broke the awkward silence. "How could I be so rude? Can I get you somethin' to eat, hon?" asked Sally. "We got a special on steak and mashed potatoes. It's really good. Al adds a little of that Carnation cream in the mash, makes the potatoes super creamy."

"Naw, I'm not hungry. So, is she here?" said Tara.

"Who? Gloria?"

"Yeah, she working today?"

"She's here. She's on her break."

"Can you tell her I would like to speak to her?"

Sally beamed with excitement. "Sure, hon. I'll get her. She's gonna be so excited to see you." She rushed away behind the counter.

Back in the kitchen, Gloria was leaning against the back door of the diner, holding it open for fresh air. Her checkered waitress apron was loosely tied around her full-figured waist. Al cooked the food obscured behind a partitioned wall but still gleaned the sunlight beaming inside from the opened door.

"Glo, you know that door is an emergency exit only. You're not supposed to have it open just for the heck of it," he said from the other side of the wall.

"I need some fresh air. Mind your business," Gloria said.

"Okay, then I'll start putting the padlock on it again. How do you like that?"

"That's a fire hazard."

"You keeping that door open is a fired hazard."

"Can you just cook the food, Al, and stop talkin' to me? I couldn't care less what you think," she said.

Sally burst into the kitchen. "Glo?"

Gloria stepped back inside and closed the emergency door.

"You're not gonna believe who's here to see you," said Sally.

"Who? The IRS?" said Gloria jokingly.

"Tara," said Sally with a wide grin.

"My Tara?"

"She's sitting at table seven. She really wants to see you."

"She said that?"

"Yeah, she did."

Gloria tugged at her dress and straightened her apron. "How do I look?"

Sally teased Gloria's bangs with her fingers until they fell just right. "You look perfect."

Gloria hurried away into the dining area and scanned the room until her eyes found Tara. It was the sight of her daughter's kind eyes after two years of being estranged that almost brought her to tears. Gloria regained her composure, straightened her dress, and walked over to her daughter's table. Tara looked up at her mother with a perfunctory smile. Gloria wanted to hug her, but Tara refused to stand, so Gloria just sat across from her instead.

"Hey sweetie, how have you been?" said Gloria.

"I've been okay."

"I left messages on your voicemail. I even went up to the salon a few times. Nobody knew how to reach you, or they just didn't wanna' tell me."

"I only work part-time at the salon, and I've been busy doing other stuff," she said and took a sip of her water. "Why does that man keep looking over here?"

Tara eyed the man three tables away with the clean-shaven head and curled-up mustache. Gloria waved, and he waved back at her.

"That's Harold Bruner, one of our regulars. He's harmless," said Gloria.

Tara took another drink of her water.

"That's all you gonna have is water?" said Gloria. "I can get you whatever you want. It's on me."

"Water is all I need. I'm not hungry."

"You look thin. You really need to eat something. Let me get you some breakfast. It doesn't have to be a lot. Just somethin' to carry you over until you—"

Tara interrupted her. "Gloria, please. I'm fine, really."

"I wish you wouldn't call me that."

"It is your name."

"Yeah, it is my name, and I don't need a reminder. I'm still your mother, Tara, no matter what."

"We obviously have very different opinions on what mothers are, but I'm not here to talk about that. What I want to say is that I need your help."

Gloria paused. "You need *my* help?"

"Yeah. Believe it or not, I do."

"Of course honey, anything you need, just tell me."

Tara was reluctant to talk about Clay. He had been part of the reason for their rift. It didn't feel right to bring her mother back into her life, but her options were limited. She had prepared herself to swallow her pride for Clay's sake.

"What is it?" asked Gloria.

"It's about Clay."

Gloria nestled in closer. "What did he do to you, Tara? Did he hurt you?"

"No, he didn't hurt me. He would never hurt me. He loves me. And apparently it doesn't matter how many times I tell you that. You still ask me the same thing."

"I'm sorry. I should be listening, not talking so much."

Tara took in a deep breath and exhaled, reluctant to expose her vulnerability to her mother. She needed her help and had no other choice. "Clay is missing, and I'm concerned about him."

"What do you mean he's missing?"

"He went on a hunting trip early this morning. He was supposed to have been back a long time ago. When I call his phone, it says that the number I dialed is not a valid phone number. I know what his number is. He's had it for years. Something is wrong. I called the police station, but they won't do anything. They say a person must be missing for at least forty-eight hours before they can start lookin'. I can't wait forty-eight hours. I have to do something now."

"Honey, what do you need?'

"You used to work at the station. You're friends with Sheriff Jenkins, right?"

"Yeah, but that was a long time ago."

"You still have an inside connection there. Maybe they can track his phone."

"You need a warrant for that," said Gloria.

"Can't you pull some strings and get a warrant?"

"Honey, you have to establish probable cause for a warrant, and even after that it would still take a few days before the judge could sign it."

"I don't have a few days," Tara said.

As Tara had expected, Gloria had to speak her mind, no matter the consequences or how offensive it might be to her. It was her mother's nature and what irked Tara the most about her.

"What makes you so sure he's missing?" asked Gloria. "He could've gotten over his head on somethin'. He's a thief who only cares about himself. Maybe he's just runnin' away from somethin' criminal he did and waiting for the right time to show his face again. It wouldn't be the first time."

Tara questioned why she was so stupid to share something personal about Clay with her mother. She regretted the entire conversation. "You don't know him," said Tara. "Who are you to judge anybody anyway? You should still be in prison for what you did to my father."

"If it makes you feel any better, I still feel like I am."

There was a moment of silence between them. Gloria reached out to touch Tara's hand. She pulled back.

"Honey, if there was somethin' I could do, of course I would do it. It's too early."

Tara had a good reason not to believe her; Gloria had twitched her nose. She could always tell when her mother kept secrets; her nose twitched. It would happen so fast that if you blinked, you would miss it. Tara fired back. "If he was Black, it would be a whole different story, wouldn't it?"

"It's already hard enough out here, honey. This world is cruel and vindictive. People treat you a certain way not because of who you are but because of how you look and who you're with. Why make your life even harder than it has to be?"

"So my life would be easier if Clay was Black? Is that the ridiculous thing you're trying to tell me?"

Gloria stared out the window, speechless.

"Tara sighed. "You know you sound like Clay's father. Can I please be alone?"

"You want me to leave?"

"Yeah, I do."

Gloria got up and trudged back into the kitchen. Tara dialed Clay's phone number, and as it did many times before, it connected her to a recording that said the number was invalid.

CHAPTER 15

SHERIFF JENKINS STEPPED out of his squad car just as the back door of the coroner's van swung open. As a gesture of respect for the unknown victim, Sheriff Jenkins removed his Stetson before he pushed aside the yellow caution tape and walked through the front door. No sheriff in the state wore that type of old-fashion cowboy hat except Sheriff Jenkins who chose to wear it with a purpose. In the past, his father and his grandfather were both Stetson wearing sheriffs in rural Kentucky towns. By wearing one himself, he kept their memory and legacy alive.

Two EMT's rushed past him on their way out carrying an empty stretcher as a crime scene photographer snapped pictures of the home's interior. Sheriff Jenkins placed the Stetson firmly back on his head and examined the floor and the walls, searching for blood or any evidence of a struggle. He found Rosalind in the hallway, jotting something down on a pad.

"Where's the body?" he asked.

"It's in the bedroom," said Rosalind.

The sheriff followed her into Henson's bedroom. Edie's body was lying face-up on the floor. Sheriff Jenkins probed the periphery of the room before he finally settled at Edie's body. He knelt next to her, removed a pair of plastic gloves from his shirt pocket, and squeezed them over his hands. The sheriff turned Edie's face from one side to the other. Blood had dried in the corner of both eyes. He lifted her head and found a patch of blood on the back of her skull. The sheriff examined her hands and fingernails, noting how pristine they were.

"What are you lookin' for?" asked Rosalind.

The sheriff stood and removed his gloves with a snap. "The reason why she's dead and most of all why she didn't fight back."

"The husband found her," said Rosalind. "He looked pretty banged up himself, so they took him to the hospital. He says he can't really remember anything but thought it might have been a home-invasion-robbery situation."

"Oh, really?"

The sheriff wandered around the room, examining the walls.

"He's hiding something," said Rosalind.

"What makes you think that?"

"There was blood on his shirt. The house wasn't even ransacked, expensive jewelry and electronic equipment haven't been touched, plus his story doesn't add up."

Sheriff Jenkins took the pen from behind his ear and drew a circle around a dent in the wall above Rosalind's head. She stepped to the side out of the way. "You think that's connected?" asked Rosalind.

"Maybe," the sheriff said, his eyes still fixed on the dent.

He found another dent in the wall and drew a circle around it. He searched the perimeter walls for more but didn't find any.

"Most cases like this end with the husband or the disgruntled boyfriend as the perpetrator," said Rosalind.

"In most cases it is," he said.

Sheriff Jenkins returned to the body and discovered something on her arm he had missed. He knelt over her and examined it closer.

"The coroner says the cause of death appears to be probable asphyxiation, that she was strangled or smothered to death with the pillow," said Rosalind.

"That opinion may change," the sheriff said.

With a pair of tweezers, he removed something from Edie's arm and stared at it.

"What is that?" asked Rosalind.

"A very long strand of black hair."

"It can't be hers. She's obviously a blonde."

Sheriff Jenkins bagged the strand of hair and placed it in his pocket.

"So you don't believe she was strangled either, huh?" asked Rosalind.

"There are bruises on her neck that look similar to a cause of strangulation, but there is no bruising on her face or petechial hemorrhages that would normally be present in the event of someone strangling or smothering you with a pillow. She was deprived of oxygen, but not because she was strangled or smothered."

"Then how?"

"That's a question I would like to ask her husband," said the sheriff.

○   ○   ○

Self-described computer nerd Mohammed Shirani, better known to his family and friends as Mo, got a kick out of pranking his friends. The latest victim of his newly acquired skill would be his best friend, Connor, and with all the elements of a planned hack worked out in advance, the tall, lanky sixteen-year-old was ready to put his hoverboard prank into action.

He hid behind two parked cars in the Milton High School parking lot, kneeling on his hoverboard as he waited for Connor to step out and head home. Students poured out of the school's back entrance, unaware of Mo's hiding spot. Connor strode through the parking lot with a backpack over one shoulder and his hoverboard under the other arm. Still hiding behind parked cars, Mo quickly typed in a code on the rogue app he had created on his cell phone. Connor put his hoverboard on the ground and mounted it. When he leaned forward to accelerate, the hoverboard jutted straight ahead at top speed. Mo pushed *enter* on his cell phone app. Connor's hoverboard abruptly stalled, and the momentum flung Connor to the ground.

Mo ran out from between the cars over to Connor, laughing hysterically. "Dude, you shouldn't be going top speed if you don't have the skills."

Connor got up and brushed the dirt off his jeans. He checked the remote in his pocket. It was turned off. "You cloned my remote, didn't you?"

"Now why would I do such a thing?" Mo answered with a mischievous grin.

Connor shoved him. "If my wheels are cracked, you're gonna replace 'em," he said.

Mo picked up Connor's hoverboard and examined the wheels. "Nope. Don't see any damage. You're golden. But if I were you, I wouldn't ride it until you've charged it up. The clone should expire by then."

"Delete the clone, Mo."

"It expires in a few minutes."

"I said delete the clone now or I'll tell your mom how you hacked her boss's computer."

Connor's threat was serious enough to make Mo capitulate. If his mother ever found out he was the one who had cost her company lost time and monetary damages, he would be grounded for life.

Mo typed in the deletion code on his cell phone and pushed *enter*. He showed it to Connor. "There. Are you happy? It's deleted."

They mounted their hoverboards and rode down Covington Street on their way home.

"Have you noticed anything strange about the people here lately?" asked Mo.

"Here as in Lynch? Or do you mean the school?" Connor said.

"Both."

"Most people I know are strange," said Connor.

"I'm serious. People aren't acting the way they normally act. You haven't noticed that?"

"Dude, would you like to give me some kinda clue of what you're talkin' about? Normal is subjective. I think I'm the most normal person I know, but my lunatic family would probably disagree with that."

Mo leaned back slightly on the hoverboard, decreasing the speed. Connor followed his lead.

"Okay, get this," said Mo. "Both my geometry teacher and my history teacher were asking me the same question about how long my parents have been together."

"What? What does that have to do with anything?"

"I don't know. I told them they met at a school in Pakistan when they were young. Then I was asked if I knew the name of the school they went to."

"Dude, tell them to get out of your parents' business," said Connor.

"It's weird, right? Then I have this neighbor. He's friends with my dad, always coming over, always talking, and never shuts up. He has this serious fear of heights to the point where he can't even drive past an airport without freaking out. He even takes a bus or a train whenever he goes out of town just so he won't have to take a plane. It's that serious, and it's been that way for as long as we've known him. Now all of a sudden he's climbing twenty-foot ladders, walking across his third-floor window ledge, and dangling from his roof, daredevil stuff. So I asked him what happened to his fear of heights, and he said he's never been afraid of heights and that I was making stuff up. Then he got right up in my face and said I should stop talking to him because we don't know each other that well. I'm like, dude, I've known you for years. Why are you lying?"

"Teachers are weird by nature," Connor said. "But your neighbor— he's not so strange. He was just playing around with you.

"Naw, if you could've seen him, you would know he was dead serious. Somethin's up with him."

Connor leaned forward, and his hoverboard picked up speed. "Somethin's up with *you*. See ya later." He made a right turn at the end of the block while Mo continued straight ahead.

Mo arrived home minutes later at the sight of shingles being flung from his neighbor's roof to the ground. He recognized the clean-shaven head and curled mustache of his next-door neighbor, Harold Bruner, the one he had just mentioned to Connor. He was on the roof, four stories high, tearing off damaged tiles with his bare hands and tossing them over the edge. Mo was baffled to see there were no stops planted on the roof to prevent him from falling off. Harold trod around the acute-pitched roof as if he walked on flat solid ground. Mo stood there watching him, perplexed by his delicate balancing act. That's when Harold overstepped, lost his footing, and slid off the roof. Mo gasped as Harold fell four stories to the ground but amazingly landed erect on his feet.

"Mr. Bruner, you okay?"

"Why wouldn't I be?" Harold snapped.

"Um…maybe because you just fell off your roof?"

Harold Bruner's palpable disdain for Mo radiated from his piercing stare. As Harold walked into his home without any signs of injury, Mo found himself puzzled by the absence of broken bones or even a hint of a limp. It only intensified his determination to uncover the mystery behind it.

○ ○ ○

Henson was sitting up in his hospital bed watching the news on a mounted TV when Bailey entered the room.

"Hey, how you doin'?" she said.

Henson's arm and forehead were bandaged and his eyes bloodshot, but they lit up at the sight of her. He had a wide smile on his face until he caught sight of Eric walking in behind her. His elated expression morphed into an indifferent one.

"They say I got a broken rib, a collapsed lung, and a concussion. Other than that, I guess I'm doin' peachy," Henson said.

"What about Edie? Is she okay?" asked Bailey.

"You don't know?"

"What?"

"She's dead, Bailey. She didn't make it."

Bailey sighed. "Oh my God. I'm so sorry. What happened?"

"I don't know. I mean, I can't…" Henson said as he glanced at Eric. "Can I talk to you alone just for a minute?"

"Whatever you can say to me, you can say in front of Eric," Bailey replied.

"No, no, it's okay, honey," Eric said. "I need to make a phone call anyway. You guys are comrades. Have your talk. I'll be in the waiting room."

Eric gave Bailey a peck on the lips and left the room. Henson had made her angry, but he didn't care. It was crucial he talk to her alone.

"What was that about? There's no reason for you to be rude to my husband," said Bailey.

"Bailey, what I have to tell you you're not gonna believe. This is some crazy-wacko stuff, and I don't know where it's goin'. The less people know, the better."

"If you know what happened to Edie, you have to tell the police," said Bailey.

"I can't."

"What do you mean you can't? They're gonna think you did it."

"It wasn't me. It was that woman."

"What woman?"

"The woman we saw in the mine, Bailey."

Bailey gazed at Henson, speechless. He expected her to doubt his story, but he was not letting her leave the room until he convinced her he was telling the truth.

"She drove up to my house in the company van," said Henson. "She had on our uniform. I remember her pointing her hand at me, and the next thing I knew I was on the ground. When I woke up she was gone, and that's when I found Edie lying on the floor dead."

Bailey turned away in disbelief.

"You think the police would believe that story?" asked Henson. "They would for sure think I did it if I told them that."

"It couldn't have been her. She's dead, Henson. MSHA confirmed it," said Bailey.

"MSHA never found her body. I know what I saw. And you know what you saw in that mine. We're not crazy."

Bailey stepped away to the other side of the room and peered out the window. "It's possible your head injury is causing you to remember things differently than what actually happened."

"If the company van is still parked at the mine, then I'll be relieved to admit I have a few screws loose," said Henson. "If it's not and is missing, then we got problems."

○ ○ ○

Abby turned into her driveway. Through the front windshield, she glimpsed someone sitting on her porch. As she drove closer to her home, it became clear who it was, Octavius. Fear consumed her, and dread overwhelmed her thoughts as she parked on the driveway path. She contemplated turning her car around and leaving, anything to avoid a confrontation, but in the end, it wouldn't matter; he would just return and torment her even more.

Octavius was sitting on her porch whittling a piece of basswood with a pocketknife. Abby grabbed a switchblade from the glove compartment and placed it halfway in the back of her jeans. She opened the door and slowly stepped out of her car.

Octavius had his head down and focused on his whittling. Abby approached him, taking careful steps.

"Where is he?" said Octavius without looking up at her.

"It's too late. There's nothing you can do. The Wheel has claimed him," said Abby.

"He is only half Ocran, half of what we are. If he turns the Wheel, it will kill him instantly."

"As it should. They are a disease, and if they are allowed to keep spreading, they will destroy this world—our home. Why do you insist on helping him when his very existence threatens ours?"

"Because he's proof that our life forms can merge," said Octavius.

"Merge?" she repeated derisively. "Merge into what? An abomination? Kaden will not allow our purity to be tainted by human subspecies."

Abby put her hand behind her back and clutched the handle of the switchblade. Out of Octavius's view, she pushed the release button, and the blade extended with a snap.

When Abby took another step toward him, the ground beneath her sank. The switchblade fell from her hand, and she dropped into a fissure engulfed up to her knees. The spiral tattoo on the palm of Octavius's hand glowed.

Abby lifted herself out of the fissure and retrieved the switchblade from the ground. The tattoo in her palm pulsated as the soil in the fissure rose to the top and instantly sealed itself over level ground.

Indifferent to what had just happened, Octavius kept whittling away at the piece of wood. "Kaden is deceiving you," he said. "We can coexist peacefully with them. Tell me where you sent Clay Krutcher."

Abby answered him in Latin. "Ludis lusum periculosissimum." – *You're playing a very dangerous game.* "Kaden will summon the power of the Council to severely punish you for your betrayal," she said.

Clutching the switchblade, she took another step toward Octavius. He stopped whittling and gazed at her. The ground beneath Abby formed a crevice, and she dropped into another fissure up to her shoulders.

Octavius spoke to her in Greek. "Den eímaste ágrioi." –*We are not savages.* "Neither I nor the others will allow an entire species to be annihilated."

Abby struggled to lift herself out of the hole. Each time she inched closer to her escape, her grip on the loosened soil waned, sending her back to the bottom.

They are destroying the land, the waters, and the atmosphere," she said, as clumps of soil crumbled down over her shoulders and arms. "If they are allowed to live another twenty of their years, this planet will be permanently uninhabitable, even for us."

Octavius stood up from the porch, walked over to her, and held out his hand. Though apprehensive, Abby grabbed hold of it anyway. He pulled her out onto solid ground as if she weighed only a couple of pounds. Abby brushed the dirt from her hair and jeans and wiped the sweat from her forehead. "We who follow Kaden greatly outnumber you," said Abby.

"Either you tell me where Clay Krutcher is, or you won't be coming out of the next hole you fall into," warned Octavius.

It wasn't a threat; it was a promise, and Abby quickly capitulated. "He's in Oceola, in Appalachia, Virginia, but you will fail. The very ones you are trying to save will never accept you," she said.

Jimmy's car came up the driveway, interrupting their standoff. He parked in front of the house and rushed over to Abby. "Hey, who are you?" he said to Octavius.

Octavius glanced over at Abby. "Ask the one you call your wife. I don't answer your questions," he said as he walked away, still whittling on the piece of basswood.

○ ○ ○

Jeb walked out of Bennington Middle School into the rain. Charlie trailed a few steps behind wearing a grocery bag on his head like a hat. Jeb turned and glared at him. "You know you look like an idiot with that thing on your head."

"If my hair gets wet I'll smell like a dog," said Charlie as they strolled down the sidewalk together.

"You always smell like a dog. Stop blamin' it on the rain," said Jeb.

"Shut up. You're the one with doggie breath."

Jeb laughed. "I'm just sayin.' It's not even raining that hard."

"It might in a minute."

"Or not." Jeb snatched the bag off Charlie's head and held it behind his back.

"Hey, what're you doing? Give it back!" Charlie yelled, trying his best to reach around Jeb to grab it.

"It's my duty as your older brother not to let you look stupid," said Jeb, laughing at Charlie's feeble attempts to grab it back.

"Give it to me," Charlie pleaded, desperate to get it back.

Jeb relented and handed it back to him. Charlie didn't waste a second putting it back on his head.

"Where did you get a crazy idea to put a plastic bag over your head anyway?" asked Jeb.

"It's not crazy. Travis does it. Nobody says he's crazy."

"You're not Travis. Anyway, you seen him lately?"

"Who? Travis?"

"Yeah."

"I saw him at his locker and gave the creep a thumbs-up," said Charlie.

"Why is he a creep?"

"Because he pretended like he didn't know who I was."

Charlie's comment induced Jeb to reflect on his encounter with Travis and how he treated him the same way—like he didn't recognize him. It only proved Jeb's suspicions.

"Listen to me. I want you to stay away from him, Charlie."

"Why?"

"I can't explain it, just trust me. Stay away from him, okay?" said Jeb.

"Does Travis have the cooties?"

"It's not the cooties. It's worse than that."

A car horn blast got their attention. When they turned to look, a silver Nissan drove up to the curb next to them. Charlie took the bag off his head. "Is that Dad?"

They hadn't seen or heard from him in weeks. Their father's surprise visit to their school baffled Jeb, and when he lowered the window, Jeb approached the car with suspicion.

"Dad, what're you doing here?" asked Charlie.

"I'm here to see my boys. How you been?"

"I'm okay."

"What about you, Jeb?" asked his father.

Jeb eyed him warily. "Does Mom know you're here?"

"Your mom doesn't have to know everything, does she? You guys wanna come spend the weekend with me? I figure we could go fishing and work on that fastball pitch of yours, Charlie."

Charlie's eyes lit up. Jeb wanted to be excited, but something was off about his father just showing up out of nowhere for no apparent reason.

"So what happened?" said Jeb. "You got bored and decided you had nothing else better to do?"

"That's not it," their father said, shaking his head. "I know I haven't been the best dad to you guys, but I'm gonna change that starting today. Come on and get in before it starts pouring. I'll call Susan and let her know you guys are with me."

Charlie couldn't open the rear door fast enough. He climbed inside and slammed it shut. Jeb lingered outside on the passenger side, debating whether to get in or not. His father had never been apologetic or remorseful about anything and hearing him refer to their mother as "Susan" instead of Sue was odd enough to give him second thoughts. Something about his father's demeanor and his insistence that they go with him didn't *feel* right.

Their father reached over and opened the glove compartment. "Remember the Pokémon cards you wanted, Jeb?" he said. "I got 'em for ya."

His father took out a card and held it up so Jeb could see it. Instead of the card, Jeb glimpsed a part of the same spiral tattoo on his father's palm that he had seen on Travis's palm. Startled, Jeb took a step back from the car.

"What's wrong?" asked his father.

"Charlie, get outta the car," said Jeb.

"Why?" Charlie answered. "I wanna go with Dad."

"Charlie, do what I said and get outta the car right now."

When Charlie didn't comply, Jeb reached for the door handle. Before he could pull it open, he heard a click. Their father had triggered the automatic door locks, shutting him out and trapping Charlie inside. Jeb pounded on the window and tugged on the door handle. "Open the door!" Jeb shouted. His father ignored him and peeled away with tires screeching.

CHAPTER 16

SHERIFF JENKINS DROPPED two files on his desk and thumbed through them. After a quick comparison, he dialed a number on his speakerphone. It rang eight times before someone finally answered.

"Virginia State Records. This is Nathan, how may I help you?" said the voice.

"Nathan, this is Sheriff Jenkins over at the Lynch station in Kentucky. How's it going over there in Appalachia?"

"Hey, Sheriff, we're okay. Just tryin' to implement all the new changes to the state law code before the deadline. You guys get any changes for Kentucky?"

Naw, not this time," said Sheriff Jenkins. He took off his Stetson and placed it on his desk. "Listen, I need a favor. Is it possible I can get a DMV listing of all your registered owners of a red Honda Civic 2001 to present?"

"What's goin' on?"

"I got a missing persons case I've been workin' on for a few months. A witness claimed she saw a red Civic speed away from the vicinity where the child was most likely abducted. I checked out all thirteen of that make and model we had here in Harlan County, and they're all clean. Since then, a new witness came forward who swears it had Appalachia license plates."

"That make and color are very popular here," said Nathan. "You want just Appalachia or the whole state of Virginia?"

"I'm thinkin' I better get the whole state just in case. Whenever you get a chance to put it all together and send it to me, I would appreciate it."

Rosalind stuck her head through the door. Sheriff Jenkins motioned her to step in and hold what she had to say until he was off the phone.

"That's gonna be a long list, Sheriff," said Nathan. "It's gonna take hours to print out copies of everything, and who knows how long it's gonna take to get to you in the mail. You sure you don't wanna just take a trip down here and pick out what exactly you need? That would be quicker and a lot less expensive."

"I don't have the time either way. I got a homicide I have to deal with along with everything else."

"A homicide in Lynch? That's unheard of."

"Small towns have big secrets," the sheriff said. "Can you make the DMV list happen?"

"Sure, if that's what you really want."

The sheriff looked up at Rosalind. "You know what? Scrap that. Don't send it. I'll have someone over there in a couple of days to make the copies and pick 'em up for me."

"It'll be ready," said Nathan.

Sheriff Jenkins hung up and pushed the Stetson back down on his head.

"So I'm assuming the person who's going there in a couple of days to pick it all up is me," said Rosalind.

"If you don't mind. I'd appreciate it," Sheriff Jenkins said. "And when you get a chance, can you take a look at these?"

He handed the files he had reviewed to Rosalind. "See if there are any similarities between the two cases."

"What kind of similarities?"

"Any kind."

Rosalind nodded and walked out of the office.

Ansley, the Lynch police public relations manager, was seated at her desk on the opposite side of the sheriff's office, signing and dating the month's police reports. The receptionist stepped into her cubicle. "There's a lady up front who wants to file a missing person's report, but I can't get any information out of her," said the receptionist.

"Another missing person?" said Ansley, stunned. She got up from her desk and strolled up to the front counter. Tara waited on the other side, visibly upset.

"Hi, ma'am, can I help you with something?" said Ansley.

"I need to file a missing person's report. Is this where I do it?" asked Tara.

"Who is it for?"

"My husband."

"Okay, let's step over to my cubicle."

Tara followed Ansley to her desk, and they both took a seat. Ansley retrieved a form and a pen from her desk drawer.

"What's your name, ma'am?" said Ansley.

"Tara Krutcher. It's Krutcher with a K."

"And your husband who's missing?"

"He's Clayton Krutcher."

"How long has he been missing?"

"I haven't seen him since this morning, but he called—"

Ansley interrupted her. "Ma'am, he would have to be missing for at least forty-eight hours before we can file anything.

"I know," said Tara. "They told me that already, but this is an emergency."

"It's very possible your husband wants to be where he is."

"I know my husband. He's not just hiding away somewhere."

"Ma'am, I can't help you right now. It's too soon."

Tara fumed. "Will you just listen to me?"

Sheriff Jenkins walked into Ansley's cubicle with Tara seconds from losing her temper. "Is this about Clay Krutcher?" he asked Ansley.

"Yeah, I was just telling her about the forty-eight-hour requirement," said Ansley.

Sheriff Jenkins gazed at Tara, concerned. "Is Clay Krutcher your husband, ma'am?"

"He's missing," said Tara. "And I know something must've happened to him, because—"

Sheriff Jenkins cut her off. "Go ahead and help Mrs. Krutcher fill out the form," he said to Ansley.

Ansley's face contorted. "But Sheriff, it hasn't been forty-eight hours yet. Not even twenty-four."

"Ansley," he said sternly, "help her fill out the form." He smiled at Tara. "She'll take care of you," he said. "I'll have a squad car out by your place sometime this evening to get more information, and we'll try for an emergency order from the judge for his phone records. I can't make you any promises, but we'll find out what's goin' on. Hopefully, he's just playin' hooky somewhere."

"Thank you so much, Sheriff," she said.

"Your mother is a very determined woman. You can thank her," the sheriff said.

○ ○ ○

Mo hurried into his bedroom, shut the door, and tossed his book bag on his bed. His room was unusually neat and organized for a teenager. Even his collection of Nike and Air Jordan sneakers were organized and mounted on the wall on separate tiny shelves, as if they were being displayed in a department store. LED lights he had installed himself highlighted the brand from underneath each shelf. Every bit of money Mo had earned from his summer jobs and allowances went into his sneaker collection, with the most expensive pair costing nearly $550. Some on the display were still brand new, and others he had worn only once or twice, afraid the more he had them on the greater the chances of nicking the soles. He made sure to walk cautiously in his most expensive ones so he wouldn't diminish the resale value that could sometimes be double or triple what he had originally paid.

On the opposite wall was a poster of Nyjah Huston kneeling on a hoverboard, and below it was one of Kid Cudi, the same picture plastered on the t-shirt he had on.

Mo was ten minutes late for their favorite NBA video game that he and Connor had set up to play online. He rushed to turn on his game console and switched to online play. Connor was already logged into the game at his home, battling two other players that he was easily defeating. Mo sat down in front of his laptop, put on his headset, and logged on to the DisContent party chat, opening the path of real-time communication with Connor while they played. Once Connor discovered Mo had logged on, he ejected the other players from the game and started a new one with Mo. They instantly began battling each other's team, making shots, tossing free throws, blocking, and fouling each other.

"You're late, dude," said Connor. "You just missed me kicking butt with amateurs who thought they were pros."

"Well now you're playing against a real pro. I promise not to eviscerate you too soon. You need to suffer for a little while first," said Mo.

Connor laughed. "I'm already destroying you," he said after he made another three-pointer.

"Hey, guess what I saw my neighbor do today," said Mo.

"Are we talking about the Bruner guy again?"

"Yeah, my neighbor, Harold."

"What did he do now, leave a bomb at your doorstep?" Connor joked.

"He fell off his four-story roof and just walked away like it was nothing."

"Yeah, right."

"I'm tellin' you, dude. I saw him slip and fall off his roof onto raw concrete and land on his feet just like a cat. He didn't even tumble."

Connor scored another ten points. Mo rapidly clicked on his controller and maneuvered his team into a scoring position.

"What is that? Fifteen feet? That's not a big deal," said Connor.

"What are you talkin' about? My house from the roof to the ground is at least twenty-five, and his house looks taller than mine.

"Okay, so?"

"Remember that girl who fell from that amusement park ride? That was twenty feet and she barely survived. Harold landed right on his feet, straight up."

"Who is Harold?"

"The neighbor. Are you listening to me?"

"Nope, I'm too busy kickin' your butt," Connor said.

"Don't you get it?" said Mo. "This guy is not normal. We need to check him out, see where he came from."

Connor didn't respond. Ten minutes later he had racked up a total of ten additional points, surpassing Mo's score by fifty. Mo pretended to be worried, but all along he had planned in advance how to change his odds of winning. Days before, he had found a hacking package online. After he downloaded it into his laptop, he transferred it onto a USB and downloaded the files directly into his game console. The hack enabled Mo to extract the IP addresses of whoever was on the server playing on their game console.

Using his coding skills, he entered Connor's IP address into his laptop and used another hack via the Internet to slow down Connor's Wi-Fi connection. Connor's playing ability was stalled, and Mo used the advantage to outmaneuver him enough to take over the lead.

"My team is moving slowly for some reason," said Connor.

"Naw, I'm just better than you at this game. Admit it," Mo said.

Mo scored another twenty points around Connor's team now moving around at a snail's pace. It all started to look suspicious to Connor.

"Somethin's wrong with my Wi-Fi connection. I should be moving way faster than this," he said.

"I don't think it's your Wi-Fi. It's you. You can't handle the butt-kicking I'm delivering."

"Wait a minute," said Connor. "You hacked my Wi-Fi, didn't you? How did you do that?"

Mo scoffed. "You're delusional. How could I be so incredibly smart and capable of hacking somebody's Wi-Fi? I would have to be brilliant or some kind of genius to pull something like that off."

Connor paused the game. "I'm logging out. You hacked it."

"Really? Where's your proof?"

Connor snatched off his headset and logged out of the server, leaving Mo online by himself.

"Sore loser," Mo said out loud as he took off his headset.

He clicked on Google on his laptop and typed in the name *Harold Bruner*. When he pushed the *enter* key, a list of obituaries and tributes appeared on the screen under the Harold Bruner name. Mo scrolled down until he found a newspaper article with the heading *Harold Bruner of Brandenburg, Kentucky*. After he clicked on the heading, a newspaper article appeared titled: *"Man pronounced clinically dead revived two hours later."*

Mo continued scrolling down to the bottom of the article. He stopped at the picture. It was Harold but ten years younger with a head full of hair and without the curled mustache.

There was a knock on his door, and he quickly closed his laptop. Mo's mother stuck her head in.

"Don't forget we have to pick up your sister from her campus in the morning."

"I know. You told me three times already," said Mo.

"Just making sure."

"Hey, have you talked to Dad?"

"I haven't heard from him today."

"Can I call him? I need to tell him something important."

"No, you're not calling him. It's 4:00 a.m. in Pakistan right now. He'll be home in a few days. You can tell him everything then."

She left the room, but seconds later stuck her head in again. "And don't forget the garbage. It has to go out tonight," she said and closed the door.

○　○　○

Henson sat up in his hospital bed when Sheriff Jenkins barged into his room disrupting his peace and quiet. "Jared Henson?" he said loud enough for the entire floor to hear.

"Yeah, who are you?" said Henson, ignoring the badge and uniform.

"I'm Sheriff Jenkins."

"I told the deputy woman everything I remember," said Henson. "There's nothing else I can tell you."

"I'm aware you spoke with Rosalind. I'm here for a follow-up."

Henson scoffed. "You guys think I did it, don't you? It wasn't me. If you wanna waste your time investigating an innocent person, go ahead."

"I need a few more questions answered, and I'll be out of your hair, Mr. Henson. I'm a straightforward kinda guy, so don't take any of this personally. Were you and your wife on good terms before she died?"

Henson grinned, oddly amused by the question. "Are you married, Sheriff?"

"Yeah."

"How many times in a month, or better yet how many times in a week are you and your wife on good terms?"

"The way it works is I ask the questions and you give me the answers. Let's try this again. Were you and your wife on good terms prior to her death?"

"Though it's none of your business, we were always on good terms until we weren't, and that's pretty much every married couple I know. So what? Why would that be a reason for me to kill her?"

"I never said you did. You have any idea who might?"

"No, I don't."

"Did you love your wife, Mr. Henson?"

Either the sheriff was intentionally pushing his buttons to get a rise out of him, or he was just a jerk, period. Henson refused to let him win. "What does that have to do with anything?"

"You don't seem that grief-stricken about her death," said Sheriff Jenkins.

"People grieve in different ways."

"Yeah, that's what they say. Do you have an insurance policy on your wife's life?"

His question confirmed it. Sheriff Jenkins aimed to get under his skin in order to elicit a reaction that he could then use against him. It made Henson more determined not to take the bait. No one commanded his emotions but himself. "We have insurance policies on each other," he said, undeterred. "What does that prove?"

"It's not meant to prove anything. It was just a question, and I appreciate the answer. Now, have you ever hit your wife, Mr. Henson?"

Henson hid his disdain for what the sheriff asked him behind a smile. "What do you mean? Punch her?"

"Punch, slap, push, choke, kick, beat up, any of the above," said the sheriff.

"I don't hit women. I'd sooner punch a hole in the wall before I would do something like that."

"Funny you would mention that. Have you punched any holes in your walls lately?"

"Are you serious?"

"Yeah, I am. You ever get angry enough at your wife that you took it out on the wall, Mr. Henson?"

"No, never."

"So you would have no idea why there are dented holes in your bedroom wall where your wife was found dead."

Flummoxed by the question, Henson squinted. "What? I don't know about any dented holes. There were no holes in our bedroom walls. The perpetrator had to have done it."

"The hole in the wall would explain the skull fracture we found in the back of her head that looked like someone pushed her back into the wall."

"I know what you're tryin' to do. I didn't kill my wife, and I have never laid a hand on her either. Whatever it was that killed her must've attacked me first. I didn't beat myself up."

"What does that mean, Mr. Henson? 'Whatever it was.' What is '*it*?'"

"I meant whoever it was. My wife is dead, and someone beat the crap out of me. I'm lucky to be alive. And who's to say the person who did it might not come back to finish the job?"

"You need to give me some names, Mr. Henson," said the sheriff. "Who would want to see you and your wife dead? Give me a motive, give me a name of an enemy, give me somethin'."

"I have nothing to give. I told you I don't know. We don't have any enemies."

Sheriff Jenkins smirked. "Apparently you have at least one."

"Maybe it was a home invasion, someone trying to rip us off that went horribly wrong," said Henson.

"What about a vindictive mistress? Brunette, long hair, wanting to get your wife out of the way so you two can ride off into the sunset?"

The sheriff searched Henson's face for a reaction. He didn't give him one.

"I didn't cheat on my wife. I would've left her first."

"Duly noted. Tell me what you remember before you found her."

"I told you I had this conversation already with your deputy."

"Now you're gonna have it with me. Tell me what you remember."

Henson sighed and wiped his face with both hands in frustration. "I remember that I was in the garage working on my car, and then the next thing I knew I woke up on the floor with this killer headache. I went into the house and found Edie on the floor. It's all I remember."

"Has the doctor diagnosed you as having amnesia?"

"I have a concussion. Temporary amnesia is normally a result of it." Henson pushed the nurse call button on the side of his bed and turned off the TV. "I'm tired, and I said all I have to say."

"I have a couple more questions," said the sheriff.

"Didn't you hear me? I'm not answering any more of your questions. If I need to get a lawyer to make that clear to you, I will."

The nurse walked into the room with a clipboard. "You ready for your dinner, Mr. Henson?"

"I'm not hungry, but I would like to get some sleep without the sheriff hammering me with questions about my wife that I already answered. She's dead, for God's sakes."

"Do you mind coming back at another time?" said the nurse to

Sheriff Jenkins. "Mr. Henson needs to rest. His doctor has him scheduled for several lab tests in the morning."

Sheriff Jenkins laid his business card on the table next to Henson's bed. "I've been in this line of work for thirty-five years," he said. "You know more than what you're tellin' me. When you're ready to talk, give me a call, but don't wait too long. I would hate to have to return with an arrest warrant and handcuff your arm to that bed. It's way more satisfying to arrest the right person."

CHAPTER 17

MO PRESSED THE remote button on the wall and the garage door lifted above his head. The sweet aroma of surrounding cedars was no match for the offensive odor seeping from his trashcan. He held his breath as he dragged it out of the garage and onto the front curb. *Why is it so dark out here?* The unlit lampposts across the street were the answer to his question. *But why aren't they on? They're always on by this time.* Without the lamppost lights, the neighborhood appeared shrouded in complete darkness. There was no sound in the warm still air, only a dead silence; not even the cicadas were singing. Someone might be lurking in the shadows, waiting for an opportunity to ambush him. Mo dismissed the wild thoughts that had crossed his mind and when he turned to walk back into the garage, something in his next-door neighbor's side window dared him to take a closer look.

Harold Bruner's curtains were halfway open, and Mo could see Mrs. Bruner sitting at the dining room table, staring straight ahead. Her arms hung loosely down by her side, and she wasn't moving or talking, just staring at the wall like she was in some kind of hypnotic trance.

Behaving like a peeping Tom made Mo feel a little sleazy, but it wasn't enough to make him turn his eyes away. Why was Mrs. Bruner sitting frozen in her seat unresponsive? Maybe he drugged her; that would explain why.

Mo crept under Mr. Bruner's window and hid behind the five-foot-high bushes that separated their two homes. He waited there patiently, and after minutes of silence he lifted his head above the windowsill and peered into Harold's window. Mrs. Bruner was still seated at the dining room table, her eyes locked in a stare, when suddenly her eyelids fluttered, and she fell back unconscious into the chair. Harold walked in the room and waved his hand in front of his wife's face as if he was checking to see if she was fully unconscious. Satisfied, Harold walked out of view and returned seconds later with a miniature cardboard box and placed it on the table in front of his wife.

"What are you doing, weirdo?" Mo whispered to himself. He retrieved his cell phone from his back pocket, convinced he needed to have video proof of what Mr. Bruner was up to.

Peering in the window through his cell phone camera, Mo recorded Harold as he opened the box and emptied what appeared to be blue colored sand onto the table in front of Mrs. Bruner. Mo gaped in disbelief at what happened next—blue sand particles floated off the table into the air and entered Mrs. Bruner's nostrils. He nearly dropped his phone when the palm of Harold's left hand glowed. The light pulsated like a heartbeat as it outlined the shape of a spiral.

Harold turned his attention to the window as if he sensed he was being watched. He gazed for a split-second into the lens of Mo's phone. Mo gasped and dropped behind the bushes, his heart racing. He whispered to himself, "He didn't see me... he didn't see me." Harold stepped over to the window, scanned his yard and then yanked the curtains closed. Relieved, Mo exhaled, and when he stood up to leave, Harold's fist came crashing through the window above his head.

Mo bolted into the garage panic-stricken. His heart pounded like a drum in his chest. He slammed the button on the wall and the garage door started its descent. Anxious seconds ticked by as he watched it lower. A couple feet more remained, and his nerves were on edge. Mo breathed heavily, desperate for the door to reach the ground and shield him from the threat that loomed beyond. Someone wearing pristine white loafers rushed forward and stood frozen mere inches behind the descending door. Mo sighed as the garage door sealed shut, separating him from what had to be Mr. Bruner. He checked his side pocket for his phone. It wasn't there. Mo frantically checked his back pocket. It wasn't there either. Harold Bruner discovered it lying on the ground outside his dining room window among pieces of broken glass. He reached down and grabbed it with his bloody hand.

○   ○   ○

Rebecca stared out her bedroom window into the dark. *Where is he?* She glanced at her wristwatch, concerned about how late he was at a time when the confrontation was close to fruition. Her freckled porcelain face seemed too young to bear worry lines, yet there were several in the corners of her eyes. If they didn't get there soon enough, everything they had tried so hard to contain would be released to wreak havoc. Finally, headlights from Octavius's EV flashed three times, signaling his arrival as he pulled up to the front of her house.

Rebecca grabbed her bag, tossed it around her shoulders, and carefully pushed her bedroom door open. She tiptoed out of her room using the light from her cell phone to illuminate her way down the dark hallway. She took small steps, extra careful not to make noises that would wake her parents as she went past their bedroom door and down the stairs. It wasn't until she had made it out the front door that she took a deep breath and relaxed. Rebecca rushed to the EV, threw her bag in the back, and hopped into the passenger seat. Octavius was seated on the driver's side, looking out the rear-view mirror.

"You're late," said Rebecca.

Octavius made a quick U-turn and sped off down the road. "There was a problem," he said, matter-of-factly.

His admission of a problem made her nervous. She responded in Hebrew. "Hatzlatchta lefatos et ze?"–*Were you able to solve it?*

He answered her in Latin. "Curam est habita." –*It's taken care of.*

○   ○   ○

Bailey searched her closet until she settled on three different dresses. She brought them out on hangers in front of the mirror and placed the first one up to her body. "Too slutty," she said and tried the next one. "Too pretentious." She took the second one away and placed a third one against her torso. "Hmm… Maybe too over-the-top? I don't wanna look overdressed. What do you think?"

She glanced over at Eric, who was standing in front of the bathroom mirror, preoccupied with examining his face from different angles for razor stubble.

"Honey, which one?" said Bailey

She held all three dresses against her body. Eric stepped away from the bathroom and took a quick glance. "I like the slutty one," he said.

Bailey gave him a disdainful look. "And which one is that, Eric?"

"I meant the red one."

"I'm not gonna wear a dress you think is slutty."

Eric laughed. "You bought it, and you're the one who said it was slutty."

"Yeah, but I was kidding."

"So was I."

"No you weren't," said Bailey.

"Why would you think I was serious?"

"Because I know you, Eric. I know when you're serious."

Eric stepped back into the bathroom and buttoned his shirt. "What I was trying to say before you so methodically twisted it was that the red one looks sexy, but, honey, they would all look hot on you."

Unconvinced, Bailey tossed the red dress on the bed and put on the black one.

"So what was so private between you and Henson that I wasn't allowed to hear?" asked Eric.

Bailey finally got what she wanted out of Eric—a reaction.

"Eric David Bailey, are you jealous?"

"I don't know. Should I be?"

"He was just having a hard time," said Bailey. "It's a lot to handle. Bailey sighed. "You know I would be perfectly fine with staying home with the kids tonight. We could just order some pizza and do this another time."

Eric walked over to her and gently placed his hands on her shoulders. He smiled as he looked her in the eye. "I planned this especially for you because you deserve a night out. Sitting at home and worrying is not gonna help. I just want you to relax and have a good time for once."

"It just bothers me that I can't figure out how that woman made her way into the mine," said Bailey. "And why we couldn't just drag her out."

Eric groaned. "Because you have to follow protocols for everyone's safety. Honey, would you please just let it go. Nobody expects you to risk your life for someone with a death wish. So stop stressin' over it. She's not your responsibility."

"I know, but there had to be a reason, a purpose for her being there, right?"

"A purpose for standing in the middle of a collapsing coal mine? You said they searched it and didn't find anybody in there, right?" said Eric.

"No, they didn't."

"Then why are you worried? She probably ran out just after you guys did, and you didn't notice it. She's alive somewhere, honey. Hopefully in an institution by now," said Eric.

Bailey turned her back to Eric. "Zip me up."

He gave his wife a protracted kiss on the neck as he zipped up her dress. Her blaring ringtone interrupted the moment.

"Great timing," Eric said sarcastically before stepping back into the bathroom. Bailey grabbed her cell phone off the bed and answered it.

"Hello?

Stanley was calling from the Pineville mine, standing outside the trailer with a cell phone in one hand and a flashlight in the other.

"Bailey, it's Stanley," he said with urgency.

The doorbell interrupted her. "Hey, Stanley," she said, surprised to hear his voice on the line. "Hold on for a sec."

Bailey lowered the phone. "Hey, honey, that's the sitter. Can you let her in?"

"I got it," said Eric. He walked out of the bedroom into the hallway.

Bailey placed the phone back to her ear. "Sorry about that. What's goin' on?"

"Someone broke into the mine and stole the company van," said Stanley.

Bailey was shocked into silence. She believed what Henson told her about the woman attacking him was all part of his imagination, and that the company van he witnessed drive up to his house would still be parked at the mine, proving him wrong. Stanley's confirmation that the company van was stolen meant Henson had not imagined it. Bailey dropped her cell phone and rushed out of the room. Eric was already at the front door. He opened it to a woman in her mid-thirties standing on the other side. She couldn't be the sitter, he thought. Bailey had told him she was seventeen.

"Can I help you?" said Eric.

Without warning, she lunged forward and grabbed him around the throat with both hands. The woman yanked his face close to hers and forced her lips against his. Eric's eyes opened wide, bulging. He tried to pull away, but her grip around his neck was vise-like. His arms and hands were frozen in place by his side, unable to respond to his brain's commands and preventing him from defending himself. Eric struggled to detach his mouth from hers. The intense suction she created drew his eyes inward. His body quivered as she literally drained the life out of him.

Bailey rushed into the foyer, intending to stop Eric from opening the door. She froze at the sight of him standing motionless with the door wide open.

"Eric?" she said, fearful.

Eric's body quivered as Bailey cautiously took a step toward him. "Eric, what's wrong?"

He dropped to the floor like a sack of potatoes, his face shaded pasty gray, revealing the dark, empty cavities where his eyes once were. Bailey was too terrified to scream. She recognized the woman standing at her door: the woman from the coal mine, dressed conservatively in

Henson's wife's gray pantsuit. Her onyx-black hair was down past her shoulders, and her eyes were ocean-blue.

"Oh my God, it's you," said Bailey.

"Where is Clayton?" the woman said.

The spiral tattoo on her palm glowed and pulsated. She opened her mouth inhumanly wide, and a gust of wind and sand shot forward. The sheer force of it struck Bailey in the chest, lifted her up off the ground, and hurled her backward. She slammed face-up unto a table twenty feet away. The glass top shattered beneath her as she landed unconscious on the floor. The woman closed her mouth, and the wind abated. She stepped over Eric's lifeless body and stooped down next to Bailey, whose fingers twitched, a sign she was still alive.

The woman placed her hands around Bailey's throat just as a child's voice interrupted her. "Don't hurt my mommy."

The woman peered up at the staircase. Bailey and Eric's twin five-year-old girls were standing on the stairs in their pajamas, holding hands, teary-eyed, watching it all.

o   o   o

Still writhing from the pain, Clay grimaced as he struggled along the forest trail. The wound on his hand had metastasized all the way up to his forearm, discoloring it to a deep-purplish hue. He ignored it, took the shotgun from around his neck, and placed it on the ground. Clay winced as he quickly removed his undershirt and wrapped it around his wounded hand. He tied a knot and tightened it with his free hand and clenched teeth. Clay returned the shotgun around his neck and resumed trekking full speed ahead across the trail. By the time he arrived back at the parking lot, he was exhausted. He checked his cell phone again— still no signal. His frustration calmed at the sight of his truck parked in the space where he had left it.

He tossed the shotgun in the cab, hopped inside, and exhaled hard. Finally, he was on his way back home. Clay pulled the napkin from his pocket to make sure the diamonds were still there. Satisfied, he placed them in the glove compartment and locked it. He turned the key in the ignition. It didn't start. Before he turned it again, a young girl's voice yelled out to him. "Wait!"

Rebecca hopped out of the passenger seat of Octavius's EV and ran toward him. She reached his truck, desperate and out of breath. "Don't go! He knows you're in that truck," she said. "Come with me. I can help you escape him."

Clay lowered the window and gazed at her, bewildered. "Who are you?"

"It doesn't matter," Rebecca said. "We don't have much time. You have to come with me."

"Look, I'm not goin' anywhere with you. I'm gettin' the heck outta this wacko town. I suggest you get back in the car with whoever you came here with and do the same."

Clay turned the key to the ignition again. The engine sputtered but didn't start. He turned it again. It sputtered a little longer but quickly went dead. Frustrated by everything that had happened to him, he beat the steering wheel with his fist. "Come on!" he shouted.

Clay turned the ignition once more, and the truck started up. He peered out the window. Rebecca was still standing there, looking defeated.

"Please, he'll try to eliminate you, and when he gathers enough power, he'll kill everyone else like you," said Rebecca.

She spoke with such urgency that it rattled Clay. "Why would anyone want to *eliminate* me? What have I done?"

"He wants you dead because he's afraid of you. He's afraid of what you'll become and what we might eventually become because of it."

Clay had enough of Rebecca's riddles and gibberish. It was all nonsense, everything that had happened to him in Oceola—crazy nonsense. He shifted gears and sped out of the parking lot, leaving Rebecca behind.

Relieved to finally be back on the road to Lynch, Clay took a deep breath and exhaled. There had to be a reasonable explanation for what had happened to him. Once he made it home, he could tend to his wound the right way and sort everything out. Things would go back to normal after some food, a shot of tequila, and some sleep. *What about Tara? She must be worried.* Clay looked through the rearview mirror. There were no cars behind or in front of him. He glanced down at the bloodstained shirt wrapped around his arm.

"This can't be real," he whispered.

Clay reached for his cell phone. It finally had a signal. He pushed the redial button.

At the same time, Tara was at home in the shower while her cell phone was lying in the room across the bed. Clay's name appeared on the screen, followed by a melodic ringtone too faint to penetrate over running water pounding the basin floor in the bathroom. Tara's ringtone played over and over until the call finally switched over to voicemail.

He shifted gears and slowed to make a right turn on a pitch-dark rural road that led to KY 160. A single headlight glimmered in the distance. Clay squinted to see what was behind the single headlight that appeared to be close to the ground. He flipped on his high beams. To Clay's shock, it wasn't a motorcycle but Kaden, pedaling his bike in the middle of the road toward him. A dim headlight mounted between the handlebars illuminated Kaden's path through the darkness.

"What the–?" Clay blurted. He slammed his foot down on the brakes. His truck came to a screeching stop. He watched through his front windshield as Kaden dismounted and dropped his bike in the middle of the road thirty yards away. Clay's high-beam lights had no effect on Kaden's ability to see right through to him. He gazed directly at Clay through the blinding light and stretched out his hand. The spiral tattoo appeared on his palm, glowing and pulsating.

"Goodbye, Clayton," Kaden said softly to himself. He knelt and pressed his palm against the pavement. A jagged rift appeared beneath Kaden's hand. It surged forward at lightning speed, ripping the road apart into chunks of concrete. Shards of debris scattered in every direction as the crevice raced toward Clay's truck. Before he could react, the intense tremor led to a crash impact under his truck and catapulted it into the air. The truck flipped and then rolled over sideways six times until it landed upside down in the adjacent field. Kaden smiled as the truck ignited and then exploded into a huge fireball lighting up the night sky.

"Why did you do that?" Jeremy asked in a soft, innocent voice.

"I didn't give you permission to speak," said Kaden harshly. "Stay quiet or I'll permanently silence you."

Two distinct life forms occupied Jeremy's body, one human, the other inhuman. The human six-year-old Jeremy was still there, barely clinging to consciousness. The inhuman presence of Kaden had taken dominion over Jeremy's mind and body. It would only be a matter of time before Kaden would completely overtake Jeremy's consciousness, but for now he would keep him alive so that he would have access to the boy's memories.

While Clay's truck burned in the background, completely engulfed in flames, Kaden hopped back on his bike and rode away in the opposite direction, singing,

"Twinkle, twinkle, little star, how I wonder what you are.
Up above the world so high, like a diamond in the sky.
Twinkle, twinkle, little star, how I wonder what you are..."

CHAPTER 18

OFFICER HOLT'S SQUAD car came to a screeching halt in front of Jeb's father's house. Jeb promptly leaped out and made a mad dash toward the front door with Susan and Officer Holt following closely behind. Frantic, Jeb pounded on the door, praying that it wasn't too late to rescue Charlie from the enigmatic force that had seized control of his father's being. Getting no response, he hammered on it a dozen times more. When his father finally swung the door open, Jeb's relief shifted to a paralyzing sense of fear.

"Jeb? Hey, what's going on?" his father said, looking concerned. Jeb read it as phony.

"You know what's goin' on!" he shouted. "Where's my brother?!"

"Calm down," Officer Holt said to Jeb before eyeing Jeb's father. "Mr. Aaron, I'm Officer Holt. Jeb says that you took Charlie home with you. Now, if you don't have a visitation order from a judge, then you need permission from the parent who has full custody, which I understand to be his mother."

"I never took him home. I haven't seen either of my boys in weeks," said Mr. Aaron. He pointed at Susan. "She'll tell you."

"He's lying," said Jeb. "He came to our school and tried to get us to go with him."

"No, that's not true," said Mr. Aaron.

"Then where is he?" asked Susan.

"I told you that I don't know. When you find him, tell him to give his dad a call. I have something nice for him."

His smug response enraged Jeb. He balled up his fists, straining to suppress an oncoming outburst. His brother had to be subdued somewhere in his father's house. If he could just get inside and look around, he would find him.

"Jeb has always had a vivid imagination, Officer. That's one of the things I love about my son, but on the other hand it can be misleading," said Mr. Aaron.

On the verge of tears, Jeb's cheeks reddened. He lifted himself up on his toes to meet his father's height and pointed his finger in his face. "Stop talkin' like you're some kinda' expert. You don't know anything about me! I hardly even see you, and I'm not imagining things."

Jeb turned to his mother. "Look at his hand, Mom. There's some weird symbol engraved in his palm."

Mr. Aaron raised both hands so that Susan and Officer Holt could get a clear view of them. "What's wrong with my hands?" he said derisively as he examined them closely in front of them. The tattoo Jeb had spied in his father's palm had vanished, just as it had from Travis's palm.

"Look, this is nonsense. I don't know where Charlie is," said Mr. Aaron. "Have you checked with his friends? He may have stopped by Travis's home."

Jeb sneered. "Travis is not his friend. He would never go to Travis's house."

"Why not?" asked Officer Holt.

"Because I warned him not to," said Jeb as he peered into the open space between his father and the door, attempting to get a better view inside the house.

"Just so everyone can be at ease, you mind if I take a quick look around inside?" asked Officer Holt. Mr. Aaron paused to think about it. The moment he nodded, Jeb rushed around his father and into the house. He knew exactly where to look for Charlie: up the stairs and in the attic where they used to hide and play when they were much younger. Susan waited outside as Officer Holt entered. He glanced inside all the rooms until he was satisfied that Charlie wasn't there. Moments later, Jeb came down the stairs.

"You find anything?" asked Officer Holt.

"He must've taken him somewhere else," said Jeb.

Officer Holt sighed. "Sorry to have bothered you, Mr. Aaron."

Jeb and Susan followed Officer Holt out the door.

"If he stops by, I'll give you a call," said Mr. Aaron. "I wouldn't be surprised if he's back at his mother's house by the time you return."

Jeb and Susan climbed back into Officer Holt's squad car. Where else could his father have taken him? No one spoke a word the entire drive back to their home, and when Officer Holt parked in front of their house, Jeb hopped out and hurried inside, hoping he would find Charlie in his bedroom, playing computer games.

Susan stepped out of the squad car and thanked Officer Holt for his help.

"No need to thank me, ma'am, just doing my job," he answered. "So, do you believe him?"

"Do I believe what?" asked Susan.

"Do you believe your ex when he says he hasn't seen Charlie, or do you believe your son who says he has?"

Susan shrugged. "Honestly, I don't know who to believe. My kids told me they saw a stag pull a boy from the lake, and you claim that's impossible. To answer your question, I don't know."

Susan got out of the car, and Officer Holt started the ignition. "If Charlie doesn't turn up in the next two hours, give me a call, and we'll take it from there."

"I will. Thank you," said Susan as she walked toward her front door.

"By the way, Miss Aaron, I've come to the conclusion that nothing's impossible, especially in this town," said Officer Holt before driving off down the road.

Susan was halfway through the front door when two young boys walking together down the sidewalk appeared out of the corner of her eye. She waited by the door until their faces came into view. Susan shouted for Jeb. He stepped out the door just as Travis and Charlie were walking by. Charlie's shirt and jeans were heavily wrinkled and his hair disheveled. His tired bloodshot eyes were what worried Jeb. He rushed up to Charlie and grabbed his arm to stop him from walking away.

"Charlie, what happened?" asked Jeb.

"Nothing happened."

"What's goin' on? Where have you been?" asked Susan. She stepped toward him and tenderly pushed back a lock of Charlie's hair from his face. Charlie pulled away from Jeb's grip and stepped inside the house without answering either of their questions. Susan followed him inside while Jeb remained outside, studying Travis as he turned and walked back in the direction he'd come from.

"What did you do to my brother?" Jeb snarled.

Travis winked at him and walked away. "Charlie is my friend, and there's nothing you can do about it."

○ ○ ○

Rebecca braced herself in the passenger seat as Octavius raced toward the ball of fire. Billowing clouds of black smoke hovered over the distant wreckage. Octavius swerved and maneuvered around fragments of broken-up concrete slabs scattered across the section of road that Kaden had literally destroyed. Melting plastic mixed with oil and gasoline created nauseous fumes that poisoned the air through the open car window, but Rebecca's concern was not about the toxic fumes she and Octavius inhaled—it was about getting to Clay in time to save his life.

She hesitated to think that if the crash hadn't killed him already, the fire would surely do the job, and Kaden would have won. Clay's very existence to him was like a disease destined to spread and infect his kind. Kaden deemed Clay's birth impure and believed that if he was left alive the disease would eventually spread among the Ocran, first corrupting them then causing them to produce offspring that were neither Ocran nor human but a disgusting hybrid anomaly.

For Kaden, Clay's elimination was necessary and inevitable, and it would only be the beginning. Rebecca and Octavius could only hope to prevent it by preoccupying Kaden until they could devise a viable plan to extract him from Jeremy's body.

Rebecca directed Octavius to pull over a safe distance away from the fiery wreckage. Though they both cringed from the scorching heat from the fire, they jumped out of the car and hurried toward it.

"We don't have much time. We gotta get to him," said Rebecca.

"Look at the fire. It's impossible that he could have survived that," replied Octavius.

She ignored him and trampled through the tall grass leading away from the burning wreck. "He's not in the fire. He's somewhere here. Astatee an ashur bujooduh," *–I can feel his presence*, she said in Arabic.

Octavius followed her until she abruptly stopped and stood still. Rebecca turned her head from side to side as if she had heard something and was trying to determine what direction it emanated from. Zeroing in on the source, she trampled eastward and spotted Clay a short distance from the smoldering flames. Rebecca headed toward him, but Octavius grabbed her arm and pulled her back. "I can see from here, he's dead. There's nothing we can do."

"No, he's alive," said Rebecca. She pulled away from him and rushed over to where Clayton lay face down in the grass. When she touched his shoulder, his body jerked.

"I told you he wants to eliminate you," said Rebecca. "Why didn't you listen to me?"

With his clothing singed and his hands and face covered with cuts, Clay ignored her scolding and tried to stand. "I can't move my leg," he whined.

A dog barked in the distance. Rebecca glanced across the open field. A white Jack Russell terrier with black and brown patches had been sitting and watching them the whole time. The dog was drenched, as though it got caught in the rain. It vigorously shook, but instead of shaking off rainwater, blue dust particles scattered in all directions. The dog's sudden appearance worried Rebecca. "Kaden will know you're still alive soon," she said to Clay. "We have to get you out of here."

"Wait, I have to get back to my truck. The diamonds…" said Clay. He broke away and limped toward the wreckage.

"What diamonds?" asked Rebecca.

"The diamonds I found in the creek. They're worth a lot of money."

"No, it's too dangerous. Leave them," said Rebecca. Clay ignored her warning and kept limping toward the truck until the BOOM! The wreckage exploded, jolting, and tossing them all to the ground. Debris shot straight up into the sky, and embers fell around them like fireflies in the night. The wreck was engulfed in a raging fireball.

Octavius helped Rebecca to her feet. "You okay?" She nodded. Octavius placed Clay's arm around his shoulder and lifted him to his feet. Clay wailed from the pain the entire way back to their car. His femur had fractured and was protruding through a cut in his bloodied khakis. After they helped him onto the back seat, Rebecca took Clay's hand and placed it over the exposed bone. "Keep it there until it's better," she said as she hurried into the passenger seat and shut the door.

Octavius searched through a wallet and tossed it in the back seat. "I think that's yours," he said before he sped off down the road.

"I saw it with my own eyes," said Clay. "He put his hand on the ground, and pieces of it came crashing at me. I need you to tell me who is this boy, and why is he trying to kill me? He knows things about my family, my wife, my unborn kid. How is he doing these things?"

"He had someone watching you, following you and your wife. I tried to warn you," said Octavius.

"That was you who left the note at the bar?"

Octavius cast a glance Rebecca's way, a silent signal that conveyed the moment had arrived to reveal everything to him. She turned around in the passenger seat and looked Clay in the eye. "His name is Kaden. He's in a child's body, but he's not a child. We are the Ocran, and so are Kaden and many others in this town. We took refuge underground a very long time ago after the arrival of your kind, but now the planet's resources you are destroying is systematically eradicating us. Only the strongest have been able to surface to save themselves. We are like dust particles in our natural form, having no shape or density. The only way to maintain our survival on the surface is to enter a human host and take over the mind and body—*changing them*. Kaden mistakenly believes that if he destroys every human here on this planet, it would save us from extinction, and we would thrive in our original form here on the surface without the human threat to this world. He's wrong. There's nothing that can stop our kind's extinction now. Me and Octavius, and many others believe it is immoral to annihilate an entire species to save another."

"Are you seriously trying to tell me you're some kind of alien?" asked Clay.

Octavius bristled. "Alien?"

"We're not aliens, silly. We're more like you—well, sort of," said Rebecca.

"I'm human," Clay replied.

"And you're also partly one of us," said Rebecca.

"You're crazy."

"You had to have seen the signs," said Rebecca. "The changes in your body. The illusions caused by the Wheel and the ability to heal yourself. That's not what humans can do."

"My mother died from lupus, and my father is Gerald Krutcher," said Clay. "They are human beings."

"Gerald is not your father," said Rebecca. "Your father is Ocran, and he uses the name Zarian. He took a human host when he encountered your mother. It was thought inconceivable for a human and Ocran to mate, but it happened with your father and your human mother, and you are the offspring of what we believed was an impossibility. Kaden assumed this trait was passed down to you—the ability to procreate and contaminate our life-form."

Octavius interrupted her. "That's why he manipulated the Council to choose you to turn the Wheel. He knew that because you're not fully Ocran, it would destroy you and your potential offspring. At that moment you refused, the Council granted him unlimited power to eliminate you, and he's using that same power to get everything else he wants. Kaden believes your existence is a threat to the purity of the Ocran species."

"Octavius and I and so many others of our kind know the only way we can survive is to assimilate with humans," said Rebecca. "You're living proof that assimilation is possible. You are the future of the Ocran's survival and the survival of every human."

Clay was silent, and Rebecca couldn't tell if they were getting through to him just how vital it was to stop Kaden. What he asked her next convinced her he was paying more attention to what she was not telling him and what she didn't want to discuss.

"Whose bodies have you and Octavius taken over?" asked Clay.

Octavius glanced at Rebecca as if asking her how to respond. She shook her head.

"It doesn't matter," said Octavius.

"What do you mean it doesn't matter?" Clay replied. "You're lying to those who believe you're their family members when you're not. You're just pretending—deceiving people, and for what purpose? The people you've changed aren't there anymore. They're dead inside."

"No," said Rebecca, "a part of them lives within us. We can access their thoughts, their feelings, their memories. We care for them."

Clay balked. "You *care* for them? You stole their bodies and took their lives away. It's wrong, and I won't be a part of it."

"You're half Ocran. You're part of us whether you want to be or not," said Octavius as he sped through the yellow street light across the intersection.

"What are you to her anyway, some kind of bodyguard?" asked Clay.

"I'm more like a protector," said Octavius.

"Where is he taking us?" Clay asked Rebecca. "I need to get to a hospital."

Octavius smirked. "We're not going to a hospital. There's nothing they can do for you that you can't do for yourself."

Clay still had his hand pressed firmly over his leg wound. "Take your hand away," said Rebecca. When Clay moved his hand, the injury was gone. The fractured femur appeared healed. Only the cut in his khakis where the bone had protruded was there.

"You're able to heal yourself," said Rebecca. "But you already knew that, didn't you, Clay?"

CHAPTER 19

MIRIAM POSITIONED HERSELF on the couch with her gaze squarely facing her front door. She didn't bother to turn on the lights, she welcomed the pitch-black darkness that concealed her presence. She had resolved to sit there in her unlit living room and wait patiently. Her maternal instincts would not allow her to keep silent any longer. Confrontation loomed, an inevitability she had prepared herself for. As Miriam peered at the outline of the door through the darkness, her emotions wavered, oscillating between fear, anxiety, and concern as she anticipated the doorknob turning. It took only minutes for the door's slow, deliberate creaking to break the silence.

Rebecca stepped inside and carefully shut the door, trying to dampen the sound of any noises. When she directed the light from her cell phone to illuminate the stairway, Miriam flicked the light switch on the lamp that was positioned on the table next to her. Rebecca gazed at her like a deer caught in headlights.

"Your father said I was imagining things," said Miriam in a subdued manner, "that I was being overly dramatic, that because of what you must've gone through you were traumatized and it would take time before you could begin to heal. I want to understand it. What happened to you, honey? Those five days you were missing, tell me what happened?"

"Nothing happened. Everything's fine," said Rebecca.

"My eight-year-old daughter is sneaking out of the house, riding around in a car with a stranger at three in the morning, and you're telling me everything's fine?"

"He's not a stranger. He's a friend."

Miriam stood up from the couch, infuriated. She firmly grabbed Rebecca by the arm. "A young child does not have adult friends, and they certainly don't go riding around in a car with an adult man that the parent doesn't know. I am three seconds away from calling the police. Who are you? Because you're not my Rebecca. You look like her, but you don't speak like her, and you don't think like my daughter, so who are you? Tell me. I want to know now what happened to my daughter."

Rebecca just stood there and stared at Miriam, trying to decide whether to tell her the truth or nothing at all. After making Miriam wait an uncomfortable amount of time, Rebecca bluntly answered. "I've changed her."

Miriam assumed that she had misheard her. "What did you say?"

Rebecca repeated it louder, though still in a calm and controlled voice. "I said I've changed her. I have taken over her body, Miriam. In order to save the majority of you, a minority had to be sacrificed. Your daughter was chosen. I'm sorry."

"No, it's not for you to make a choice for her. I want my daughter back the way she was. What gives you the right to take over her body? She's just a child. Please, give her back to me," she said as tears welled up.

"You seem to be one of extraordinary empathy—an admirable trait, but if I'm extracted from your daughter's body, she will die. As long as I am a part of her, her memories and her subconscious thoughts will remain intact."

Miriam walked back over to the couch and sat down hard, not sure what to think.

"What is your name?" asked Miriam.

"My name? You know my name is Rebecca."

"Your name is not Rebecca, it's my daughter's name."

"Why do you want to know that?"

"You've taken over my daughter's body. I have the right to know who you are."

"It's not important. My original name is not pronounceable in your form of speech. What matters is that we're here to help your kind survive what's coming," said Rebecca.

"So there's more of you out there doing this to people—taking over the lives of their children. This can't be real."

"We're only doing what is necessary, Miriam, in order to save as many of you as we can."

"Save us from what?"

"From us," said Rebecca.

○ ○ ○

Mo opened his laptop and logged on to the DisContent chatroom linked to his video game. He typed a new message under the heading *Spiral Tattoo,* asking if anyone had seen one on a friend or relative or even a stranger and to describe where on the body they saw it. He suspected there were more out there like Mr. Bruner, but they were hiding in plain sight among regular people. Exposing them was the only way to protect the public from whatever deviant acts they were up to.

The doorbell rang as he was sending it. His mother answered and the familiar voice speaking back to her startled him. Mo walked out of his room toward the front door. Mr. Bruner was having a conversation with his mother, his worse fear personified. Mo's pace to the door stalled, and his hands twitched from nervousness. It was too late to dash back to his room. His mother had seen him already, and she gazed at him, concerned. "Mo, did you lose something?" She asked the question in an inquisitive tone of voice that conveyed she knew that he had. All Mo could think to do was to shake his head. "Really? You didn't lose your phone?"

Mr. Bruner flashed a disingenuous smile. Mo played along. Neither of them wanted his mother to know the truth.

"Oh yeah, I lost it yesterday. I forgot," said Mo.

"You forgot that you lost your phone? That doesn't make sense," his mother replied.

"I thought I may have left it at a friend's house."

"You didn't leave it at your friend's house. You know where Mr. Bruner found it?"

Mo remained silent, pretending not to know the answer.

"Mr. Bruner found it on the ground on the side of his house. You know how it got there?"

"Nope."

Mr. Bruner handed the phone to Mo. "You should always know where your phone is. Most people have private information on their phones. If it gets in the wrong hands, the sky's the limit to how it can be used against you," he said.

"Thank you for bringing it back, Harold," his mother said. "That phone cost us a lot. I wish my son was more mindful of that."

Mo took that as his cue to walk away. "Mo, come back here," his mother demanded.

"What?"

"I didn't hear you thank Mr. Bruner."

Mo sighed and walked up to Mr. Bruner, who now had a stupid grin on his face, enjoying Mo's humiliation. "Thank you," Mo said without looking at him.

He went into his bedroom and shut the door in a hurry. He had to know if the video he took of Mr. Bruner the night before was still there. Just as he expected, it was deleted, as were all his videos on his phone. He checked his texts, and not only were his back-and-forth texts to Connor gone, but all his texts from the previous six months were also deleted. Mr. Bruner had even erased the same videos and texts from his cloud account. Mo nodded. "Oh, you're good, Harold, but you can't outsmart me, dude," he said out loud. "Do you really think I can't get the videos back?"

A week before, Mo had installed a program that would back up his phone every four minutes to an encrypted secret cloud account only he could access. All he had to do now was connect to the program on his laptop and transfer the files. After he restored them on his phone, he used Mr. Bruner's GPS location at the time he erased the files and retrieved his IP address. "Booya! Gotcha dude," he said.

Mo entered Mr. Bruner's IP address into his computer program and within minutes had access to the files. After skimming through his files and copying them, Mo called Connor. He picked up immediately.

"Why did you stand me up? You were supposed to be here an hour ago," said Connor.

"Dude, he tried to erase the videos on my phone. I told you!" said Mo.

"You got your phone back?"

"Yeah, he brought it back today, but not before he tried to wipe it clean. I was able to get his IP address, and I copied all his documents and folders off his computer. They're encrypted in some kind of code I've never seen before."

"You serious?"

"I just forwarded you a copy of the video," said Mo. "We have to come up with a plan. We have to expose him. Call me back after you watch the video."

Mo hung up and logged in on the DisContent chat platform again to see if there were any responses to his spiral tattoo post. There was one from someone with the screen name *JBop*.

○　○　○

Jeb stopped using the screen name JBop months ago thinking it was corny. By the time he started posting on the DisContent chat platform, JBop sounded cool enough to use again. Mo's spiral tattoo post had immediately caught Jeb's attention. The revelation that what had happened to his brother Charlie was also happening to others outside of Virginia was both comforting and disturbing. Jeb left his phone number and his email address in the reply, hoping Mo would respond so that they could share their experiences and find a way to fix it. Charlie shuffled into the room as Jeb finished typing. He peeked into the closet then searched under the bed.

"What are you looking for?" said Jeb.

"Where's Sebastian?" asked Charlie.

"Sebastian? Who is Sebastian?"

"The cat. Where is it?"

Charlie's question perplexed him. "The cat's name is Sherlock, not Sebastian."

"Well, he doesn't like Sherlock. So we call him Sebastian. He likes it better."

Sherlock ran into the room, hopped up onto the windowpane, and jumped into Charlie's arms. He petted him, and the cat purred in appreciation.

"Sebastian, where have you been hiding?" asked Charlie.

Jeb scratched his head. *Why is Sherlock so attached to Charlie now when he used to be afraid of him?*

"You said *we call him Sebastian*. Who did you mean by *we*?" asked Jeb.

"I never said that."

"Yes, you did. You said *we call him Sebastian*. I know what I heard."

"You're confused," said Charlie.

Jeb stood up from the computer and got right in Charlie's face, ready to say what he was too afraid to say before. "I'm not confused. I know you're not my brother, and I know that wasn't the real Travis. I'm gonna make sure Mom knows everything about what you really are too."

"Mom might get hurt if you told her," said Charlie. "And we would both be sad to see that happen, wouldn't we?"

Charlie snatched the computer's power cord from the outlet and calmly walked out of the room with Sherlock in his arms. Jeb didn't see him again until later that night just before he went to bed. He would usually stay up hours later than Charlie, but that night he fell fast asleep in a matter of minutes. He awakened in the middle of the night to Charlie in his bedroom standing over him. Jeb shot up from his bed. "What are you doin'?"

Charlie's face dripped with sweat. "Jeb, I'm scared," he said in a muffled voice and bloodshot eyes.

"Charlie? Is it really you? Can you hear me?"

Charlie's facial expression hardened, and the tone of his voice changed to a slightly lower pitch. "Of course I can hear you. I can't sleep because I'm hearing your snoring all the way in my room," he said.

Charlie walked out and went back to his own room leaving Jeb to ponder whether his brother was trying to convey some kind of message–maybe that he was still in there, still alive and needed his help. Jeb worried that if he went back to sleep, the thing that had taken over Charlie's body might return to change him into something weird, so he kept himself awake until the next morning by placing rags he soaked in cold water across his face.

CHAPTER 20

TARA TURNED THE key and entered her trailer without having to unlock the deadbolt. She always locked the deadbolt when she left home, especially after spotting the weird homeless man in their trailer park. It made her nervous, but the slim possibility that it might have slipped her mind and she had just forgotten to lock it was enough to calm her. She locked it for sure this time, dropped her keys and purse on the table, and headed toward the bathroom.

Clay's laptop was sitting on the counter, open as if someone had used it. Fear raced through every vein in her body. She was certain she hadn't left it that way, and there was no trace of Clay's truck out front. Someone had been in her home. A muffled thump came from the direction of her bedroom. Tara opened the counter drawer and grabbed a hammer. As she crept into her bedroom, she held it over her shoulder, ready to strike at whatever came at her. When she turned the corner, a hand reached out and grabbed her by the wrist.

"Tara, what're you doing?" said Clay.

"Oh my God, Clay, you scared the crap out of me."

She let go of the hammer and threw her arms around him, hugging him as tightly as she could. "I didn't see your truck. Where have you been? I filed a missing person's report on you."

"Why would you do that?"

"Because you've been gone for two days and not returning my calls,

Clay. What did you expect me to do? Edie and Eric are dead. I was trying to reach you to tell you."

"What? How?"

"No one knows yet."

Clay wiped the line of sweat from his forehead and gazed around the room.

"What happened?" asked Tara. "Why didn't you call me?"

Clay took a seat on the bed. "I was in a car accident. I totaled my truck."

Tara sat down next to him, even more concerned. "Why didn't the police contact me? Where did this happen?"

"Near the county line in Appalachia. There was a fire and—"

"What? Have you been to a hospital?"

"I don't need a hospital. I'm okay."

"Clay, you should get checked just in case."

"I said I'm fine. What I need is a beer. Do we have any left in the fridge?"

Tara nodded and followed him into the kitchen, relieved to have him home but puzzled why he offered such a feeble explanation. There had to be more to the story, and she wanted to ask him more until she caught sight of something odd about his face. When Clay grabbed the beer from the refrigerator, she took a good look at him. It was his eyes. One of his hazel eyes was ocean blue. More perplexed than alarmed by it, she stepped in front of him and held his face gently within her hands. "What's wrong with your eye? Why is it blue like that?"

Clay gazed at her as if he didn't believe it. He hurried into the bathroom and stared at his face in the mirror. Tara waited for a response, but he didn't give her one. He went back to the kitchen and opened his beer like he hadn't seen it.

"Something could be seriously wrong with your eye, honey. What are you gonna do?" said Tara.

"I'll have a doc look at it," he replied.

"Is it painful or blurry?"

"I have never seen things so clearly."

Clay took a swallow of his beer and immediately spat it out in the kitchen sink. "Ugh! What's wrong with this?" he muttered to himself. The beer had a bitter metallic taste that made his stomach turn. He poured the rest of it into the sink and grabbed another bottle. It was his favorite, Avery Ellie's Brown Ale. He took a swallow. It had the same bitter metallic taste as the other. Clay twisted off the tops of every bottle of beer left in his refrigerator and after tasting every one of them poured them all out into the sink. He glanced at Tara. "I don't feel right. I'm gonna take a shower," he said.

He went into the bedroom and took off his shirt. Tara stood by the doorway as he undressed. "Why did you tell Abby about my pregnancy?" she blurted out with her arms crossed in front of her.

"What're you talking about?" said Clay, dumbfounded. "I didn't tell her anything. We agreed we wouldn't tell anyone until we were ready. Why do you think I would do that?"

"She knew, and she was very rude to me about it. What about Jimmy? Did you tell him?"

"No, I told you I didn't tell anybody."

Tara sighed. "Then I don't know how she found out."

"I don't either," said Clay as he walked away into the bathroom and stepped into the shower. The cold water against his skin soothed his body, despite his mind being somewhere else. *What if Abby is one of them?* She and Kaden somehow knew about Tara's pregnancy, and Abby had even given him the map to where he ended up meeting Kaden. How would he tell Tara what really happened to him in Appalachia? Or was keeping silent about it the only way to protect her and his unborn baby from all the madness swirling around him?

Clay rinsed the soap away, overwhelmed by his dilemma and the peculiar metallic taste in his mouth. Rebecca was right—he had always been aware of the changes in his body. How could he not? He remembered how during his childhood the same metallic taste would return whenever he was angry or stressed over something. He never paid much attention to it. It was the other things he noticed about himself that he had never told anyone, like how he fell out of a tree when he was six years old and broke his ankle. He assumed he had broken it because it was twisted in the opposite direction. He felt no pain, just the metallic taste in his mouth, and when he massaged it, his ankle straightened to its normal position. He remembered standing up and walking home like nothing ever happened.

Another incident was running with a bottle of soda pop in his hand and tripping on the concrete sidewalk. The bottle shattered in his hand and severed the vein between his thumb and forefinger. He bled profusely at first, but minutes later the bleeding stopped, and the cut had all but disappeared. As a matter of fact, he couldn't remember a time when he was ever sick or hurt as a child or even had a cold. While his brother, Jimmy, suffered from measles and the flu and was sometimes made to stay home from school because he had a fever, Clay himself never experienced any maladies. There were so many things he didn't understand physically about himself, odd traits he had ignored or denied throughout his youth, and now it had all culminated to a realization he wanted to escape as an adult—that he would never have a life like everyone else.

Clay reached for the towel to dry himself and glimpsed the vein in his arm protruding and pulsing through his skin in sync with his heartbeat. Translucent and bluish in color, it stretched from his wrist all the up to his shoulder. The sight of it didn't alarm him. He had seen it all before. It would appear and then vanish minutes later, though this time it remained.

Accepting the state of his changing body would mean that he would have to face the reality that whatever had made him that way was inherited. And not from Gerald, the man he had always believed was his father, but instead from someone or something inhuman that he had yet to encounter. Clay's body was changing from the inside out, and there was no use in denying or fighting it any longer. What was destined for him, no one would be able to stop.

Doug rushed inside his home, went to Kaden's door, and opened it. Kaden was sitting on his bed with his back turned, enthralled by a new cube puzzle. "You're supposed to knock, Doug, before you enter. Try it again," said Kaden.

Doug didn't say a word. He closed the door and knocked three times. "Who is it?" said Kaden derisively.

Doug gritted his teeth. "It's me, Doug."

"You may enter."

Doug stepped in and sat down next to him. "I have good news."

"What is it?" asked Kaden.

"Your puppy has returned."

Kaden's eyes lit up. "As what?"

"A Jack Russell terrier, and he's in the field next door," said Doug.

Kaden dropped the cube on the floor and ran out of the room. The moment he stepped out his front door, a Jack Russell with black and brown patches rose from the field next to his house.

"Puppy!" he shouted. The dog honed in on him, and they ran toward each other. The dog leaped up onto Kaden's shoulder and was licking his face and wagging his tail in excitement. Kaden carried him into the house and placed him down on the living room couch. Pamela stepped into the room.

"Look, Puppy is back," said Kaden.

"That's wonderful. Is he hungry?" Pamela asked.

"I don't think so."

Doug entered. "He might be thirsty. Most are the moment they return," he said.

Kaden sat down on the couch, picked up his dog with both hands, and stared directly into its eyes. The dog gazed back at Kaden as if they were silently communicating. He placed the dog down on the floor, and it scurried away into his bedroom. Enraged, Kaden grabbed the vase from the table and hurled it against the wall. It shattered into tiny pieces. Without saying a word, Pamela quickly grabbed the broom and started cleaning it up.

"How can he still be alive?" said Kaden.

"What are you talking about?" asked Doug.

"Clayton, Doug. Who else? Clayton Krutcher is still alive."

○   ○   ○

Bailey awakened in the hospital to Henson and Stanley sitting there by her side, looking dismal. They came ready to support her and to help break the tragic news that her husband didn't make it. She didn't cry; she was too proud for that. After hearing what they had to say, she stared out the window as if they weren't in the room with her anymore.

What sort of person would kill her husband for no apparent reason? She remembered the entire incident in vivid detail—how she was attacked and how Eric was horribly mutilated–the life sucked out of him. The woman from the coal mine had left him for dead before coming after her with an unworldly force that hurled her across the room like a rag doll. She was not an ordinary woman, she had to be some kind of monster. What troubled Bailey the most was this monster was still somewhere out in the world, capable of coming after her again.

CHAPTER 21

ONE WHACK ACROSS the head and it'll all be over.

The time to do something was now. Travis had some kind of creepy sway over his brother that prevented him from being the Charlie he was before. If he got rid of Travis, maybe whatever had taken over Charlie would leave his body. Travis's weirdness was the beginning of it, and it made sense that he needed to be gone to end his bizarre connection to Charlie. Without giving much thought to the consequences, Jeb readied himself to act. He grabbed the bat out of the closet.

The fishing pier overlooking the lake where they would meet up and hang out seemed the most logical place to look for him. It had become their sanctuary playpen where they would share their secrets and escape the rest of the world. They met there every day after school around the same time, and when Jeb made it down the lake, that was where he found Travis, standing on the pier, just as he expected. Travis teetered on the edge with his back turned as he tossed the line of his fishing rod out into the lake. Jeb crept toward Travis with the bat in his hand, ready to swing. His attempt to catch Travis off-guard backfired when one of the rotted-out wooden planks he trodded on made creaking noises.

Travis glanced back at him. "Hey, watch your step, don't crush the worms. It's our fish food."

Jeb gazed at the floor. Hundreds of worms slithered and oozed across the wooden planks, moist and foul-smelling. "Ugh," he grunted in disgust and jumped back.

"Remember how we used to fish here for trout and carp?" said Travis. "Guess what? I know a better way to catch 'em. Watch this."

Travis raised his palm and pointed it at the lake. A carp shot fifteen feet out of the water and splashed on land. One by one, dozens of fish were shooting upward like mini-rockets out of the lake and into the air and then splashing back into the water. Some jumped as high as twenty feet in the air and landed twice the distance away. Travis dropped his fishing pole and shoved his hand forward at just the right moment to grab a carp out of the air. The fish flailed back and forth as it fought to break free from his grip.

Travis turned to Jeb and held it out to him. "It's yours if you want it."

Spooked, Jeb said "I don't want it."

"Why not? We can have as many as we want."

"It's not the same as catching it fair and square," said Jeb.

Travis smirked at him. "Since when did you care about fairness? Was it fair that you and I both polluted the lake with motor oil and garbage? We poisoned and killed innocent animals that depended on this lake for sustenance. We should've been punished. Me, you, and Charlie are all responsible and should pay the price for what we did."

"Why are you talking like the kid at the lake? Who are you?" said Jeb.

Travis grinned. "Now that's a ridiculous question, Jeb. You know who I am."

"You're not Travis," said Jeb. "We only went fishing once, and it wasn't for carp or trout. It was for catfish, and we both hated it. I dunno who you are, but you're not Travis."

Travis's grin faded. He tossed the fish back into the lake and to Jeb's astonishment slapped himself across the face. "Your friend lied to me," said Travis to Jeb.

Jeb stood there stunned, not sure what was going on or what to do.

"He thinks he's clever, but he's not," said Travis. He slapped himself again so hard that his handprint was left outlined in red on his face.

Out of fear, Jeb raised the bat over his head, ready to swing if Travis came at him.

"So you're gonna hit me with that?" asked Travis.

"Yeah, I will if you take another step toward me," said Jeb.

"No, you won't, Jeb. I'm your friend. Besides, if you hit me with that bat, you'll hurt Travis, not me."

Travis punched himself right in the jaw with a closed fist. Jeb flinched at the sight and sound of the impact.

"See? I didn't feel that at all," said Travis. He spat a bloody tooth on the ground, and a line of blood dripped from one of his nostrils. He wiped it away with his hand. "Unfortunately, your friend Travis felt it. As a matter of fact, he just told me that it hurt pretty bad. What a complainer, huh?"

Jeb stepped back. He gripped the bat so tight that his hands ached. "You're crazy," he said as he took a ready-to-swing stance as if waiting for a pitcher to throw the ball.

"Put down the bat, Jeb," said Travis.

"Not until you leave his body."

"I can't do that. Give the bat to me."

Jeb didn't budge. He held his stance, ready to swing.

"That bat is light as a feather when there's no gravity surrounding it," said Travis.

Jeb's bat broke free from his hands and floated up into the air above him. He gazed up at it, astonished. *What just happened?* The bat floated in mid-air, repositioned itself, and then dropped right into Travis's waiting hands. He swung at Jeb's head. A rush of air brushed Jeb's cheek where the bat had missed its mark. He sprinted, and Travis took off after him. Jeb tore through bushes and jumped over tree stumps in his best effort to outrun him. In the thick of the chase, he glanced back. Travis was still right there on his heels, breathing through his mouth like a wild animal. When Jeb glimpsed a rotted tree branch ahead, it was too late to put the brakes on his momentum. He ran smack into it, stumbled, and fell over. Travis was only two steps away when the ground opened beneath him. Travis dropped into a deep crevice up to his chest. Jeb looked ahead. Rebecca was on her knees with her palm pressed against the ground. "C'mon, before he finds his way out," she shouted.

As Travis struggled to extricate himself from the crevice, Jeb and Rebecca ran until they had cleared the lake area and were safely entrenched in the residential part of the neighborhood. Jeb took a moment to catch his breath as they strolled down the sidewalk together.

"Listen to me," said Rebecca. "Stay away from him. If he believes you're a threat, he'll eliminate you or find a way to change you."

"What happened to him? Why is he doing this?"

"Do you remember the little boy who confronted you at the lake?"

"Yeah, a stag dragged him out of the lake, but nobody believes us."

"I do, and I know it was Kaden. He summoned the animal for help. He's not really a little boy. He's stronger than any of the others. He's taken over the boy's body, and one of Kaden's followers is controlling Travis from within. I'm afraid there's nothing you can do to help him."

"There's gotta be something," said Jeb.

"The Ocran inside of him has taken authority of his mind and body. Travis is most likely dead inside by now."

"The Ocran? What's an Ocran?"

"It doesn't matter."

"The real Travis isn't dead," said Jeb. "He tricked the thing inside of him. He gave him the wrong information. I know he's in there, still alive," said Jeb.

"I'm telling you he's gone, and there's nothing you can do to get him back," said Rebecca.

Jeb's eyes watered. "What about my brother, Charlie? He's been changed too. I gotta help him. I can't leave him the way he is. My mom would kill me."

"You can't bring him back if he's already dead," said Rebecca.

"Stop saying that. He's not dead."

"I have to say what I feel, and I feel he is."

Jeb dropped his head and stopped walking. Rebecca continued ahead of him.

"Charlie said you never lie, and he really believed it, but I don't," said Jeb. "Everybody lies. It's human nature."

"I'm not human," said Rebecca.

Jeb's look of defeat and his genuine concern for his brother engaged her empathy. She walked back to where he stood and placed her hand on his shoulder. "All right, I'll tell you a way," she said, "but it's very dangerous."

"I don't care. I wanna know," he replied.

"Are you sure that Charlie has been changed?"

"I saw the tattoo on the palm of his hand," said Jeb, "the same one I saw on Travis's. Charlie knows I know it's not him, and he threatened to hurt our mother if I told her."

"Most likely you will end up killing your brother if you try to extract the Ocran from him, and Travis will do everything he can to stop you. It's not worth risking your life."

"He's my brother. It's my life."

Rebecca shrugged. "Okay, if that's what you really want. What you should know is that the Ocran that dwells in Charlie will only leave him if it senses the body is near death. You have to bring Charlie to the point of dying, and when you see the Ocran life form leave his body, that's the only chance you'll have to bring him back to life before it's too late. Remember to cover his face and yours so the Ocran doesn't reenter him or change you."

"I don't understand," said Jeb.

"It's why you shouldn't do it. It's too risky," Rebecca replied. She sauntered away down the sidewalk. "Don't blame me if you end up killing your brother," she said.

○ ○ ○

After making copies of vehicle registrations for Sheriff Jenkins, Rosalind left the Appalachia Department of Motor Vehicles in a rush to get home to Lynch before evening traffic. She needed to take her cholesterol medication but had forgotten to bring her water bottle. She pulled over at the nearest gas station. It was busy inside when she entered, and after she grabbed a bottle of water from the cooler she stood in line behind several other customers. She didn't have to wait long before she paid and was on her way out the door when she saw him.

Gazing at a shelf of assorted candies was a little boy who looked the same age and had the same facial profile as the pictures she had seen of Jeremy. *It can't be possible.*

Rosalind walked over to where the boy was standing and touched his shoulder. He turned around and glared at her with the same face that was on the missing persons flyer—Jeremy's face, except for the eye color. She remembered Jeremy's eyes were brown in all the pictures she had seen of him, but the boy in front of her had eyes that were a striking light-blue color. Still, the resemblance to Jeremy was uncanny.

"Hi, you look very familiar. What's your name?" asked Rosalind.

"His name is Kaden," said a harsh voice coming from over her shoulder. "And he's my son. Why do you ask?" Doug stepped up and took Kaden's hand in a defensive posture. Rosalind noted that the boy's father bore no resemblance to his son. His eyes were deep brown, almost black, and he looked irritated that she had spoken to his son.

"I'm sorry, sir. He looks so much like a boy I know in Lynch, Kentucky, named Jeremy."

"My son's name is Kaden, and in this day and age, miss, it's inappropriate to put your hands on or interrogate someone else's child."

Doug gave her a menacing look, and Kaden just stood there, scowling.

"No worries, I'm a police officer."

"A police officer dressed in a denim jacket?"

"I'm off duty right now, sir. Again, I'm sorry about that," said Rosalind. She brought her phone out of her pocket. "You mind if I take a picture of the two of you? I would like to show my friend the resemblance."

"Yeah, I do mind," said Doug.

Rosalind put her cell phone back in her pocket and walked back to her car, thinking something wasn't right. She dialed Lily's number and interrupted her before she could say hello.

"Lily, this is going to sound strange, and I don't want you to read a lot into this, but I'm here in Appalachia, Virginia, at a Fairview convenience store, and I just saw this little boy who looked almost identical to Jeremy."

"What do you mean? How identical?" said Lily.

"The only difference is that his eyes were blue."

Lily sighed. "It's not him. My Jeremy has brown eyes."

"I thought so," said Rosalind. "I'm sorry I even bothered you with this. He just looked so much like him."

"It's okay. Thanks for call—"

"Lily, wait, don't hang up. Does Jeremy have any distinguishing marks on his body?"

"He has an oval-shaped birthmark on his right arm. Why?"

Rosalind spied out of her rear-view mirror at Doug and Kaden leaving the convenience store and getting into a red Honda Civic, the same make, model, and color spotted at the scene of Jeremy's disappearance.

"I gotta go, Lily. I'll call you later."

Rosalind hung up and grabbed her pen and a pad from her glove compartment, and as Doug drove out of the gas station, she jotted down his Appalachia license plate number. Her next phone call was to Nate at the DMV to get the home address associated with the plate.

CHAPTER 22

ABBY WALKED ACROSS the gravel driveway to the mailbox in her usual routine of retrieving her mail at 3:15 in the afternoon. She reached inside and found it uncharacteristically empty. Scattered about on the ground beneath it were whittled shards of basswood. She closed the lid on the mailbox and looked around, now suspicious of her surroundings. More whittled pieces of basswood lied on the ground, and she followed the trail of shavings all the way around the side of her house. Footprints in the soil continued to the rear of her home, too large to belong to Jimmy. It could only be the work of one person—the one who loved to torment her and leave evidence of his presence. She spoke his name. "Octavius, I know you're here." She continued in Latin, "Te non timeo." —*I'm not afraid of you.*

Instead of Octavius, it was Clay who stepped out from behind her house wearing dark sunglasses. Abby turned white as a ghost.

"What's wrong? You look surprised to see me," said Clay. "By the way, you draw horrible maps, Abby. It sent me straight to Kaden. Or maybe that was your plan from the beginning."

Abby backed slowly away as Clay stepped closer. "I was right all along," he said. "You're not really who you say you are, and you're not who my brother thinks you are either."

"Why are you speaking as if you're not part of us?" said Abby.

"I don't kill people and steal their bodies. I'm not a part of you or your plan."

Jimmy stumbled out the back door dragging a trash bag of garbage. His eyes widened at the sight of his brother. "Clay, where the heck have you been?" He dropped the bag and hugged him. "What happened on the trip? I wanna hear all about it."

"So Abby didn't tell you?"

"Tell me what?"

Clay rolled his eyes at Abby. She glanced back at him, nervous.

"I had an accident in my truck," said Clay. "Totaled it."

"Are you serious? You okay?" said Jimmy.

"Yeah, banged up a little bit, but I'm okay."

"Come on in. I have to take a quick call," said Jimmy. He put his cell phone to his ear and rushed back into the house, and as soon as the door shut, Abby pulled a switchblade from her back pocket and hurled it at Clay's face. He caught it with an open hand, a millimeter from penetrating his eye. It sliced through his skin and the blade protruded out from the other side. Clay showed no emotion. He yanked the switchblade from his palm and tossed it. Seething, he charged Abby, grabbed her around the neck and forced her backward, lifting her off the ground and slamming her into her car. He had her back pressed up against the driver's side window with his bloody hand. Her feet dangled inches off the ground. "I *know* my brother," he said. "And I'll know if he's being controlled by one of you. If you harm one hair on his head, or I discover that he's been changed, I will hunt you down, and I promise you, I won't be as nice as Octavius," said Clay, through gritting teeth.

Abby cringed at the oversized bluish vein protruding from Clay's arm. It pulsated in a staggered rhythm. When he released his hand from her neck, she collapsed to her knees, gasping to catch her breath. *How could he have such abilities without the image appearing on his palm?* "You're still evolving, aren't you?" said Abby. "And you have no idea of the monstrosity you're becoming."

Clay ignored her and stepped into the house. Abby lifted herself off the ground and brushed the dirt from her jeans. The bloody handprint Clay left on her shirt couldn't be easily wiped away.

○ ○ ○

Mo left the school in a hurry. After traveling a couple of blocks at top speed on his hoverboard, he spotted Connor walking ahead with his board under his arm. Mo sped up and hopped off his hoverboard in front of him, blocking his path. "Hey, you were supposed to wait," said Mo.

Connor stepped around him and kept walking. Mo followed behind.

"I said I could only wait five minutes, dude," Connor replied. "I have to be home by three."

"Then why aren't you riding your board?"

"Because I need a charge, and I forgot to bring my charger."

Mo mocked him. "Oh, my son, will you ever learn? You should always keep a spare charger in your locker like most incredibly intelligent people like me do."

"Shut up," said Connor.

Mo flicked on the power switch to his hoverboard. It lit up in a rainbow of colors. "See? I'm still fully loaded with power."

"Good for you. You're gonna need it to get away from Mr. Bruner."

"That's not funny. The dude is a psycho," said Mo. "Did you look at the video?"

"Yeah, your video was a dud," said Connor.

"What're you talking about?"

"Dude, your video was nothing but white noise and static."

"You're kidding, right?"

"Nope, I'm not kidding. Did you accidentally erase it?"

"I swear it was there when I sent it to you. Unless my dad…" said Mo, looking away contemplating.

"What about your dad?"

"He came home from Pakistan last night, and I told him everything."

"*Everything?*"

"Yep, everything. All the weirdo stuff I saw Bruner do with my own eyes."

"Did he believe you?"

"He said he did after I showed him the video. He knows a guy at the FBI. He's gonna have him do a thorough background check on him."

"You know, it's possible that this Bruner guy is just a guinea pig for some kind of experimental superhuman drug that the government is hiding from the rest of the world," said Connor.

"That had crossed my mind, Watson, but that's highly unlikely," said Mo. "I met another gamer on the DisContent message board named JBop. Of course, I ran his IP address and found out his real name is Jeb. Anyways, he saw the same thing–the spiral tattoo and the super-strength stuff. His brother and his best friend are both acting strange like Bruner, and they live in Appalachia. Whatever is goin' on, it's not just happening here in Lynch, and it's not just Mr. Bruner."

Mo handed Connor his hoverboard. "Here, take it, since you need to get back. I'll take yours, and we can swap tomorrow."

Connor handed it to him and took off at top speed down the sidewalk. When Mo turned the corner, his dad's car was parked in front of their house instead of the garage, where he usually parked it. Mo entered and walked straight to the refrigerator, grabbed a hot pocket, and nuked it in the microwave. "Dad, you want a hot pocket?"

When he didn't get an answer, he went looking for him in the other rooms. The only place he hadn't checked was the backyard, and when he peeked out from the curtains, his father was laughing and talking with Mr. and Mrs. Bruner like best friends having a light-hearted conversation. His father had betrayed him. How could he be friendly with Mr. Bruner after he had warned him of all the strange things he had done?

○   ○   ○

Rosalind parked across the street with a clear view of Doug and Pamela's house. The red Honda was parked out front, confirming that Nathan had given her the correct address and that she was staking out the right house. She debated going to the door. What would she say? *Can I examine your child's arm to see if he has the birthmark of another child?*

She didn't have a search warrant, and no judge on the planet would grant her one based on a hunch. But it was more than a hunch. It was a gut-wrenching feeling that the boy was hiding something and maybe too afraid to say anything with his father around or someone pretending to be his father. Kaden resembled Frank in so many ways. If she could just talk to him alone without his father around and verify that there was no birthmark on his arm, it would put her suspicions to rest, and she'd drive home to Lynch convinced it was just an extraordinary coincidence.

Rosalind concluded the chances of that happening were next to impossible and started her car, ready to return home, when Kaden strolled out the front door. He had on a safety helmet as he marched to the side of his house, where his bike was on the ground. He hopped on and pedaled away, creating an opportunity for Rosalind to talk to him alone.

She waited until he was well ahead of her before she started trailing him. Kaden sped down the road as fast as he could go. Even with the excessive noise Rosalind's car made traveling on the gravel road, Kaden never bothered to look back at how close her car was to him. He just suddenly stopped, dropped his bike on the ground, and ran into the adjacent woods. *Where is he going? There's nothing in there but trees.*

She parked next to his bike and with the car still running stepped out and hurried over to where she had seen him enter the woods. There was no sign of him, so she walked deeper into the wooded area, paused, and just listened. The quietness seemed unusual. No crickets chirping, no birds cawing—no noises of any kind, nothing. Thinking he might have found another way to get back to his bike, she turned to go back to her car. Kaden was standing there in front of her, frozen and staring at her curiously. Rosalind flinched. It was Jeremy, except for the eyes. Ocean-blue and translucent, they were more haunting than innocent. Rosalind placed a hand on her chest and caught her breath.

"Hey, are you okay?" she asked as she took a step toward him. He responded by taking a step back.

"Why are you here?" he replied.

After he spoke, a cool breeze brushed against her face, and then came the smell—metallic, like burning copper.

"I just wanted to make sure you were okay," said Rosalind. "What's your name?"

Rosalind's eyes locked on a birthmark on the upper part of his arm. She looked away when Kaden caught her fixation on it.

"You know my name," he said.

Minutes later, Kaden walked out of the woods alone, with no trace of Rosalind. He opened the driver's side door of her car, climbed in, and turned off the ignition. Kaden locked the door and rode home on his bike.

CHAPTER 23

CLOSING TIME AT the Derby Diner was always stressful for Gloria. She and Sally would end up scrambling to clean the tables, count the receipts, refill all the condiment jars, and set the alarm all before the clock struck 10:30 p.m. Often, stragglers refused to leave until the very last minute, and Gloria would drive herself into a frenzy afterward to get everything done on time. She was certain it wouldn't be one of those nights. Business had been so slow that Al had shut down the kitchen an hour early and left for the day. Only four customers remained, two at each table. They paid their checks and were chatting as they prepared to leave, so it was especially irritating for Gloria to see a new customer enter the diner five minutes before closing. She was ready to turn her away until she recognized it was Tara.

Considering how disastrous their last meeting had turned out, Tara was the last person Gloria expected to see at the diner again. She smiled, hoped for the best, walked up to Tara, and hugged her. To her surprise, Tara reciprocated.

"Honey, the kitchen is down, but we have some dessert ready I can get you if you want," said Gloria.

"I don't need anything," Tara replied. "I know you're closing, so I'm not gonna stay long."

Gloria took off her apron. "C'mon."

Tara followed her to an empty booth in the middle of the diner, where they sat across from each other.

"Sheriff Jenkins told me how you insisted that he help me. It was because of you that he went beyond what he would do for anyone else. That was very nice of you. I just wanted to thank you in person."

"Honey, you don't have to thank me for anything. You know I would do anything for you. Did you hear from Clay? Is he okay?"

Tara nodded. "Yeah, he's back home. He's okay."

Gloria sensed there was more to it than Tara was willing to tell her, but she didn't want to push it and create a reason for her to become defensive again.

Sally stopped at their booth on her way out the door with her purse and jacket around her arm. "I'm gonna leave a little early," she said. "My sister needs some help with her little ones. You gonna be okay?"

"It's not much left to do. I'm fine, go ahead," said Gloria.

"You sure?"

"Yeah, I'm sure."

"I refilled all the condiments, so you should be good to go," said Sally.

"What would I do without you, Sally?"

"You shouldn't do anything without me," she replied. Sally winked at Tara and smiled. "It's so good to see you two together again," she said before she hurried out the door.

Tara turned to Gloria. "I have some news I want to share with you, though you probably would've noticed it anyway."

Gloria perked up. Tara had not shared anything personal with her since she was a teenager. "Are you gonna tell me or keep me in suspense?" she said eagerly.

"I'm pregnant," Tara said.

Gloria's facial expression changed from disbelief to shock and ended in excitement. "Oh, honey, that's wonderful." She took hold of Tara's hands and squeezed them. "I am so happy for you."

"It's not just my baby. It's Clay's too. I want you to be happy for both of us."

"I know you think I don't like him, but—"

Tara cut her off. "Don't talk like you've been misunderstood. Everyone knows how much you dislike him. It's not like you kept it a secret that you didn't want me with a white guy."

Gloria sighed. "I know what I said, but it's not what I meant. I just wanted you to have somebody who's going to take care of you, and I didn't feel he was the right choice for that."

"It's my choice," said Tara.

"I know. It is your choice. And as long as he's a good father to my grandchild, I can overlook all the other stuff."

"Nobody's perfect, but he'll be a great father, you'll see."

Tara's comment caused Gloria to reminisce about her father and how Tara reminded her so much of him. Gloria found herself staring at her.

"What?" said Tara.

"You look so much like your father," Gloria said dryly.

"You make it sound like a bad thing."

"I didn't mean it that way. He was a very handsome man. It was one of the reasons I fell in love with him."

"That's not how you said it. It must be hard for you that when you see me you see him."

Gloria paused, unsure how to answer without upsetting Tara. "It's not at all. I loved him. Period."

Tara shot her a curt look, her annoyance evident. "Then why did you shoot him?"

Gloria sighed. It was the last thing she wanted to talk about. "I've explained it to you many times, Tara. You know why," she answered.

"I know what you told the court, and it was enough to get you acquitted, but I deserve to know the whole truth. My father didn't just suddenly turn violent one day to the point where you had to shoot and kill him. There has to be more."

"I told you everything that happened that night," said Gloria, defiant. "I didn't shoot him for no reason, and I have no clue why he attacked me, but he did, honey, and I felt I had no choice. I wish I could go back and change it, but I can't. I'm sorry. Why do we always end up here?"

"I didn't bring my father into this conversation. You did."

Gloria wanted so badly to confess to Tara what really happened the night she shot and killed her husband. How when she tried to run away from him up the basement stairs, he grabbed her ankle and dragged her back down and viciously beat her. The kick she landed on his kneecap had given her enough time to run into their bedroom and lock the door before he came and kicked it off its hinges. When he stepped into the closet, Gloria was waiting and pointing the .22 caliber handgun she had taken out of the shoebox at his chest. She couldn't remember how many times she fired, only that she kept pulling the trigger until it wouldn't fire anymore, and even that was only half the story. If she told anyone about the blue particles she witnessed floating out from his nose and mouth and finally out the opened window, it would get her committed to a mental institution. Why would her daughter believe what at times she found hard to believe herself? It was best to leave things the way they were.

Lightning flashed and thunder suddenly rattled the building. The sound of raindrops tapping on the windows followed.

"I know you have to close," said Tara. "And I need to get back before it starts pouring." She grabbed her things, and Gloria escorted her to the exit.

"Thanks for stopping by, honey. I love you," said Gloria. She waited for Tara to repeat the same words to her. Instead, Tara flashed a perfunctory smile and walked out without even giving her a courtesy hug. Her feelings were hurt, but at least they were talking to each other again. She closed the blinds on the door, optimistic about the future of their relationship, and overwhelmed by all the things she needed to do in preparing the diner for the next day.

A customer was left seated at the table in the corner. His baseball cap obscured his face. Gloria wanted to tell him she'd soon be locking up and he had to leave, but she changed her mind and wiped down the booth where she and Tara had sat. She'd give him a minute or two longer before she made her final closing announcement.

Upon her walking back into the kitchen, he whistled a familiar melody: 'Close to You' by The Carpenters. She paused and listened intently to her husband's favorite song. Hearing it whistled by a stranger in the same way was surreal. It made the hairs on her arm stand up. Her husband had whistled the song before it happened…before he *turned* on her.

When Gloria walked back into the dining area, the customer had finally made his way to the exit, and was standing with his back turned, not moving, though still whistling the same melody. She recognized the stature and his clean-shaven head, hidden under the baseball cap. "Mr. Bruner?"

The whistling stopped. He pushed the door open to leave, but he didn't walk out. He pulled the door shut and turned the deadbolt latch, locking himself inside with her. Mr. Bruner turned and gazed at Gloria through eyes that were dilated and crystal blue, mimicking the eyes of a Siberian husky. "We have unfinished business, don't we, Gloria?" he said in a commanding voice.

She stepped back, aghast, as he walked toward her. Her heartbeat spiked. *This can't be happening all over again*, she thought. The tone of his voice was what she remembered the most when he turned, the same unnatural tone of voice that came out of her husband the night he attacked her. She smelled the foul, toxic odor of burning metals again as he continued to take small steps in her direction.

"What do you want, Mr. Bruner?" asked Gloria, trembling.

His lips were chafed and sweat dripped from under his cap down both sides of his face. His eyes never blinked. They stayed laser-focused on her.

"I want to share my secret with you," he answered.

"The manager is coming back. He'll be here any minute," she said, hoping it would get him to leave. She stumbled behind the bar area as she scanned for anything she could use as a weapon.

"I know when my wife is lying," he said.

"I'm not your wife, and you, whatever you are, are not my husband."

Mr. Bruner lunged forward with both hands aimed at her throat. Gloria grabbed the glass pitcher of water behind her and slammed it across Mr. Bruner's head. His baseball cap flew off to the other side of the room, and he dropped to the floor among shattered pieces of bloodstained glass. Gloria rushed to the door. She tried to open it. It wouldn't budge. Mr. Bruner had twisted the lock and jammed it shut. The back room off the kitchen was the only other exit, and she would have to step over Mr. Bruner to get there. Blood oozed from a laceration across the top of his skull as he lied unconscious.

With her eyes locked on him, Gloria stepped over Mr. Bruner's legs and hurried to the back door. She turned the doorknob and pushed. It wouldn't budge either. She looked above her head. Al had made good on his threat—he had placed a padlock on an emergency exit door, violating the safety codes. "Damn you, Al!" she yelled as she hammered at it with her fist. Out of nowhere, Mr. Bruner grabbed her from behind in a chokehold and dragged her back into the dining area as she kicked and struggled to get away. He managed to pin her down to the floor and straddled her.

"I never forgot about you, Gloria," he said. "I hoped you hadn't forgotten me."

Mr. Bruner opened his mouth wide. Gloria cringed in horror at the sight of blue dust particles floating out of him. She had escaped what she thought was a hallucination a long time ago, and now it had returned. The halo formation of blue particles hovered above her head, and before she could scream, the particles entered her nose and mouth. She went silent, and her eyes froze in a terrified gaze at the ceiling. Mr. Bruner fell over on the side of her, dead. Almost immediately, Gloria's eyes blinked. She sat up with her eyes wide open and pushed Mr. Bruner's legs off her and lifted herself from the floor. Gloria cleaned up the dining area so no trace of a struggle would be found. After she set the security alarm, she stepped out into the pouring rain, effortlessly carrying Mr. Bruner in her arms as if his 190-pound body only weighed twenty.

The rain splashed against her face, but she had no feeling at all in her arms, legs, and hands, nor did she have any control over their movement. She existed only as thoughts encased in a shell of a body that did as it pleased. Gloria hoisted Mr. Bruner's lifeless body into the backseat of her car. She sped off down the rain-slick road, traveling east through the high-elevation black mountain range.

"Where are you going?" asked Gloria.

The Ocran entity inside of her answered. "You will see soon enough," it said in a lower- pitched voice that sounded like Mr. Bruner's.

"They'll know you're not me. And you can't fool Sally."

"I won't have to. Your thoughts will reveal everything I need to know, but first we're going to bury Bruner. And when that's completed, we will visit your daughter."

"No, I won't let you hurt my daughter."

"If you keep speaking, I'll shut your voice off permanently."

"You're not going near her." Gloria slammed her face into the steering wheel, causing the car to swerve into the opposite lane.

The Ocran quickly regained control and continued driving uphill with a bloody nose. "That was a stupid thing to do, Gloria," it bristled. "You are only hurting yourself. I don't feel your pain." It wiped the blood from her nose. "You will not keep me from fulfilling my mission."

Gloria wavered in and out of consciousness. Each lapse of time returned a faint sensation of feeling back to her extremities. She timed the space between intervals, and when she regained consciousness for the third time, she stomped the accelerator and steered the car with her knee toward the guard railing. "I love you, Tara," she whispered. It was too late when the Ocran entity regained control of the steering wheel. The car skidded across slick, wet pavement, hit the guardrail, flipped, and catapulted over the cliff, plummeting eight hundred feet down into a ravine.

CHAPTER 24

DOUG SLOWED TO a crawl when he came upon the abandoned car on the side of the road. He had never seen the make and model in the neighborhood and thought it suspicious that someone would be lurking in an unassuming wooded area. He made a U-turn and pulled up behind the car. The license plate appeared to be government-issued, heightening his suspicion. He peered into the driver's window at a purse lying on the passenger-side seat.

Doug followed his instincts and wandered into the wooded area next to where the car was parked. He didn't see anyone or anything out of the ordinary except for a particular area on the ground where dried leaves were curiously stacked neatly in a pile. He kneeled next to it and brushed the leaves away. The cuff of a denim jacket was sticking up. He dug around it, removing dirt and placing it to the side. Doug stopped cold when he uncovered a portion of a hand still attached under the cuff. Someone had been buried alive in the vertical position where they stood. Unaffected by the gruesome discovery, he covered it over again with dirt and leaves and left the scene in a hurry.

Kaden was sitting on the stairs waiting for Doug when he returned. "It's her, isn't it?" said Doug. "The woman who approached you at the store. You eliminated her, didn't you?"

Kaden gritted his teeth. "Was she your friend? Why do you care?"

He waited for Doug to respond. He chose to remain silent.

"She came searching for me," said Kaden. "I had no choice but to rid myself of the problem. It was the appropriate solution because it was the only viable one, and that's all you need to know."

"She's a police officer. It's tagged on her license plate. Now more of them will come to investigate her disappearance," said Doug.

"And they will find nothing because you will dispose of her car after sundown." Kaden tossed Rosalind's car keys at Doug. He caught them and put them in his pocket.

"Park it in the garage and cover it with a tarp until it's clear to move it," said Kaden, "and as a warning for the future of our father and son relationship, it would be in your best interest not to question my decisions again."

○ ○ ○

Clay waited at Bailey's doorstep for her to answer. In all the years they had worked together at the Pineville mine, it was only the second time he had come to her home. The first time, he was uninvited, but this time it was a welcomed visit. Henson, Stanley, and Lars had all been there to support her and her twin girls in the aftermath of her husband's death, but Clay had been absent the entire time. Bailey wanted his support, but more than that she wanted answers. She hugged him and invited him in. Henson and Stanley were seated around her kitchen island. Oddly, Clay wore sunglasses on a day when a flurry of stratus clouds had quelled the sun. He looked Bailey in the eye. "You okay?"

"I'm all right," said Bailey.

"What about the twins?"

She sighed. "Well, they're handling it the best way they can. They don't talk about what happened, and I don't try to push it. It's hard. They loved their dad so much. I'm just hoping with time it'll get easier. I'm glad you're here, Clay."

"I can't stay long. I have to get back to Tara. You sure you're okay?"

"Has anyone told you the woman who we found in Pineville was calling your name, searching for you?"

"What woman?" asked Clay.

"The woman who killed my wife and her husband," said Henson.

"She asked for you, Clay," said Stanley. "We wanna know why."

Shocked by the revelation, Clay stuttered. "I don't–I don't know."

"What do you mean you don't know? You have to know something," said Henson.

"It could've been someone else who has the same name," Clay replied.

"Yeah, it could've been someone else, but you're the only Clay who works at that mine," said Stanley.

Bailey poured herself a cup of coffee. "Look, he said he doesn't know. Leave him alone."

Her hopes of learning the woman's identity evaporated at that moment. She had no reason not to believe him.

Henson popped the top off a can of beer. "We're not talkin' about a normal woman here. She did unexplainable things to me and Bailey. Who's to say that this crazy woman won't come for Stanley and you next Clay?"

"What do you mean by *unexplainable*?" Clay asked.

"Tell him, Bailey," said Stanley.

She didn't want to talk about it. Getting justice for Eric and Edie depended solely on finding the woman and learning her identity. Nothing else mattered.

"What unexplainable things did she do?" Clay asked again.

Bailey wouldn't answer, so Henson blurted it out. "She threw Bailey across the room without touching her. The wind or some kind of force came out of her mouth, and there was something in the palm of her hand that was glowing, just like it did when we first saw her at the mine," said Henson. "She didn't just kill Eric and Edie. She mutilated them." He handed Clay the beer. He didn't take it, just waved it away, still looking dumbfounded.

"I don't drink anymore," Clay replied.

Henson chuckled like he didn't believe him. "Since when?"

"Since I started loathing the taste of it. Why are you offering a drink to someone you've accused of being an alcoholic?" said Clay. Henson didn't answer him. Clay turned to Bailey. "This woman, what did she look like?"

"She had long black hair, my height, blue eyes. That's all I can remember," said Bailey. Clay denied he knew her, so why was his face suddenly etched with worry and his fingers wringing his hands? *He's hiding something.*

"She kept repeating your name, Clay. Are you sure?" asked Bailey.

"I told you, I don't know her. I really have to go," Clay said and abruptly walked out. He hurried to his car and peeled out of the driveway and down the road.

Bailey closed the door. "When the sheriff comes," she said to Henson and Stanley, "I'm gonna tell him everything."

Henson took in a big swallow of his beer. "I thought you did already."

"Not about her asking for Clay. I never told him that the woman was asking for him by name. I didn't think it meant anything, but now I'm not so sure."

Stanley excused himself and went to the bathroom. Henson walked up to Bailey, face-to-face, and put his hands on her shoulders. "We're gonna get through this."

Bailey gazed at the floor.

"Bailey, look at me," said Henson. He gently lifted her chin. "We're gonna find her. We're gonna get justice for what she did. I promise you."

Henson went in for a kiss, but before his lips met hers she pulled away from him. "I think you got the wrong impression," said Bailey.

Henson capitulated. "I don't know what I was thinking. I didn't mean to—"

"You should leave," she interrupted.

"I'm sorry. If you need anything, you know my number."

Bailey nodded, and Henson left her home just as the sheriff pulled up and parked in front.

Sheriff Jenkins was in his squad car on the phone, trying to reach Rosalind. After several attempts with no response, he called Nathan at the Appalachia DMV, asked him if he had seen Rosalind, and told him she was due back in Lynch hours ago. Nathan confirmed that she had picked up the registrations from him earlier in the day, but he had not seen or heard from her since. Concerned, Jenkins put on his best poker face, hopped out of his squad car, and approached Henson as he was leaving.

"What a surprise to see you here," said Jenkins facetiously.

"Bailey is a friend. I hope you're done wasting time going after me for this and you find that demented woman who actually did it. We have to stop her," said Henson.

"There's no *we*," said Sheriff Jenkins.

○   ○   ○

Clay sat in his car a few doors down from Gerald's auto shop, contemplating whether to go inside and confront him. Rebecca's straightforward explanation of his half-human, half-Ocran origin was only a small part of an unfathomable story. Gerald had to know more. If he was not his biological father, then he most likely knew who was. The story Bailey told him about the woman who had taken Eric and Edie's life left no doubt of a connection to Kaden and what was happening to him and his body. The revelation that this woman knew his name and was searching for him was worrisome, not that he feared for his own life, but rather that there was a killer out there who was somehow linked to him. Finding out what Gerald knew would be the first step in making sense of it all.

He entered the auto shop just as Gerald was preparing to close for the evening. Clay leaned up against the wall and waited for Gerald to notice him there. He glanced at Clay, grabbed a rag from the counter, and used it to wipe the oil from his hands. "Good to see that you made it back in one piece," said Gerald. "You had people worried you had gone missing."

"What about you? Were you worried?" asked Clay.

Gerald took a drink from his bottle of water. "I have enough to worry about."

195

He offered a bottle to Clay, who declined. "Why do you have sunglasses on when there's no sun out?" said Gerald.

"I caught an eye infection. It helps clear it up. Pops, I need to ask you something, and I want you to be honest with me."

"I've never had a problem being honest with you. That was always your issue. Anyway, where's Tara? I know how much she likes to insert herself into everything."

"It's just you and me. I need to ask you this, and I don't want you to take it the wrong way." Clay searched for a benign way to phrase it before deciding to just ask him outright. "Are you my biological father?"

Gerald's eyebrows furrowed in confusion. He tossed the rag on the counter. "Take off the sunglasses," he said.

Clay was reluctant to remove them. He didn't want the changing pigmentation of his eye to shift the focus. Surprisingly, Gerald had no visible reaction at all when he took them off.

"Now why would you ask me that?"

"I just need to know."

"What difference does it make? You've been my kid from the beginning. Biological means nothing to me."

"So, it's true. You're not my biological father?"

Gerald remained stoic and didn't answer.

"It's important that I find out where I came from," said Clay, insisting.

"So that's what this is all about. You wanna connect with him, and you think I'm the only one around who can help you do that. Well, I'm sorry, I can't. I've seen him only a couple of times, and that was a heck of a long time ago."

"When was the last time?"

"When your mother was having an affair with him. She and I had our problems, but I respected our vows. She made the decision not to, brought this man to our home, and introduced him as a guy she met at work who needed some repairs done on his car."

"Did he look—" Clay struggled to find the right word. "—normal?"

"What does that mean? *Normal?*"

"My biological father–did he look normal to you?"

"As normal as a no-good womanizer can look."

"That's not what I meant."

"He took advantage of a married woman who was vulnerable. Why do we need to rehash this, Clay?"

"You said my mother died from Lupus. I saw her death certificate. It wasn't Lupus. I wanna know the truth, Pops."

Gerald shot him a stern gaze. "So you really wanna know the truth?"

Clay nodded. "I do."

Gerald clenched his jaw. "Truth is your mother died giving birth to you. I guess Karma caught up to her," he said with a smirk that revealed how much her death gratified him. Clay's heart dropped. It was a cruel thing to say about the mother he longed to know. For a moment he wished he had never asked, but the truth needed to be revealed no matter how much it hurt to hear it. Clay suppressed a reaction so that Gerald wouldn't use it as a reason not to reveal more about her.

"I was so angry at her for what she had done to our marriage, and for birthing you into the middle of all of it, that I couldn't grieve," said Gerald. "Each day that would go by, I would wonder if this was the day this guy was gonna come back and claim custody over you and how I could fight it."

In a surge of boldness, Clay sputtered out what he had always wanted to say to his father since childhood. "You never wanted me. Why did you wanna fight it? You sent me away to live with Grandma and Grandpa Ellis while you kept Jimmy with you," said Clay.

Gerald looked away, irritated. "You were a newborn; Jimmy was four years old. What did you expect?"

"I didn't expect anything, I was a kid."

"I took you back when you turned eleven, didn't I?"

Yeah, that's when you started telling me that I would never amount to anything in this world. Proving you wrong was all that ever mattered to me."

Gerald shook his head–denying it. "I never said anything like that to you."

"Yeah, you did. It's okay, you were right, Pops. I didn't amount to anything."

"That's not how I remember it."

"Can I tell you what I remember? I remember how you never missed a game," said Clay. "Every practice that Jimmy had you were there sitting in the front row rooting for him—*the good one*, you called him. You never had a problem missing work to be there for him, but for me—"

Clay paused. He needed to maintain his composure in Gerald's presence and not let his emotions cause his voice to quaver. "—all I ever got from you was a *sorry I can't make it*," Clay continued. "I guess I wasn't important enough for you to miss a day of work, and I didn't matter enough for you to come sit on the bleachers and root for me."

Gerald crossed his arms and his tone sharpened. "Is that the story you tell to get people to feel sorry for you? I did the best I could with the cards your cheating mother dealt me. What else do you want from me?" he snarled.

The crassness in Gerald's voice tempered Clay's response. "I need to find my biological father," he mumbled.

"Why?" asked Gerald. "If he gave a crap about you, he would've been in your life."

Clay's chest tightened at Gerald's malicious comment. "I can't tell you why right now."

"You mean you won't."

Clay sighed. "Will you help me, Pops?"

Gerald gulped down the last bit of water left in the bottle and crushed it. "I hope you find what you're looking for, but I can't help you. I have no clue who or where he is, and honestly, I couldn't care less." Gerald tossed the crushed bottle in the trashcan and gazed at Clay's eye. "That looks a lot worse than an eye infection. If I were you, I'd get it checked."

CHAPTER 25

A COOL BREEZE surged through Miriam's home. She searched for the source and found her front door wide open and Rebecca standing outside, gazing into the morning sky. Miriam stepped outside and stood next to Rebecca without saying a word. She looked up but didn't see anything unusual.

"What's wrong?" asked Miriam.

"It's him," Rebecca said.

"What do you mean?"

Rebecca pointed up at the only cloud in the sky. The puffy cumulus cloud changed before their eyes from white to gray then from gray to a dark overcast, lingering above in an otherwise clear blue sky. "It's Kaden's work," said Rebecca.

"It's just a storm cloud. Who is Kaden?"

"He's a malevolent force that has to be stopped," said Rebecca. She rushed down the porch stairs.

"Rebecca, wait," Miriam said. Rebecca turned and faced her.

"Whatever it is you feel you have to do, be careful," said Miriam.

Rebecca walked back up the stairs and ignored what the Council had forbidden her to do: she hugged Miriam, fully embracing her. She had accessed her host's memories and learned that it was the kind of embrace she would give her mother as a way of thanking her for buying the gift that she always wanted or taking her to the amusement park with her friends. Rebecca had not embraced her in that way since before the abduction. If only for a moment, she wanted Miriam to experience her daughter's presence.

"Why did you do that?" asked Miriam.

"She would've wanted me to," said Rebecca.

"That means she's gone, isn't she? You can tell me the truth. My Becca is not alive, is she?"

Rebecca paused. She dreaded having to confirm what Miriam feared the most. The painful look in Miriam's eyes evoked a peculiar sadness that penetrated Rebecca's Ocran life form and overwhelmingly distressed her. Unable to avoid her question, Rebecca nodded. "Her consciousness has died, it's true. All that I have access to is her memories. I'm sorry," she said with a whimper.

Rebecca rushed down the stairs and around the back of the house, leaving Miriam standing alone and devastated on the porch. She wiped the tears from her eyes as she ran toward the open meadow where she had seen Kaden before. Thunder roared and quickly dissipated. A clear, sunny day was concealing Kaden's deviance. Rebecca reached the meadow, and, just as she had assumed, Kaden was standing below the storm cloud, making a circular motion with his hands in the air, maneuvering it. The cloud shifted into an oval shape, and the beginnings of a whirling vortex appeared. It swirled rapidly in a circular motion, forming a tight, spinning gyre of air. Flashes of lightning emanated around it every few seconds, and the cracking of thunder returned. As the vortex descended into a deadly tornado, it created wind currents that flung rain droplets across her face.

Inside the barn, the Wheel spun erratically on its own, spurting out sand as Kaden accessed the power of the Council through it. Rebecca feared he planned to eliminate someone, and while he still had his hands in the air, she ran up to him from behind and shoved him to the ground. The vortex disappeared, and the cloud stopped circling. It was frightening enough that he had gained the ability to extract any one of them from their human host, but now he had somehow convinced the Council to empower him with the ability to form storm cycles.

Kaden picked himself off the ground. "What did you do that for?" He scowled and clenched his fists.

"You were gonna use that to hurt people."

"I wouldn't have to if you hadn't helped him. It's your fault he's still alive," said Kaden, as he brushed the dirt off his kneecaps.

"He's just a human. He can't harm us."

"Clayton Krutcher is not human. He's an abomination, the weakest of our kind merged with the most flawed of theirs. He's neither human nor Ocran, but he is a threat to the purity of our life form. What's so difficult to understand about that?"

"I *do* understand. It doesn't mean I have to agree with you. We know it won't stop with Clayton. You'll find a way to eliminate them all," said Rebecca.

"You wanna believe that you're superior, but you're no different than the rest of us. Whose human form have you stolen, Rebecca? And what innocent eight-year-old girl did you have to eliminate to get it?" When she didn't respond, Kaden sneered. "I'll eliminate whoever I wish."

"I can't let you do that," said Rebecca.

"The Council chose me to lead. I'm stronger than you now, much stronger," he said, backing away from her. The tattoo on his palm glowed. "I had a conversation with your father…well, the one you pretend is your father. It was sort of amusing that the poor man knew nothing about what or who you really are."

Rebecca's eyes widened, and she covered her mouth with her hand. "Did you hurt him?"

"Of course not. I didn't want to, but he has been changed."

Rebecca masked her devastation. She had already caused Miriam an overwhelming amount of pain and despair by taking over her daughter's body, and now her husband had been taken over by an Ocran undoubtedly controlled and manipulated by Kaden. She had failed to protect her parents, something she had promised herself she would do from the beginning.

"Oh, I'm sorry," said Kaden. "Did you care for him too? He told me you were afraid of snakes. I hope not, because there's one behind you."

A hissing sound caught her attention. When she turned around to look, a black six-foot-long cottonmouth snake was slithering toward her. The neck pivoted into an S-shaped ready-to-strike position. It threw its head back and gaped at her. Razor-sharp fangs protruded from the startling white lining of its mouth, and its tail vibrated. Swiftly, she conquered her fear, assuming Kaden had summoned a reptile to carry out what he didn't want to do himself.

Rebecca slowly backed away. She glanced over her shoulder and froze. Another cottonmouth was slithering toward her. Both snakes gaped at her while emitting a musky odor that was so pungent it penetrated her nasal cavity. Kaden watched gleefully.

Both snakes lunged at Rebecca's bare leg. One missed its mark, but the other managed to lock its jaw into her calf below her pleated skirt. She fell to the ground, moaning from the excruciating pain. The snake recoiled as blood droplets surfaced from her wound. Both snakes jerked their heads back in sync, pivoting to strike her again. The tattoo appeared on the palm of Rebecca's hand and produced a faint glow. She clenched her fingers over it while closing her eyes and summoning help. In a matter of seconds, a feral cat trotted out from the vegetation, grabbed the head of one of the snakes in its jaws, shook it, then slammed it against the ground. It lied there motionless.

The second snake lunged at the cat but was unable to make contact because of its keen agility. The cat circled the snake, moving counter to its striking range. It swatted it with its paw, and when the cottonmouth struck back, the cat ducked and leapt away just in time to avoid the bite. It finally grabbed the snake's tail, twirled it around in its mouth, and dragged it away into the vegetation. Rebecca's leg swelled as the venom surged through her body, weakening her to the point of paralysis. She placed her palm over the bite and pressed down on it. When she looked again, it hadn't changed. *Something is wrong. Why is it still there?* She pressed down on it again, and the hissing sound returned. The snake had regained consciousness and slithered toward her head.

Rebecca closed her eyes and summoned what was left lurking in the meadow. Seconds later, she opened her eyes upon a raccoon scurrying down the tree. It picked up a small rock, and as the snake gaped inches away from her face, slammed it down on the snake's head, flattening it. After the raccoon was satisfied the snake was dead, it climbed back up the tree and hid between the branches.

"Interesting that in spite of your betrayal of your own kind, the Council still empowers you to summon," said Kaden. He resumed forming and maneuvering the storm cloud, making a circular motion with his hands above his head. Thunder roared, and the vortex reappeared and began its descent. It swirled rapidly in circles, expanding and creating surging winds. "Your healing ability is weakening, isn't it?" said Kaden. "Or maybe there's no healing ability left in you at all."

To prove to him wrong, Rebecca forced herself to stand, fighting her paralysis with every bit of healing force she had left. The winds from the vortex pushed her back, preventing her from reaching him. "It's shameful and a waste that you're not on my side," said Kaden. He opened his mouth wide and pointed it up toward the storm cloud. Winds gushed out from his mouth, forming a funnel that linked the descending vortex. The funnel encapsulated Kaden as it reached the ground and formed the tornado. "It's your choice to keep fighting me, but you will lose," he said.

The funnel swept Kaden a hundred feet in the air, and he disappeared into the eye of the storm. Turbulent winds pushed then pulled Rebecca as she used every bit of her innate command of the gravitational force to keep herself from being swept up along with him. Kaden reappeared from above and descended the vortex, landing steady on his feet. The powerful wind currents had no effect at all on his ability to walk in and around it. He took a deep breath, filled his cheeks with air, and exhaled it at the tornado, causing it to move northwest in the direction of Lynch.

CHAPTER 26

CLAY STARED AT his eye in the bathroom mirror. The blue pigmentation in the iris had become so translucent that it now had a subtle glow. Though it appeared abnormal, it didn't *feel* abnormal. Compared to his normal-looking eye, his vision in the translucent one appeared sharper and clearer. He flinched when a sharp pain migrated from his shoulder to his arm. Clay rolled up his sleeve. Blood surged through his veins like hot liquid flowing into his arm from an IV. The stinging sensation spread from his arm to his fingertips, numbing them.

Hundreds of tiny blue veins resembling plant roots were clearly visible through his pale skin, and his vertebrae slightly protruded from his back. *What's happening to my body? What am I?* Tara pulled on the bathroom doorknob. It wouldn't turn. "So you're locking the door now?" she said from the other side.

Clay rolled down his sleeve in a hurry. "I'll be out in a second," he said.

It would be so much easier to drive down to the Black Mountain Sports bar and chug some brews and avoid her questions, but the taste of alcohol had become bitter and nauseating for him. Besides, the last promise he made to Tara meant something—no more secrets. He had to tell her, and if necessary, show her. No matter how unbelievable or crazy or nonsensical it would make him sound. At least it would be the truth, whether it was believable or not to anybody else. He needed to lay everything on the table for her, even the bizarre changes to his body, and she would decide whether she wanted to accept what he had become, or what he was becoming.

When Clay opened the bathroom door, Tara was standing there waiting for him. The lines on her forehead creased at the sight of his translucent eye. "Clay, it's getting worse. We have to go and get it checked by a doctor." She cradled his face with her hands. "Your vision isn't cloudy? Do you feel any pain?"

He sighed and took hold of her hands. "I can see just fine, and I don't feel any pain in my eye," said Clay. "I didn't tell you everything that happened to me on the hunting trip and in the car accident because I was afraid you would think that I was mentally ill or outta my mind. Even that would be better than the truth."

Clay revealed everything that had happened to him in Oceola, from his encounters with Kaden, Rebecca, and Octavius to what he had seen happen with the Wheel and the diamonds that he thought would end their problems. He didn't leave out any details. He told her everything he could remember. Tara didn't say a word, just listened. When he finished, she gave him a *you-must-be-kidding* look. Instead of trying to convince her that everything he told her was the truth, he took off his shirt. The blue veins protruding from his pale skin and the vertebrae protruding from his back were enough to make her gasp.

"Oh my God, Clay," she said as she leaned away from him.

An aggressive knock at their door startled them both. Clay put on his shirt and buttoned it as he headed to the door. When he opened it, Sheriff Jenkins was there with a somber look. "You must be Clay Krutcher?"

"Yeah, what's this about?" said Clay.

"Glad to see you made it back in one piece. Your wife was worried sick about you."

"We're fine. We don't need the cops."

"I'm not a cop. I'm the sheriff. I need to talk to your wife. Is Tara here?"

Clay nodded.

"You mind if I come in? It's important."

When Sheriff Jenkins entered, Tara stood up from the couch. "No, Miss Krutcher, you should take a seat," said the sheriff.

Tara returned to the couch. "What's wrong?"

"It's about Gloria, your mother."

"What happened? Is she in trouble?"

"Gloria was in a car accident. She's deceased, Miss Krutcher."

"What? No."

"It was raining pretty hard," said Sheriff Jenkins. "We found skidmarks on the road where her car went over an embankment. I'm so sorry."

Tara sighed. Clay sat down next to her and embraced her. "I just saw her at the diner two days ago. Are you sure it's her?" said Tara.

"I'm afraid so, ma'am. I've known Gloria for twenty-three years. I'm very sorry."

Silence hung heavy in the air as the news of her mother's death sunk in. Tara's eyes remained void of tears, and her facial expression didn't change. What kind of daughter remained unshattered by the death of her own mother? Tara sensed the sheriff's unspoken judgment of her and accepted it. It was impossible that he could know the gnawing guilt that enveloped her. For years, she had lived a life estranged from Gloria, distancing herself from the mother who had broken their family by killing the one who adored her the most. Her detachment from her mother was the only tool she had to punish her for what she had done. Death had come to Gloria just as Tara had resolved to forgive her in favor of her child's future relationship with his grandmother.

Sheriff Jenkins broke the silence. "I hope you don't mind me asking about your mother's companions. It's part of the process of our investigation.

"I don't know about any companions."

"Do you know if she was dating or had a boyfriend?" said the sheriff.

"We haven't been close for a long time, so she never shared that with me. Why do you ask?"

"There was a man in the car with her who was also found deceased.

His name was Harold Bruner. We're trying to determine the basis of their relationship. Did Gloria ever mention that name?"

Tara shrugged. "No," she said, and then she recalled her mother calling a man by that name at the diner. "Wait a minute. I do remember a man by that name, but he wasn't a boyfriend. He was just one of her regulars."

"All right," said the sheriff. "I appreciate your time."

After giving his condolences again, Sheriff Jenkins returned to his squad car and called Ansley at the station. He inquired if Rosalind had shown up or at least called to say she was okay. Ansley informed him that no one had heard from Rosalind, but the GPS tracker on her unmarked squad car pinged from a tower in Appalachia. Sheriff Jenkins considered Rosalind a formidable woman, more than capable of taking care of herself. There had never been an instance where he worried about her safety—until now. Something was off. He contacted the Appalachia police department and requested that an officer track Rosalind's vehicle GPS coordinates.

Back inside their trailer, Tara went into the bedroom and grabbed her purse and jacket. Clay followed her. "Where you goin'?"

"I'm gonna work at the salon."

"Honey, it can wait. We need to talk about this."

"I don't wanna talk about it. I need to breathe, okay?" She opened the door and stepped out.

"Tara, wait. What about what I showed you?"

She turned to him. "I don't know what you want me to say? I don't even know what you are, Clay. What have I married?"

His head dropped. "I don't know what I am."

Tara glimpsed the vulnerability in his voice, and it frightened her. It was all too much to absorb. She walked out the door, leaving him standing there alone. A gust of wind pushed her forward, and she dropped her keys on the ground. She picked them up and gazed at the sky. It was a beautiful sunny day except for a storm cloud forming strangely above their trailer park. It rotated and the beginnings of a vertical vortex descended from it. The wind speed increased, and the storm cloud began to spin faster and faster.

She stood there perplexed as the wind shook the trees and rattled the windows of the other trailer homes. A flash of lightning and the thunderclap that followed weren't enough to convince her to go back inside. *It can't be a real storm. The sun is still shining.* Tara pulled a folded piece of paper from under the windshield wiper of her car and unfolded Jeremy's missing persons flyer. Clay grabbed Tara by the arm and pulled her back inside. The moment he shut the door, a lightning bolt shot out from the sky and struck a tree, causing it to fall. It slammed to the ground on the side of their house with a loud boom.

"Get down!" Clay yelled. She didn't move fast enough, so he shoved her down to the floor and covered her with his body. A roaring gust of wind blew out all the windows. Tara shuddered at the broken glass falling all around them. They remained motionless on the floor for a few seconds until the noises stopped and the wind calmed. Clay helped Tara to her feet. "You okay?" he asked.

"Yeah. What was that?"

"It felt like a tornado," said Clay. He stepped outside the door. Debris was scattered across their and their neighbors' lots. A giant oak tree had been forcefully uprooted and was tossed in front of their trailer. If it had fallen inches to the right, they would have been instantly crushed. The enormous branches reached all the way to Tara's car, blocking it in. Clay went over to the base of the tree, put both his palms on the trunk, and to her astonishment pushed it away from her car. He walked calmly back into the house. "I'll clean up the glass and cover the windows until we can get them replaced," he said, deadpan.

Tara, still in shock over seeing him lift and move a giant tree, wasn't listening. "How did you do that?"

"The tree was blocking your car. I don't want anything to stop you from leaving, if that's what you really wanna do," said Clay.

"I didn't ask you why. I asked you how, Clay," said Tara. "That tree had to weigh tons. How were you able to push it away so easily?"

"I don't know."

Tara glared at him, suspicious that he kept avoiding answering her question. No matter how long it took, she would get an answer out of him. After a long pause, Clay explained. "Look, I don't know what's happening to me. I don't have the answers," he said. "I'm trying to figure this thing out and it's scaring me, Tara." He spoke as if he were all alone in the world, surrendering to the inevitability that she would leave him, repulsed by what she had seen on his body. It was far from the truth. Tara made a commitment from the beginning to be faithfully in his corner and vowed to stay beside him no matter what. The guilt she carried was that she had failed to make him feel secure in her commitment.

Tara walked up to Clay and hugged him. They stood in the middle of their disheveled trailer and held each other.

"I love you," she whispered.

"I love you too."

"I know we're gonna get through this together," said Tara, "but I can't help being afraid of what this is doing to you." She handed him the flyer. "I found this under the windshield wiper of my car."

Clay stared at Jeremy's picture, baffled. "It's him."

"What do you mean it's *him*?"

"It's the kid I told you about. The one who I saw in Appalachia."

"Clay, it can't be. It says he's been missing for months."

CHAPTER 27

JEB CHECKED THE clock on the wall for the eighth time. For every minute that ticked by, beads of sweat gathered on his forehead, and he would nervously wipe them away. While the other students had their books open and were reading the assignment, Jeb sat at his desk with his book closed, doodling on a piece of paper. The last class was ending soon, and it was hard not to think about worst-case scenarios.

Once all the students had cleared the classroom before leaving, Jeb peered around the corner of the congested school hallway and spotted Travis standing at Charlie's locker, waiting for Charlie to grab his jacket and lock up. It didn't surprise him that Travis was hovering around his brother like an unrelenting housefly. It had been that way ever since Charlie left their father's house and had transformed into someone he didn't know. From that day forward, Charlie and Travis were always together. Their unnatural bond frightened Jeb as much as it made him `jealous. *If Travis can make fish jump out of the water and things float up in the air, who knows what other crazy weird things he can do?* The link between Travis and Charlie needed to be severed, and since Jeb couldn't overpower Travis enough to separate him from his brother, his only choice was to cut off his brother from Travis.

First, he had to wait for the most essential component of his plan, a day of rain. When the early rain showers came that morning, the clock started ticking. If he didn't follow through with it now, he would never again get the opportunity or the courage to do it.

While Charlie and Travis hovered talking at the lockers, Jeb hurried out the school's rear exit door, trying not to be seen. He ran until he reached a vacant house a few blocks away. It was the corner where Travis would break off from Charlie to go to his house and Charlie would continue through the field in the opposite direction to his. Jeb patiently waited in the rain at the back of the house, peeking out intermittently for a sighting of Travis and his brother strolling down the sidewalk. Minutes later, he spotted them walking together in mid-conversation. Jeb waited until Travis broke away from Charlie and went in the direction of his home. When he was completely out of sight, Jeb caught up with Charlie and walked beside him through the field.

"I know you were following me," said Charlie. "It's creepy."

Jeb scoffed at the irony. "What's creepy is how you're pretending to be my brother when you're not really him."

Charlie fretted. "If I'm not your brother, then who am I?"

"I dunno what you are, but I want my brother back the way he was."

"Is that why you attacked Travis with a bat? Because you didn't think it was him? You know how crazy that sounds?"

Jeb paused. He didn't plan on Charlie being told of his encounter with Travis. Anything that could cause Charlie to become suspicious of him might thwart his plan.

"I never attacked him," said Jeb. "He made the bat float away out of my hand, and he attacked me."

Charlie narrowed his eyes at him. "No one will believe you, Jeb-the-stalker."

"I don't care. You can't accuse me of stalking you when we live in the same house, moron. This is the quickest way home."

"Fair enough," said Charlie dryly.

"I wanted to give you this before you got wet," said Jeb. He pulled out a plastic grocery bag and handed it to Charlie.

"What's this for?" said Charlie.

"Don't you remember?"

Charlie seemed flustered for a moment, then his eyes widened as if he just had a eureka moment. "Oh yeah, so I don't get my hair wet."

"Well, it's already wet, but at least it won't get worse," said Jeb.

Charlie covered his head with the bag, and Jeb pulled another from his pocket and placed it around his. They walked through the field, and as planned he fell behind and let Charlie walk in front of him. Jeb struggled to remember everything Rebecca told him. *What if she's wrong? What if it all goes bad and he doesn't make it?* The courage he had stored up was fading fast; if he didn't go for it now, it would never happen.

Behind Charlie's back, Jeb removed a surgical mask from his pocket and put it over his nose and mouth. Charlie instinctively stopped in his tracks. "You said I looked like an idiot with this on my head, didn't you?" said Charlie, still with his back turned. "So why would you put something on your head that you think is stupid?"

Jeb stood behind him, frozen. The rain stopped, and he could feel his own heart beating through his jacket. There was no turning back. Jeb rushed Charlie, yanked the bag down over his face, and tackled him to the ground. Charlie squirmed and kicked wildly. "What're you doing?" he screamed out. Jeb ignored it. With his weight pushing down on Charlie's back, he tightened the bag around his brother's neck, intending to suffocate him.

"Stop it! I can't breathe," Charlie shouted, his cries muffled by the bag.

"Just let it happen, Charlie," said Jeb, teary-eyed.

Charlie fought back ferociously in an adrenaline-fueled struggle for his life, gasping for air for what seemed like forever. It didn't play out at all like it did in the movies, where it took only seconds for someone to suffocate. Jeb wanted so badly to let go of the bag and to let his brother breathe, but he kept playing in his head what he had promised his mother, that he would take care of his little brother. Pushing him to the point of death was the only answer, and according to Rebecca the only way to rid him of the Ocran entity that had taken over his mind and body. The chance that he could end up killing him was terrifying, but as long as the Ocran entity remained in Charlie he would always be dead.

Finally, Charlie stopped struggling, and his body went limp. Jeb snatched the bag off Charlie's head and turned him over. Blue-tinted dust particles floated out from Charlie's nostrils. Jeb's eyes bulged. The particles floated upward and hovered in a continuous halo formation, inches from his face. Jeb stood still as he was being studied by it, too frightened to move. Now it made sense why Rebecca stressed that he cover his face. Once extracted, the particles would immediately search for a way inside another living body, and since he was the closest, he would become its next target. He prayed his face mask was enough to keep it from entering him.

The wind began to whirl, and the particles dispersed until nothing was there. Jeb gasped at Charlie's pasty face. His cheeks and lips were purple.

"No, no, no, you're not dead, you're not dead," he muttered in a feeble effort to convince himself. He put one hand on top of the other and pressed down on Charlie's chest with short compressions. "One, two, three, four," he shouted out for each compression, and then he repeated it again as he had learned in his physical ed class. "One, two, three, four, come on, Charlie." Jeb checked for a heartbeat. He couldn't feel one, so he did more chest compressions but at a faster pace.

He put his ear to Charlie's chest. A heartbeat. The purple faded from Charlie's cheeks. "Charlie?" said Jeb. Charlie opened his eyes and coughed violently. Relieved that he was alive, Jeb wiped the tears from his face so that his brother wouldn't know that he had been crying. *Who wants a crybaby as an older brother?*

Jeb helped Charlie sit up, and he cleared his throat. "Why am I on the ground? And why do you have a mask on?" asked Charlie.

Jeb completely forgot he still had it on. "Oh, I was just playin' around," he said.

He took it off and tossed it. Jeb contained his excitement that his plan had worked or at least appeared to have.

Charlie stood up. His clothes were covered in mud. "How did I end up on the ground?"

"Uh, you tripped on something," said Jeb. "You might have landed on your head. Who knows? Let's go home."

Maybe the extraction worked. Jeb wasn't one-hundred-percent sure if Charlie was back to himself or if the entity was still inside of him.

"What's the last thing you remember?" said Jeb.

Charlie scratched his head. "I remember getting into Dad's car and going somewhere."

"Where did you go?"

"I can't remember," said Charlie as he bit his fingernails. Jeb exhaled, relieved. Charlie's nervous twitch was uniquely him.

CHAPTER 28

OFFICER HOLT RECEIVED the order to pursue the GPS tracker on Rosalind's vehicle. After driving for thirty minutes around the area designated by the coordinates, the green locater arrow on his onboard computer flashed yellow. He had reached the vicinity of the signal, and the area looked strangely familiar. He'd been in the neighborhood before but couldn't remember when or why. It wasn't until he drove past a ranch house with a chicken coop in the back that it all came flooding back to him. Doug and Pamela Lofton lived in the neighborhood with the kid he had investigated. It didn't make sense that Rosalind would be in a rural part of town so far out of the way from the Appalachia courthouse. Still, his computer confirmed she was, or at least her vehicle was somewhere in the area.

On a hunch, he drove directly to the block where the Loftons lived, and instantly the arrow on his onboard computer flashed green, signaling he was within a hundred and thirty yards away from the source. The GPS locator on his onboard computer beeped three times and shut down. He parked in front of their home and the signal disappeared. After multiple failed attempts to get it back, he gave up.

This doesn't make sense. Officer Holt exited his patrol car, walked up to the Loftons' attached garage, and peered through a corner window. Parked next to a red Honda was another vehicle covered by a tarp.

Rosalind drove a black Jeep Cherokee, and by its shape and size it looked possible one could be underneath. It was a ridiculous notion that her vehicle could be in the Loftons' garage and most likely a malfunction of his onboard computer system, but it had to be checked out nonetheless. While Holt peered through the garage window, Doug stepped out his front door and approached him.

"Excuse me. Can I help you?" asked Doug.

When Officer Holt turned and faced him, Doug's countenance sank. "Officer Holt? What are you doing here?"

"Do you know a woman named Rosalind Stallworth? She's a detective with the Lynch, Kentucky police department.

"No, I don't," said Doug. "You thought you might find her in my garage?"

Officer Holt took note of his flippant remark. "Both cars in there belong to you?

"Yeah, why?" said Doug.

"You mind if I take a look at what's under the tarp?"

"What's in my garage is none of your business."

"Actually it is. This woman and her black Jeep Cherokee are missing."

"And what does that have to do with me?"

Officer Holt's expression hardened. "You sure you don't know her?"

"I answered your question, now I want you to get off my property. You have no reason to be here except to harass me and my family," said Doug.

The cordial, friendly, and hyper-hospitable Doug Lofton he had encountered at his first visit to their home had vanished. This new Doug seemed irrationally defensive, inhospitable, and easily angered. Officer Holt couldn't discern which personality was the façade because both were capable of lying to him.

Kaden walked out of the house and stood next to Doug. Officer Holt assumed Doug would react as any other normal adult and order his child back inside. He didn't. Contrarily, he appeared comfortable with Kaden standing there next to him.

Officer Holt ignored Kaden's snarky glance and focused on Doug.

"I got a missing woman's GPS tracker emitting from this vicinity, a woman you say you don't know. I'm gonna need you to open the garage."

"I don't know who you're talking about," said Doug, "and I'm not opening anything unless you have a warrant. Do you have a search warrant, Officer?"

"If that's the way you wanna do it, I'm happy to get one, and you can believe it'll give me the authority to search more than just your garage."

Convinced he meant business, Doug went over to the garage keypad and typed in the numerical code. The garage door panel slowly rose with a loud mechanical hum until it reached the top and cut off. Officer Holt was even more convinced he had his black Cherokee there under the tarp. He tensed and instinctively repositioned his hand over to the handle of his revolver. Heaven forbid he would have to use it if Doug made a false move.

"Can you please remove the tarp?" said Officer Holt. Doug instantly had a troubled gaze. His fidgeting hand gestures betrayed his unease in the moment. He shot Kaden a quick glance. Kaden nodded as if he was giving Doug permission to uncover it. Doug grabbed the corner of the tarp and lifted it back onto the hood in one swift move. To Officer Holt's surprise, beneath it was a Jeep Cherokee, but the color was white. It couldn't be Rosalind's car.

Doug relaxed and reclaimed his confidence. "Have you seen enough, Officer?"

Officer Holt nodded. His tracker had malfunctioned, he assumed, and it had directed him to the wrong house. Without a functioning GPS signal, there was nowhere else in the area he could check.

"Goodbye, Mister Officer," said Kaden.

Officer Holt left the scene no less suspicious of Doug Lofton. His relationship with his son wasn't natural or normal. They were hiding something—both of them. He may have been wrong about Rosalind's vehicle being stowed in the garage, but one mishap in judgment couldn't minimize what he had successfully relied on most of his life. His gut instincts had always steered him in the right direction.

When Holt drove away from the Loftons' house, the glow from the tattoo on Kaden's palm faded away. He had kept it hidden behind his back as he created the illusion in Holt's mind that the black Jeep beneath the tarp was white.

CHAPTER 29

CLAY PARKED IN front of Lily's home just as she gathered the last bit of hedge trimmings into a garbage bag. She halted her yard work when he got out of the car and approached her. Though sunglasses were necessary to hide his eyes, they made him look more intimidating. Lily tipped her sunhat, squinting to see if she recognized him. The concerned look on her face was expected and justifiable. She didn't know him. His unexpected appearance at her home might be enough to discourage her from telling him what he needed to know. He smiled at her, attempting to make his expression as friendly as possible.

"Can I help you?" she asked.

"I'm looking for Lily Astin," said Clay.

"What for?"

He unfolded Jeremy's missing persons flyer and showed it to her. "Is this your son?"

"Yeah, what's going on?"

"Ma'am, I don't know how to tell you this, but I've seen him."

Clay expected her to have some kind of reaction, but neither her expression nor her demeanor changed.

"What do you mean you've seen him?"

"I mean I've seen him in person. I've talked to him. He was fine."

"And where did this happen?" asked Lily, dubious.

"Just over the state line in Virginia."

It perplexed him that she still had no visible reaction to his sighting of her son.

"Come inside," said Lily, "before you get sunburned."

Clay followed her inside into a quaint living room decorated with furnishings from a time long ago. Someone much older than Lily most likely lived there as well. Clay found himself staring at the framed family pictures scattered about. Most of them featured Jeremy.

"Please, have a seat. I'll be right back. I need to check on my mother," said Lily.

She disappeared into a room and returned minutes later. "I'm sorry, I didn't get your name," she said.

"I'm Clay. Clayton Krutcher."

"You got somethin' to hide, Clay?"

"I don't understand. What do you mean?"

"There's no sun in this house, and I prefer to look a person in the eye when I'm talking to them."

Clay had no choice but to take off his sunglasses. She glanced at his eyes and smiled.

"Can I get you something to drink? Water? Soda? I might have some iced tea left if you prefer that," said Lily, as if she didn't notice anything abnormal about his eye.

"No, thank you, ma'am. I'm okay."

Lily took a seat on the couch next to a stuffed animal panda. "My address was not on the flyer. I'm a little concerned about how you found me."

"Ma'am, you can find just about anything on the Internet if you put the time in to look."

"I know you're being respectful, but you don't have to call me ma'am. It makes me feel old. Just call me Lily."

"Yes, ma'am...I mean Lily, sorry. I wasn't trying to invade your privacy. I thought this was urgent—something you should know. A phone call didn't seem good enough."

"So you saw my Jeremy?" she said warily.

"Yeah, I did. More than once."

"Did you go to the police?"

"Uh, no, I didn't. Jeremy told me his name was Kaden. I didn't think anything was wrong until I saw the flyer."

"And where exactly did you see him?"

"I was on a hunting trip, and he was there by himself in a town near Appalachia."

"By any chance you remember the color of his eyes?"

"Um, yeah, I remember they were really, really blue."

She sighed. "It's not him. My Jeremy has brown eyes. I have a friend who's a detective. She saw the same little boy out there in Appalachia. It must be my son's doppelgänger, but I appreciate you taking the time to come here and tell me what you saw."

Clay picked up on Lily's cue that it was time for him to leave and stood up. "So you don't wanna see him? Maybe go there and find out for sure?"

She paused, pensive. "Do you have any children, Clay?"

"No, but my wife is pregnant with our first kid."

"Congratulations," she said, smiling. "Children are the most precious gift God has given us. I never felt there was meaning or purpose to my life until Jeremy came along. His battle with autism challenged me to be a better mother, but when it mattered the most, I failed him because I couldn't protect him from this cruel world."

Tears welled up in her eyes. "Nothing hurts like the pain of losing your child, and I hope and pray you never have to experience it. It's already unbearable to face the truth that someone—some stranger took my child from me, but to go through it all over again based on a whim that a boy who looked like my son might actually be him would break me. I would give my life for my Jeremy if I knew it would bring him back alive, but it's not possible."

Lily regained her composure and stiffened. "My son does not have blue eyes. I don't need to go there and see him," she said. "I truly appreciate you giving me the information, Clay. Really, I do."

When she stood, she accidentally knocked the stuffed animal onto the floor. It played a nursery rhyme sang in a child-like voice: "*Twinkle, twinkle, little star, how I wonder what you are. Up above the world so high, like a diamond in the sky. Twinkle, twinkle, little star, how I wonder what you are.*"

Clay cringed at the familiar melody while Lily beamed at hearing it. "It's Jeremy's favorite," she said. "—his panda friend. Having a best friend was very important to him."

Lily sat the stuffed animal panda back on the couch. After she thanked Clay again for coming, he left her home haunted by the nursery rhyme and the sound of Kaden's singing voice in his head. Jeremy and Kaden were the same. He was convinced that the Ocran entity of Kaden had taken over an innocent kid, robbing him of his childhood and his future from the mother who so deeply loved him. It was wrong and unfair, and he needed to be stopped.

CHAPTER 30

MO WALKED DOWNSTAIRS, curious to hear the protracted conversation his father was having with the sheriff at their front door. Sheriff Jenkins questioned him about Mr. Bruner, specifically if he had conversed with him recently and if he mentioned having trouble with anyone. When his father answered no to the sheriff's question about witnessing any unusual behavior from Mr. Bruner, Mo raised his hand and interrupted them.

"I did," said Mo, standing behind his father. "I witnessed some unusual, freakish behavior by that dude."

His father turned and gazed back at him, surprised and irritated by his sudden outburst. "He's kidding, Sheriff," his father said with a faux grin.

"No, I'm not. I saw Mr. Bruner with my own eyes doing weird things," said Mo.

"Really? What kinds of weird things?" asked Sheriff Jenkins.

"He did something to his wife and—"

Before he could complete the sentence, his father stepped in front of the sheriff to block his view of Mo. "He's exaggerating," said his father. "You know how teenagers like to make something out of nothing."

"Stop speaking for me. I'm not exaggerating," Mo said.

"Mohammed, go to your room now," said his father as he pointed his finger at him. "I mean it, right now!"

The anger in his father's eyes was threatening enough to get Mo to follow his orders. He trudged upstairs to his bedroom and flopped across the bed. He dialed Connor's number on his cell phone. His father entered and closed the door. "Put the phone down," he said.

Mo didn't want his father to take his phone away, so he complied.

"Now what was that all about?" asked his father, seething.

Mo hopped out of bed and stood face-to-face, ready for a challenge. "All the things I told you about Mr. Bruner, you said you believed me. You saw the video. So why are you trying to make me look like a liar, like I'm crazy or somethin'?"

"Harold Bruner is dead, Mohammed. Stop behaving like a spoiled brat and give the man a break, for godsakes!"

Mo gazed at his father, bewildered. "What's wrong with you?"

His father sighed. "Look, I'm sorry for yelling at you. I don't think you're crazy, nor am I trying to make you look like a liar. Why would I do that, Mohammed? I love you. You're my son."

What Mo's father said was not just awkward—it was cringe-worthy. He knew everything about his father, yet he didn't know anything about the man standing in front of him. "My father would never tell me that he loved me," said Mo. "He would tell my mom sometimes, and she would tell me, but my father would never say that to my face, and he never calls me Mohammed either. I wasn't sure at first, but I am now. You have his face, his body, and his voice, but you're not him. Just like Mrs. Bruner is not Mrs. Bruner anymore."

"Do you know how ridiculous it would sound if you told someone that?"

Mo didn't answer him. His father's question confirmed he was right—the man standing in front of him was not his *real* father.

"It doesn't matter who I am, Mohammed," said his father. "We can mutually help each other as long as you remain discreet about my presence here."

"I don't need your help. I want my father back the way he was."

"No, you don't. You wouldn't want him back in the state he was in."

"Why wouldn't I?"

"I see your mother chose not to tell you."

"Tell me what?"

"Your father had stage-four cancer. He was dying. That's why he left to go to Pakistan. Your parents told you he was going there to visit his family, but he didn't go to Pakistan at all. He went to Switzerland for an experimental treatment for his cancer. He was there for months because he needed to recuperate from the surgeries. It was not successful. Instead, it accelerated the spread of his cancer. Your father was nearly dead when I was brought to him in the clinic. Unfortunately, his consciousness died moments before the cancer went into remission. I have access to his memories, and they are being sustained through me. If I depart from his body, you will have nothing but an empty shell. I am all that is left of him until the cancer returns and kills the body completely."

Mo stepped back, shaking his head. "No, I don't believe you. My father is not dead. I want you to leave his body or I'll expose you and all your friends to the police. I decoded Mr. Bruner's encrypted files on his computer. I know where all you people live."

"Are you sure that's what you want?"

"Yeah, without a doubt. I want you to leave him now," said Mo.

His father stopped moving and froze in place. The olive color of his skin darkened, and his cheeks sank in. His face hollowed into an expression of extreme pain. "Mo, is that you?" he whispered in a gruff tone that was positively his father's. His arms and hands remained motionless down by his side.

"Dad?" Mo answered, terrified.

His father's eyes bulged. He fell back against the door and slowly slid down until he was seated on the floor with his legs stretched out in front of him. Mo gasped when blue-tinted dust particles floated out from his father's nostrils. The particles drifted upward and hovered in a perpetual circular formation above his father's head. They were the same blue-moving particles that entered Mrs. Bruner's nostrils when he eavesdropped at their window. His father's eyes closed. He exhaled his last breath, and his head fell limp to the side. There was no further movement, only silence. Mo had never seen anyone die, but this was what he imagined it would be like.

"Dad?" said Mo. He placed his hand on his father's chest; there was no heartbeat. He checked for a pulse on his wrist—nothing. "No, Dad!" Mo blurted. He gazed at the formation still hovering above his father's head. "Don't let him die. I'm sorry. Go back, please. Go back. I believe you. Just don't let him die."

The dust particles reversed and reentered his father's nostrils. His body jolted forward, and he opened his eyes.

"Dad? Are you okay?"

His father held out his hand. "Help me up," he said. Mo took his father's hand and pulled him to his feet. Having a semblance of his father was better than nothing at all.

"So my mom knew you were dying from cancer the whole time?" asked Mo.

"She made the decision not to tell you and your sister. It was what your father wanted."

"How do you know that?"

"As I said, I have access to your father's memories, but not his emotions."

Mo sighed. "I don't understand why you're doing this. What do you want?"

"We want to save this world," he said.

CHAPTER 31

AN OFFICER RUSHED into Sheriff Jenkins's office, excited. "Sheriff, you gotta see this," he said, positioning his laptop in front of Jenkins's face. "This was last night around 3:00 a.m. at a QuikStop on 14th and Sarasota."

"What is it?" asked Jenkins.

"You'll see."

The officer pushed the spacebar on his laptop, and a surveillance tape played. A van drove up to the front of the gas station. Sheriff Jenkins recognized the Pineville Enterprises insignia on the van's side door. They had been looking for the vehicle ever since Lars reported it stolen and Henson claimed to have seen a woman with long black hair driving it up to his home at the time of his assault. The sheriff focused on a woman dressed conservatively in a pantsuit stepping out of the van and walking up to the QuikStop front door. She placed her palm against the glass. Tiny cracks grew into large ones until the entire glass door was covered in them. The door shattered, and the shards of glass crumbled to the ground. The woman stepped into the gas station, grabbed bags of chips, bottled water, and food items, as much as she could carry, and loaded it into the van. The vehicle backed up and casually pulled out of the parking lot like nothing was wrong.

Did she just use her bare hand to shatter a one-inch reinforced glass door? That's not possible. She can't be more than a hundred and twenty pounds soakin' wet... Is it some kinda' martial arts move?

The officer broke into Sheriff Jenkins's chain of thought. "Weird, huh? How did she do that?"

"All sorts of ways," said Sheriff Jenkins, though he couldn't think of any plausible explanation for it. "Put a copy of that in my box. Oh, and do we still have that BOLO out on the Pineville van?"

"Far as I know, yeah."

Ansley walked in, looking concerned. "Sheriff, there's someone here at the front desk who needs to see you."

Sheriff Jenkins stood up to leave. "Find that van," he said to the officer before he walked out of his office to the front desk. Lily was there, waiting for him. "I don't have any new news I can give you, Miss Astin, about your son's case," said Sheriff Jenkins.

"Where's Rosalind? She hasn't returned my calls. It's not like her."

"I'm trying to figure that out. She was supposed to be back here in Lynch yesterday, and to be honest with you I'm not sure what's going on. She hasn't responded to me either, but we have a GPS on her vehicle, and I have officers tracking her whereabouts. We'll know something soon."

"Are you tracking her in Appalachia?"

"Yeah, how did you know?"

"She called me on her way back to Lynch and said that she was at Fairview convenience store in Appalachia. She saw a boy she thought looked like my Jeremy. She said she would call me back, but I never heard from her after that."

"Like I said, Miss Astin, we got officers on her trail right now. I'll let you know when we reach her. Most likely her car broke down on the freeway or something, and she requires some assistance."

"I wish I hadn't told Frank about her call. He sounded like he's going out there to Appalachia to see the boy, but it's not him. Rosalind told me his eyes were a different color," said Lily.

Ansley interrupted. "Sheriff, you have a call on line two. It's urgent."

"Miss Astin, I have to take this. I'll call you when I get more information."

Sheriff Jenkins went back to his office and picked up the phone. Officer Holt was on the line. He explained that the GPS tracker on Rosalind's car malfunctioned, and he had lost her locator signal. He asked for suggestions on what to do next, but Jenkins was at a loss on what to tell him. He settled on having a follow-up call the next day.

"By the way," said Holt, "what was she in Appalachia for?"

"We're investigating a missing persons case. I sent her to get records on the make and model of the vehicle that was at the scene of the abduction. We have cause to believe that the tags were from Appalachia."

"Can you fax me the information on the missing persons and the vehicle you're looking for? Maybe I can do a follow-up on it."

Sheriff Jenkins agreed and hung up. Until that call from Officer Holt, he never considered asking the FBI for assistance. His missing persons cases and unsolved homicides were stacking up, and none of the evidence made any sense. *A woman steals a van from a coal mine and goes on a killing spree? And as an added bonus, she's shattering bulletproof glass with the palm of her hand.* He didn't want the FBI involved, but if he couldn't make sense of it, who else could?

CHAPTER 32

FRANK SPED THROUGH the red light. Within minutes of Lily informing him of her call with Rosalind, he was on the road, laser-focused on finding them. He discounted Rosalind's observation that the boy had blue eyes and Lily's conclusion that it couldn't be Jeremy because of it. Rosalind might have been mistaken. No one knew his son better than him. He would make that determination, and he had already convinced himself that the boy Rosalind saw at the convenience store had to be Jeremy. It didn't matter who had taken him or why; he just wanted his son back.

The hour-long drive put him right in the heart of downtown Appalachia. There was no plan on where to go or what to do next. Frank parked in a strip mall overwhelmed by the feeling that Jeremy was being kept hidden somewhere in someone's home nearby. The only information he had was of a red Honda Civic and a sighting of his son there in Appalachia. It was possible a worker at the DMV could translate that limited information into an address.

He walked into the building searching for someone who looked like they'd broken some rules in their past. Frank settled on a clerk standing in the corner using the copy machine. He proudly sported a mohawk haircut and had piercings on every facial crevice available—not the type you would normally see working at a government job but a perfect candidate for manipulation.

"Sir, can I ask you a question?" said Frank.

"How can I help you?" replied the clerk.

"I was just involved in a hit-and-run. Somebody just rammed into my car and when I tried to get their information they sped off. I can't afford to get it fixed, and if I report it to my insurance, they'll raise my premium to some ridiculous rate. I need to find the person who hit my car."

The clerk checked the clock on the wall. "I'm sorry to hear that, sir, but there's nothing we can do."

"Look, he almost ran over a lady walking across the street. It was a red Honda," said Frank. "One of the newer models. If you could just give me a list of all the red Hondas in this area, the newer models? I can narrow it down from there."

"Oh, no, we can't do that, sir. You're better off going to the police."

"C'mon, you know the police won't pay any attention to this kind of thing. They got bigger fish to fry. How hard can it be to print out a record of red Hondas just here in the town?"

"Sir, I can't help you. We're not allowed to give that kind of information out to the public."

"So you have it?"

"You need to go to the police."

"Look, what if he's drunk and instead of almost hitting a lady, he runs down a child? He needs to pay the consequence now before he really hurts somebody."

Frank pulled an envelope from his pocket and handed it to the clerk. "You'll be doing more than just helping me. You'll be getting a dangerous driver off the road."

The clerk opened the envelope. Inside was a fifty-dollar bill. "No one has to know," said Frank with a wink.

The clerk stared at it, contemplating, and finally nodded. "Okay, but you can't share this with anybody."

"No worries. It's between you and me," said Frank.

The clerk stashed the envelope into his pocket and went to work on the computer in his cubicle. He returned with a printout two pages long and gave it to Frank.

"There are forty-six newer-model red Hondas registered in the town," said the clerk. "Good luck finding the right one."

Frank reviewed the list as he exited the building and walked back to his car. Using a GPS app on his phone, he searched for the addresses closest to Fairview convenience store, where Rosalind had seen the child she thought was Jeremy. Only one name and address were less than two miles from the store, while the other forty-five names were either six miles or more away. Douglas and Pamela Lofton at 6449 Wolcott Avenue would be his next destination.

His heart raced as he approached the rural neighborhood where his son was most likely being held. Should he break down the door or wait to see if they brought him outside, where he could take him back? Calling the police was not an option. It would have to wait until he had undeniable proof that the boy they were holding was his Jeremy.

Frank parked across the street from the house at 6449 Walcott. He took a deep breath, exhaled, and collected his thoughts. "He's here… I know he's here," he kept whispering, though it failed to drown out the doubt that still hovered in his mind. He left his car and trudged across the street to the front of the house. It boasted a manicured lawn, and, in stark contrast to the surrounding two homes, a well-maintained exterior.

An old station wagon approached and slowed to a crawl. As it passed by the house, the driver locked eyes with Frank, revved up the engine, and then floored it down the road. It spooked Frank, but it failed to intimidate him. He continued up to the front door and peered through the glass door window. He didn't see anyone inside, so he headed back to his car. Within minutes of sitting and waiting, he glimpsed something in the middle of the road, traveling toward him.

He got out of his car to get a closer look. It appeared too small to be a motorcycle. Someone was riding a child's bike. He walked toward it. The scene reminded him of the day he had taught Jeremy how to ride his bike and how excited his son was riding up to meet him at the end of the block without the help of training wheels. The difference was that the boy on the bike coming toward him was not wearing a helmet.

Frank picked up his walking pace. With each step he took, more of the boy's features became clearer, and all of them were a spitting image of Jeremy. Frank froze in the middle of the street, waiting for him to get closer. Instead, the boy slowed down and came to a stop a short distance away.

Frank's eyes widened at the sight of his son's face. "Jeremy?" he said, on the verge of tears. He had been right the whole time. His son was alive, but why didn't he recognize him? *Maybe he's been brainwashed.*

The boy sneered at Frank. "I'm not Jeremy. I'm Kaden," he said.

Kaden turned his bike around and rode away in the opposite direction as fast as he could. Frank ran after him, chasing him on foot down the middle of the street.

"Jeremy! Wait!"

Kaden ignored him and kept pedaling. When he took a quick glance over his shoulder, Frank was closing in on him. Kaden waved a hand in the air. A flock of squawking blackbirds flew out from the trees above them. Soaring through the wind on their trail was a tiger owl. It swooped down at Frank and with talons sharpened like polished knives scraped his face, leaving a bleeding laceration across his cheek. Kaden put on his brakes. He glanced back the moment the tiger owl whiffed around Frank and soared back into the air. The owl emitted a piercing shriek and hissed at Frank before it darted again for his head. Frank shooed it, flailing his hands, but the owl's long talons struck him again and penetrated his scalp. Frank managed to strike back at the bird, yanking away the long feathers on its legs and feet. The injured owl flew away into the woods with its damaged wings beating the wind.

Frank was left with a second bleeding laceration across his forehead. He wiped the blood away while Kaden just stood there holding his bike and staring at him, expressionless.

When Frank motioned toward him, Kaden dropped the bike and ran into the adjacent woods. Frank followed but lost him. He found himself trudging through a wooded area where wet leaves brushed against his face. In a place where an owl would attack, anything could happen, but there was no way he was leaving without his son.

Frank stepped around a row of overgrown bushes and spotted Jeremy ahead, leaning against a tree, looking at him. An overwhelming smell of burnt metal wafted through the air. There was something different, even strange about the way Jeremy looked at him. It was in his eyes. Why and how were his eyes blue?

"Dad?" said Jeremy with a whimper.

Kaden jerked his head to the side and spoke to himself. "If you say another word, I will bury him underground, and you will never see your father again."

"Jeremy, it's okay. You can come to me," said Frank. Jeremy calling him *Dad* gave Frank hope that his son's memory was returning and the trauma he had endured could be reversed.

Kaden stepped back. "Leave me alone. I told you my name is Kaden. Kaden Lofton. My parents are Douglas and Pamela Lofton. I live at 6449 Wolcott Avenue," he said as if he was reading from a script. Frank wanted to rush and grab him but was afraid he would frighten him away. He needed to speak to his son soothingly and win back his trust first.

"Your name is Jeremy Astin," said Frank in a soothing voice. "They're not telling you the truth because they're not your real parents. I'm Frank Astin, your dad, and your mother is Lily. We've been trying to find you for months. Someone stole you from us."

"You're wrong," said Kaden. "I was not stolen. I belong where I am."

Frank viewed the birthmark on Jeremy's arm. There was no doubt he had found his son, though the way he spoke was not the way Jeremy would speak or the words he would use. Because of his acute autism, Jeremy had struggled his entire young life to do normal things. It was difficult to speak clearly, and he struggled just to express his feelings. Something had changed in him, and it wasn't just his eye color.

Frank took small, careful steps toward Jeremy. The adrenaline that had muted the effects of the owl attack had worn off. The stinging pain from the lacerations finally hit him, and maybe that was the reason he was hallucinating that Jeremy's palm was glowing.

A crack formed on the ground under Jeremy's foot. It surged across the ground until it reached the area under his foot and halted. He stared at Jeremy, baffled. "What's going on? Did you do that?"

Blue dust particles rose out of the crack in the ground in front of Frank's face. It formed a halo, circling in midair. "Relax, Frank. It'll be over soon," said Kaden.

Kaden walked out of the woods, mounted his bike, and rode away. Minutes later, Frank stepped out from the same area with a deadpan expression. He walked down the middle of the road to his car, hopped in, and drove away.

CHAPTER 33

WHEN CLAY ARRIVED home from Lily's, he found Octavius and Rebecca sitting in their parked car, waiting for him. He marched up to the driver's side window, annoyed by their presence.

"What're you doing here? How did you find me?"

"I returned your wallet, remember?" Octavius replied. "Your address is on your driver's license. It wasn't that difficult."

"We need to talk to you. It's urgent," Rebecca said.

"I've talked enough with you people. I just want you to leave me alone," Clay replied.

"We can't do that. You're just as much a part of this as we are. And look, your eye has changed. You're still evolving."

"I'm not evolving," said Clay. "I am what I am."

Rebecca and Octavius stepped out of the car onto pieces of broken glass. The setting sun cast long shadows across Clay's debris-strewn front yard, where a downed tree served as a reminder of the storm's volatility.

"The tree—he sent a lightning bolt, didn't he? It didn't accomplish what he wanted, so he created a tornado," said Rebecca, scanning the scene. "I can't stop him. The Council has made him stronger. His plan was to eliminate you and your family."

"Are you kidding? No one can create a tornado," Clay said incredulously.

"You've seen with your own eyes what Kaden can do," said Rebecca. "What makes you think the elements are off-limits for him?"

Rebecca confirmed what Clay had already suspected about the tornado's origin. But why would someone with that kind of power and ability use it against him?

"We really need to talk to you. Can we go inside?" Rebecca asked again.

Clay paused, not inclined to let anyone he didn't really know into his home.

Octavius scoffed. "Your cohabitor doesn't know, does she?"

"She's not my cohabitor. She's my wife, and I told her everything," Clay replied.

"Then it shouldn't be a problem for us to be candid with you in her presence," said Octavius.

Reluctant to admit his uncertainty about whether Tara believed him, Clay headed for the front door. Rebecca and Octavius followed him into his trailer, and they all sat down in the living room.

"You wanted to talk," Clay said, crossing his arms. "So go ahead. Talk."

Tara entered the room. "Clay, who are these people?"

"I'm Rebecca. That's Octavius," said Rebecca, pointing at him. "Clay said he told you about us."

Tara gazed hard at Clay. "What did you tell me?"

"Honey, I told you all about them," said Clay. "I just never mentioned their names."

Tara eyed Rebecca suspiciously. "You can't be more than eight or nine years old, and you're all a part of this? You're the ones who found Clay at the accident?"

"It wasn't an accident," said Rebecca.

"So you're gonna tell me you were a witness to this little boy flipping Clay's truck."

"We tried to warn him in advance about Kaden. He's determined to eliminate Clay by any means necessary."

"Eliminate him? Kaden is just a boy—a child, right?"

"No, he's not. He's Ocran, and so are we, and so is your husband. At least part of him," said Rebecca.

Tara took a seat, flustered. "If you are what you say you are, and Clay's a part of your kind, then explain to me how he was able to move a tree away from my car with his bare hands. Tell me. How did he do it?"

"Tara, if I knew, I would have told you myself," Clay interjected.

Tara locked eyes with Rebecca. "Tell me how he did it," she said.

"He didn't move the tree," Rebecca said. "He unknowingly manipulated the gravity around it. That's what caused it to shift at his whim. Because he's half-human, his Ocran abilities are evolving, even though he doesn't want to believe it." She turned her attention to Clay. "I assume you now see a yellowish-cerulean haze when the wind blows, and transparent blue outlines around objects. Is that true?"

Clay paused. He didn't want to admit it, but he nodded anyway.

"It's the gravitational force you're seeing," Rebecca continued. "We can see the elements that are invisible to the human eye, like the wind and gravity. We see their true shapes and colors. You can't control what you cannot see, and we can see the elements all around us."

Tara sighed.

Rebecca addressed Clay in Arabic. "Alam taqbal bi-man takun?" *—Has she not accepted what you are?*

Clay responded in Latin, "Quomodo exspectas ut accipiat quod nondum accepi?" *—How can you expect her to accept what I haven't yet accepted?*

Tara's forehead creased, and she squinted at Clay. "When did you start speaking another language?"

"What're you talking about?" Clay replied.

"He doesn't know when he's speaking or hearing the old languages," said Rebecca. "It's an ability of the Ocran that flows naturally from the Wheel."

Tara shrugged, exasperated. "How do you expect me to deal with all of this, Clay? How much of this is real? Do I even know who you are?"

Overwhelmed, Tara abruptly walked out of the room. Clay raised up to go after her.

"Clayton, it's in her best interest that you remain here and listen to what we have to tell you," Rebecca said in a gentle but firm voice.

He returned to his seat; his jaw clenched. "You got two minutes before I throw you out," he muttered.

"He will do it," said Rebecca. "He will eliminate millions of people. It's been his plan all along."

The thought of millions of people dying at the hands of what appeared to be a kid seemed unimaginable to Clay. "How is that even possible?"

"He's been testing his power over the elements for weeks," Octavius revealed. "Forming a tornado and sending it to eliminate you is just the beginning. Kaden has taken dominion over the Wheel. He's using it to corrupt the Council to help him halt the rotation of this planet's inner core."

"Do you understand what that would do?" asked Rebecca, her voice rising. "It will disrupt the entire gravitational force of this planet. In every country in the world, there will be earthquakes, releasing millions of Ocran from underground to the surface. They will enter millions of humans all at once, and when Kaden gives the order, they will extract themselves simultaneously, killing the millions of people they changed."

"Why are you telling me this?" Clay said. "Even if I believed you, what do you expect me to do about it?"

"The Wheel is the conduit for the source of his power. Without it, he can't access the Council. We have to destroy the Wheel," said Rebecca. "It's the only way to stop him."

"If that's what will stop him, then do it. Destroy the Wheel," Clay said.

"We can't," Rebecca replied. "The moment we opened the barn door, the Wheel would inform Kaden of our presence and he would direct the Council to instantly extract us from our human body. We can't get near the Wheel without Kaden knowing. But because you are only part Ocran, there is no entity within you to be extracted."

Octavius added, "Once the Wheel is destroyed, Kaden will be imprisoned in the boy's body, harmless, with no abilities over us or the elements, as all of us who have taken over human bodies will be the same way until the body grows old and dies."

"And what about the kid, Jeremy?" Clay asked. "Kaden will be in control of his body until he dies?"

Rebecca and Octavius exchanged glances as if they were deciding who should be the one to answer his question. "Most likely Jeremy is already gone. The human side of the consciousness eventually dies. Some must be sacrificed in order for the majority to survive," Octavius said.

"He's an innocent child," said Clay. "He has a name, and it's not Kaden, it's Jeremy. I've spoken to his mother. The kid has a right to live, to grow up, like everyone else. His mother has a right to be with her child again."

"It's too late for him. There is no other choice," Octavius replied. "You have to help us destroy the Wheel."

"No, I'm not doing it," said Clay.

"Kaden cannot be extracted from Jeremy's body without killing him, and there's nothing you or I or anyone can do about that. What we can do is stop him from releasing millions of Ocran to the surface, which would eliminate every human alive. He will no doubt extract me and Octavius and disperse our dust into the lake, terminating our existence if we attempted to destroy it. You have the ability to do something," Rebecca said.

"And I said I'm not doing it, and your two minutes are up. I want you to leave."

Rebecca sighed and followed Octavius to the door. "Please, Clayton, consider the consequences if we do nothing. Kaden will win," she said.

"I have an idea," Clay replied. "Get me the diamonds, and I'll do it. I'll destroy the Wheel. Whatever you want. I just want something for my trouble."

Rebecca frowned and dropped her chin. "Diamonds are a toxic by-product of the Wheel. They're dangerous and harmful to our life form. We don't touch them or go near them."

"They're not dangerous for me," Clay countered. "It's money and a ticket out of this nowhere town. You want me to get rid of the Wheel? Then get me the diamonds."

Octavius chafed at his request. "And how do you expect us to do that?"

Clay shrugged. "That Wheel contraption was nearly spitting them out. I'm sure you'll find a way."

Tara's scream startled them. Clay rushed back into the bedroom to find Tara bent over, grasping her stomach.

"Tara, what's wrong?" Clay asked.

"I don't know. All of a sudden…this pain. Clay, it's the baby. I need to get to the hospital."

CHAPTER 34

LILY HADN'T HEARD from Frank since the morning she told him about Rosalind sighting a boy resembling their son in Appalachia. It worried her that after leaving several messages on his voicemail she had not received a response. It spurred her to visit his home, assuming he might be isolating himself again. Her concern heightened at the sight of his car parked out front. She knocked on the door and rang the bell but didn't get an answer. Dread came over her as she contemplated the possibility that Frank had harmed himself. Ever since Jeremy's disappearance, he had been prone to depression; anything was possible with him. It was crucial that she get inside to make sure he was okay.

Lily circled around to the rear of the house, retrieved the spare key he kept under the mat, and unlocked the door. The only sound she heard in the eerily silent home was her own breathing.

"Frank? It's me. Are you here?" she shouted. "Frank?"

Lily searched the rooms on the first floor and then headed upstairs. "Frank?"

The door to his bedroom was closed. She knocked and entered. "Frank, it's me," she said as she walked in. Lily had never seen the bedroom so clean and organized. *He must have hired a cleaning service.*

An ornate box sitting on his dresser sparked her curiosity. As she lifted the top, Frank appeared from behind, startling her. "What're you doing here, Lily?"

She quickly replaced the lid before she had a chance to see what was inside. "You weren't answering my calls. I was worried. Rosalind is missing. I thought you might've gone to Appalachia looking for her."

"No, I've been here," said Frank.

"Why didn't you answer the door or return any of my calls?"

Frank sniffed and pulled his earlobe. "I've been sleeping a lot. I probably didn't hear it."

Lily's eyes were drawn to the cuts across his forehead and cheeks. "What happened to your face? What are all those marks?"

"It's nothing," he said, dismissively.

As she reached to touch his face, he grabbed her hand. "So you're curious to know what's in the box, huh?"

"It's none of my business," she said.

Clay released his grip on her hand. "If you want to see it, Lily, I'll show it to you."

Frank sniffed, pulled his earlobe, and sniffed again. It was an odd tic that he never had before. "So you never went to Appalachia?" asked Lily, pretending not to notice it.

"Why would I go to Appalachia?"

"Why do you do a lot of things, Frank? I don't know—to make sure the boy Rosalind saw there wasn't Jeremy?"

"Jeremy is dead," said Frank dryly.

"What did you say?" said Lily.

"I said Jeremy is dead, Lily. Rosalind must've been mistaken."

"How do you know he's dead?" she asked, tearing up.

"We have to face what happened to Jeremy and move on. He was taken, and he was killed. It's as simple as that," said Frank in a deadpan tone.

Lily stared at him, bewildered. "But you said you believed he was alive. You told me not to give up on him, that you felt his presence."

"I don't anymore," said Frank. "He's gone, Lily."

Frank had maliciously snatched away her hopes of Jeremy's safe return. His insistence that their son was still alive had been her only light in a dark existence. She had latched on to Frank's optimism and his sense of hope for the safe return of their son, but now he had taken all that away from her. The sudden reversal didn't match his character. Something about Frank had changed. Standing in the same space with him made her uncomfortable, and she walked out of the room in a hurry.

"Where are you going?" said Frank. He grabbed the box and followed her down the stairs. "I want you to see what's inside the box. It's gonna surprise you, Lily."

"I don't wanna see anything. I'm going home. I'm glad you're okay," she said. His presence alone made the hairs on her neck and arms stand up. She needed to leave his house as quickly as possible.

"It's a gift. I bought it for you," said Frank as he pulled on his earlobe. She didn't know why she was afraid, but her heartbeat pounded through her chest. *Why does he keep insisting?* She had a gut feeling not to turn around and look at anything he had to show her. She twisted the knob on the front door. It wouldn't open. She yanked at it again. It didn't budge. Frank's breath grazed the back of her neck, repulsing her, still she wouldn't turn around and look at him.

"You don't have to leave. Just because we're divorced doesn't mean we can't get to know each other again. Why don't you stay for a little while?" said Frank.

It was bizarre that he was coming on to her. His words seemed forced and unnatural. "I can't stay. I have to get home to give my mother her medication," she explained.

Lily yanked on the doorknob again. "Why won't it open?" she said as she pulled on it, her hands shaking uncontrollably.

Frank reached around her, turned the knob, and gently pushed the door open. "There's nothing wrong with the door, Lily."

Relieved, she hurried out, got in her car, and sped off without looking back.

CHAPTER 35

TARA AWAKENED WHEN Sally entered her hospital room and gently squeezed her hand. "How are you, sweetie?" Sally asked. The sound roused Clay from his slumber in the chair beside Tara's bed.

"I'm okay," Tara said. "Just had a little scare."

"How's the baby?"

"The baby's fine. Everything looks normal for a twelve-week pregnancy. They did a prenatal blood test. It's a boy."

"Oh, sweetie, that's wonderful! And he's healthy?"

"Yeah, whatever came over me, the doctor said it was probably stress-related. They want to keep me another night to do more tests and to make sure everything is working right."

"You can't be stressing out over anything at this point," Sally chided, casting a suspicious glance at Clay. "You stressin' her out, Clay?"

"I'm tryin' not to," he replied, rubbing the back of his neck. "Haven't seen you since the wedding, Miss Sally. You still at the diner?"

"For now, but I don't know how much longer."

Sally turned back to Tara, her expression softening. "It's been hard showin' up there without Gloria. Your mother is really missed. She told me a few things before she died."

Tara sensed from the way Sally looked at her that she wanted to talk to her privately. She turned to Clay. "Honey, you've been here all night. You should go and get some real sleep. I'll be fine."

"You sure?"

"I'll keep her company," Sally answered. "We have a lot of catching up to do."

Clay leaned in and kissed Tara on the forehead. "Call me if you need anything," he said before exiting the room.

Sally gazed at Tara, concerned. "You think you'll be well enough to go to Gloria's funeral tomorrow?"

Tara exhaled. "I'll be there for her, well or not. I just don't know if I'm ready to see her in a casket, Sally. She seemed happy the last time we talked. I wanna remember her that way."

"You won't see her, honey. She requested a closed casket. You know how she was about the way she looked. It was important for her to always look her best."

"But why cremation? And she said she wanted her ashes poured out over Buckhorn Lake? It doesn't make sense."

"It was in the *just-in-case* letter she left me," said Sally. "I can show it to you. Why doesn't it make sense?"

"Buckhorn Lake was where she met my father, and we both know what she thought about him."

"Believe it or not, in her own way, Gloria loved your father. She told me how sorry she was at what she had done to him, but she swore he wasn't himself that day, that she had no choice."

"What does that mean, Sally? *He wasn't himself?*"

"I can't explain it either. She left a just-in-case letter for you too."

Sally pulled an envelope from her purse and handed it to Tara. "You don't have to read it now," she added. "She was so excited about your pregnancy. She would've been such an awesome grandmother." Sally wiped her watery eyes dry. It caused Tara to tear up. "I never told her I loved her," said Tara. "I wanted to so many times, but something just wouldn't let me."

Sally squeezed Tara's hand again. "She knew you loved her, honey. She knew it."

Tara debated whether to confide in Sally what was physically happening to Clay. She yearned to share the burden, but the changes in his body were just too bizarre to be believed and certainly not worth the risk of her being labeled crazy.

○　○　○

Outside the hospital, Clay reached Tara's car and was greeted with another folded note tucked beneath the windshield wiper. He didn't have to guess who left it there. Clay pulled out the note and read it: *When you return from destroying the Wheel, the diamonds will be at your doorstep.*

His brother's voice called out his name. "Clay!" Jimmy shouted. He waved and hurried toward him. Clay quickly folded up the note and stashed it in his back pocket.

Jimmy gave him a quick hug. "Hey, we heard about Tara. I thought I'd come by and check on her, since both of you never answer your phones. How is she? How's the baby?"

"She's good. They want to keep her another day for more tests. It's a boy, Jimmy. I'm gonna have a baby boy."

"Congrats, but why do I have to hunt you down to have a conversation with you? Where have you been?"

"I'm dealing with a lot right now," said Clay.

"You wanna talk about it? We can go get a bite somewhere."

"Nah, I have to go," Clay said, his voice strained. He climbed into the car and rolled down the window. "Out of all the crazy things Pops has said to me over the years, there's one thing I do agree with…" Clay looked Jimmy in the eye. "*You are* one of the good ones, Jimmy." Clay started the ignition and drove away.

○　○　○

Jeb and Officer Holt were waiting in the hallway for Charlie when he stepped out of his classroom.

"Hello, Charlie," said Officer Holt. "I need to chat with you and your brother. Would you mind following me out to my car? It'll only take a few minutes."

"We haven't done anything," said Charlie.

"It's nothing like that. C'mon," said Officer Holt. Jeb and Charlie followed him outside and into the back of his patrol car. "First off, I want to apologize for not believing your story about the stag. I know I said it wasn't possible, but now I see that anything's possible. I'm not ready to accept the part about it dragging the kid out of the water, but I can concede that for some unknown reason a stag was there at the lake. Anyway, that's not what I wanted to talk to you about. The situation with you and the Lofton kid is done and over with. I don't want to rehash it. I want to know about Travis."

Charlie bit down on his thumbnail, and Jeb stared aimlessly out the window. Travis was the last thing they wanted to talk about. Their reaction piqued Officer Holt's curiosity even more. "Have you noticed something about him? Anything? Something unusual?"

Charlie shook his head, no. Jeb didn't respond at all.

"What about you, Jeb?" asked the officer.

"I don't know anything," said Jeb.

"I didn't ask if you knew anything. I asked if you noticed anything unusual about him lately."

"You won't believe me."

"Trust me, I'm listening."

Jeb exhaled. "He's not the real Travis. He has abilities."

Officer Holt frowned. "Abilities? What kind of abilities?"

"He can make things move."

"Make things move? You mean on command?"

"Yeah, with his voice or his thoughts. He's not like us. He's not human."

Officer Holt sighed and stared out the car window.

"I said you wouldn't believe me," said Jeb.

A call on the officer's radio interrupted them. Dispatch alerted him of Rosalind's car, discovered abandoned off-road in Appalachia, and requested he get there as soon as possible to collect evidence.

"I have to go, but we'll talk again," said Officer Holt. "Let's not mention this to your mom, okay? I wouldn't want her to worry about anything."

Jeb and Charlie climbed out of the patrol car and entered the school. Before they could return to their classrooms, Travis marched down the hallway with a smirk on his face and blocked their way. He stepped up to Charlie and stood in front of him, gazing at him curiously from his head down to his feet.

"Get away from me you psycho" said Charlie.

"What did he do to you? You've changed." asked Travis.

Jeb rushed ahead and moved Charlie behind him, interrupting Travis's ruthless stare at his brother.

"You extracted him, didn't you?" asked Travis. "But how? How could someone as inconsequential as you perform an extraction? It's improbable that your brother survived it without an inhuman assisting you," he said. "Tell me, who helped you? Was it the one called Rebecca?"

"Leave me and my brother alone," Jeb demanded, clenching his fists. "I'm not afraid of you. I'm gonna tell everyone just what kind of *thing* you are."

"I don't think so. Who will believe it, Jeb?" said Travis.

Jeb and Charlie walked around him, leaving Travis standing alone in the middle of the school hallway. Jeb escorted Charlie to his classroom. "Okay, meet me after fifth period," said Jeb. "We'll walk home together, just in case he comes back."

Charlie scratched his head and his shoulders sagged slightly forward.

"What's wrong?" asked Jeb.

"He said you extracted me. What did he mean? Did something bad happen to me?"

Jeb masked his nervousness. There's no way he could tell his brother the truth. It would only make things worse. "Nothing happened except you hit your head, dude. That's why you can't remember. I told you he's insane. Don't listen to him and don't go near him Charlie, ever!"

CHAPTER 36

CLAY NEVER IMAGINED he'd return to Oceola, the very place where his life had unraveled. Anxiety churned his stomach as he considered the possibility of Kaden appearing and thwarting his plan. Yet his most pressing concern was the strange transformation overtaking his body. How long would it be before he morphed into something that even Tara would find repulsive? Would he even live long enough to witness the birth of his son? He couldn't go back in time and change anything, but he could make the best of it. Destroying the Wheel would get him what he wanted: a better life and a better future for his family. Having the financial stability the diamonds could bring would, in the end, finally allow him to be happy. He was willing to risk the unforeseen consequences of its destruction.

Jolted from his thoughts, Clay reached for the gas can resting on the back seat of the car. He navigated the thicket of foliage, making his way to the base of the embankment with an unobstructed view of the barn. Heart pounding, he waited, scanning for any sign of movement. Minutes ticked by as he gauged the opportune moment to carry out his plan.

As soon as he resolved to go through with it, the convenience store attendant emerged from the barn. Clay observed intently as he secured a padlock to the door, ensuring it was locked with a key before departing.

Seizing the opportunity, Clay rushed up the embankment, gas can in hand, intent on reducing the barn to ashes with the Wheel trapped inside. He doused the barn door and the entire perimeter of the weathered structure in gasoline, his movements deliberate and systematic. With the gas can emptied, he reached into his pocket for the matches, only to have the world around him suddenly plunge into darkness.

Clay didn't register the initial impact, only the searing pain that followed, hitting him like a ton of bricks. He found himself lying flat on his back, his head throbbing and vision blurred. Slowly, the fuzzy image of someone standing over him came into focus.

As the haze cleared, he recognized the convenience store attendant's uniform. He held a rotted plank in his hand, its corners crowded with protruding bloody nails as if it had been ripped from the barn's exterior. It wasn't until Clay touched something wet on his scalp that the pieces fell into place. Blood stained his fingers. If he didn't get up, his situation would only worsen. He attempted to rise, but the attendant swung the plank at his head once more. Clay instinctively shielded his face with his arm, the nails piercing his skin and sinking deep into his palm. When the attendant yanked the plank back, Clay's blood sprinkled across his face.

"There are consequences for your actions," said the attendant, remarkably calm.

Grimacing, Clay forced himself back onto his feet. The holes in his palm healed in front of his eyes and faded away. The attendant dropped the plank, his palm revealing the tattoo as it began to glow. Clay retreated several steps, bracing himself for whatever might come next.

Birds cawed in unison, and a resounding crack echoed through the air. The attendant gazed at the branches high above them causing a ten-foot branch as thick as a small tree to break off. It hurtled down and landed across Clay's chest, pinning him to the ground. The air was forced from his lungs, and the pressure on his ribcage made breathing nearly impossible. Clay internalized the pain and focused on the faint blue outline around the tree branch—an outline invisible to the human eye but visible to the Ocran—the gravitational force that Rebecca assured him he had the ability to manipulate.

Clay lunged forward, envisioning himself pushing the outline toward the attendant. The branch lifted and rocketed through the air, striking the attendant in the chest, and sending him crashing unconscious to the ground over a hundred feet away.

Relieved, Clay gasped for air, struggling to stand. He limped back to the barn, struck a match, and tossed it onto the gasoline-soaked structure. The dry wood caught fire instantly, flames leaping skyward and engulfing the barn in mere seconds. The intense heat forced him to retreat farther. Whatever lied within the barn would soon be reduced to ashes.

Clay headed back to his car, anticipating blowback from the Wheel's destruction. So far, nothing within his body had changed.

A burst of laughter echoed, and the attendant stepped out in front of him, his store uniform tattered and soiled. Clay froze.

"You destroyed an old barn, that's all you've done. The Wheel was moved a long time ago," he sneered. Clay's jaw tightened as the attendant's words sank in.

"I don't believe you," Clay said.

"If the Wheel is burning, then why has everything remained the same?"

The attendant's tattooed palm was still aglow. Something should have happened. Why hadn't he considered the Wheel could be moved to another location where it wouldn't be found? Rebecca and Octavius should have warned him.

The attendant spat on the ground. "What a foolish thing to do," he said. "While your father Zarian is dying on the surface of your Pineville mine, longing for you instead of his own kind, you're here attempting to destroy the very thing that's keeping him alive. How pathetic. You both deserve each other."

CHAPTER 37

STANLEY AND LARS huddled in the Pineville mine trailer pouring over new equipment specifications when the harsh crunch sound of tires on the gravel interrupted their focus.

You expecting somebody?" Stanley's voice carried an edge of unease.

"Nope, what's on the cameras?" said Lars, his brow furrowing.

"Cameras aren't working, remember? They don't fix those until Tuesday."

Stanley pushed the window blinds aside, his eyes narrowing as he peeked outside. There, parked next to Lars's vehicle, sat the company van. The very same van they hadn't seen since it vanished into the night days ago.

"You won't believe this," Stanley muttered. "Someone just returned the van."

"Are you freakin' kidding me?" said Lars.

Stanley pointed out the window. "It's right there. See for yourself."

Lars shot up from his seat and joined him at the window. His jaw dropped in astonishment. "Call the sheriff," he ordered.

Lars stepped out of the office trailer with a feeling of dread gnawing at him. As he cautiously approached the van, the driver's side door swung open, revealing the woman. He immediately recognized her, now fully clothed, her long jet-black hair disheveled, yet still appealing.

The intensity in her eyes remained, striking fear that raced through his entire body. *How was she still alive?*

"Have I awakened your memory?" the woman asked, her voice raspy, yet articulate. "When I encountered you in the mine, you reacted as though you had never seen me before, or was that just an act to keep the others from suspecting what you did to me?" She paused to think about it. "Well, not what you did to me, but what you did to her."

The woman took a step toward Lars. He responded by taking two steps back, shaking his head, speechless.

"I thought you pulled over to help me," she said. "My good Samaritan. Little did I know, you had other plans, didn't you, Lars? You took advantage of a woman whose car had broken down on the road. It was pitch-black that night. No one else was around, and no one would see or hear anything, so you hit her over the head with something, knocked her unconscious, and then you dragged her—you dragged her by her hair through the back woods with her hands bound, helpless and vulnerable to you."

The scene flashed through Lars's mind as she retold it. Her description made him sound like a monster, but he didn't feel like one. He had made a mistake that spiraled out of control, and not until she had reminded him of what he had done that night did he feel remorseful. "I'm sorry," said Lars. "I didn't mean—"

"You didn't mean what?" she interrupted. "You didn't mean to savagely rip her dress and undergarments off of her, leaving her naked in the cold? You didn't mean to unbuckle your belt and unzip your pants? It startled you when she opened her eyes and kicked you in the groin, didn't it? It was her only chance to escape, her chance to get away from you. Since her hands were bound, she couldn't run fast enough. You caught up with her as she was trying to hide, and when you threw her to the ground, you got on top of her. She begged for her life. She had so much to live for—a daughter in preschool to raise and nurture, but all you cared about was satisfying your urge to dominate and control. You put your hands around her neck and squeezed until her screams were stifled. She fought back as hard as she could, but it was futile.

You kept strangling her until she went limp, until she breathed her last breath." The woman smirked. "But you were mistaken, Lars. She wasn't dead yet. She was barely alive when I felt her desperation. I decided she would be my way back to the surface. Her death would not be in vain."

The spiral tattoo materialized on the palm of the woman's hand. She clenched her fist to keep Lars from noticing it. "Before she took her last breath, I ascended from the ground next to her, and out of the crevice I ascended as dust in the wind," said the woman. "I entered her body, giving her life again. I share her memories now, and I hear her thoughts. She hates you, Lars, and she demands retribution for what you did to her."

Lars contemplated escaping to his car but remembered he had left his keys in the office trailer. He turned to go back inside.

"Where are you going?" asked the woman. The ground beneath him shifted, and a crack formed under his feet. Lars hastened toward the trailer. The break formed into a crevice and split the ground open as it followed behind him, expanding at his heels. The crevice spread ahead of him and formed a five-foot-deep fissure so fast that he didn't see it until it happened. Lars fell into the ditch up to his neck. When his foot impacted solid ground, a sharp pain surged through his kneecaps up into his chest.

The woman walked up to where he was entrenched into the ground, only his head above the hole. Lars had a horrified look on his face, not because of the tattoo glowing on her palm but because of how the walls of soil around him crumbled and shifted before they slowly began filling the cramped fissure he was stuck in. Fearing that he would soon be buried alive, he clawed at the dirt walls, trying to lift himself out. The woman stood there above him, staring, motionless, waiting for the soil to cover his head completely.

○ ○ ○

Pineville mine protocol required the security gate code to be changed immediately after an employee dismissal. Clay hoped Lars's inexperience in updating the security system hadn't prompted him to have someone change it for him. As he approached the Pineville mine entrance, it became clear that the code wouldn't be necessary. The gate had been torn from its hinges as if someone had rammed through it with a diesel truck and continued onward. Clay sped around the debris and into the parking lot, screeching to a halt in front of the office trailer. The bizarre scene unfolding through his front windshield left him baffled. Lars was submerged in a hole with only his head sticking above ground, and a woman stood over him, her left palm glowing. Despite the way Lars had treated him, firing him and then humiliating him in front of Henson, Clay didn't think he deserved to be buried alive. He leaped out of the car.

"What're you doing? Let him go," Clay demanded.

The woman turned and gazed at him. The tattoo on her palm faded away, and the soil stopped crumbling into the hole around Lars. She paced around Clay, examining him from head to toe as she methodically circled him a full three hundred and sixty degrees.

"Except for the protrusion on your back, the discoloration of your eye, and the translucent veins in your left arm, you have fully maintained the human image—amazing," she said in her raspy voice.

Clay didn't understand what she meant by "maintaining," so he ignored it. "Let him go," he repeated. "The people who work at this mine are harmless."

The woman bristled. "There is nothing harmless about this man. He is full of deception." She glanced sharply down at Lars's face with disgust. "Tell him what you did to her," she ordered. Lars remained silent.

"I said tell him what you did to her—what you did to an innocent woman."

The spiral tattoo reappeared on her palm, glowing.

"It was an accident," Lars muttered.

"Liar," she shouted. The woman pointed the palm of her hand at Lars, shifting the gravitational force around him. He floated up out of the fissure, spinning in midair.

"What's going on?" Lars shouted. Suspended twelve feet high, he flailed his arms and kicked aimlessly into the wind. "Krutcher, what is this? Let me down, please," he begged.

"Go ahead, tell him," said the woman to Lars. "Tell him how you assaulted her before you violated her and left her for dead."

"I didn't want to hurt you. You wouldn't stop screaming. I snapped," Lars stammered.

"You didn't just hurt me—you killed me."

"But you're not dead. You're alive," said Lars.

"She's dead inside, but I'm very much alive."

"Krutcher, please, help me," Lars pleaded.

The woman lifted him higher in the air. Stanley stepped out from the office trailer, his eyes bulging in disbelief. He sprinted to his car and started the ignition.

"Let him go," Clay insisted. "He's a monster, but how are you any different? You're the woman they've been looking for. You killed Henson's wife and Bailey's husband, Eric."

The soft glow on her palm subsided, and the gravitational force around Lars returned to normal. He plummeted through the air like a stone. Clay lifted his own palm and retracted the blue outline enveloping Lars, slowing the gravitational pull. Lars's descent halted mere inches from a head-first collision with the ground. He toppled over and vomited, reeling from the zero-gravity-induced motion sickness. Shaking it off, he picked himself up and trudged toward the passenger side of Stanley's waiting car. They tore out of the parking lot, tires screeching and sending a plume of dust into the air.

CHAPTER 38

CLAY FACED THE woman, resolved to get an answer from her. "I wanna know why you took Edie and Eric's life. What did they ever do to you?"

"I didn't take the life any human who wasn't already dead," she replied. "Others of the Ocran had changed them both long before I arrived. Their bodies were merely empty shells when I encountered them."

The calmness in her voice and her subdued reaction to his accusations convinced Clay that she was being truthful. Her presence at the mine was unexpected; she wasn't the one he had come to confront. "Is there someone else here with you? Someone named Zarian?"

"So you've come for your father."

"I came here to get answers."

"Whatever questions you might have, your father is more than capable of answering them."

"Where is Zarian?" asked Clay.

"I know you sense my presence. Why won't you accept it? I am Zarian."

Clay mocked. "You're Zarian? That's impossible."

Gathering her hair to one side, she tied it in a knot. "Why do you think it's impossible?"

"It's obvious you're a woman," Clay said. "You can't be anyone's father."

"The host I now inhabit is female. I first appeared on the surface decades ago and took a male human host. Your mother was enamored with him. No Ocran believed it was possible for a human changed by an Ocran to mate with a pure human, and yet it happened with your mother and me. You are the offspring of that union. I am neither male nor female. I am not of flesh, blood, or bone. I am Ocran. Nevertheless, I am your father."

Clay didn't want to believe it, but what else could explain the sudden mutation of his body and his intrinsic ability to manipulate gravity? It all seemed unreal, like a wild, crazy dream without an ending. The thought of being a descendant of some kind of inhuman life form was too extraordinary to believe but admittedly equally plausible. Clay scrutinized her face for similar features but found none.

"If you're looking for a physical resemblance between us, you won't find it," she said. "Your physical similarities are with the first human I changed, who has since expired. My hope is that we share a deeper connection—a trait that is meaningful and virtuous."

"I don't share anything with you," Clay said.

"Really? You insisted on sparing Lars's life even though you despised him. Why?"

Her question made him uneasy. She clearly knew the answer and it disconcerted him. "I don't owe you any explanations," he shot back.

A vein bulged beneath her skin, snaking from her wrist up her arm to her shoulder. She didn't flinch or acknowledge it. Clay's eyes followed the protrusion as it spread from her shoulder to her neck. "What's happening to you?" he asked. She glanced at the raised vein in her arm. "The process of cessation has begun. My time here is ending, and I need to reconcile with you—my offspring before I expire. The fact that you're still alive means that Rebecca and Octavius succeeded where I had failed in finding you. They are the last ones left who believe as I do. They must have told you that we're in a silent war against Kaden and the other Ocran. Kaden doesn't only want to eliminate you, Clayton; he wants to eradicate all humans from this planet.

In a matter of days, he will have stored up enough energy to slow the rotation of this planet's inner core. It will cause massive earthquakes that will unleash an innumerable number of Ocran from underground around the world. They will change millions of humans, and the remainder they will bury alive. Listen to me carefully: there isn't much time. Kaden's power is expanding, and he will succeed unless the source of his power is cut off. Without the Wheel, he has no access to the Council. The Wheel must be destroyed."

Another vein appeared, but this one throbbed beneath the skin of Zarian's neck. It spread upward into her cheek, constricted, and swelled to three times its original size, pulsating under her skin like a pounding heartbeat. *Why is she reacting as if what was happening to her was normal? Is this what awaits me?*

"I will not change and destroy another human in order to survive here on the surface," said Zarian. "You must finish it. Destroy the Wheel, and Kaden will be weakened. That's when you can permanently extract and eliminate him."

Clay kept shaking his head. "I tried to destroy the Wheel, but it's been moved. I don't know where it is. There's nothing I can do."

He turned and walked away.

"Wait," said Zarian. "You've seen it, and you've touched it. You and the Wheel are linked. Instinct will lead you back to where it's been hidden, and when you find it, you have to destroy it."

Clay turned and faced her. "You're wrong. I don't feel linked to anything, and if you really believe the source of Kaden's power is the Council, then it's obvious you need to have a conversation with them, not me."

"The Council is not a governing body of people, it's one machine," said Zarian.

Clay's brow furrowed in confusion. "You can't be serious. A machine?"

"An omnipotent machine that resides seven miles below the Pacific Ocean in what humans call the Mariana Trench. The only way to stop Kaden is to destroy the Wheel—the conduit to the Council. Once that's accomplished, you would be the only one left who could get close enough to Kaden to finally extract him and end the Ocran takeover of this world."

Clay scoffed, and his expression hardened. "Extract him? You mean kill him and the innocent kid whose body he's taken over."

"Either that, or you can accept the consequences of your inaction. Kaden is residing in Appalachia with Douglas and Pamela Lofton, who are posing as his parents. Find him."

"He could just as easily bury me alive," said Clay.

"True, it's very possible he could end your life, but without the help of the Wheel, he would be severely weakened. Once he's extracted, every Ocran that has entered a human would extract and return to their place underground. Most importantly, Kaden's life form would be swept away in the wind and lost forever."

"I'm not the one for this," said Clay. "I'm no match for him. He nearly killed me. I saw him with my own eyes uproot an entire concrete road and hurl it at me. He created a tornado and sent it to my home that almost killed me and my wife. What makes you think I can fight against that kind of force?"

Zarian looked him directly in the eye, her pupils dilated. "We will one day coexist with humans without destroying them. Don't let Kaden win."

She clenched her teeth, and the protruded vein traveled up to her forehead. Her skin turned milky white, and before he could look away it became completely translucent. She fell to her knees, having no control of her limbs, and gazed up at Clay. "Save your pity," she said and then continued in Latin, "Tam longe in itinere meo veni, quantum corpus humanum pati potest." *—I have come as far in my journey as this human body can endure.*

Her arms and hands changed into solid alabaster, and she was unable to move them.

Without realizing, he heard and spoke another language. Clay responded in Arabic. "Min fadlak, la taghader. Ladayya almazeed min al-as'ila." *—Please, don't leave. I have more questions.*

"I regret that I don't have more time," said Zarian. "I only ask as your father that you not bury my dust in the ground or allow it to be swept away in the wind. You must gather it and disperse it over the waters so that there is no possibility of entering another human and transforming them. I will be forever eradicated, as any other Ocran would be if their dust was dispersed over the waters."

There was a moment of silence followed by a barrage of crackling and popping noises. "You are the future of our kind, Clayton. You are capable of so much more," said Zarian.

In an instant, her body transformed into a solid alabaster statue. Jagged cracks formed in her plaster-like face that spread rapidly from her head to her feet. The statue imploded into tiny particles and crumbled to the ground. Only a handful of dust was left lying within her clothing. Clay stood there frozen, overwhelmed by the dreadfulness of it. He found himself tearing up, though he didn't understand why. He hardly knew her, but a part of him had died.

Sheriff Jenkins pulled up in his patrol car and stepped out with his hand firmly planted on his gun holster. "Where's the woman?"

Clay replied, "He's gone."

CHAPTER 39

REBECCA JOLTED AWAKE in bed. She glanced over at the clock on her nightstand–it read 7:35 a.m. Sensing an uneasiness around her, she threw off her bedcover and rushed to her parents' bedroom; no one was there. Rebecca hurried downstairs into the kitchen where she found Miriam staring intently out the sliding glass door at Kaden. He stood outside in the backyard with his Petaminx cube in hand, rotating the pieces to solve the puzzle. A stag towered over him in a majestic stance with its dark, piercing eyes locked on Miriam. The moment Kaden looked up from the Petaminx cube and glimpsed Rebecca through the glass door, the stag charged toward them at full speed.

Rebecca pulled Miriam away from the door just as the antlers crashed into it. The impact shook the house, and the thunderous sound reverberated throughout the room. The glass door cracked from top to bottom but the layered thickness of it kept it from collapsing. Dazed from the impact, the stag regained its footing, jumped up, and fled from her yard. Streaks of blood stained the cracked glass, and the fear of dread on Miriam's face saddened Rebecca.

"I've seen that little boy before; you were talking to him," said Miriam. "Who is he?"

"Lock the door behind me. No matter what happens, don't open it. Stay inside," said Rebecca firmly.

"You shouldn't go out there. What if it comes back," said Miriam. "Please, do as I asked and lock the door. Promise me…Mom."

"You're not my daughter. You don't have to call me mom."

"I know. I wanted to," said Rebecca.

She stepped out through the sliding glass door and closed it behind her. Miriam locked it from the inside as she was told.

"I'm giving you another chance, Rebecca," shouted Kaden. "Return to us and stop this senseless rebellion that you and Octavius have foolishly started."

With a final twist, he solved the Petaminx cube. "There is one of our kind who needs a fresh human host. I have its form with me. Demonstrate your loyalty and assist me in changing the one you call your mother."

Rebecca turned and locked eyes with Miriam, whose expression betrayed her confusion and vulnerability. She stood behind the glass door, physically frail compared to the Ocran, and oblivious to the imminent threat Kaden posed to her life. Determined to protect her, Rebecca faced Kaden again. "No!" she exclaimed. "I won't let you."

Kaden sneered. "She will be changed. You can't stop it from happening, but you can save yourself from eternal elimination if you join me. We can be best friends, Rebecca."

Rebecca answered, defiant. "Your intention is to kill people. I don't wanna be your friend."

"So what about my intentions? The atrocities they commit are killing this world and the innocent animals that depend on it."

"What you're doing is just as cruel. It's not right, Kaden. They deserve a chance."

"They've had their chance, and I'll do what I want."

"Then I will be your enemy."

Kaden sighed. "Very well. If that's your choice."

He turned and walked away. Rebecca looked back at Miriam behind the glass door. She pressed her hands against it with her fingers splayed. A tear rolled down Miriam's cheek as she mouthed the words, "I love you." Taking a deep breath, Rebecca tore her gaze away from Miriam and went after Kaden.

Clay tossed his car keys onto the kitchen table and rushed straight to the bedroom without uttering a word to Tara. She glimpsed the distress etched on his face and trailed him. His jeans were caked with mud from the knees down, and she expected an explanation. When she didn't get one, she questioned him about it.

He remained silent, removing his wet t-shirt and slipping into a fresh pair of jeans. His silence only made her more determined to get an answer. "Are you gonna tell me what happened, or do I have to keep asking you questions?"

"It's not a big deal," Clay mumbled.

Tara closed the distance between them and in a soft, insistent tone, said, "Keep your promise." It was all she needed to say—he knew exactly what she meant. He had vowed to be open with her, even if it meant losing her.

"I met the one who claims to be my father. She was one of them. One of the Ocran."

"What do you mean *she*?"

"I know this won't make sense, but Ocran are neither male nor female. They assume the sex of whatever human form they inhabit. I watched my father die and disintegrate into a handful of dust, and there was nothing I could do about it."

Clay slumped onto the bed; head bowed. The once faint, translucent skin on his arm had spread, now reaching his shoulder. "His name was Zarian," he added quietly.

"How can you be sure it really was your father? What if he's lying to you? How can you be certain if there's no way to do a DNA test?"

"Look at me, Tara. My arms, my eyes, my back. The abilities I have—it's not normal, and it's not human either. There's no explaining it away. I'm part of them."

Tara settled beside Clay on the bed and guided his hand to her swollen belly. "You're a part of *us*, and that's what matters the most.

I love you, Clayton Krutcher. We'll get through this together." She embraced him, and he kissed her. "We could still visit a doctor," she said. "Maybe they can help."

Clay sighed, exasperated. She still didn't get it. His physical abnormalities weren't a medical condition—they were hereditary and not human, and he needed her to accept it. "If they found out about me, you know what they would do. I don't want to be locked up, treated like a lab rat in some experiment. I'm not going to a doctor, Tara. There's nothing they can do for me."

She nodded, though he wasn't convinced she understood or even agreed with the point he was trying to make.

"I went to the lake. That's why my jeans were wet. My father's last wish was for me to scatter his dust over the water. It would prevent him from ever returning to change another human—taking over some innocent person's life. So that's what I did. I promised not to bury his dust in the ground or let it be carried away by the wind."

"Why did he die?" Tara asked.

Clay shrugged. "I don't know." He put on a clean t-shirt, snatched the keys from the kitchen table, and strode toward the front door.

"Where are you going?"

"There's something I have to do…for us."

Clay retrieved an ax from the closet and stepped out the door.

CHAPTER 40

THE URGENT WARNING about what Kaden planned to unleash on the people of Appalachia and consequently the entire world wasn't what spurred Clay into action. It was always about the diamonds. The wealth they represented would transform life for him and Tara. He could finally take care of her as he had always wanted and provide the financial support his newborn son would need. All he had to do was to find and destroy the Wheel, and all his problems would be solved. It was worth the risk if he could just locate it.

Clay recalled what Zarian told him moments before his transformation—that his nexus to the Wheel would guide his instincts to its concealed location, and Clay had been driving aimlessly, waiting for that moment to happen. He considered Oceola and the places he visited there. *The Wheel couldn't have been moved far*, he surmised. It had to be functioning somewhere in Oceola, where he first caught sight of it—*maybe in the place where it all began*. Clay accelerated down the highway, now confident in his destination. His instinct led him back to the pawnshop.

Clay opened the trunk, retrieved the ax, and approached the front door. A neon sign glowed red in the window, spelling *Closed*. He peered through the glass door and focused on the dim light beaming from the rear of the shop. Clay swung the ax at the glass door and shattered it.

He expected the alarm to blare, but there was no sound but the hum of the air conditioning in the room. He unlocked the door from the inside and stepped in. The air was thick with the familiar scent of burning copper, so intense he could taste it. Where was it coming from?

The smell intensified as he walked across broken glass toward the back of the shop. Black curtains hid a back room where creaking noises emanated. Clay pushed the curtains aside and entered the pitch-black space. He found a light switch on the wall and flicked it on. What he had come for was mounted to the floor in the room's center: the Wheel. It looked just as it had before, made from wood with clear blue sapphire spokes and a pulley system of rope and leather. The brass pipe extended from the Wheel into the floor. Clay's breathing quickened at the sight of it. Despite no one cranking it, the Wheel continued to creak and sputter out nothing but air.

Clay scanned the area around the Wheel for traces of sand but found none. The curtains parted and Raphael stepped into the room with fear in his eyes as he focused on the ax in Clay's hand.

"Until now, I never fully understood why Kaden was so intent on eliminating you," said Raphael. "You're only part human, but more importantly you are Ocran. And yet you're here foolishly trying to destroy what keeps us all alive."

"This thing isn't what's keeping me alive," Clay countered. "Without it, you can't change any more people."

Raphael smirked. "Is that what Rebecca told you? She's so dramatic. You have to understand, it's the human side of you that's causing you to think irrationally. Put down the ax, Clayton."

Clay raised the ax overhead, ready to strike.

"Don't," Raphael warned, extending his palm toward Clay. The spiral tattoo materialized in the center. Clay swung the ax through the Wheel's spokes then yanked it back. He struck it again, hitting the wooden frame and splitting it apart. The creaking noises faded before falling completely silent.

Raphael put his hands over his ears. "What have you done?" he cried out. His hands were pressed tightly over his ears as if he was trying to block out an agonizing clamor. Clay heard nothing but the crumbling of the Wheel's wooden structure as he struck it once more. Panicked, Raphael dashed out of the room, his hands still shielding his ears from the piercing sound that only he could hear.

○   ○   ○

The aroma of freshly picked fruit drew Abby to the produce department of Miner's Market. She wandered leisurely through the aisle before stopping in front of a table displaying plump green tomatoes. She meticulously inspected each one before settling on three and then tossing them into a plastic bag and into the grocery cart that Jimmy pushed behind her.

While he continued down the aisle, engrossed in a conversation on his cell phone, Abby's attention shifted to a display of red wine. She picked up a bottle and held it out to Jimmy. "Should we get one of these?"

Jimmy glanced away from the phone and offered a quick nod. "Get two," he said.

Abby obliged, grasping a bottle in each hand. She went to place them in their cart when suddenly she froze, her eyes locked in a frightened stare. "What's wrong?" said Jimmy. The bottles of wine fell from her hands and shattered on the floor. Blood-red liquid spread out like a stain across the polished hardwood, seeping beneath her shoes.

Agony washed over Abby's face as she bent over, hands pressed tightly against her ears, desperate to block out the excruciating sound. It mimicked a foghorn blasting directly into her eardrums, and she could neither suppress the deafening noise nor escape from it. Jimmy ended his phone call and rushed to her side. "Honey, what's going on?" He reached out to embrace her. She recoiled from his touch and paced the floor in tight circles.

She screamed, "You don't hear it! It's so loud. Something's wrong!"

He approached her again, but she pushed him away. "The Wheel, something has happened to the Wheel," she cried, her voice trembling with fear.

269

Curious shoppers cast side glances at the unfolding scene, their unease palpable as they quickened their pace to distance themselves from the disturbance. Jimmy stared at Abby, perplexed and uncertain. She still clutched her ears, hunched over as if the sound was unbearable.

The store manager appeared and cautiously approached her. "Ma'am, if you could step away from the spill, we can clean that right up," he said,

Abby straightened up and took a step back, her hand raised defensively in front of her, motioning for him not to come closer.

"Are you okay, miss?" the manager asked.

Jimmy intercepted him, offering a nervous smile. "She'll be okay. She's just tired."

Abby's gaze bore into the manager's eyes. "Can't you hear it?"

He shook his head. "No, ma'am. What is it?"

She trembled as she stammered, "It's excruciating. Why can't you hear it?"

"I can call someone for help, ma'am," he offered.

Jimmy intervened again. "You don't need to call anybody. We'll be okay. I'm just gonna take her home."

Abby's eyes widened as she stared at the manager, her voice barely above a whisper, "One of you has found it…and you're trying to destroy it."

Jimmy made another attempt to embrace her, but Abby jerked away from his outstretched arms and dashed past him. She fled through the exit doors with her hands still over her ears as the sound continued to torment her. Jimmy muttered a quick apology to the store manager and hurried out the door after her.

CHAPTER 41

REBECCA FOLLOWED KADEN all the way to the lake but lost track of him in the surrounding overgrown foliage. "I know you're here, Kaden," she shouted. "I'm not afraid of you. You can come out now."

She waited for footsteps. They never came. The silence was enough to make her nervous. "You can't stay hidden forever," she said.

A tap on her shoulder made her jerk around.

"I'm right here. I'm not hiding," said Kaden. He gazed at her with cold, empty eyes and the spiral tattoo aglow in his palm. And then came the sound—a continuous foghorn blast, a sound so deafening she had to cover her ears to protect her hearing. She glanced at Kaden. He mirrored her agony, shielding his ears to save his hearing. The energy drained from Rebecca's body and Kaden's tattoo faded away to nothing. Clay had succeeded in destroying the Wheel, obliterating their abilities. The foghorn sound abated, and the ominous silence returned.

"The Wheel is no more," said Rebecca.

To be certain, she tried summoning an animal, and the tattoo did not appear. "We are all the same now," she said to Kaden, "without the ability to manipulate the elements or the beasts of the field. We're now in many ways...human."

Kaden lamented as though he had lost his puppy again and dropped to his knees, anguishing. He buried his face in his cupped hands, sobbing.

It astonished her that he had allowed himself to cede to one of the most extreme human emotions, and letting it manifest instead of deleting it from his consciousness.

"Why are you crying? There's no need to be sad about it," said Rebecca. "The right to control the elements has always belonged to the Council. We don't need it. We can be content in this human form without manipulating things. And when our bodies fail from old age, we can extract and return beneath the surface with the others of our kind. It's not so bad, Kaden."

Rebecca reached her hand out to him. He took hold of it, got up and flung his arms tightly around her in an all-encompassing embrace. He rested his head against her chest like a wounded animal who needed her help. Perhaps she had misjudged him, and he had always possessed the capacity for redemption. She held him close to her with one hand and caressed his face with the other. It gratified her to console him in his most vulnerable state. Calmed by it, Kaden closed his eyes.

"Are you my friend?" he whimpered.

Rebecca paused. She didn't want to offend him, but she couldn't lie to him either.

"Maybe someday in the future we'll be friends," she said.

The ground cracked under their feet. Stunned, she recoiled from him. The crack spread across the ground in all directions. "What's happening? said Rebecca.

Kaden stood there smug. "The Wheel is obsolete," said Kaden. "The Council and I are intrinsically linked now."

Rebecca trembled. "It's not true, you're lying. The Council is linked to no one, only to the inner core of this world."

"I found a way, Rebecca. It is true."

Fear overwhelmed her and she turned and ran. Kaden made a swift move with his hand and the crack spread across the ground at breakneck speed toward her. The second it reached the space beneath her, it formed a fissure, and she fell straight down up to her shoulders in it. The width of it was so narrow that she could barely move her arms. Kaden had found a way to harness the power of the Council without the assistance of the Wheel. She was mortified by what he could do with its power—he could destroy everything.

Kaden walked over to the fissure and kneeled in front of Rebecca's face. "You had so much potential, and look what you've done with it—wasted it on human flesh and blood in order to save a species that has no proclivity for anything meaningful except the frivolous pursuit of riches, never for the lives of innocent animals or for the survival of a planet they forcefully occupied. Your behavior is disgusting and intolerable, and it ends now. The Ocran will reclaim what rightfully belongs to us," said Kaden.

Trampling footsteps made him turn around. Octavius was facing him.

"Octavius, be careful. He has the power of the Council!" Rebecca shouted.

"I know. It was inevitable," said Octavius, unduly calm.

Rebecca shattered in confusion. "What're you saying?"

"We can't keep fighting him. We can't win, Rebecca," said Octavius. "The Council has chosen him to lead."

"Only because he deceived the Council," said Rebecca. "You're gonna help me out of this hole, and we'll defeat him. Both of us—together."

Octavius avoided eye contact with her, sighed and looked straight ahead. "The Council has determined that the body you've inhabited is destined for infirmity, requiring you to be extracted. Kaden has found you a new human host, a body that is strong and thriving and more deserving of who you are."

Rebecca managed to lift herself several inches, but in the end, she fell back into the fissure. "I don't want a new host because I don't wanna end another human life," she fretted. "This is who I am now. How could you, Octavius? What are you doing?"

"I'm saving us from eradication," he replied,

"No, you're not. Can't you see he's deceiving you? He's going to eliminate us both. You can't believe him!"

Rebecca tried again to lift herself out of the fissure, but she couldn't get a firm enough grip on the walls of dirt that kept crumbling down around her. Her attempt at summoning the animals failed, and there was nothing she could do to manipulate the elements. She conceded her abilities were lost to the destruction of the Wheel.

"Don't fight the extraction, Rebecca, if you just let it happen it'll be over soon," said Octavius.

"Listen to me, Octavius. Please, don't let him do this," pleaded Rebecca.

"It's the only choice we have, the only way we can survive."

Rebecca melted at his betrayal. The one she had trusted with her life had handed it over to a tyrant, as if it had no value at all. She mourned for herself, but mostly she mourned for Octavius. He had weakened, and she grieved that he no longer had confidence in her or himself that they could emerge victorious, that the cause they represented, the lives that they would save, was worth it.

Kaden kneeled in front of her. The tattoo glowed in his palm, and he pressed it against Rebecca's forehead. Her eyes locked on Octavius, silently imploring for his help. He turned away, unable to bear her pleading gaze. Rebecca's body jolted three times, and when Kaden lifted his palm from her face, the tattoo had faded away and blue dust particles floated out of her mouth into Kaden's cupped hands. Rebecca's eyes closed in death and her human host's body collapsed into the fissure.

Kaden walked toward the lakeshore with Rebecca's dust particles in his hands. Octavius's eyes widened. "Where are you going?"

"To the lake to get rid of her," said Kaden.

Octavius's jaw dropped. "No! You promised you wouldn't."

"I changed my mind. She didn't wanna be my friend so why should I care?"

Kaden stepped into the shallow part of the lake and gazed back at Octavius. It amused him to see such a commanding and confident Ocran as Octavius become frightened like a human child by what he was about to do.

"Don't eliminate her, Kaden. Punish me instead."

Kaden beamed with an inflated sense of accomplishment as he held

Rebecca's dust particles in his hands. "I wanna hear you, on your knees, beg for her life right now."

Octavius shot him a perplexed expression. "But you know I'm not capable of that."

A wry smile crept across Kaden's face. "And you know that once I've changed my mind, I won't change it back."

Kaden spread his fingers apart, and the dust scattered over the lake.

"Kaden no!" Octavius screamed. He charged at Kaden, dashing wildly toward him. The spiral tattoo reappeared on Kaden's palm, and he pointed it at Octavius. The force of it propelled Octavius backward across the ground and down into the fissure. The crack sealed instantly over him, swallowing both his and Rebecca's bodies alive.

Kaden stepped out of the lake without remorse for disposing of Rebecca and Octavius in such a horrific manner. Now that he had merged with the power of the Council, he was ready to ignite the surfacing and end the catastrophic reign of corrupted humanity.

He gazed up at the flock of tundra swans flying overhead. The timing of the migration was off and the flock appeared much smaller than it should have been, indicating that the health of the ecosystems there at the lake were at risk.

Kaden raised his arms and waved them back and forth. The branches shimmered in the whistling wind, and storm clouds formed and gathered in the sky. Within seconds the darkened clouds multiplied, blocking the light of the sun. The winds swirled around Kaden, tossing the autumn leaves in midair. Invigorated, he lay on his stomach, and pressed his ear and both glowing palms against the ground. The sound of the Earth's inner core rotating over three thousand miles below permeated. Above the core, millions of Ocran were roving about in the hollow underground, waiting to be unleashed to the surface. The ground rumbled, and Kaden smiled, exhilarated by it. For the first time, the tattoo appeared on both his palms.

CHAPTER 42

THE JOURNEY HOME from Oceola afforded Clay the time to reflect on what he had done. He was confident his second attempt at destroying the Wheel had succeeded, but had it really changed anything? Why did he feel the same restlessness he felt before it was destroyed?

Clay arrived back in Lynch with a gnawing suspicion that something was still amiss. Brooding storm clouds had blanketed the sky in dismal gray, and an orange hue permeated through the spaces in-between. It all looked surreal and unworldly.

Tara stood outside the door, waiting for him, the wind sweeping her hair over her eyes. He walked up to her, concerned. "What's wrong?"

"Is he causing this?" asked Tara. "Is this another storm he sent to hurt us?"

"No, he can't hurt anyone anymore."

Tara's eyes suddenly clung to something lurking beyond Clay's shoulder, her expression contorting from fear. Clay pivoted to see what had captured her attention in such a dreadful way.

"It's him," said Tara.

A frail-looking bearded man was standing on the pavement, lugging a bindle over his shoulder.

"You know him?" Clay replied. "Who is he?"

"It's the homeless man I saw at the drugstore. Clay, he's the one who was stalking me. He's been to our house before."

"Go inside. I'll be there in a minute," said Clay.

Tara stepped into her house but watched him through the half-opened door. Clay rushed over to the man who clearly didn't appear to be intimidated by his aggressive approach.

"What's your problem?" asked Clay. "Why are you following my wife?"

"How else would I find you?" replied the man offhandedly.

The snarky remark stoked Clay's anger. "If you don't leave right now, I'm calling the police."

"I'm standing on the pavement. It's public property and it doesn't matter anyway. The police are useless in what's about to happen to this world. I can see it in your eyes. You're aware of what's coming, aren't you?"

A gust blew a shard of tile off the roof of the neighbor's home. It hit the homeless man across his face, leaving a bleeding cut. He didn't budge or react to it at all. This was no ordinary man. The burnt copper odor scent he emitted confirmed it. "Who are you?"

The man placed the bindle on the ground. "Open it. Inside you'll find what you wanted," said the man.

"Why would I do that?"

"Rebecca asked me to deliver it to you."

The fact that the man knew Rebecca gave credence to what he had to say. Clay untied the bindle, reached inside, and pulled out a small leather pouch. The man stepped back as if he was afraid of it. "What is this?" asked Clay.

"It's what Rebecca promised you."

Clay opened the pouch and poured the contents into his hands. There were six crystal diamonds that resembled the ones he had left in his truck that were lost in the fire.

"I hope it fulfills your need," said the man. Clay nodded, indifferent that he finally had in his hands what could change his life for the better. He shoved the diamonds into his pocket. "How do you know Rebecca?"

"I am Ocran," he said, "and I once believed as Kaden believes, that humanity has no redeeming value. However true that might be, I cannot continue to be part of his systematic annihilation of an entire race. I renounced my allegiance to Kaden and joined with Rebecca and Octavius and the others. I expect Kaden to find me and punish me for my defection."

"He can't punish anyone," said Clay. "The Wheel is destroyed. His abilities are gone."

"You were too late. He has established his kinship with the Council now. His abilities have expanded. Can't you feel it? He's slowing this world's rotation."

The ground beneath their feet rumbled and then abruptly stopped. "What was that?" asked Clay.

"It's beginning," said the man. The wind shifted and pushed them both to the side. "There isn't much time before he causes the Council to completely halt this planet's rotation. I have accepted my final mission to return to my station and wait for Kaden's retribution—my elimination."

The ground shook again, tossing Clay about. The homeless man remained steady on his feet. "Rebecca said that you and your offspring are the future of our collective species," he said. "It's unfortunate that we will never know. Goodbye, Clayton."

The man walked away, fighting the force of the winds as he turned the corner. *It wasn't over.* After everything he had done to destroy the Wheel, it still wasn't enough to stop Kaden. He trudged somberly to the front door, where Tara awaited him.

"Did you feel that? Was that an earthquake?" she asked.

"No," said Clay.

"Then what was it?"

"I'm not sure," he said.

He followed her into the house and sat down in front of his laptop. Tara stared out the window, searching for any trace of the homeless man. Nothing stood out except the onslaught of tree branches swaying back and forth by the force of the wind. "I can't believe that man came back to our house again," she said. "You were talking to him. What did he say to you?"

"Just crazy nonsense. He won't be back here again," said Clay. He typed a name in the search engine on his laptop and started scrolling through the results until he found the information he needed. He wrote it down on a piece of paper, hurried to the closet, and grabbed his jacket.

"Clay, where you going?"

"I gotta go to Appalachia."

"Appalachia? Why? You just got home."

"I have to finish what I started, Tara."

"No, you don't. You don't owe them anything. You belong here. You're not a part of them."

"I'm sorry," said Clay as he put on his jacket.

"Then I'm going with you," she replied. She grabbed her cell phone from the table and followed him to the door.

"Tara, I have to do this alone. You can't go with me."

"Why not?" she snapped.

"Because it's not safe."

"This is about Kaden, isn't it? He's doing this—the wind and the earthquake, the cracks in the ground. It's all him."

He nodded. "Yeah."

"I don't care. I'm going."

"Tara, please, you can't go."

"You're not leaving me here alone," she said, teary-eyed. "I'm not going to sit and wait around, not knowing what's happening to you. You can't just keep me in the dark and expect me to be okay with it."

"Honey, please, I have to do this alone. It's the only way."

Tara sighed, a sign that she had given in to him. Clay caressed her face. "I don't want you hurt. I love you, and I want you and our baby boy safe."

He kissed her tenderly and looked her in the eye. "*I'll be back,*" he said and walked out the door.

○ ○ ○

Not more than a minute after Officer Holt returned to the Appalachia police department, he was alerted that he had a call from Sheriff Jenkins. He sat down in his cubicle and picked up the line.

"This is Officer Holt."

"Hey, how's it goin'? I got your message," said the sheriff. "So, you have news for me?"

"Yeah, I wish it was good news. The fact is we found Deputy Rosalind's Jeep here in Appalachia off-road in a cornfield."

"Tell me. Was she inside?"

"No, it's nothing like that. We just started combing it for evidence," said Holt.

Jenkins exhaled a sigh of frustration. "What am I gonna tell her family?"

"We still have a team of officers out there actively looking for her."

"I appreciate that. Was there any exterior damage to the car?"

"Naw, it's clean," said Holt. "We're holding it at a lot in downtown Appalachia if you wanna come down and see it for yourself."

"Yeah, I'll get there before tomorrow afternoon," said Jenkins. "Since she disappeared across state lines, I contacted the FBI about getting involved. I'll send the agent your way as well to take a look at it."

"Okay, I'll look out for 'em."

There was an awkward pause that Jenkins finally broke. "She's very important to me," he said. "If you find out anything else, no matter how trivial, please call me first."

"Will do, Sheriff. Did you guys feel that earthquake we just had?" asked Holt.

"Yeah, we felt it here in Lynch too. Very strange. There's never been a quake in these parts. Never."

"Now we have a tornado warning with cars on the highway being blown into different lanes. It's a mess out here."

"We're dealing with the same problems," said Sheriff Jenkins.

"Before you go, I wanted to tell you that I never received that fax of your missing kid, Jeremy Astin."

"Sorry about that. Ansley took a couple of days off, and it didn't get sent. I'll fax it over now," said Jenkins.

"Great, I'll be in touch."

Officer Holt stepped into the copy room and waited for it. The printer made a humming sound as the flyer slowly emerged. He did a double-take. The picture was of a child he recognized. It was the Lofton kid, Kaden.

His suspicions about the Loftons were justified. It explained why they said they were from a town in Kentucky that he never heard of. *Who are these people who have kidnapped a child and are posing as his parents?* Aside from false identities, they were covertly dangerous. To secure Jeremy's safety, he needed to remove him from their custody as soon as possible. Officer Holt hopped into his squad car, fighting the wind as he headed to the Loftons' home, prepared and ready for a confrontation.

CHAPTER 43

THE HOUSE LOOKED nothing like how Clay imagined. It was just an average dwelling nestled in a rural neighborhood. How could the one who wielded such unlimited power over the elements live such a seemingly simple life in a modest home? Kaden had shown himself to be cunning and manipulative. Was his home just another part of the facade?

Clay pondered what Zarian had told him, how millions would die if Kaden wasn't stopped and what that would mean for Tara and the future of his unborn son. Taking in a deep breath to muster up the nerve, Clay got out of his car. The wind nearly lifted him off his feet. With every step he took toward the house, cracks resembling roots of a massive tree formed on the pavement and spread rapidly around him.

Pamela stood at the door with her eyes fixed on him. He walked deliberately toward her, resolute to a mission of ending the threat of Kaden's existence. She examined her palm; the spiral tattoo never appeared. "The Wheel can't help you. It's destroyed," said Clay. "Where is Kaden?"

Pamela backed away behind the door. "You can't stop what's inevitable," she said.

She rushed to shut him out, but Clay forced the door open before she had a chance to lock it. He barged through, pushing her back against the wall. Pamela yelled Douglas's name as she grabbed a vase from the counter. She swung it at his face and missed. Clay snatched it out of her hand and tossed it behind him. Pamela growled and charged him. Her neck landed in the grip of his hand, and he used the force of her momentum to push her backward. The back of Pamela's head slammed against the cabinet counter. She slid down the wall to the floor, unconscious.

Doug edged up from behind Clay, grabbed him by the collar of his shirt, and flung him to the other side of the room. The porcelain lamp shattered across the table, and framed pictures fell off the wall and crashed to the floor one after another.

"What gives you the right to invade my home, assault my wife and vandalize my property?" said Doug.

He lifted Clay off the floor by his shirt collar and tossed him across the room again like an old rag doll. Clay landed across a wooden chair and collapsed it.

"It puzzles me why some are afraid of you," said Doug. "You're just another flawed, vacuous human, nothing more."

Clay recovered and staggered to his feet. "I'm not here to fight you. I've come for Kaden," he defiantly muttered.

"You're not going anywhere near him."

Doug took a butcher knife from the kitchen drawer and rushed back to the room. Clay reached down into his pocket and cupped the diamonds in his clenched fist. Doug raised the knife and swiped at him. Clay swayed to the side and punched Doug in the center of his abdomen. His eyes widened, and he gaped at Clay. An outline of a cloth burn in the shape of Clay's fist was left imprinted on Doug's shirt. He convulsed, dropped to his knees, and fell over on the floor. A trace of smoke eased into the air from the burnt hole left in Doug's abdomen. There was no blood. The heat from the impact singed the blood vessels in the wound closed. What Rebecca told Clay about the diamonds was true–they were extremely lethal to the Ocran, and his hunch to use them had saved his life. He placed them back in his pocket and walked over to Doug to get a closer look at the wound. Blue dust particles floated out from Doug's nostrils and ascended. He had inadvertently extracted Doug from his human host. Clay covered his nose and mouth with his hand so the particles wouldn't enter his body.

Eyes were on him. He turned and saw Kaden standing in the doorway, staring at Doug's entity floating away as blue particles out the open front door. Kaden sprinted out the back door, and Clay staggered out behind him. Storm clouds had morphed into deep, dark-gray pillows in the sky. Clay limped over to the empty lot next door, searching for Kaden. The ground shifted, jolting him. Loud, popping noises like firecrackers cut through the morbid silence. Where was Kaden?

A child's voice rang out. "Are you searching for me, Clayton? It's too late. The surfacing has already begun."

Clay scanned the area around him. No one was there. "Where are you? Why are you hiding?"

"I'm right here," said Kaden. "I'm not hiding."

Clay scanned his surroundings again and still didn't see anyone.

"What did Rebecca tell you, Clayton? That Ocran and humans can coexist?"

Kaden stepped out from behind a bush in front of Clay and smiled. "Look at yourself," he said. "You are what the human race will become if we assimilate: a skeleton with veins, arteries, and blood vessels. Look at your arms, Clayton. They're grotesque."

Clay took off his jacket and tossed it on the ground. His arms were just as Kaden described. His skin from his shoulder down to his wrist was paper-thin and translucent. All the veins and blue-colored blood vessels in his arm were visible and wrapped around raw bone. The mutation was spreading throughout his entire body.

"Is that what you want for the future of your kind?" said Kaden. "Of course you don't, and neither do I."

Kaden pointed his palms at the ground. The spiral tattoo appeared on both. A crevice surged across the ground, creating cracks that ended in a deep chasm fifty feet away. It stunned Clay to learn Kaden still had *abilities*.

"Your destruction of the Wheel has only revealed my renewed kinship to the Council," said Kaden.

"You don't have to do this. We'll accept you in your original form. We can all thrive on this earth together," Clay replied.

"You can accept us?" Kaden's anger boiled over and he yelled at the top of his lungs. "This is not your world! It has never belonged to your kind. It belongs to *us!*"

The tattoo on Kaden's palm glowed, and a surge of wind hurled Clay across the ground, down into the chasm.

Kaden trudged over to the edge, expecting to see only a dark, endless drop. Instead, Clay dangled over the edge, holding on to the surface with one hand in a desperate effort to keep himself from falling.

"I see you've learned how to restrain the gravitational element," said Kaden. "Interesting, that you still have abilities without the assistance of the Wheel. We are the same in so many ways."

Kaden pointed his glowing palm at the chasm, but the earth surrounding Clay only crumbled around him. It failed to converge over his head and seal him underground as Kaden intended.

When the glow faded, he shrugged. "It doesn't matter, Clayton. You can't hold on forever. Eventually gravity will win, and you will fall, and we will take back what rightfully belongs to us. Millions of Ocran will surface, changing human hosts and then extracting from them until all of you are eliminated."

Clay relived all the warnings from Rebecca, Octavius, and Zarian about Kaden's diabolical plan of destruction and how he had treated those warnings as exaggerations. What could he do now? His fall into the chasm was imminent. How much longer could he manipulate the gravitational force around his hand before the blue outline fades away and he lets go?

Kaden raised his palm to the sky and waved. Two rock doves flew down from the trees and landed on the ground next to his feet. "It'll all be over quickly, Clayton, if you just let go."

Clay remained silent, staring up at the fading blue outline around his weakening hand.

"You're stubborn inconsequential creatures," said Kaden. "It's astonishing how you were able to contaminate Rebecca and Octavius so easily. If you're expecting them to come to your aid again, you'll be disappointed."

"Did you hurt them?"

"That's a senseless question, Clayton. I don't hurt things. I eliminate them."

The rock doves stepped across Clay's hand, one after the other and pecked at his fingers, drawing blood. Clay squirmed, barely holding on to the surface.

CHAPTER 44

OFFICER HOLT PULLED his patrol car to a stop by the Loftons' place, tucking it in snugly behind Clay's vehicle. As he advanced toward the house, his trained eye caught a glimpse of the front door partially ajar, and an errant gust of wind pushed it wide open. His hand inched toward his holster–something was amiss. Hauling the Loftons' in for questioning may not go as smoothly as he had planned.

A voice, blurting out something incomprehensible from the neighboring lot, shattered the suspicious silence, disrupting his intended entry into the house. In a heartbeat, he veered away to where the house met the wooded lot.

There, he spotted Kaden standing perilously close to the edge of what appeared to be a massive sinkhole, one step away from plunging into its depths. Officer Holt shouted Jeremy's name. It pierced the eerie stillness as he sprinted through the foliage toward him. The startled rock doves took flight, their wings flapping erratically. When Kaden spun around to confront the approaching officer, Clay, with one hand still clinging to the precipice's edge, reached up in an act of sheer will, clutched Kaden's ankle and swung him over the chasm. Clay held on tenaciously to the edge of the abyss with a solitary hand, while he simultaneously dangled Kaden by his ankle.

"If you want to live," said Clay, "extract from Jeremy's body, or I'll drop you."

"You wouldn't hurt a little boy, Clayton. He's innocent, and his parents need him," said Kaden.

Officer Holt reached the chasm, his heart disconcerted that he had arrived too late to prevent Kaden from plummeting into its depths. As he moved closer, he couldn't believe his eyes. Suspended precariously on the precipice, were fingers tightly gripping the ledge. He cast a gaze downward to discern who the fingers were attached to and beheld a man in a harrowing scene, teetering on the brink of a bottomless chasm with one hand, his life hanging in the balance. Simultaneously, with his other hand, he dangled Jeremy by his ankle over the dark and endless drop. The bizarre scene startled Officer Holt to action. "Hold on! Hold on!" he nervously shouted.

Holt sprinted to the trunk of his patrol car and grabbed the heavy-duty utility rope he used to anchor his fishing boat to the dock. He raced back to the scene and tied one end of the rope around a nearby oak, and the other end he wrapped tightly around his waist.

Officer Holt lied flat on the ground and grabbed hold of Clay's forearm. He struggled to pull Clay out inch-by-inch until he was finally above ground. Clay kept his hold on Kaden's ankle, dragging him out of the chasm by what Officer Holt thought, was unbelievable strength.

He stood out of breath from the ordeal and hurried to untie the rope from around his waist. "Is the boy okay?"

With an eye on Kaden, Clay shrugged and sat on the ground, wiping the sweat from his brow. Kaden awakened, sobbing without tears.

Officer Holt stepped over and rubbed his shoulders in a sincere effort to console him.

"What happened? How did you guys end up in the sinkhole?" asked Officer Holt.

Before Kaden could answer, Clay interjected. "It's not a sinkhole."

Now even more confounded by Clay's answer, officer Holt looked Kaden in the eye. "What's your name? Are you Jeremy?"

Kaden ignored his question and pointed at Clay. "That man tried to hurt me. He wanted to put me in the hole and bury me."

Officer Holt gazed suspiciously at Clay. "Get up and put your hands behind your back."

"He's lying. Don't believe him," said Clay. "He's not who you think he is."

"I said stand up and put your hands behind your back. Now!"

While the officer's back was turned, Kaden stretched out his palm at him. The tattoo glowed, and when Officer Holt attempted to secure the handcuffs to Clay's wrists, he was lifted off the ground and sent soaring backward over a hundred feet. His back slammed into the side of his squad car. On impact he slumped to the ground revealing the elongated dent his head left in the driver's side door.

Clay took advantage of the distraction and shoved Kaden. He pinned his hands to the ground, preventing him from utilizing the spiral tattoo. "Extract yourself from him now," Clay demanded, "or I'll kill the kid, and you'll be trapped inside his dead body forever."

"Taking a child's life is not in your nature. I know you, Clayton."

"No, you don't me at all. I will kill him if I have to, I swear." Clay wrapped both his hands around Kaden's throat and squeezed.

"Killing my host won't stop us," said Kaden, gurgling as he strained to get the words out. "It will only delay what is inevitable. Look around you, Clayton. See all the Ocran surfacing, searching for human hosts."

Under an overcast sky, the day had darkened. Clay gazed up at swirling trails of blue dust particles ascending in every direction into the air out of cracks in the ground and the wind whistling as it carried it away.

"Millions of us will fill this world," said Kaden. "The Council and I will become one for all time, and I will return with even greater dominion over the elements. All humanity will be eliminated, and your wife and your son will be the first to be destroyed."

The conviction in Kaden's voice left no doubt that he intended to do exactly what he said. Clay squeezed Kaden's neck even tighter so that he didn't have to hear him speak another word. The happiest memories of Clay's past flashed before him: the day he met Tara, the moment she told him she was pregnant, the weekends he'd spent fishing at the lake with his Grandpa Ellis as a child. Kaden's existence threatened everything that he loved, and the worst of it all was denying his unborn son the chance to grow up and be whatever he wanted.

Clayton Michael Krutcher understood that he couldn't live his life just for himself anymore; it would be for the lives of those he loved and for the countless innocent souls oblivious to Kaden's deadly threat.

○ ○ ○

Officer Holt regained consciousness. He staggered to his feet, dazed, and checked that his revolver remained in its holster before radioing for backup. Fierce winds pushed him forward, and he covered his face to block the strange blue dust particles that swirled in the air all around him. Up ahead in the overgrown lot, Kaden was on the ground, and Clay hovered over him with his hands around his neck. The sight of an adult choking a child galvanized Holt.

He shouted, "Let him go!"

Holt rushed toward them. Clay ignored the command and maintained his grip on Kaden's throat. Jeremy's life was fading away, and it agonized Clay to see it happen. Harming a child was unthinkable, and attempting to take a child's life would label him a monster. He prayed in the end, Jeremy would survive Kaden's extraction and the child's life would be spared, but that scenario was a longshot. Now that he had come to the point of no return, he had no choice than to go through with it. Kaden's mere existence placed Tara, the baby, and millions of people in danger of being changed or killed. His moment to bring an end to it had come. Clay kept squeezing Jeremy's throat as the irises in the child's eyes turned from ocean-blue to brown. Officer Holt reached them just as Kaden's entity, in the form of blue-tinted dust particles, floated from Jeremy's opened mouth, and as Clay had anticipated, into his own nostrils. Officer Holt stood there, dumbfounded.

Clay reached into his pocket, grabbed the diamonds, and swallowed them whole, trapping Kaden's entity within his body with no means of escape. An immediate burning sensation coated his throat, and his eyes rolled back. The diamonds had in the end supplied him with what he really needed—not the promise of prosperity like what his Grandpa Ellis had taught him to value the most, but it provided the key to Kaden's annihilation. His death would assure Tara and his unborn son's survival.

"Step away from the boy, or you'll be shot," said Officer Holt with his revolver pointed at Clay's head. Clay's thoughts were drifting away, being blotted out and replaced by Kaden's. It had to be done now, before Kaden's entity attained absolute dominion over his mind. In a split second, Clay lunged at Officer Holt knowing that it would force the officer's hand. The revolver went off in rapid succession, each shot piercing Clay's chest, a trail of smoke escaping the barrel. Clay crumpled to the ground next to Kaden, his gaze locked in a frozen stare at the billowing clouds in the sky. In the end, Clay had proven Gerald wrong. His life had amounted to something–a self-sacrifice that had saved the lives of millions.

The winds stilled, and Officer Holt witnessed an eerie scene: blue-tinted dust particles falling from the sky all around him, drawn like a voracious vacuum into the very crevices from which they had initially ascended. A hushed whistling sound followed as each rift sealed itself shut. The illusion of Clay's mutation disappeared, and his body was free of deformities and of any sign of life. Officer Holt tried desperately to revive Jeremy with quick chest compressions and rescue breaths into his mouth, but despite his advanced CPR techniques, Jeremy's pulse remained elusive. There was no time to wait for an ambulance. He scooped Jeremy up and rushed his limp body to his squad car, speeding him to the hospital.

CHAPTER 45

NINETY-SEVEN PEOPLE PERISHED that day in the small towns of Appalachia, Virginia, and Lynch, Kentucky. Man, woman, and child, every human who had been changed by the Ocran, all died in a matter of seconds, the moment Kaden extracted from Jeremy. Without the sustaining power of the Wheel or Kaden's link to the omnipotent Council, the Ocran could no longer survive in their hosts' bodies. Kaden's demise had driven the Ocran back underground. The authorities blamed the deaths on the dual anomaly of the earthquake and the tornado hitting the towns simultaneously and without warning, though the coroner found no storm or quake-related injuries on the bodies. It was all swept quietly under the rug to keep the residents of Lynch and Appalachia calm. The extractions killed every human host, just as Kaden had warned, and ironically Jeremy was the only survivor. Officer Holt had managed to keep him alive long enough for the emergency medical team to resuscitate him.

After four days of hospitalization, Lily took Jeremy home, overjoyed that he survived his ordeal but devastated over Frank's unexplained death and how she would explain it to a six-year-old who loved his father so much. Jeremy had no memory of the eight-month period of his abduction or who the Lofton's were. They were both discovered deceased in their home when Holt returned to arrest them on a kidnapping charge.

He had never fired his weapon before and had assumed he would never have to. The realization that he had not only shot at, but actually killed someone, was too much for him to handle.

Officer Holt still hadn't come to terms with what he witnessed the day of the shooting–the blue dust particles swirling around him, sinking into cracks in the ground, and those same particles floating out of Jeremy, and entering Clayton Krutcher, and how he himself was somehow flung through the air by some unknown force, were all things he couldn't rationalize. He resigned from the Appalachia police department and started a new career in real estate near his hometown of Billings, Montana, hoping to forget it all. He found solace in knowing he had saved Jeremy, an innocent child, and deemed it enough to justify what he had done to Clay Krutcher.

It was not enough for Tara. The Internal Affairs division for the Appalachia police department cleared Officer Holt of all wrongdoing in her husband's death even though what Clay had been accused of was not possible. He would never hurt a child. It infuriated her that a follow-up investigation never transpired, or any subsequent charges filed. In a matter of days, Officer Holt stood completely exonerated, denying Tara the justice and answers she deserved. Clay's fellow coalminers: Bailey, Stanley, and Henson, never returned to the Pineville coal mine after his death. The appearance of the woman and the phenomena that followed had tarnished what they believed was a decent and respectable job. Lars replaced them with new hires, but the earthquake anomaly had damaged the mine so severely that MSHA designated it a safety hazard and shut it down permanently. The Pineville mine closure ended a dark period in Lars's life, and he trusted that Clay and Zarian's death meant that his deadly assault on an innocent woman would now remain a secret.

Miriam's dark period stretched on endlessly. To find solace in the loss of her daughter Rebecca, she purged her life of reminders, disposing of every possession that could conjure the memory of her precious daughter, who she had lost twice in the same unforgiving year. Amongst the relics, a discovery—inside her daughter's desk—a drawing.

A portrait of them, their cheeks touching, smiles radiant, captured in rich detail and intricacy, reminiscent of a happier time in their shared past. She kept the only item of her daughter's adorned on the wall of her bedroom, encased in an ornate frame. Miriam pondered whether the drawing had been a gift from Rebecca or the entity that had taken over her daughter's body. But in the end, it scarcely mattered. They were both her daughter, and the drawing left behind, their way of saying good-bye.

o o o

Sheriff Jenkins search for answers in Rosalind's disappearance came to a somber conclusion a year later when a man walking his dog discovered her partially surfaced remains. The guilt of losing his deputy on an assignment he had placed her on overwhelmed him. He stayed on as sheriff, yet he never came to terms with her death, nor did he wear his Stetson ever again because of it. Conversely, the extraction deaths of Mo, and Jeb's fathers had brought the teens closer together and sealed their friendship. They communicated frequently through the DisContent chat board, and Mo's sister had even driven Mo to Appalachia to meet up with Jeb and Charlie twice in the same month.

Tara had never heard much about Appalachia until Clay mentioned it as the place where he had gone hunting. It was an ominous forewarning that ultimately would be the place where he would lose his life.

The day after Clay's death, Tara powered up his laptop. After four attempts at guessing his password and failing, she typed in *Carmel-by-the-sea*, and the screen unlocked. An icon at the bottom titled "For Tara" stood out in red on the desktop. She clicked on it and a video opened to Clay gazing into the camera, looking pensive but relaxed. "Well, you're seeing this, so I guess that means it's not good news for me," he said. "I'm sorry I'm not there. I hope you know I tried my best to make it back home to you, but this was the only way I could guarantee you and our baby's safety and the safety of so many others. Honey, I need you to do this for me. I wanna be cremated, and this part is important… I need you to spread my ashes over the lake, like I did my Ocran father, Zarian. Please don't bury my ashes in the ground where they might be dug up somehow and carried away in the wind to take someone else's life. It's extremely important that you do this, Tara. Do that for me, honey, please, spread them over the lake. I love you always and take care of our son. Make sure he knows how much I wanted to be there with him, and even though I never got a chance to meet him, I love him so much. You were the best thing that ever happened to me, honey," said Clay.

Tara wiped her eyes dry and powered off his laptop.

It took two years for her even to consider carrying out Clay's wishes. Living in the trailer without him had caused her distress so she kept his urn on the dresser in the bedroom. His unconventional presence had become a part of her healing process that never ended. Only because of their son, Reed Brandon Krutcher, was she able to find the strength to let Clay go in the manner that he wished. She planned a play date with her son on the freshwater beach at Buckhorn Lake, where she had for the first time, mourned the death of her mother and released her ashes. It felt like the most appropriate place to finally release Clay's remains as he had instructed her to do.

Reed relished the moment, digging holes and building houses in the sand with his toy bucket and shovel. Tara worried her entire pregnancy that he might inherit Clay's mutation or the genetics of his inhuman side. To her relief, Reed's birth was without complications, and the doctors assured her he was a perfectly normal and healthy child.

A month shy of two years old, Reed was rambunctious, curious, and always laughing. Other than his sandy-blond curly hair, he resembled Clay in so many ways, especially his deep-set hazel eyes that undeniably mirrored his father's. While still engrossed in building another sand house, Tara took the opportunity to carry Clay's urn to the edge of the beach. She stepped into the water up to her ankles, preparing to release his ashes into the water just as she had done there with Gloria's ashes two years before.

She opened the urn and immediately had second thoughts about going through with it. Clay wanted his death to be his end; he wanted to be gone forever. Could it mean that if she didn't do as he asked, that there was a slight chance she might see him again? Maybe not as he was but possibly in some other form. It was crazy thinking that made no sense at all, but she succumbed to it, nevertheless.

Tara took the urn over to one of the holes that Reed had dug in the sand and emptied Clay's remains into it. How strange that his ashes had a bluish tint. She covered it over with the sand and left Buckhorn Lake without the guilt of having ended his life forever.

CHAPTER 46

FOUR YEARS HAD passed since Clay's death, and Tara had told no one about the origin of his father or how his physical appearance had mutated into something beyond human. She moved on with her life raising Reed, as he had become her source of joy, comfort, and purpose she had lost with Clay's death. While she contemplated whether she would take her son to the park or the zoo, the doorbell rang. She stacked the last dish in the dishwasher and opened the door. The last person in the world she expected to see stood on the other side with an envelope in his hand. "Gerald?" she said, surprised. "What are you doing here?"

"I know you weren't expectin' me. I just wanted to give you this," he said and handed Tara the envelope. "I never trusted the mail delivery service."

"What is it?"

She opened the envelope and glanced inside. "Isn't this the check I wrote you a long time ago?" said Tara. "Why didn't you cash it?"

"I didn't want to."

"Clay owed you the money, so I'm paying it back."

"You guys don't owe me anything. Keep it."

"I appreciate it, but you don't have to do that. Clay wanted to settle your differences."

"They're as good as settled," said Gerald.

"Are you sure?"

"Yeah, I'm sure. Hey, I wanted to say this to you for a long time, but I didn't know how."

"What is it?" she said concerned by his serious expression.

"I felt my relationship with my son was our business alone and you were just there in the middle of it stirring the pot, but I was wrong. You're his wife, and I should've respected that. There's no other way to justify it except that I was a jerk for no reason other than I was angry at Clay, and I rightly blamed myself for his shortcomings. I wasn't a father to him as I was to Jimmy, at least not the father he deserved. I guess what I'm tryin' to say to you is what I couldn't say to him to his face—that I'm sorry."

Tara was left speechless. An apology from Gerald was something she never thought she would hear in her lifetime. Perhaps under that rough exterior there did exist a man with a heart and feelings. She relaxed her defenses and nodded. "Thank you for that," said Tara.

"So you accept my apology?"

"Of course, and we'll let the past be the past. Deal?"

"Deal," he replied and exhaled, relieved by her response. "I imagine you've been busy workin' and tryin' to take care of Reed, but if you ever need a babysitter, I'm here. I am his grandpa, you know, a retired grandpa with a lot of free time, and I would love to see him more, if that's okay with you."

Gerald's interest in Reed surprised her and the look on his face portrayed his sincerity. Tara wanted Reed to have a relationship with his grandpa, and it touched her that Gerald had taken the initiative after so many years of their strained relationship. She remembered how Clay cherished the relationship he had with his Grandpa Ellis, and she wanted the same for Reed.

"That's really nice of you, Gerald. We can do that," she said. "He's taking a nap right now, but I can wake him up. You wanna come in?"

"Naw, don't wake him up. A kid needs his sleep to grow. So, how you holding up? You okay?" asked Gerald.

"I'm doing the best I can. I still can't help but think about him."

"I think about him too. Clay may not have been my biological son, but he was *my* son. Sometimes I wonder if he knew I loved him."

Tara sensed his insecurity. The question seemed directed at her, and she was more than willing to answer. "He knew. That's one thing I'm certain of."

Gerald smiled—expressing his gratitude and walked away. She stood at the door and watched him slide into his truck and drive away. When she returned to the kitchen, she froze. The back door was standing wide open. Tara panicked and rushed into Reed's room. It was empty. "Reed!" she screamed, and ran out the back door searching for him. She glimpsed her surroundings. No one was around. Tara rushed back into the house to call 911. Before she could find her phone, the doorbell rang. She rushed to open it. On the other side, stood a tall African-American man with thick dark eyebrows and eyelashes over friendly eyes, holding Reed's hand.

"He says he lives here," said the man.

Tara sighed in relief and took Reed's hand. "You scared me. You know you're not supposed to go out that door without me. Why did you open it?"

Reed shrugged. "I don't know. I can't remember."

"And I told you not to talk to strangers," said Tara.

"He's not a stranger, Mom."

"Yes, he is. Now go play with your truck. Mommy will be there in a minute."

Tara watched him just to make sure he made it into his room before turning her attention back to the stranger.

"I'm sorry," she said. "Thanks for bringing him back."

"There's nothing to be sorry about."

"Where was he?"

"Two trailers down, wandering behind your neighbor's backyard. He said he chased a rabbit."

"Yeah, he loves rabbits. You live in the area?" asked Tara.

"I have relatives who do, but I'm pretty familiar with it, at least

I thought I was. It's funny how things change. I don't remember it looking this way when I was here before."

"How long has it been since you've seen Lynch?"

"A few years. Believe it or not, Lynch is my hometown."

Tara's interest spiked. "You're from Lynch? I don't know anyone who was actually born in this place except for the elderly."

"Now you do. Born and raised. I found my ticket out of this nowhere town a couple of years ago and moved to California."

His mention of California aroused her curiosity. "Really? What part?"

"Seaside. It's a little north of Carmel."

Tara paused, baffled. Besides Clay, no one she knew had ever talked about Carmel. "Lynch is a long way from California," she said.

"It is, and after I tie up a few loose ends here, I'll be heading back to finish moving. I just relocated my trucking business to the Carmel area. Now I'm looking for a place there."

"A place in Carmel? That must be expensive."

"It's worth it. As they say, Carmel-by-the-Sea, it's the best place to be."

He said the phrase in the same way that Clay had in their private moment. It was surreal and strange. Tara grinned through her apprehension about what was happening. How much of a coincidence could it all be? He looked nothing like Clay, yet his demeanor, his mannerisms, and even the cadence of his speaking voice were more than similar.

"It was rude of me not to introduce myself. I'm Atlas," he said, extending a hand to her.

She lifted an eyebrow. "Atlas?"

"Yeah, I get that look a lot. It's not your most common name, but I've learned to own it."

His show of confidence impressed her. She gave him a firm handshake. "I'm Tara."

Away in his room, Reed was on his knees tinkering with his toy dump truck, scooting it across the floor while he emulated the engine sound with his voice. A wheel broke off, and he stood up, trying to reattach it when something outside his window commanded his attention. He went over to get a closer look. Blue dust particles hovered continuously in a circular formation just outside his window. The bright pastel color and the way it danced about mesmerized him like a Saturday morning cartoon. Eager to reach out and touch it, he placed his step stool under the ledge and stood on top. It elevated him just enough to reach the lock and push the window open.

Tara had just finished her conversation with Atlas at the front door. After saying goodbye to him, she stepped back into her home, curious, confounded, and fascinated by the experience of meeting him. She sauntered to the back of the trailer with a smile on her face and opened Reed's bedroom door. He was standing on the stool with his back turned to her, staring out the window.

"Reed? Honey, what are you doing?" said Tara. "Get down from there right now."

Reed remained planted on the stool. He swayed his hands in the air at the shimmering tree branches outside his window with eyes as blue as the crystal-clear waters of a tropical bay. He broke free from his mesmeric gaze and faced Tara, singing,

"Twinkle, twinkle, little star, how I wonder what you are..."

ACKNOWLEDGEMENTS

Special thanks to my family for their support. In addition, I would like to thank the following people for not only their name, but more importantly for their friendship and inspiration during the writing process: Mohammed (Mo) Murtuza, Jeb Stewart, Charlie Musick, Eric Trimble, Ansley Youngerman and my colleagues: Zarian, Octavius, Rosalind, Travis, Raphael, Caden and Connor. Thanks to Doriano Carta and Vickie Boff and my editor; Allister Thompson and proof editor Jason Letts for their much-needed expertise and my language translators; Kenya Coffey and Anaes Ahmed. Special thanks to Lorenzo Pelosini for his encouragement and the push I needed to finish the story.

ABOUT THE AUTHOR

Terrance Coffey is a bestselling author, screenwriter, songwriter, and composer with a predilection for science fiction thrillers and Egyptian history. He has written numerous short stories, screenplays, television pilots, and was the composer of the iconic Always Coca-Cola music jingle. His debut novel "VALLEY OF THE KINGS: The 18th Dynasty" is a 2017 National Indie Excellence Awards Finalist for Best Historical Fiction and a #1 Amazon Bestseller. Hailing from Chicago, Illinois, Terrance Coffey currently calls Atlanta, Georgia, his home.

Join the mailing list at www.TerranceCoffey.com for free giveaways of "VALLEY OF THE KINGS: The 18th Dynasty," and please remember to leave a review on Amazon or Goodreads. Your feedback is always appreciated. ☺

Twitter/X: @terry_coffey
TerranceCoffey.com